George P. Lathrop, Rose H. Lathrop, Nuns Visitation

A Story of Courage

annals of the Georgetown convent of the Visitation of the Blessed Virgin Mary

George P. Lathrop, Rose H. Lathrop, Nuns Visitation

A Story of Courage
annals of the Georgetown convent of the Visitation of the Blessed Virgin Mary

ISBN/EAN: 9783337332013

Printed in Europe, USA, Canada, Australia, Japan

Cover: Foto ©Andreas Hilbeck / pixelio.de

More available books at **www.hansebooks.com**

A STORY OF COURAGE

ANNALS OF THE GEORGETOWN
CONVENT OF THE VISITATION OF
THE BLESSED VIRGIN MARY

FROM THE MANUSCRIPT RECORDS

BY

GEORGE PARSONS LATHROP

AND

ROSE HAWTHORNE LATHROP

BOSTON AND NEW YORK
HOUGHTON, MIFFLIN AND COMPANY
The Riverside Press, Cambridge
1894

PREFACE.

"As cheerful as a nun" is a phrase which certain Catholics (whom we chance to know intimately) always use, to express the acme of serenity, light-heartedness, and the sweetest good spirits. Indeed, there are no happier or cheerier persons on earth than the members of religious sisterhoods.

Clear consciences, methodical lives, temperateness and self-denial, with the cultivation of a habit of contentment and gratitude and the marvelously re-fining, uplifting influence of constant prayer and devotion, all tend to this result. The pure heart is like a transparent lake that ripples or sparkles ex-quisitely, at the slightest touch of a healthful breeze or the gleam of a ray from heaven. And even un-der the shadow of agitation or tempest, its depths are calm, clear, fed from innumerable springs, not of the earth, but spiritual and eternal.

Often, however, we hear just the contrary idea ex-pressed, — namely, that religious communities are stagnant pools where life stops; into which people drop inertly, from disappointment or because they are of no use anywhere else. It is our hope and conviction that these records of the earliest Visitation Convent in the United States, which we are now privileged to lay before the public, will do much to disperse misty and mistaken notions of this sort, and to establish a firmer and clearer point of view for those who have hitherto lacked eyesight, or, possessing it, have refused to avail themselves of it when contemplating monastic institutions.

The courage of the founders and maintainers of the Visitation in Georgetown — which is the next to the oldest convent for nuns in the United States — is not only a tribute to God; it is likewise a shining instance of the integrity of human nature when aided by grace. This foundation is a historic monument of great value, as marking the progress of our general civilization and as an early realization of true spiritual advancement. Further, it appeals to us in our modern day as the work of women, who have demonstrated through it their power in practical, executive management as well as in the exercise of holy influences. And these women have toiled with express devotion to the Blessed Virgin, inspired by that act of charity which prompted her to visit Saint Elizabeth before Jesus the Incarnate God was born. Their achievement and the manner of it remind us that the whole modern movement for the "advancement of women" took its impetus from the veneration and honor paid by Catholic Christianity to the Blessed Virgin —

" Woman above all women glorified,
Our tainted nature's solitary boast " —

as the Protestant poet Wordsworth wrote of her.

We hear so much discussion as to possible new ad-
justments of society, and so many experiments have
been made in forming secular community associations, that it seems proper to point out here the
important bearing which religious communities have
upon these problems, agitated more or less in nearly
every century and conspicuous in ours. The religious orders of Christianity are the only organizations, it seems to us, which have solved the question
of community life on a great scale, and have made
their solution good, year after year, century after
century. They have succeeded in doing this because
the basis on which they rest is one of reverence, of
humility, and of absolute good-will thoroughly and
practically set forth, made real in daily thought and
conduct. Not all people are fitted to share in such
a life, but only a picked contingent of souls equipped
for it by special qualities of nature, guided by God's
grace. How, then, does the success of religious orders bear upon the struggle which the majority of
civilized men and women are constantly brought to
face, — the struggle of somehow bettering the condition of the masses by a closer and more kindly association among human beings than is now generally
practiced?

We think its bearing is simply this: that the

great Catholic Christian Orders, forming communities of men or of women under rules of perfect obedience and of absolute, unflinching fulfillment of every precept of Christ, keep alive from age to age the ideal type of association, after which society must pattern if it wishes to be truly happy or to please God. By this we do not mean that all men and women are, or ever will be, called upon to become celibates and enter such communities; or that those are the only organizations in which life can be led well. What we mean is that they supply the type, the model; and that the spirit of religious communities must be transferred to or infused into the family and all groups of families, before society can allay the difficulty of mutual relations, over which it now wrangles so savagely.

Another point requiring mention here is, that while religious communities thus preserve the purest Christian types in humanity, and keep example alive for us, they are not — as is often erroneously asserted — a burden upon the rest of society. On the contrary, they are a benefit and a gain to it, even according to the principles of political economy, and as a source of addition to the national wealth. Hippolyte Adolphe Taine, who was by no means favorably disposed toward Catholicity, writing of the religious orders in France, said of the monks and nuns that they "are benefactors by institution and voluntary laborers, choosing to devote themselves to dangerous, revoltant, and at least ungrateful services, — countless charitable and educational works, primary schools, orphan asylums, houses of refuge and prisons, and all gratuitously or at the lowest wages, through a reduction of bodily necessities to the lowest point, and of the personal expenditure of each brother and sister."[1] He quoted at the same time, in support, the calculation of Emile Keller that the value of the useful labor performed by the monks and nuns of France (1880), over and above their expenses, gave a net gain to the public of 80,000,000 francs, or $16,000,000 per annum.

From this, and various other testimony, it would appear that religious communities not only set the best kind of spiritual example, but also show forth the true principles of industry and thrift.

Regarding one point, touched upon in certain chapters, it may be well to offer a word of general explanation, in order to forestall possible misunderstanding as to those visions which are said to have been experienced by some of the persons in this history. Even among people who hold identically the same view respecting the supernatural and its *capability* or power of visible and material manifestation, there is a diversity concerning the exact force of meaning which ought to attach to the term "vision." By some,

[1] *The Origins of Contemporary France. The Modern Régime.* By Hippolyte Adolphe Taine, D. C. L., Oxon. Translated by John Durand. Vol. ii., Book v., p. 100.

also, visions, taken as things external to one's self, are thought to be of common occurrence, while, in the opinion of others, they are extremely rare, all but impossible, and should always be doubted in the first instance and subjected to the most rigid test of evidence, or, since evidence is hardly obtainable, should be thrown aside entirely. We prefer, therefore, to let each reader consider in his own way the dreams or visions mentioned in the narrative. We have aimed to avoid leaning towards either side of any discussion to which they might give rise, while setting down the facts or appearances as they presented themselves to the persons concerned. For this much, at least, is certain, that the thought or action of persons of holy or ascetic life, who believe themselves to have beheld visions or received counsel in dreams, is often distinctly influenced by these.

It remains for us to say, here, that the courtesy of the Georgetown Sisters of the Visitation gave us access to their manuscript Annals, and that we have consulted the Sisters at every point in our work. This book is based on the manuscripts, from which we have quoted occasionally. But the arrangement of the material is ours; the account of the origin of the Order, and the biographies of Saint Francis de Sales and Saint Jane de Chantal are our own work; as the whole form and expression of the narrative also are. In brief, this volume is not a mere piece of editing, or a compilation, but is an original work, though following closely and accurately the authentic records from which it is derived.

GEORGE PARSONS LATHROP,
ROSE HAWTHORNE LATHROP.

CONTENTS.

VII.

LIST OF ILLUSTRATIONS.

A STORY OF COURAGE.

I.

ON THE THRESHOLD.

THE time of year at which we first saw the convent was perhaps not unfitting for our first impressions; since the December leaflessness, the unornamented aspect of the ground and the stone walls, whose vines were mere shadows, typified the stern simplicity of the life which the sisters have adopted; while the bursts of delicate but cheery sunshine resembled their good spirits, which are so entirely spiritual.

The open landscape, disburdened of veiling foliage, and thus disclosing the opalescent colors of the distances and of the sky, and revealing the draughtsmanship of nature in the arrangement of trees and hills, seemed to mirror the clear outlooks of a life of unselfishness and unworldly schemes, where the larger and more beautifully tinted composition of God's intentions is seen, as in no other season of the mind and soul. Raphael gave backgrounds of such airy landscape to his holy pictures, and in so doing followed an accepted fashion in religious art, with surpassing skill.

To those who are keen for color, the most delicate

effects become the most powerful; and, to the holy
mind, that beauty which is the least garish, self-evi-
dent, and crude, and therefore the most refreshing, is
spiritual beauty.   It calls into action the most sensitive kind of perception.

To eyes which know how to find it, there is in the
least luxuriant season of the year a beauty which is entirely sufficient; and, to the perception of a nun, the
quiet and solemnity of a convent contain all the loveliness she needs ; because, just as there is no season
without its peculiar beauty, so there is no health of
soul without beauty; and the beauty of holiness is
the truest and loveliest of all.   It is very necessary to
acknowledge that this delicacy of which we are speaking is satisfactory, with a far higher satisfaction than
a redundant beauty can give, if we are to put ourselves into a proper relation with conventual life,
while trying to understand its virtue and attractive-
ness.

It is as necessary to do this, for instance, as for a
man who looks at a supremely fine painting to know
what supremely fine painting is.   Why should an ama-
teur in the study of convents expect at once to comprehend their value, any more than a tyro in art the
virtue of a Millet or a Michael Angelo?   Many people
see no beauty in the highest art, who never confess
their blindness.   Is it not almost as mortifying to
confess that we dislike holiness of life?   Yet it is
a fact that many people consider a convent dedicated
to the Blessed Virgin of less consequence than an old
master's portrayal of the Blessed Virgin.   The convent has the unassuming virtue of expending its ener-

gies for others; while the picture has the charm of costing a fortune. Hence, half the world knows but little of conventual life.

There is a seriousness at hand, all the time, upon setting foot within the monastic door, which means that the silent endurance of Christ, and the *unsmiling* courage of his life, are never forgotten by the religious of either sex. It is easy to see that the religious are, as a class, never, for a single moment, intoxicated by any sense or perception. The rare exceptions which we have seen to perfect self-control in the cloister have all been on the lofty plane of loving enthusiasm or genial interest, which " in the world " would be called beautiful exhibitions of feeling. It is with an effort that one measures the higher principles of " feeling " in a convent.

Human waywardness, doubtless, is sometimes there, but so well barred with law and observance that it no longer tears the heart. This principle of recognizing the undying force of nature, and counteracting it by rigorous remembrance, is indorsed by every scheme of wisdom ever made, and is figured by the knotted cord of the saints. Those who complain that, on this account, the religious life must be a morbid life, might find illumination in the question, — Was the Christ-child morbid?

The religious celibate cheers other human creatures, but never relies upon being cheered by them; she brightens the lives of others, but she never throws aside her solemn adoration of Christ. She smiles, it is true, and even turns a happy phrase, or jokes daintily, with a laugh of genuine mirth; but her eyes are

calm, the while.   Always there is something that
tells of the heart once and forever pierced with the
sword; the peaceful dwelling of a nature which has
been touched and tamed by God. This seriousness
strikes cold through one's less pure and generous
nature; the whole aspect of the convent is too sudden
a contrast from luxury and confusion to spare one
a gasp of dread. The poorly equipped rooms, the
meagre cells, the intense clearness of the skin of these
still human sisters who have clasped hands with the
superhuman; the firm lines of their mouths, which
tell so much in their silent way of battles won; in
short, the evidence of law as stern as that which takes
away a man's life, — but in this case, giving life instead of taking it, — all this is like new wine to the
intelligence which has hitherto been occupied with
caressing its own desires, upon the level of food, drink,
and gayety, with death to-morrow. Our master, "the
world," has trained us to beds of roses, — if we can
afford them, or get credit for them. He has taught
us to follow luscious waltz tunes and broken rules; he
has loaded us with wasted hours, with muscles relaxed
and flesh tender with indulgence. God trains the
sisters to laws that cannot be broken; to a system
that holds back from sin and all intemperance of feeling; to hours devoted to the good of the many and
never to the gratification of self; to muscles tense
with constant self-denial; and to a sight which can
see, whenever the spirit thirsts and hungers for it,
Christ upon the cross, dying to save mankind.

This image, far from being a spectacle of horror,
comprises all that went before in his divine existence

upon earth. It comprises, to a refined perception, his loving sermons, his tender glance and touch, his radiant though never smiling face, and the voice which blessed the child and the leper with impartial holiness. Who will say that this vision of the devoted man or woman of the monastic life does not console them for their own energy and suffering and effort? The truth is, we who are incapable of understanding the reward which a keener knowledge of Christ brings are in a lower order of development; are weeds, not flowers; are sinners, not children of God; are mastodons, great in our own conceit, and monstrous as lords of creation; are devoid of many points of perfection reached by our more fortunate because more sanctified brothers and sisters, who have been actually *taught* by Christ; while we have heard Him, and yet perhaps have not always literally accepted what we have heard.

II.

INTRODUCTION TO THE CONVENT.

I. THE HOUSE, THE GARDEN, THE GROUNDS.

THE Convent of the Visitation in Georgetown, as it exists to-day, is (with its academy) a large three-sided structure of brick, enclosing a great garden. The front faces on Fayette Street, a cheerful thoroughfare which runs straight northward up the hill, in this venerable suburb of the capital city of the Union.

Across the street is a row of cosy little dwellings, standing somewhat back from the sidewalk. Georgetown College, conducted by the Jesuits, is close by, gracefully overlooking the Potomac and the Virginian heights of Arlington just beyond that historic river's current. The city and the suburb have been gradually welded into one, by a continuous and expanding web of streets and houses, so that now they stretch up to the very border of the convent demesne, which was of old a quiet and almost remote rural solitude. The refreshing wildness of a somewhat open woodland is still preserved, in the tract just behind the convent and its academy. But on its front, to the east, runs the rectangular street; and up to this street, at the southern corner of the convent, the patient horse-car from the heart of Washington plods its equine way.

A large edifice is the convent, as we have said; and added to it at the north is the still more imposing building of the academy, under charge of the good sisters. The convent proper — or, as it is often called, the " monastery " — is a long, plain four-story brick house, the windows of which are firmly shuttered with green blinds up to half their height, with another blind that may be pushed upward to cover the rest of the glass; so that no one may gaze in from idle curiosity. The inmates have no desire to gaze out; for their time is fully occupied with duties of teaching, of religious observance, and of their household tasks. Their thoughts are fixed on God, not on the world; still less on the casual street that runs by their door. A narrow strip of grass, railed in by a light iron fence, separates their dwelling from the sidewalk, and gives them an added safeguard in their retirement. All this is in accord with the aims of a community like that of the Visitation. Their object is not so much to prevent the inmates from passing out, — because no one ever becomes a member there without long preparation and decision, and a firm resolve to remain in the ideal service of religious devotion, — but rather to prevent the intrusion of careless, worldly, noisy people, who may be inclined to invade the seclusion and sanctity of a life wholly ordered and consecrated to spiritual purposes.

The countenance, then, — if one may so describe it, — of this religious building is calm, neutral, neither repelling nor inviting. Although it stands high on the hill of Georgetown, it is in no way de-

monstrative. From a distance you cannot even dis-
tinguish it among the other buildings. It does not
dominate them. It does not tower up, or threaten,
or warn you away. Neither does it, by its promi-
nence, invite you to come towards it; although it is
established on a lofty plane.

It simply stands there, and waits. When you
have reached it, — whether by horse-car, or by the
electric road, and part way on foot, — you recognize
that you have arrived at a limit, a barrier-line.
Turn, then, and direct your steps, if you choose, to
some other quarter. You cannot penetrate the sacred
enclosure of the convent. It is a line drawn, a barrier set up, between the loose, miscellaneous world
and the things of God.

If you wish to approach it, and to see and know
something of those who inhabit this enclosure, you
can do so only through reverence and sympathy.

The convent and the academy make practically one
front along the street; being connected interiorly,
and united midway by the chapel, except for a narrow
recess between the latter and the school building
proper; and the three structures, though distinctly
differing in style, — each one characteristic and suggestive — form together a massive and interesting
total effect. The convent part, in the lines of its construction as well as in its whole appearance, is modest
and self-effacing. The chapel (to which low steps and
a pointed door give ingress from the street) has
arched and mullioned diamond-leaded windows; the
lower ones being iron-grated, part way up; and its
four tall classic pilasters on the front, with Doric

capitals, aid in giving it a look of repose, of peaceful meditation. Above, rise a Greek pediment and gable, surmounted by an unobtrusive gilded cross; while farther ·back, about at the middle of the roof and over the nave, there is a square tower, shuttered and loopholed, ending in a quaint balustraded belfry spire, on the tip of which, again, is poised a still more slender cross. Upon a tablet on the street wall, just over the entrance door, is inscribed a text from the Seventy-fifth Psalm : *Vovete et reddite Domino*, " Vow ye, and pay unto the Lord your God."

Set in such a place, this admonition may suitably be construed to mean that we must not only make vows to God, but must pay them as well, by constant service and self-sacrifice. It is easy enough to *say* that we vow so and so ; but it is only by life-long devotion and self-denial that we can *pay* what we have promised. In these words of Scripture, then, the convent sums up and declares to the whole world, quietly, its principle and its practice. Close by, on the left or northern side of the chapel, — which, it may be said here, covers and includes the spot on which was reared the first Catholic Christian sanctuary ever set upon this ground, — stands the ample, prosperous new building of the academy, of brick trimmed with brownstone ; a stately edifice, with tall embrasured windows crowned by heavy ornamental mouldings, a canopied porch, high dormers and pavilions in the mansard roof ; with, in fact, quite an air of mundane comfort and even ·of display, as contrasted with the meek home of the nuns and the quiet, serious home of worship that adjoin. Is it not eminently fitting that this house of worship, the chapel, with such memorable thought and counsel imprinted on its open brow, should stand between the cloistered convent and the hospitable school, uniting religion and education?

As the academy has its door, independently of the rest, and the chapel its little portal (never opened now to the public), so the convent has its own entrance from the street, an entrance thoroughly in keeping, and used but rarely. For the nuns never emerge from their dwelling and their grounds; that is, none of them but the "out sisters," who are detailed to carry on such communication with the external life as may be necessary, or to escort their young charges, the academy pupils, when they have to go into the city. It is very seldom indeed that any visitor is admitted by this approach; nor is any one ever allowed to go into the actual convent interior without a special permission from the ecclesiastical head of the archdiocese of Baltimore. This permission is never granted for other than exceptional and momentous reasons. People are constantly applying for this privilege, at the convent door, impelled by curiosity or respectful interest. But it is quite useless for them to do so. This calm abode is never, under any circumstances, penetrated by even a single sight-seer. In the academy parlor, furnished as is the little convent parlor with a heavy grating, so that the sisters who are at times called there may observe their fundamental rule, — that of enclosure, — the pupils are allowed to see their relatives or friends sent by their parents, on Wednesday and Saturday

afternoons. The convent has a reception-room behind its well guarded door ; but into this no one may
pass who does not come with suitable credentials.

The door, solid and painted a dark ivy-green, is set
back in a deep embrasure, within which one may
stand sheltered. So standing, we rang the bell and
waited, with a curious mixture of feeling in our
minds, and not a little agitation at the thought of
the unusual privilege and experience which was about
to be ours. For we were expected, and it had been
duly arranged that we were to go through the house.
Presently a panel in the shadowed door was drawn
aside, showing a heavy grating, with the face of a
serious woman, the portress, behind it. She discovered who we were, and, according to previous
orders, asked us to enter the parlor to our right,
which was really outside the boundaries of the convent, being provided with a separate threshold. The
parlor was very small, and seemed to express, at once,
the modicum of communication with social affairs, as
they are usually carried on, which the sisters are
called upon to undergo. However, the little room
immediately asserted that gentle fascination of quaint
age that some of us find so sweet. In the next
moment we were impressed by the large and sturdy
wooden grating across one side of the parlor; behind
which was another little room, hung with a few tiny
pictures, and ornamented by one of the most ethereal
and diminutive air-tight stoves it had ever been our
fortune to see. Probably its last warmth emerged
from a silvery birch stick, flickering in its delicate
grasp, fifty years ago. We waited for the Mother

Superior long enough to observe the sundry small portraits and religious pictures here and there upon the walls, — a likeness of St. Francis de Sales, another of St. Jane de Chantal, and one of St. Francis of Assisi. The spirit of the convent bade us pause. Then the Mother entered (behind the grate), accompanied by her assistant. The two sisters were somewhat constrained, as we ourselves certainly were to a great degree. Probably they instinctively drew back from the moment when we were to penetrate the sacred precincts of the enclosure, where the turmoil and distresses of uninspired life were utter strangers; while we two visitors were weighed down by a definite sense of the absurdity of that spiritual ignorance and cowardice, by which those who dwell in the outer world are always more or less influenced and infected. All our worldly wisdom and ordinary knowledge seemed to take flight, and to be of no account whatever. We felt like children who have strayed into some privacy which does not belong to them, which they are hardly qualified to share. Nevertheless, the Mother met the situation graciously, and by her pleasant words and manner soon put us at our ease. Among other things, she said that our friend (a friend through interchange of letters), the Sister Procuratrix, whom we had never seen, would soon come to speak with us. She also said that we were about to do what had not been done by mere visitors since her residence in the convent of more than twenty years; and that was, to cross the threshold of the large entrance door, usually inaccessible to the world, unless physicians or workmen were imperatively needed. As we were finally admitted (and those twenty years seemed very long), the Mother stood at the door, and took us kindly by the hands. She exclaimed most gently: "You would be excommunicated for this, if you had not received a special dispensation."

We were ushered into the Treasurer's, or Procuratrix's office, where everything was comfortably business-like. Then we chatted for a while, and the sister into whose domain we had penetrated expressed amusement at our having so much mail matter, piled up on her table, which had been awaiting us for several days before our arrival. The collection included great rolls of newspapers. "I told them," she cried, "that I was glad I was not literary by profession, if it would entail my reading all that!" Various convent matters were discussed, both as to historical records and observances, and nuns of remarkable, saintly character, who had lived and died within this enclosure. It was not long before we proceeded to examine all the apartments, the garden, and the extensive grounds.

One of the first places we visited was the refectory. The board-like tables upon which the few dishes of the nuns are placed are the same that were set up for the nuns who were here nearly a hundred years ago. A raised desk called a pulpit, in the middle of one side of the room, is where the sister sits who reads aloud, during the meals; at which, by the way, no conversation is allowed. The spiritual food she dispenses is usually the Life of a Saint, or passages from saintly writings. At one end of the

long refectory, somewhat isolated, is the table for
the Superioress. The sisters showed us the coarse ·
towel which envelops the knife, fork, and spoon of
each nun; which towel, at the signal "In the name
of God" from the Superioress, they open, laying the
corners down on the table, so that the utensils are
revealed spread upon the cloth. After the meal is
over, they wash their knives and forks in a large
bowl, of which there are a number at intervals along
the narrow tables, holding pitchers of water. The
dishes are washed outside of the refectory by those
appointed. The vow of poverty is indeed never lost
sight of. The sisters were full of a merry recognition of the poverty here enforced. A gourmand or
an epicure — or a French cook — would have with-
ered away in the healthy, noonday intelligence of the
convent, which refused to subscribe to the monar-
chical reign of the stomach (that unkind tyrant of
long dynasty) and had declared for the republic of
abstemiousness.

Bread, coffee, and meat, at half past seven, usually
constitute breakfast. Dinner at twelve consists of
meat and bread and two or three vegetables; and, for
occasions, a little molasses with the bread. On feast
days, there is dessert. The bright, happy young
sister — a talented musician — who gave us these
items, was surprised, we could see, at our having a
special interest in food statistics. The gulf is great
between the refectory and a "pink lunch," that very
shoppy freak of too often shoppy fashion. The
many windows are all on one side of the hall-like
apartment, and look out on a garden, which is attrac-

tive even in winter because of pretty trees and box
borders, where, central amid the pathways and the
verdure, stands a statue of St. Joseph, white and
beneficent. The whole outlook is made more impressive by pillars of whitewashed brick, forming a
cloistral arcade outside the windows, and framing the
view.

In the refectory, as all through the convent, everything is beautifully clean and neat. The long corridors, the large rooms, the little " cells " or bed-cham-
bers of the sisters, are innocent of dust and nearly
as pure as a spotless conscience. The floors are
scrubbed almost to whiteness. What peace and pleas-
antness reign in this interior! Here in the refectory,
the only seats are benches ranged along the walls.
There are no chairs. The nuns do not gather *around*
a table, in the ordinary social way, but sit in order on
the long, hard benches, at one side of the continuous
tables, against the wall, and face the middle of the
room. None of them sit on the opposite side of the
table, which is left empty and clear, so that the serv-
ers, who constitute in turn all the sisters, from the
Superioress to the novices, can conveniently place the
dishes for them, from that side. Thus the arrangement and the position of the nuns is like that of the
apostles, in the traditional pictures of the Last Supper, with which the world is familiar. The rule of
silence which governs them, at their meals, may well
remind the rest of us, taking our daily bread amid a
pleasant babble of the family, around a social table,
that there are thousands of pure and noble women in
convents all over the world who, when they submit

to the necessity of eating, do not think of their material sustenance, or of chat and gossip, but are absorbed in thoughts of holiness. The Mother Superior was even moved to apologize for the fact that they fared well at table. "Oh, we have very good meals," she said, — "often much better than those of other poor people who have not taken any vow of poverty."

Once a year only is there any social diversion among them at meal-hours; any break in the silent routine. This little relaxation comes on the eve of Epiphany, in January, — the festival which commemorates the spreading of the Gospel to the Gentiles; that is, to all human creatures. On the evening before that festival, the sisters, at supper, have a bag full of black beans, among which there is one white one. Every sister has the right to draw a bean; and she to whose hand the white one comes is crowned as Epiphany Queen. General conversation is also allowed at supper, on that occasion. The Epiphany Queen is entitled to receive gifts from the whole community. But what is the chief gift? Not one of the common worldly kind, you may be sure. It is a holy communion, with many prayers, partaken of by all the sisters. The queen may request them to offer this communion for some special object that she has at heart; or she may, at her pleasure, transfer it to any other member of the sisterhood. From this, the sole annual amusement allowed them at their table, we may judge how rigorous and self-denying is the rest of their existence.

It was a quick and striking change from the sober

yet cheerful refectory to the burial-vault beneath the chapel, which we visited next. Here is the tomb of the Most Reverend Leonard Neale, second Archbishop of Baltimore, the founder of the monastery; and here, too, lies the body of Father Clorivière, who after Archbishop Neale's death became the spiritual director of the monastery; and, by his substantial generosity as well as by his devoted service, placed it on a firm footing and established its success as an institution. The mortal frame of Archbishop Neale was buried here in the stone-work sustaining the chapel; and below his memorial tablet there is a Roman-arched recess containing a plain marble cross, a crucifix, and a shelf holding vases for flowers. In front of this, just at the centre of the vault, stands the severely unadorned marble sarcophagus in which Father Clorivière was laid to rest. Around the walls, too, are marked on little boards the names of the nuns who have been buried in the niches under or behind them. Five of the former sisters sleep in the earth, in the deep alcoves on either side of Archbishop Neale's resting-place. These are Sister Teresa Lalor, the first Mother of the house; three members of the Neale family; and Miss Yturbide, daughter of the former Mexican emperor; and to each of them there has been accorded a small plain tombstone. Black crosses fastened 'into the earth underfoot indicate the lowly place of repose of other nuns. On a wall at one side hangs a picture gently and pensively reminding us of "the hour of our death," — a picture of a Visitation nun lying in her coffin ready for burial, with white flowers on her sombre habit and dark veil. There is something so calm, so sweet, so unutterably resigned, about this quiet figure — crude and perhaps inadequate though the painting be, technically — that the sight of it at once relieves, wonderfully, the melancholy which at first gathers around us on stepping into this mortuary place and seeing the memorials of those who have passed away. The life of the good and the sincere, on earth, is something that we are always loath to lose; and we cannot help regretting the noble dead of the past, even though we know that it was a happiness for them to journey to another region of God's universe, where they still live. This burial vault, though lighted cheerfully by windows on the garden, certainly leads one without preamble into the valley of the shadow; but it seems at the same time to demonstrate how the terrors of death, burial, and corruption are not the stupendous *finale* we are accustomed to consider them. By meeting the bugbear, Death, face to face so abruptly, we see his gruesomeness more clearly; but also comprehend his pettiness and grotesqueness in the scheme of the spheres, and of salvation. As well might the butterfly turn to worship the coil he has shuffled off, as the soul stoop in submission to its dead frame and to its coffin or its walled-up tomb. While every change in physical life is important, the process itself is often decidedly humiliating and transient. The apotheosis of death seems a distorted respect; and we were glad to have that necessary transition relegated, by the convent's attitude, to the unadorned and useful but somewhat mortifying level where it belongs. But the black crosses in the earthy ground were painfully pathetic enough to turn away from and forget; except that one might naturally hasten back again and again to repeat a *Hail Mary* for the risen soul, once buried in human life, at the very spot where sympathy becomes the most generous, and perhaps most effectual. One of the sisters told us that she thought Walter Scott's tales of nuns buried alive might have been caused by the finding of their bones in the walls of ruined convents, where apertures only large enough to receive their bodies may have been made, and then evenly bricked up, as is the arrangement in the mortuary wall here. This allusion to Scott's genius, even though it referred only to one of his picturesque mistakes, gave a brighter coloring to our mood, as we moved away.

There was another graveyard at one side of the garden, which is embraced by the large quadrangle of the convent. The same kind of plain black crosses as those in the mortuary chapel vault were stationed over these graves; but they were larger. Some of the names inscribed on them were nearly obliterated; yet the loving sisters knew every mound. Here Sister " Stannie " (Sister M. Stanislaus Jones) was buried. She was one of the most piquant as well as most devout and remarkable of all their religious. She was small but very handsome, her biographical sketch says, and full of talent. However, she none the less made a most spiritual and self-sacrificing nun; and she understood *silence*. She was cured once of disease by a miracle. "But," said another sister, "she would not tell us anything about the particulars of it, until we drove her to! Oh, what a little rogue she was!" Think of it! she had nearly robbed the sisters of any knowledge that this convent contained *yet another* miracle, of which there had already been several, and all for the sake of that violet-like humility and reticence which the rule enjoins. How virtuous the roguishness of a nun can be! That the sisters do not lose their interest in the bones of their dear ones, hidden away in dusty death, is made manifest by the following unpretentious verses, which were written by a young nun, as one of the sisters says, "for an old one, who felt that we should not leave our ancient dead, when laying out the new graveyard, without a farewell sigh of regret."

One summer eve, when weary day
  Had closed its amber wings to rest,
And zephyrs wafted o'er the brake
  The fragrant wild flowers' rich bequest,
In thoughtful mood I strayed alone
  Unto a quiet, shady dell,
Where trembling lights and changing hues
  All Nature wrapped in mystic spell.

The woodland songsters sweet and low
  Their vespers chanted in the trees,
Whose sombre boughs but faintly stirred
  'Neath evening's soft caressing breeze;
And twilight shadows creeping fast
  O'er distant hill and winding vale,
Seemed resting with a sadder touch
  Around this calm, sequestered dale.

No sounds of harsh discordance came
  To mar the landscape's blessëd peace;
The solemn hush of eventide
  Bade all unquiet longings cease.
Amid this sylvan solitude,
  Within the wildwood's tangled bound,
Afar from din of worldly strife,
  Our convent resting-place is found.

A lonely spot, whose verdant sward
  Unbroken yet by lowly grave,
Awakes the thought — which virgin soul
  Will first its quiet shelter crave ?
Will some young member of our band
  Whose pathway bright seems just begun,
With joyful heart all here resign
  For heavenly crown so quickly won ?

Or will death's summons come to her
  Who bears the burden of the day,
Whose ceaseless round of arduous toil
  Is stamped with virtue's shining ray ?
Perhaps 't will come to one who yearns
  For that safe port and silent shore,
Where she may rest with folded hands,
  Life's troubled, anxious voyage o'er.

For old and young alike will find
  A home within this quiet glen,
Whose peaceful beauty brings repose
  From all that pains in haunts of men.
The convent bell tolled twilight's hour,
  As wandering homeward lost in thought,
I paused before another spot,
  With deepest, holiest memories fraught.

Dear honored dead ! who sweetly rest
  Within the cloister's hallowed shade,
Will ye forgive the stern demands
  That bid us seek yon burial glade ?
Oh ! would that coming years might see
  A band as noble, pure and brave,
As those whose lives fore'er are hid
  Within each lonely mossy grave !

With high courageous love they toiled,
  Nor faltered in the rugged way,
Till Jesus called his dear ones home, —
  Their labors crowned with endless day.
Then, chosen souls ! sleep on in peace !
  With loving hearts your place of rest
We 'll guard, until, life's conflict o'er,
  We, too, are numbered 'mong the blest.

The ground was very damp, forming into puddles
where we stood; and the sisters had no rubbers on;
so that our inquisitive anxiety for their health led us
to glance at their shoes, which we discovered were
extremely solid.   They take general precautions, but
leave shivering dread to worldlings, and a stout shoe
or a thick dress are considered in conventual life
quite good enough for rain and wind, or dry weather
and summer days.

At the end of the garden there is a wall, thickly
mantled with ivy; and here on the academy side we
found a structure of rock-work representing, or sug-
gesting, rather, the grotto at Lourdes where the
Blessed Virgin appeared to Bernardette Soubirous,
the devout and unsophisticated peasant child.   A
figure of Bernardette, kneeling in prayer and holding a candle, is placed at the foot of the rocks, praying to the Blessed Virgin, who is seen standing with
clasped hands in a niche near the top of the grotto,
over which there clambers a profusion of leafy vines.
Those who know the marvelous and carefully authenticated results which have come from that vision
granted to the French peasant girl at Lourdes, and
from her inspired discovery of the healing spring,
may well pause here for a moment to breathe an earnest thanksgiving and a prayer for grace.   Just at
this point, however, it is fitting to remark that many
of the children and young ladies who study in the
academy of this convent are Protestants; the parents
of such children having discovered, by long experience, that they can obtain here the benefit of certain
rare qualities in the training of character which can-

not be had elsewhere. These pupils, doubtless, know little or nothing of Lourdes and its miracles. They probably are quite willing to believe in the miracles of the New Testament time, because that is now conveniently far away ; but would find it more difficult to believe in miracles which happen every day in this enlightened but prosaic nineteenth century, right under the eyes of living men, women, and children. Yet, while they may be ignorant of Lourdes and of contemporary Christian miracles, it certainly can do them no harm to be confronted with mute memorials of holy things. They are never interfered with, nor pressed to give their attention to these things. But the lesson of self-abnegation, the quiet influence of prayer, and the silent benediction of the Blessed Virgin, at the typical Lourdes grotto, have most probably influenced them for good, even though they knew it not.

From the convent garden we proceeded to the new graveyard, laid out in 1887, where one of the sisters, a cherished friend, the niece of Ralph Waldo Emerson, and formerly an intimate visitor in the household of Nathaniel Hawthorne, is buried. The pretty bit of ground is reached through an extremely attractive path, winding along under the protection of the high stone wall, and called "Saint Joseph's Walk," since in the angle of the wall turning towards the graveyard is an old oratory dedicated to this great saint; and the last object seen upon leaving the convent quadrangle, or garden, is his benignant statue ; while the first object to greet the eye in the new graveyard is Saint Joseph's likeness again, as if to say, " Here, too, all is well." Different sorts of trees and flowering shrubs border the right-hand side of the path; and vines at intervals beautify the high wall on the left. Here, in summer, there is a wealth of bloom and verdure, and the sweet orchestration of birds accompanies the flickering play of sunbeam and shadow along the peaceful, charming promenade. Upward from the path rises the gentle acclivity of the hill, not very high, but still stately and broad, where trees and sward are brightened by sunlight. The gate of the graveyard is made admirable by the grouping near it of some very graceful oaks; while the ground itself is somewhat curved, convexly, and is surrounded by many trees, outside the tall board fence. The hill-like shape of the little enclosure is just sufficient to display all these trees on two sides, and to give a view of fields beyond.

There is no attempt to ornament the severe fact of bodily extinction, even in this sweet spot. There are no funereal cottages of marble or granite; no open-air galleries of sculptured art; there are no cascades of potted plants or dressy shrubs to hide the mound of the grave. Saint Joseph, the patron of a happy death, is not far absent, as his effigy reminds us, and a rosebush hangs over our friend's last resting-place; while the trees soften all the outlines in accidental loveliness, as if Nature herself had sympathized; and, indeed, precisely as though she knew more of heaven, and human systems in relation to heaven, than we usually admit to be possible.

In the convent our friend was called Sister Jane Frances (in veneration for Saint Jane Frances de

Chantal); but we had loved her as Phœbe Ripley, one of the warmest geniuses, in music, and one of the most reticent women we had ever met; though, like all reticent women, flashing a fire of feeling at certain chords of thought. She became a nun here, and for several years was directress of the Academy of the Visitation.

Farther on swells the hillside and the elevated brow of land already mentioned, bordered or crossed by paths, provided with seats, and at the summit a small rose-embowered oratory. The slope stretches upward, and rises far enough into the world to obtain several fine glimpses of the neighboring Georgetown College, with its effective points of pinnacled architecture. This hill-crown also gives us a glance in the opposite direction, at the House of the Good Shepherd. Hereabouts stand more oaks, — one pleasant slanting spot being known as " Under the Oaks," — and, among them, a great specimen six or seven feet in diameter. The nuns come to its shade in summer at the approach of sundown, to "recreate." The Mother Superior said (alluding to the convent seen in the distance) in a particularly gentle voice and with a gleam of tears : " The sisters of the House of the Good Shepherd are doing a wonderful work. Among them are many ladies of the greatest refinement and sensitiveness ; yet they devote themselves to the poor, wretched creatures who come to them, and *make good women* of them, very often ! "

Under the sky and the trees the Mother's energy became still more apparent ; and the unconscious intonations of her voice suggested laughter now

and then, but instantly melted back into the mono-
tone of solemn remembrance. Her mind was fresh
with a healthy joy of rectitude; and her calm eyes,
with innocent faith, looked further than we could
see. The Mother seemed to regard all the features
of the convent grounds, familiar to her for more
than thirty years (since she had herself been a pupil
in the academy before entering the sisterhood), as
though they were intimate friends; and called our
attention to a hundred pretty things. At the oratory
we found rosebuds soft and ruby-tinted, and sprouting
ivy. To see was to gather, with the Mother Superior; and she made us a bouquet in the twinkling of
a dewdrop.

One elderly sister, a convert from Lutheranism,
many years ago, had toiled bravely after us, up to
this moment, with inky cloak and skirt held at a safe
distance from the wet path; but now went back.
The other dear sister of our party, also elderly, but
with the glow of youth not yet extinguished in her
heart, began to show signs of breathlessness, too.
She gave us a bright history of the pecan-trees,
whose beginnings were interesting, and then also
bade us a temporary adieu, and turned back to Saint
Joseph's Walk.

The pecan-trees stand on the borders of the estate. They have grown from nuts, as tradition and
probability have it, which were sent to Georgetown
by President Jefferson. This will be inferred from
the subjoined literal copy of a note to Mr. Threlkeld,
grandfather of one of the nuns of the Visitation.

WASHINGTON, MARCH 26, 1807.

SIR, — I thank you for your kind offer of the trees mentioned in your letter of yesterday. the peach apricot which you saw at Hepburn's, was lost on the road: but I recieved with it from Italy at the same time a supply of the stones of the same fruit, which are planted at Monticello, and from which I hope to raise some trees, tho' as yet I do not know their success. should these fail I will avail myself of your offer the next fall or spring. the two peach trees you propose will be very acceptable at the same time. I am endeavoring to make a collection of the choicest kinds of peaches for Monticello.

presuming you are attached to the culture of trees, I take the liberty of sending you some Paccan nuts, which being of the last years growth, recieved from New Orleans, will probably grow. they are a very fine nut, and succeed well in this climate. they require rich land. between the two lobes of the kernel there is a thin pellicle, excessively austere and bitter, which it is necessary to take out before eating the nut. Accept my salutations and assurances of respect.

TH. JEFFERSON.

MR. THRELKELD.

The existence of pecan-trees in this locality is a most unusual thing; but they have so well consoled themselves for their exile from warmer latitudes as to be still tall and healthy.

From another source we learn of a legend that some pecans were sent from Texas and planted by a Mr. Grayson, of Georgetown, on these grounds. There is no documentary evidence of this. On the other hand, the tradition in the community is that the nuts from which the trees sprang were of Jefferson's gift, and his letter seems to support it.

The Mother Superior led us on, showing us the place where the girl students of the academy play lawn tennis; and where a number of swings were ready for the youngest to romp and scream over; where there were seats for on-lookers at the games, sheltered by trees; where the farmyard flourished, and the limpid spring, down in a glade, rejoiced the temperate cow, speaking collectively. Returning slowly towards the inner garden (under the convent windows) she told us of the May-day festivity of olden times, when up the path and terraces to the hill the girls used to come, two and two, to crown the May Queen, who stood under a flourishing pear-tree, noticeable even among the tall, towering growth of boxwood, and the many other trees all around. The terraced lawns make two distinct waves of green-sward, forming a fitting *entourage* for the sway of the queen of springtime. A band of music, in other days, added further merriment. Many women, after-wards of note in the social world, have been May Queens at the Convent of the Visitation. The Mother pointed out to us two English copper beeches, flourish-ing of course, and so similar, as they stand side by side, that they are called the twins. Her tranquil voice became cheerfully sympathetic as she described the phases of loveliness of the beeches, which, she said, pass through, *really*, almost every shade of color in the world, beginning with the tenderest tints in earliest spring, and so going on and on in their enchanting variety of shades, until winter at last gathers away every one of the leaves. If the Mother Superior ever desired "variety," it was apparent that the twin beeches gave it to her in abundance. The nuns are poets in actual life-verses, and all the more classical because they are Homeric in their respect for practical detail.

Passing along an avenue arched by tall sycamores, on our return to the garden, we stopped and inspected the new brick steam-laundry, where all the washing for more than two hundred persons is carried on. Mother was proud to say that it had not required more than three months for the sisters to learn from an engineer the use of the apparatus, so that now the laundry has been conceded entirely to their unaided skill. A strong, large, pink and white cheeked sister was busily stirring the clothes in a caldron, as we stepped in at the door. Very little, to be sure, these sisters care to say to people from the fretted world; and their gentle reserve and downcast eyes (yet happy peace, withal) are very soothing, and suggestive of possible peace for one's self, likewise. The great boiler and engine, indeed, seemed too large to be manipulated by even a stalwart woman; but these monsters of steel and iron really had succumbed to feminine intelligence.

We now wound our way back through the gate in the lofty wall of the convent garden, and, through the green box-bordered paths of the latter, reached the academy, where we were to take lunch. The Sister Procuratrix had met us again, in the white cloister under the first veranda of the nuns' house, — the three verandas, in fact, provide convenient cloisters for each floor, running the whole length of the convent's rear, — and she urged us to take a cup of tea without a moment's delay. We were ushered into the inner parlor of the academy, coming upon an appetizing luncheon-table, decoratively arranged for us; and a tall, elderly out-sister attended to serve us, earnestly setting aside any idea that she was of clay too fine, or culture too good, to stoop to service when required. A connoisseur in convent luncheons can affirm that good cooks often get caught in the golden meshes of that wise life; — golden, because nowhere is silence so well observed. Everything they cook is of the best, and concocted in the best way. The sisters do everything perfectly, with an exquisitely faithful and neat workmanship, from cake to portraits of Bishops.

Mother sat by, for a short time, while we gratefully began to feast; thinking of the meagre benches we had lately seen in the refectory, and that no such china — a present to one of the sisters — as we were now using was allowed on the tables there. "You will excuse me, I'm sure," she said. "I do not refrain from joining in your lunch because of lack of hospitality; but our rule does not allow us to eat in the reception-room." We somewhat rashly answered, having in mind the long excursion we had taken in the damp, appetizing air for an hour or more: "But will you not have your lunch in the refectory while we are having ours here? Dear Mother, it cannot be according to your rule to go without eating altogether!" Our excessive alarm, or something else, — probably the consciousness of the ease of fasting when you know how, — amused the Mother and made the good-natured out-sister smile.

After a little pause of indifference and demur, the Mother Superior kindly accepted our proposition, and swiftly disappeared.

Luncheon finished, we met several of the sisters. One was the Directress,[1] a lady of noble looks, impressing us as a person of the highest intellectuality. She had long been in charge of the academy, to which she had given her best talent and attention, endearing herself, through disinterested inspiration for their welfare, to the many bright graduates who remember her vividly in the midst of present worldly cares. Another sister had been a special friend of Sister Jane Frances Ripley. We perceived at a glance that she was a very sweet and sympathetic person, and we were glad that Phœbe Ripley had had the solace of her companionship, in the absence of her own sisters by birth, and the still greater absence in want of sympathy with her religious views and aspirations. We met, moreover, the sister who teaches literature; nor shall we ever lose the pleasure that meeting gave us. To those who know her, need more be said? We now went to the infirmary, and saw first the cell in which Sister Jane Frances died. It is one of the largest, just capable of making room for two single beds, and a small stove, with a chair or two against the wall; the beds old-fashioned and utterly simple, curtained with dimity, and appearing to be too narrow for tempestuous death. However, they were suited to those calm farewells to this life which the deaths of nuns are most apt to be; and such a placid ending was Phœbe Ripley's.

[1] Sister Loretto, since deceased.

We were especially moved by the little rooms we
saw in the infirmary; for in these were very ancient
nuns, sitting out the old year of their earthly existence ; nuns fading into aged death, who would have
given even to palatial apartments a tinge of melancholy.   But, after all, it is humanity, and not the
convent, which makes the scene so sombre.   Turn
down a street in New York, where an accident has
happened.   Perhaps a fashionable woman has been
run over, and lies upon the pavement.   The body is
surrounded by brilliant shops, splendid carriages, and
handsomely dressed people, just out from a performance by Sothern or Sarah Bernhardt.   Why do you
see, in all the burly glitter of the hurrying city, only
the searching whiteness of this dead woman's cheek?

And further, death "in the world," in a luxurious
room, among a group of relatives and friends, may
(possibly) be more agreeable to *us*.   But let us
remember that to our relatives and friends our death-
scene must be an almost unmitigated suffering.   Is it
not fortunate, then, to be a nun, dying in braver
solitude ?   Yet, while we are adjusting ourselves to
the right point of view, we shiver.   The bedroom of
a person "in the world" is supposed to contain
sundry dear mementos and luxuries and ornaments;
sundry easy-chairs and soft pillows and cosy nooks,
which are considered adequate to console the bruised
spirit after its daily tussle in the arena of men.
Withdraw hither, and you are, for a brief and delicious hour of change, in a sphere of your own; with
a good novel, or other book of leisure, or with some
subject of study in hand, so congenial as to be a

blessing. But in the nun's life her cosiest, quietest nook is an altar before which to pray. Are we strong enough to keep in reserve no lair, no robber's cave, where we can steal away from God, nursing our pet fancies, or handling the fairy gold of self-indulgence? Are we generous enough to merge ourselves wholly in the unselfishness of divinity? If not, we recoil from the frank simplicity, the austere plainness, of a nun's cell. Here there is no place for withdrawal into a self which is mere selfishness. Over each door stands the name of a saint, and the mention of some special virtue to be remembered and cultivated. The little beds are prim and hard; the pictures are few, and in their intention point heavenward. Cold, literally, the tiny rooms are; — the only heat coming from registers in the halls, — with one big window apiece giving plenty of light and air; no carpet, one chair; and the only richness to be detected in all this region of simplicity is that richest blessing — the consolation of faith. But, behold, we soon felt that the nuns (and we felt it with the whole heart) had *cheerful* rooms!

There is arithmetic in all this; and one is at a disadvantage until one learns to figure it out. A religious life is very nice in its calculations. If you follow the deductions of the cloister, you find out what seems good and remunerative in worldly life, and what is good and remunerative in a cloistered life, by a perfectly clear process of division and subtraction. The delusive speciousness of elegance in what we can buy is challenged by the genuine values of what the virtues can give us, even out of the seem-

ing barrenness of a convent cell; and victory follows
" God, and the right ! "

The rule of the Convent of the Visitation is strictly
according to its earliest traditions in America; and
wherever bleakness appears, it is the pride and joy of
the sisters ; a pride and a joy that never yet hurt or
overbore, so sweetly unselfish are these traits when
transmuted by self-sacrifice. It must be admitted
also that even kings have, by a like preference,
occupied small and primly unornamented private
chambers ; that is, the kings who have accomplished
things and have been " heard from." For, as that
wise man and monarch Marcus Aurelius said : " Even
in a palace, life can be led well."

Before leaving the portion of the convent above
described, we met the Infirmarian, a sister as white
as her veil was black, and possessing that gentleness
of expression which Rembrandt could so well portray
with what seems a positive movement of light over
the features. It was near the dispensary that we
found her ; and this department is well worth noting,
with a comment. Neat and pretty as a toy it was,
this quiet little dispensary, with its wholesome medi-
cinal jars, its glasses and paraphernalia for com-
pounding pills, draughts, or electuaries, and its reassuring aromatic odor of drugs. One felt inclined. to
stop there and play apothecary for a while. The Sister Infirmarian who has that privilege is to be envied.
And now the serious comment to be made is as follows : Those who, in their vague thoughts, associate
with convents only mortification of the flesh — in
fasts, self-denial, plain living, early rising, hard toil

— generally are ignorant of, or forget, that other equally Catholic principle and practice that the body must be respected and preserved, must be treated as a temple of the Holy Ghost; and that a sin of disregard for health is to be dreaded as other sins are. If the sisters overtax themselves, it is not with an intention of self-injury; and the efficient, though simple, appointments of their little cabinet of drugs and their infirmary show how well they provide for maintaining or restoring health. Although naturally not undertaking to practice medicine, they have gathered much experience, which is passed on by tradition from one to another, so that there are always two or three members of the community competent to preside in the dispensary and prepare simple remedies.

Stepping from the corridor, a little farther on, we went into the long choir, whose clear windows look out over the garden; a spacious room fitted with numerous dark stalls on either side, where the sisters sit, or kneel, chanting their offices; matins and lauds, the last devotion at night, then prime, terce, sext, and none; at different early hours of the morning; vespers in the afternoon; and, in the evening, compline. It is in this place — which is not a part of the chapel, but is a room in the convent, simply looking into the chapel — that they hear mass and perform their other religious exercises; their voices heard, themselves unseen by the young girls and children of the academy, who come to the chapel. The choir, though on the second floor, is on a level with and opens directly into the sanctuary, the opening taking up the whole end of the room. It is

closely grated with iron, and is furnished with fold-
ing screen-shutters of cloth, so that it can be closed
entirely, if this be desired. Its position at right
angles from the chapel nave also protects the occu-
pants of the choir from being seen. In the centre
of the long space between the stalls is a lectern, and
on the walls, opposite or between the windows, hang
many interesting religious pictures, old and new,
oil paintings, engravings, or colored reproductions;
among them a copy of the famed, miraculous picture
of Our Lady of Good Counsel, the original of which
is at Genazzano, in Italy. The "little gallery" for
the infirm or invalid sisters is just above the grated
opening of the choir, and from this the sisters can
look down into the sanctuary. This little gallery is
reached from the second floor by ascending a flight of
steps, and passing down a long corridor on each side
of which is a row of "cells."   Here, in the small
room, we found wooden chairs, glistening with the
polish of a hundred years or more, and probably contrived by carpenters who were learning their trade, in
a country then, at best, largely experimental. But,
by their very quaintness, the chairs were particularly
attractive to-day. They were part of the long-treas-
ured furniture brought to the house by sister Mary
McDermott.

Into the gallery the light fell from a window reaching to its floor. Below, the chapel looked narrow,
high, sacred, mellow with mingled colors, and lovely
in its vague richness and calm. Portraits of St.
Francis de Sales and St. Jane de Chantal are to be
seen, in what may be called *dark* luminosity, on

either side of the sanctuary; and an ancient picture, browned by time, represents Martha and Mary in a composition of much dignity, and hangs directly over the altar. This picture was painted by order of Charles X., and presented by him to the Georgetown chapel, through Rev. Father Clorivière, S. J., whose family were devoted French royalists. Descending to the second story again, from the gallery, we found the grated confessional, adjoining the chapel. It is a wholly unadorned apartment, where the nuns kneel to make confession; the Father confessor being on the other side of the grating; for no habitual intrusion upon the privacy of the actual convent enclosure may be permitted, even in the performance of this holy office. In this room, General Winfield Scott — the " hero of Lundy's Lane," victor in the Mexican War, and, at the outbreak of the war for the Union, general of the army of the United States — was allowed to see his daughter Virginia, dying of consumption, who had entered the order of the Visitation, here, under the name in religion of Sister Mary Emmanuel Scott. The old warrior, who had served his country with so much ability and patriotism, had also a conception of his duty to his God; and, although he did not share with his daughter the faith she had won, he fully consented to her taking the vows of religion. It was in this very room that she died; and her father visited her here, only after it became evident that her health, always delicate, was hopelessly broken.

We were led to the assembly room, an ample apartment, where the sisters gather for an hour after dinner, and about two hours in the evening, meeting

socially for what they call their "recreation." Then
they busy themselves with knitting or plain sewing,
or with any fancy-work or embroidery they may have
to do; being careful to keep their fingers alert, on
account of the advice of St. Jane de Chantal — that
the hands should be employed whenever possible.
No games are indulged in; but much pleasant chat
goes on, and a harmless joke pleases every one.

Even here, in this apartment chiefly designed for
rest and leisure, for pleasant chat and light occupa-
tion, there are many reminders that a higher purpose
is always to be kept in view. One of these is a
written scroll of paper attached to the wall, near the
fireplace, and called the "Challenge." But it assur-
edly is the gentlest challenge ever known, and, by its
character, seems to neutralize its own title. For the
purport of this paper is simply to remind the sisters,
at each and every season of the Christian year, that
it is desirable at that season, in their social intercourse
and recreation among themselves, to give special attention to some particular virtue — patience, humility,
gentleness, cheerfulness — whichever it may be that
is specified on the scroll. Briefly, it is a quiet appeal
to them, putting them on their mettle or their honor
and conscience, to make an additional effort to excel
in that virtue. There is a challenge for Advent, for
Christmas, for Epiphany, for Lent, for Easter, for
Pentecost. It establishes among the sisters a friendly
competition, not a rivalry. No award is made, no decision is rendered as to who among them has surpassed
the rest. The arbitrament is solely of the conscience
and God.

Now it may seem, to those who are wholly unaccustomed to such methods of thought and action, that this ever present watchfulness of self, and this constant endeavor to rise to the higher plane even while engaged in amusement or social converse, must become intolerably monotonous and a frightful strain. But, on the contrary, this conventual system of mingled self-examination and unselfish activity results in the greatest buoyancy of spirits, and in a healthy, happy life. There are no human beings so deliciously light-hearted as the nuns. They turn their whole natures in the direction of adoration, and of every virtue, as easily as they walk, talk, eat, sleep, or wake.

Their system, too, is absolutely the one that has been copied in every religious society or brotherhood or league formed for spiritual and Christian purposes outside of the Church; with this difference, that these organizations outside follow the lead only so far as it is convenient and in accord with self-indulgence to do so. They adopt the general principles, to a certain extent; but, while trying to arouse emulation in well doing, they seldom deny themselves the selfish gratifications of the world; and they insist upon having individual superiority in goodness promptly rewarded with prizes, honors, distinctions of some kind, flattering to the unconsecrated life. But the sisters work without expectation of material reward, or even of an honorary one. They succeed in making religion and self-sacrifice perfectly natural, unaffected, joyous, day by day, at the same time that both it and they are enveloped in and sustained by the fine, sweet, enlivening atmosphere of the supernatural.

The prevailing gray tone of the convent creeps into the community room, as well as into the broad corridors, graced on each floor by altars. But there are interesting pictures on the walls; likenesses of the patron saints of the order, so constantly repeated in different parts of the house; and purely sacred groups. The phalanx of windows on the outer side of the room, overlooking the garden and its trees across the cloistered piazza, gives decorativeness to the long room, as a similar phalanx does in the refectory. There is a large painting over the mantelpiece of the Blessed Virgin meeting St. Elizabeth. The tone is a pale nut brown, and the figures are rather indistinct, as if the voluntary pensiveness of the general deportment of the convent had embraced this picture of the Visitation. A truer example of the underlying and frequently manifest good cheer of the nuns is given by the sturdy portraits of the saints, and the beaming representations of angels. Within the clear monochrome of these pictures is caught the bright courage of religious zeal and sublime law. Their firm glances, their steady poise of head, their sweet but uncompromising lips, express the only genuine satisfaction and happiness; namely, those which last through eternity. They remind us of the sort of people we trust, — not those who profess most. They remind us of those faces which, throughout our own lives, have given us the most solid comfort and the deepest refreshment. Were those the faces of gay young companions, laughing too much, and quick to pout in disappointment or even anger? Or were they the faces of eager beginners of life, willing to expend

themselves lavishly in all pleasurable ways for each
other, but crushed or indignant when called upon to
expend themselves for each other in suffering? Are
not the faces we look back to as being sublimely encouraging, lastingly good, those of mothers, sisters,
nurses, that smiled gently in the hour of calumny or
sickness; faces which were merciful in their expression, when *we* were fiercely unjust; which were sternly
strong in the wild hours of anxiety or anguish well
known to every life? Such faces are the faces of
religious superiors.

There is a story of St. John the Evangelist, who,
while at Ephesus, took a young man of great promise
under his care. Afterwards he was himself called to
Rome, and the youth became dissipated, and the
leader of a band of robbers. On St. John's return
he sought the outlaw, discovered him, talked with
him. He noticed that the young man tried to conceal his right hand (which had committed so many
crimes) from the eyes of the apostle. St. John seized
it, kissed it, and bathed it with his tears. We recall,
too, that St. Francis de Sales was so "charitable,
tolerant, and gentle towards those who disagreed
with him, as well as those who led wicked lives,"
that he was sometimes remonstrated with; and then
he would reply: "Had Saul been rejected, should
we have had St. Paul?"

In evidence of the charity illustrated by those two
episodes, the pictures of religious devotees in the
assembly-room made it reassuringly pleasant and
restful. Sundry tables stand adown the centre of
the floor, and numerous simple little chairs of quaint

outline, like those in the invalids' gallery, bring with
them the memory of Madame Yturbide, ex-empress
of Mexico, one of the first benefactors of the convent,
who gave these chairs to the community about a hundred years ago. They are now especially prized by
the sisterhood on account of their associations, their
antiquity, and their freedom from undue luxuri-
ousness.

II. THE ACADEMY.

In our conversation with the Superioress we realized that the academy, as conducted from its origin,
had been permitted only by a special dispensation
(which will be referred to later on).[1] The intention
of the holy founders of the Visitation order was that,
when perfected, the institute should rank among the
contemplative, rather than the active orders of the
church, without question of utility to the outside
world, other than the utility of prayer.

Nevertheless, even during the lifetime of the founders, it was deemed well to receive into certain parts
of the monastery children called "sisters of the little
habit," who were to be reared either for the religious
life or for the world, as their vocation might develop.
Somewhat later, many of the Visitation houses of
Europe were compelled to resort to regular teaching
as a means of livelihood; although this did not force
them to depart from even the least of their rules and
customs. In a new and non-Catholic country the
case was different, and some divergence from these
became necessary. When the Georgetown convent

[1] Chapter xiv. of Annals, in this volume.

was founded, there was great need of a good Catholic school for girls near Washington; and this work was undertaken by the rising community, which looked to it for material support, having no endowment or other means. The points of variation from the strict rule thereby involved were about as follows: a change in the hours of meals, on account of the climate, as well as the arrangement of classes and recitations; the admission of day-pupils, with a more frequent opening of the academy door, consequently, than would otherwise have been allowed; compliance with the wish of parents and guardians to inspect the academy building, on bringing their children to school; the employment of " externs " as teachers, if needful; a benevolent school for the parish children, kept by the sisters (within their own enclosure, however, very near the academy); and some minor, nonessential changes resulting from these.

In their honest, earnest endeavor to place their school on a level with the best in the land, the first object held in view by the pioneer sisters was to preserve and spread the faith, to save souls; an object often better forwarded and more surely attained when sought for in connection with the highest cultivation of mind and heart. The foresight of the ecclesiastical superiors who obtained these privileges from the Holy See (without which there would probably have been no school at all) has been fully justified. All through the country the good results are witnessed to by grandmothers, mothers, and children, who turn with grateful hearts to their Alma Mater as the source from which they imbibed the faith more precious than life itself. Some of the sisters of the present day bear similar testimony.

But, in order that readers may not misapprehend the nature and extent of the dispensation just referred to, we may add a few words here. As privileges are always liable, at one time or another, to be counted on too far, though not necessarily leading to abuses, the power of authorizing " the changes which may perhaps in process of time be made on account of the circumstances of place and government "[1] were intrusted to the Most Reverend Archbishops of Baltimore. These same superiors, as years passed on, wisely reminded the sisters to hold themselves in readiness (as every religious community is in duty bound to do) to return to the primitive rule in strict observance, or to adopt it as nearly as possible, when there should no longer be need of privilege or dispensation. Such injunctions the sisters hold from the archbishops of fifty years back; before which time the convent was much more assailed by attacks from ignorance and prejudice than has been the case in subsequent years. Thus does the church, in the person of her chief pastor or his representatives, either loosen or draw more closely the lines of a monastic rule, according to circumstances, for the true benefit and use of those cloistered few who separate themselves from the world in order to live closer to God.

In view of the work done for souls in the Georgetown House of the Visitation, this authorized departure from some details of the rule may be regarded as a circumstance of great and happy moment. The im-

[1] Chapter xiv. Annals, *ut supra.*

pression that it is so is deepened when one enters the
spacious, the almost immense academy, which has ex-
panded so vastly since the days of Madame Yturbide
and Sister Mary McDermott. The academy building
is large and stately, towering above the convent, yet
as we have before pointed out, closely attached to it;
like a tall, strong child still clinging close to the de-
mure little mother whom it has outgrown in size.
When you step into the hall beyond the reception
room, connecting with the chapel and the convent's
sacred and sombre precincts, the Mother tells you that
all is now in sharp contrast to monastic quiet and
poverty. Yet you will have your opinion, because it
is too agreeable to relinquish, that the calm of the
cloister fills and softens and hushes the regions devoted to the girl students; whose rippling chat and
laughter is not louder, in these large spaces, than the
merriment of a brook. The girls move about in
groups or singly; in black dresses, but rosy of cheek
and golden or glistening-dark of hair, and as pretty
as pictures; often with a style about their dresses as
unmistakably fashionable as it is simple in general
effect. Sometimes the girls we came across bowed
gracefully and with delicious respect to the Superioress, the figure in black veil and white barbette, and
with a glimmering smile upon its lips, which had suddenly appeared among them.

Everything about the academy has the effect of
largeness. The staircases are of a noble width; the
rooms and halls are very high. Here and there,
beside the wide passageways, hang large paintings,
sometimes only excellent in intention; but that — a

religious expression of holiness — made the pictures
lovely. The laboratory was the most interesting place
of all. Some fine old brass electrical instruments of
handsome proportions, and some modern specimens as
well, a portrait of Father Curley — and twenty other
things — were pointed out to us, and filled us with
admiration. The Mother turned a wheel, making the
sparks appear with a sudden crackling sound of
power; or, touching her finger to the brass cylinder,
emitted a resounding star of electricity by the gentle
contact. In this charming room she teaches physics
and chemistry to the older girls. Other very attractive rooms are the art studios, where the severities of
the monastic rule really are merged in those elements
of life which do no more than soothe and please
through the eyesight. Some of the work was very
good, and all of it imbued with artistic feeling.

Still another pleasant spot was the library, every
inch a library. Then we saw the large hall for musical
entertainments, lectures, and graduating exercises,— all
confined to the pupils, except the last, to which the parents and friends are invited. With accommodations
for seven or eight hundred listeners, its qualities are
admirable for its purpose, in that it has no suspicion
of the oblong shape which seems to relegate some people
to the second-best place; and its acoustic properties
are excellent, under the proper conditions of a large
audience. Opposite the entrance there is a spacious
platform, over which is placed a picture of the highest excellence. It represents the Blessed Virgin and
Infant Saviour, with St. John. It was given to the
sisters by the father of General Meade, the famous

commander of the Army of the Potomac at the Battle
of Gettysburg. Mr. Meade had a fine collection of
paintings, obtained while he was on a visit to Spain,
and this was one of them. For a long time the sisters supposed it to be a Murillo; but while it was
on exhibition at the Metropolitan Museum in New
York, George William Curtis and other critics in art
decided that it must be a Vandyke, which opinion was
confirmed by the art authorities of Seville, to whom a
photograph was sent.

We had come to the hall to hear some remarkably
good piano playing and singing, and to learn how
gifted some of the Georgetown Academy pupils can
be. A young creature, whose ardent enthusiasm was
somehow conveyed across the spaces of the hall in
spite of her quiet demeanor, played for us; and the
piano being a superlatively good one, her melodies,
nobly modulated and phrased, rolled out with fine
expressiveness. The next number was a piece of the
utmost religious sweetness, played very beautifully by
another young woman; and then a sparkling child in
her teens sang, with the pure fire of a girl's ardor,
and with an astonishingly strong, clear voice, a rich,
naïve love-song. These three ingenuous girls, one
could easily see, were immensely happy. Success and
the joy of earnest endeavor glowed all around them.
The young sister, their teacher, was a healthy-minded,
spirited nun, possessed of a graceful air; yet there
was something about her quite as distinctive as her
sombre dress, to bring an elevating influence of " recollection " and self-correcting humility to these pretty
débutantes, who are soon to shine in the world with-

out. The tolerant and gently kind superiority of the
sisters towards the inevitable girl of society, who must
be cultivated and then cast upon her cruel, though
fair-seeming fate of usefulness to creation, is typical
of their state of mind towards the world. The nun is
a kind of woman so entirely appreciative, that she has
all a woman's geniality towards feminine charm and
talent. But in being also, as all nuns must be, different from all other kinds of women, she proves
clearly that all this charm and talent is mere fanci-
fulness, in comparison to the life of spiritual adoration; that consciousness which embraces the whole
system of religious science, of which the science of
humane love of our kind — usually "in the world"
exemplified perfectly only in a mother's love — is but
a part. In the world we are apt to think this "brotherly" love among the human family is the most spiritual thing possible, the *summum bonum*, the complete circle of everything *not* material and selfish. To
the nun, this mother's love, brother's love, love of
the friend, is the mere *a b c*, or beginning, of the
language of spiritual works; — the instrument of the
poetry of highest action, which must be brought into
play towards all human creatures alike.

But if the girls of the academy are happy, are
gently treated, and are fully appreciated as the
mothers of the future, still the good sisters would not
deprive them of a little flavor of discipline, without
which their lives might, of course, become so vapid as
to weigh upon them! The vehicle of justice, used
for discipline in the academy, is a pretty and modest
old-fashioned article of furniture, seemingly alive. It

is nothing less than a venerable clock, standing in
a corner of the large hall on the first floor, and lit
whitely by an adjacent window. It is one of two
timepieces given to the community by Sister Mary
McDermott, the early teacher and benefactress of
the convent, whom we have mentioned before. The
clocks must therefore be a hundred, and may more
probably be a hundred and fifty years old; but they
both keep perfect time (one in the convent itself, and
the other in this academy hall), deriving, you imagine,
not a little benefit from coming under the dominion of
the ascetic rule of St. Francis de Sales and St. Jane,
and could not possibly stoop to falsifying time or losing vigor, like clocks devoted to secular uses. To tell
the truth, much of the merit involved must be due to
the faithful care which the quiet sisters give to every
farthing's worth of commodity which finds itself
under their charge. This old clock of the academy
has a subordinate executive, an ally in the punishment
of offenders, that looks as if it had been originally
designed for nursery merriment and dolls' play. It
is a very small old-fashioned chair, which has been
reserved, time out of mind, to bring rosy-cheeked and
pouting delinquents to repentance, when the mischief-
makers are guilty of insubordination of any sort. For
untold years — so a girl of sixteen would call the interval — to "sit by the clock" has been a penance at
Georgetown Convent Academy, bringing misery to
those who have, a moment before, experienced the
brief joys of revolt. The clock of justice proudly
bears a mirthful moon upon its disk of numerals,
which seems, in its semicircular orbit, to peep over

the whole world at the little girl who has had the
audacity to defy the Sisters of the Visitation. We
can see her ourselves with distinctness, seated with
bowed head, and an eye carefully observant; a small
handful of wickedness, not by any means so very
wicked. It is justly considered to be a terrible retribution to be ordered " to sit by the clock; " and yet,
strange to say, and easy to understand, those women,
now alumnæ of the academy, who were once rene-
gades of the chair, look back with ardent affection to
Sister McDermott's clock and its tiny stool of discipline.

One day, one of the brightest and naughtiest of the
scholars (who was it?) had been doomed to sit out
her punishment at the feet of time. Who should
come along, through the large, dark-wooded hall but
her papa and a party of friends, accompanied by a sister who was the very directress who had sent the young
damsel " to the clock." The papa and his friends
were bent on seeing the child, to congratulate her
upon being in so safe and beneficial and happy a
home; — the sister directress may have hoped that
the encounter, fraught with humiliation, would do
much to subdue her little charge. The observant eye
of the delinquent took in the whole situation at a
glance, and her tender and guileless youth arose in de-
fence. She rapidly decided upon breaking the iron
law not to leave the small, humorous-looking chair
until the last moment of penance had been ticked out
by the stately clock. What was the directress's astonishment to see her rise, advance towards her proud
papa and his surrounding friends, and explain that

her teacher had asked her to watch and see if the
clock kept regular time! She enacted the part she
had assumed, of useful little clock-superintendent, to
perfection; and was commended for her patience and
reliability, even by her father; who had nevertheless
guessed the truth of the matter at once. The directress had not the heart to interfere, for, after all, discipline in the convent academy is loving.

Near the academy clock was a little anteroom,
where were hung a number of pictures of flowers and
fruits, which we were told belonged to one of the novices who was in that state which may turn either wholly
spiritual, or back to the wholly worldly. At least, up
to a certain point the postulant, no matter how fervently
religious, is regarded by her superiors as one who
may find that, after all, her vocation is not for a life
of such complete abnegation, and may at the final
hour decide to recede from the great renunciation of
worldly pleasures. Our religion, in its wisdom and
generosity, asks of us all our perishable possessions,
before filling our hands with the imperishable; and
even the ordinary layman, if he has life at all, must
labor for that bliss which he receives back from his
faith a hundred fold in excess of his deserts. These pictures before us belonged, as we have said, to a young
woman still in the doubtful phase; and were to be returned to her if *she* returned to "the world." They
produced the same sensation as does the reading of a
dead person's will. The nothingness of them beside
the great beauty and value of the heavenly life argued
very forcibly that it would be unwise to retrace one's
way for their sake. They were a gay and tempting

illustration of the mess of pottage for which we often
resign our inheritance, unless we bravely launch ourselves upon the mists of eternity, — when, in response
to our faith, angels hold us up ; and, rising as we
surely do above the mists, clear visions fill our sight,
which we never need and never can forget.

In the reception room, to which we at last returned,
where we met several interesting and charming nuns,
there is a portrait of Archbishop Leonard Neale,
whose twenty years of faith in response to a vision
of the Order of the Visitation, was at last crowned
with success in the establishment of this convent.
The portrait is supposed to be by a Dutch painter, and
is eminently fine ; homely, exquisite, touching, sweetly
stern, in the true Dutch contradictory style of fascinating art.   And so, as we came away, we bore
with us in our minds and hearts the gentle, firm, and
earnest visage of the American Founder.

A word, and more, should have been said here of
the clusters of girls trooping out merrily along the
walk of the garden, into the wider domain of the
grounds, under charge of some watchful yet smiling
and companionable sister ; of the indoor play-rooms,
where the younger or more delicate children — whom
it was not advisable to emancipate into the dampness of
that day, out-doors — frolicked mildly, but gayly, like
so many lambs or fledglings of various age and size.
Then, too, there was the shiningly neat, commodious
academy refectory, sparkling with plain glass and china
on white tablecloths ; and with a high shelf around
two sides of the wall, where dessert-plates stood
arrayed on edge with expectation, and rosy apples

glowed invitingly. Up-stairs, the long dormitories extended their vistas of snowy little beds and linen curtains in a peaceful series; with statues of the Blessed Virgin or of St. Joseph at either end of the apartment, and a small ever-burning crimson lamp before every statue, like a heart aglow with love and charity. On a floor above these dormitories were special rooms for young ladies domiciled there to take some special course in music or languages, beyond the regular curriculum. And, highest of all, at the very top, were the music-rooms, each one — like a big melodious bird-cage — enclosing a captive piano. In this high and airy precinct, also, may be heard the warbling of violins.

From the windows of the music-rooms we became suddenly aware of broad, far-reaching, and delightful views over the whole realm of Washington, with the wide and winding flood of the tan-colored Potomac eddying along its southwestern verge, and the picturesque, fast-growing city far below our feet. The mass of houses, interspersed with abundant trees, appears, because of the irregularity of the ground, to heave and billow away beneath us like a material surge of Time; and across and beyond it rises again, majestic, the white-pillared Capitol of the United States, its pure dome crowned by a solemn figure of Columbia, typifying Liberty, in dark bronze. As we stand here in "the upper room" of a Catholic Christian convent, it is interesting to reflect that the figure presiding there on the summit of the nation's chief place of government was designed and modelled by the sculptor Crawford — father of one among the greatest and

most famous of American novelists, Marion Crawford,
who is an ardent Catholic.

Below us lies the city that seethes with a turmoil
of politics concentrated from all quarters of the
Union. It is the whirlpool in which all the conflict-
ing currents of jealousy or ambition meet and struggle ; in which the strivings of individuals or of parties,
for wealth, social or commercial supremacy and the
power of control, go on unceasingly. Many are
wrecked there ; some go down in the whirlpool and
are lost completely. A few survive, for a while.
On all this we can look down calmly, though with
intense compassion, from the serene point of view of
the convent school. But it is well that the sombre
statue which represents civic Liberty there, on that
eminence of Capitol Hill — overlooking so much of
intrigue and corruption, so much of angry rivalry,
greed or disappointment, mingled with virtue and
honest endeavor — should be able to exchange glances
always with the spirit of self-sacrifice and self-control,
dominant ever in the holy house of the Visitation, on
the Georgetown heights. For pure religious faith,
true self-renunciation and self-sacrifice are always the
basis and the beacon-light of a people's genuine
liberty.

In those soft, half-soliloquizing tones which are so
usual with them, the nuns bade us good-by. But,
although that parting meant the end of immediate
personal association, a link between us had been
wrought, which we gladly accepted as something that
would join us to them, in a manner, permanently.

They had confided to us the manuscript Annals of

their Georgetown Convent of the Visitation, with the privilege of arranging the contents for publication. Unassuming blank-books filled with interesting records, these volumes (some of them very old), bound in marbled boards, or carefully covered with smooth brown paper or dark cloth, hold registered in manuscript, penned by the patient, industrious sisters from time to time, the whole vivid, pathetic, and inspiring narrative of the founding and the growth of this first American house of the Visitation Order. It is from them that we have drawn the authentic Story of Courage, which is related in the course of the ensuing chapters.

As we came away, the Mother Superior said quietly, with a subdued and gently resigned fear lest we might not look upon the convent as it shone to her eyes and lived in her spirit: "It is all very old-fashioned and plain, but we love it. It is our home, on earth, and " — hesitating again — "we think it is a little above and more than earth."

The history of it, will, we believe, cause our readers to share her feeling.

III.

THE VISITATION ESTABLISHED IN THE UNITED STATES.

THE record of the establishment, in the United States, of the Order of the Visitation of the Blessed Virgin Mary — like the record of all great institutions rooted in age-long faith — leads us at once to an interesting chain of circumstances and results, which to the world's eye might seem like a series of curious coincidences or accidents. To the more discerning mind, these circumstances and results form portions of a plan in which the guiding touch of God, the far-reaching influence and help of the Holy Spirit, are clearly apparent; working simply, naturally, yet with supernatural power and design, through finite means.

The lights of history, and in especial of religious history, resemble those signals of the heliograph which are given by flashes of sunlight reflected from a small mirror. With the heliograph, men standing on high elevations can communicate at enormous distances. Although they may be so far apart as to remain invisible to each other, yet, from points where no other form or motion can be discerned, they send their messages of clear intelligence by a regular system of glancing sun rays, — so that, from mountain range to mountain range, from peak to peak, the word is made to travel on wings of illumination for a hundred miles.

In the same way, if we ascend to lofty heights of observation we may catch the lights of history, the signals of faith as they are flashed upon the mind from century to century, across the deep valleys and the heavy mists of time.

And so when, in 1893, we contemplate the fact that the Visitation Order in America had its tentative beginning here at Georgetown in the District of Columbia in 1793 (though not actually established until 1798), another luminous fact comes to us from the remote past, which — like an actual sunbeam — shows us that the foundation here is closely connected with an event which occurred one hundred and seventy-five years before that date.

The event we refer to is a prediction by St. Francis de Sales, himself the originator of the Order of the Visitation in France; and this prediction was made in 1619. He had been deputed in that year to the court of France, where a marriage was to be celebrated between Victor Amadeus of Savoy and Princess Christine, daughter of the late King Henry IV. On the same occasion he was also introduced to the youngest daughter of the deceased monarch, Henrietta Maria.

Henry IV., her father, had, as we know, entertained toward the saint a special esteem and affection;[1] shown by cordial aid given to his missionary labors in Chablais and Gex, nearly twenty years

[1] See the life sketch of St. Francis in this volume.

earlier. St. Francis, therefore, who was now Bishop of Geneva, must have taken particular pleasure in witnessing the union of the houses of France and Savoy, through the marriage of Henry's eldest daughter, Christine, to Victor. Yet even while allowing himself this pleasure, — noticing, too, the vivacity of little Henrietta Maria and her delight at the splendor of her sister's wedding, — he said, placing his hand on the younger princess' head: "*God has reserved for this child a higher destiny, a more solid glory. He designs her for the support of the church.*"

Words of great import, worthy to be noted and emphasized; uttered as they were with a confidence which only the pure heart, the clear vision of the seer and holy man could authorize! And mark in what direct manner the prophecy came true; not only in Henrietta's services to the church in England and her founding a house of the Visitation many years afterward in France, but also and especially in her planting the Catholic colony of Maryland, as well as in the work which was to be done a hundred and seventy-five years later in the United States — a nation unknown and non-existent when St. Francis spoke — by the descendants of a faithful lady attached to Henrietta's own court.

For, six years after her sister's wedding, Henrietta Maria also became a royal bride, the spouse of Charles I. of England. The earthly career of Charles ended in tragedy; but, while he reigned, Henrietta Maria, as Queen of England, did much to better the condition of the persecuted Catholics of that country. By the secret articles of her marriage treaty it was stipulated that not only she and her household were to enjoy their religion without restraint, but that the oppressed Catholics of England and Ireland should likewise be protected against the rigor of the penal law.

King Charles, in spite of opposition, did his best to carry out these articles of the contract. Tyburn gallows, which almost daily had been dyed with the blood of martyrs, now stood idle. The Tower of London and the various jails gave up those large numbers of priests and laymen who had been imprisoned for conscience' sake; and although the public exercise of Catholic Christian worship was still prohibited, Catholics were at least freed from the cruelties and oppressions which had weighed upon them heavily for many years.

Notwithstanding the general prohibition, Queen Henrietta maintained in her court ten priests and ten choir musicians, and mass was openly celebrated with pomp in her chapel at Whitehall Palace. Ultimately she erected three stately churches, to which were attached bodies of Capuchins, Oratorians, and Benedictines. But even with doing so much in England itself she was not satisfied.

Hitherto no Catholic colony had been settled in the new world. Henrietta made it her special care that one should now be organized here, under her patronage and with her aid.

Maryland, the cradle of Catholicity among the English-speaking colonies in this hemisphere, was named after her, — and thus the holy name of Mary, or Maria, bestowed upon this queen, was permanently impressed also upon a considerable territory which was afterward to become part of the United States.

But Parliament and the Puritan party became enraged with King Charles for his toleration of "popery;" and because of this, quite as much as on account of his unbending views of royal prerogative, took up arms against him. When he was defeated and had suffered death by decapitation, at the order of the ill-fated court of regicides, Henrietta — after twenty years of life in England — was compelled to fly to France, in 1649. Here she sought solace for her grief in retirement from the world, and much of her time was spent at the Visitation Convent in Paris. Worldly disaster, the piteous death of her husband, and the loss of a throne had all contributed to fulfill the destiny which St. Francis de Sales had, even in her young girlhood, foreseen and predicted for her. Yet it is plain that her choice of a convent as her place of rest and consolation was not due to a mere inert and fruitless mourning. For, two years later, she proceeded actively to build the third convent of Paris (Chaillot), where she entered into a still deeper religious seclusion. It was at Chaillot that her funeral obsequies were performed, and there, also, her heart was enshrined.

Now, between these events and circumstances and the origin of the first American Visitation house, toward the last of the eighteenth century, and its complete habitation early in the nineteenth, there is an unbroken connection. It was this very convent of Chaillot, founded by Henrietta Maria, which first acknowledged the community of religious ladies in

Georgetown as belonging to the Visitation, and sent them (under charge of secrecy) the rules, customs, and writings of the Order.

We must further observe, in the connection of Georgetown with the past, a most important and vital link, which is supplied in the life of that faithful Catholic lady of Henrietta's court, to whom a general allusion has been made, — Madam Anna Neale, ancestress of the holy Archbishop Neale and of several eminent Jesuits. Madam Neale was a favorite with Queen Henrietta; and it was by her posterity that two female religious orders were to be introduced into this republic of the United States: the Carmelites and the Visitation Order.

The story of her descendant, Archbishop Neale, founder of the Visitation in America, — a story which we are now to retrace briefly, — is of absorbing and impressive interest.

II. ARCHBISHOP NEALE.

On the outbreak of the civil wars in England, so the annals of the Georgetown convent inform us, Captain Neale,[1] — finding it impossible longer to enjoy the comforts of his faith unmolested, or to serve the captive king — left England with his wife, Madam Anna Neale, and their family, betaking himself to the all but wilderness of Maryland, in the New World. Yet even into this " Land of the Sanctuary " Protestant intolerance penetrated.

---

[1] He was also, by some persons, said to have been an admiral in the Royal Navy.

After the usurpation of Cromwell, and during the reign of the earlier Protestant princes of England, the Maryland Catholics found themselves laid under those very privations and disabilities from which they had fled in the Old World. Even before then, indeed, scarcely ten years subsequent to the landing of Governor Leonard Calvert in 1634, the Puritans — whom he had welcomed to the benefits of that gentle religious tolerance proclaimed by him for this Catholic province — rose in armed insurrection against the Catholics and their chief magistrate.

On the downfall of Charles, many Jesuits in Maryland were seized by the Protestants and sent off to England, where they underwent long and cruel imprisonment. Finally, in 1654, the Provincial Assembly deprived Catholics of their civil rights, and decreed that liberty of conscience should not extend to " popery, prelacy or licentiousness of opinion." Catholics were forbidden to build churches or maintain schools. The Mass was prohibited. Catholic Christians were not allowed even to walk with their fellow citizens in front of the State House at Annapolis, and were subjected to insult and persecution. Up to the time of the American Revolution, in fact, as the historian O'Shea tells us, Catholics were forbidden on pain of death to enter any of the other colonies except Pennsylvania; and in Maryland not a single public place of Catholic worship was permitted to exist. Some of the Jesuits, however, had succeeded in maintaining a few chapels in secret, and also a fine grammar school on their secluded farm, known as "The Bohemian Manor," upon the eastern shore.

It was in this school that Charles Carroll of Carrollton, with the future Archbishop Carroll, and Archbishop Neale, received their first education.

The generation to which Leonard Neale, afterward Archbishop of Baltimore, belonged, seems not to have been recorded with precision. But, as he was born in 1748, the opinion is probably correct, that his mother was the grand-daughter of Madam Anna Neale. She was left a widow, with six sons and one daughter. Yet, although death had taken from her the companionship of her husband, this fearless and devout woman did not hesitate to consign her life to a still deeper loneliness, for the sake of keeping her children's faith intact.

The persecution of Catholics in Maryland, the enforced secrecy of their worship, the suppressing of Catholic education by law, upon which we have touched, placed Catholic parents in the dilemma of either seeing their children grow up ignorant, or else of exposing them to the danger of losing their faith if they attended schools hostile to Catholicity. Those who could afford it, therefore, were led by a strong and high motive to send their children to Europe, for education. Mrs. Neale, the mother of Leonard, had the material means for doing so; and, with a magnificent devotion worthy of the cause for which she lived and made her sacrifice, she sent from her side all her sons and her only daughter; placing them in the Catholic schools or colleges of France and Belgium.

It is a memorable fact, to be noted here, that five of these sons (William, Benedict, Charles, Leonard, and Francis) entered the Society of Jesus. The other one made a fitting and creditable marriage. The only daughter, Ann, joined the Poor Clares in France, and remained there, " giving up the comforts of an opulent home, to embrace the poverty of Jesus Christ in a strange land."

" This heroic woman, like the mother of the Machabees, was the mother of seven children, whom in their early youth she had sacrificed, in order to secure their eternal happiness from peril." But faith made this a joy to her. Surely we may say there could hardly have been a nature better fitted than hers to bring forth and give early guidance to the character of that wise and brave archbishop who was to take so great a part in the first developments of this " Story of Courage."

Leonard and his brother Charles, having ended their preparatory course at the Bohemian Manor School, were to continue their studies in Europe. From one little episode of their departure — slight, perhaps, yet pathetic and full of significance — we may judge of the suffering inflicted on these devoted people by the bigotry which oppressed them and forced them to such a separation. It gives us an insight, also, into the heroic resolution of Mrs. Neale. When Leonard, only ten years old, was brought to the dock where lay the ship that was to carry him from home, he made such resistance to going on board that his poor mother, even in that hour of terrible trial to herself, was obliged to whip him before she could make him leave her.

But her unyielding self-denial received a tangible

reward, in this world. The reluctant blows with which she drove him from her, while lacerating her own heart, had, we may think, some premonitory touch of consecration in their scourging. Both Leonard and all her priestly sons — excepting Rev. William Neale, who died in England — returned to her long afterward. They then remained in America, and were the comforters of her old age, as well as a glory to the church in this country.

Leonard, as we have said, became a Jesuit. For sixteen years he stayed in Flanders; five years he spent in England, and four more in Demerara, South America; coming back to Maryland at last in 1783.

Many instances of Mrs. Neale's piety have been remembered; and some things were told of her which verged upon the miraculous, but have not been verified. One instance of her spirituality was, however, told by the archbishop himself to Mother Agnes, and often repeated by her to the sisters at Georgetown.

" Being ill one Sunday and unable to go to church, Mrs. Neale wished, at least, to hear mass in spirit and to unite with the congregation in prayer. Accordingly, at the hour of service she seated herself at a window looking towards St. Thomas Manor, and here — like Daniel gazing toward Jerusalem — she yearned for the holy sacrifice and for the temple. God heard her prayer, — dare we conjecture to what extent? . . . Yet this we know: that on the return of her household from church, she was able to relate to them the entire sermon, assuring them she had heard every word preached that morning at St. Thomas, three miles distant."

She lived to a venerable age, dying, it is thought, prior to 1793 ; the exact date has not been obtained.

Ten years before that date, Father Leonard Neale arrived at home from Demerara, after a perilous voyage during which he was captured by British cruisers. He had sailed in January, 1783, and he landed in April of the same year. The revolt of the colonies and the close of the Revolutionary War had brought great changes; among them a decided relaxation of the former intense hostility to Catholics. The uprising against Great Britain had made it essential to conciliate Catholics for the sake of unity in resisting the crown. And in truth they were found extremely useful in fighting the battles of freedom, contributing as they did to the continental army large numbers of gallant American soldiers and officers.

In 1774 was passed the Act of Catholic Emancipation ; and in that very month of April, 1783, when Father Neale again reached his native land, George Washington, at the head of the army, — on the 19th of April, the anniversary of the Battle of Lexington and Concord, — issued a proclamation of peace.

With its broadening light of a truer liberty and the equal rights of Catholic citizens, this was the dawn of a better day for America, when consecrated priests of the Christian faith could live and move unhindered in the country of their birth or their adoption. It was of happy omen that Father Neale, whom Providence (as we shall see) had chosen for the rearing of a living monument to Catholic faith at the capital of the new United States, should return at such a time.

He was now thirty-five years of age, and for twenty-five years of his life he had been absent from home. It is recorded that, when he came to the family mansion at Port Tobacco and asked for Mrs. Neale, she received him with the formality properly used towards an entire stranger. Father Leonard, seeing that she did not know him, feared that if he should reveal himself suddenly his mother might be too greatly surprised, perhaps overcome, by the meeting and the recognition. He asked that they might withdraw together to a more private room, since he had business of importance to communicate. When they were alone, he told her that he had been acquainted with her sons in Europe; had himself been a fellow-student with them at St. Omer and Liége; was at Bruges when the "stunning edict" of the suppression of the Jesuits was declared and was followed by the breaking up of their colleges, with the dispersion of priests and students, and the pillage of their houses.

So, by answering all her inquiries and drawing her on to questions about her Poor Clare daughter and himself, he led her to the surmise that he was no stranger, but her veritable long-lost son. The disclosure came to her then as a great happiness. Had she not well earned it ?

It was permitted to this noble mother and her noble son that they should remain together in the happiness of this reunion for ten years; Father Neale being stationed at Port Tobacco during that period. He was with her at her death, and had the consolation of administering to her, himself, the last sacraments. In this he used to say that he resembled St. Francis de Sales, who did the same for his own venerable mother. Here, again, we have one of those coincidences which are still something more than coincidence, that continually crop out like little veins of gold running through the simple, solid, unpretentious fact-stratum of this Visitation history.

After his mother's death, Father Neale was ordered to Philadelphia, to replace Fathers Grasler and Fleming, who, while attending the dying, in the frightful yellow fever epidemic there in 1793, had themselves fallen victims to the plague. Father Neale hastened to "the city of pestilence and death, where he cheered by his presence the terror-stricken flock, or soothed the last hours of the departing; encouraging all by his tender and undaunted charity."

On the reappearance of the same epidemic in 1797–98, his heroic exertions were renewed and continued, until he himself was attacked by the deadly fever. Laid prostrate, he now showed by his example of patience and resignation what he had previously taught in words. Heaven spared his life for further and greater service in the Church; and in the following summer he was nominated President of Georgetown College.

In the spring of 1799 he left Philadelphia, to assume the duties of this new post. But we must now go back for a few moments, to the time of his mission in Demerara, in order to show how the idea of establishing the Visitation in America was first presented to him.

III. FATHER NEALE'S VISION.

When the Jesuits in Europe were suppressed in 1773, Father Leonard Neale, who had become a priest of that society, was in Flanders. After this event and the dispersal of the Jesuit Fathers in all directions, his time for five years was occupied with the care of a small congregation in England. But, longing for a wider field, and being especially anxious to aid in Christianizing American Indians, he set out for the mission of British Guiana, South America, where he took up his abode in Demerara, — the English name of which, singularly enough, is also Georgetown.

The mission was a difficult and painful one; yet, during his service there, hundreds of savages were converted and baptized. Encouraging though these results of his zeal undoubtedly were, his work was constantly opposed and checked by the English settlers and authorities, who would not permit him even to build a church. The young missionary was therefore compelled to suffer all the severity of the oppressive local climate, while attending his daily duties and officiating among his scattered communicants in the vast, swampy forests, with little or no shelter from the violent showers of the rainy season, which in those latitudes continues through more than half the year.

The greater portion of the country was a lowland, which even at a distance of several leagues from the sea was flooded at high tide. The swampy soil was covered with a dense wilderness, infested by alligators, jaguars, red tigers, rattlesnakes, boa-constrictors, and innumerable venomous reptiles or insects. Archbishop Neale used to recall in later years how, at that time, the path which he trod through the forest was often so black with swarms of noxious insects that the very ground seemed to be alive and moving.

Father Neale — as he then was — bore up under the weight of labor, suffering, and continual exposure for four years. But his health at last began to give way. His robust frame betrayed symptoms of an alarming nature. Cough and fluxion asserted themselves, and never wholly left him again. The failure of physical strength would hardly have induced him to quit Demerara. But sectarian hostility, and the refusal of the British authorities to allow the building of a Catholic church edifice, made it certain that the fruit of his labors would soon wither, since his power to meet the demands of so arduous a life was continually diminishing.

Still another circumstance seemed to overrule his desire to stay and safeguard his dusky neophytes.

A mysterious vision had come to him, which beckoned him elsewhere and pointed out a work of another kind, — a work that he was indeed destined to accomplish though as yet he could apprehend it but dimly.

While he was in Demerara, the South American Georgetown, he beheld — whether in dream or in a waking trance, we do not know — a long procession of religious women, headed by Saint Jane de Chantal and clad in a peculiar costume which he afterwards learned was the prescribed " habit," or dress, of the

Visitation Order. In the picture, or vision, which thus presented itself to him, stood St. Francis de Sales, who, looking steadfastly at the missionary, said: " *You will erect a house of this Order.*"

Not far away, in this vision, was a fountain or reservoir, from which an angel pumped streams of limpid water, while crying out repeatedly: " *Pax super Israel !* " (Peace unto Israel.)

It would seem that, clear and vivid though the apparition was, Father Neale did not know the two principal persons in it as St. Jane and St. Francis. In those days, when portraits could be reproduced only by engravings, which were of limited and slow circulation, it might easily — indeed, it would most probably — be the case, that even an ecclesiastic who had spent much time in Europe would not have that familiarity with the personal appearance, the features of men and women eminent in religion, which is open to us of to-day through countless books and illustrations. Moreover, there was no house of the Visitation in the cities where Father Neale had lived. He therefore had no acquaintance with its members, their institute, or the garb of the nuns. But it is written that he was a profound admirer of the teachings of St. Francis de Sales, and in after years hoped to instill the saint's peaceful and humble spirit into the natures of his own spiritual daughters.

What the dream or spiritual disclosure meant, he was wholly at a loss to decide. How was he to execute the mandate to found a house of an Order strange to him and unidentified? What could be denoted by the angel crying out, " Peace unto Israel " ?

Although the whole thing remained an enigma to him, it yet impressed his mind so deeply that he could not forget it. All the details fixed themselves in his memory, firm, distinct, undimmed. The figure of the holy man in pontifical insignia, resplendent with glory and accompanied by St. Jane de Chantal with her train of saintly daughters, lived always radiant before his eyes; and, notwithstanding that the individuality of each was unknown to him, the words of the Bishop of Geneva rang ever in his ears. From that moment he was on the watch to discover, in each event of his life, some clue to the fulfillment of those words; some indication of God's will towards the carrying out of a behest or prophecy so direct and solemn.

As we shall see, the full accomplishment of this behest was reserved to be almost the final act in the career of this consecrated servant of God and the Church. What could the poor outcast missionary priest, struggling to perform his Master's will in the poisonous swamps of Demerara, guess of the earthly future in store for him? Did his thoughts then turn from the Georgetown of British Guiana to the Georgetown in the District of Columbia, where his final work was to be done?

We think not. For no human being could have foreseen or planned the train of circumstances by which he was to achieve, in this more northern Georgetown, the task which had been set for him in those words uttered by the St. Francis de Sales of his vision at the South American Georgetown. We know that he came home to Maryland from Demerara, and served

VAULT UNDER THE CHAPEL

as a priest at Port Tobacco and in Philadelphia for fifteen years longer, before there was the slightest hint from any source that he would be called to Georgetown in the District of Columbia, where the opportunity was given to him of realizing in solid actuality the ghostly command of St. Francis, by means and instruments which Providence had prepared.

Those means and instruments had been brought together from independent sources, without his knowledge. They were utterly beyond his touch or control, at least until 1795. And even when he came to Georgetown, D. C., in the spring of 1799, and began to realize his possible opportunity, the obstacles and indeed the actual opposition of fellow Catholics to the achievement of his task — as our narrative will soon make clear — were such as would have persuaded any man not guided by a supernatural idea, and by the Catholic confidence in supernatural aid, that it was hopeless for him to persist in carrying out the plan entrusted to him by the vision and the mandate of a saint. But, no; like St. Francis, he was inspired to feel the need of this particular Order; and when, subsequently, he was urged to merge it in that of the Ursulines, or otherwise deprive it of a peculiar virtue all its own, he would insist that the Church is a garden, the variety of whose plants (the different Orders) adds to its beauty.

It is interesting to note, that as the angel in Father Neale's vision, cried " Peace unto Israel," — an exclamation, which at the time seemed to have no special relevance, — so Father Neale, at the end of the voyage home, which was to result in realizing his dream, reached the United States in the very month when peace was proclaimed.

We leave to psychologists or natural scientists, if they choose, all disputation as to the origin or significance of Father Neale's vision. To us, these are clear and simple. We but limit ourselves to recording the plain facts. At the time when the vision came, Father Neale did not understand it. He labored patiently for many years in other directions, like the true priest that he was, without receiving any further indication as to how he was to achieve the prophecy. He worked hard, exposed himself without fear to pestilence, and was nearly stricken to death by yellow fever. At last he was brought to the scene where he was to accomplish the joyful task set for him.

Yet, all through this time, he had no exact knowledge of the Order of the Visitation. Not until *thirty years later* — when he was more than sixty years old — did he succeed in finding a picture of St. Jane de Chantal, the foundress of the order, and, when he found it, he recognized there the face and the conventual dress which he had seen in his vision in far-off Demerara; although at that time he had had no previous knowledge of it.

Daily life and observation, as well as the records of natural science, prove that there is such a thing as mirage. A mirage, under certain conditions of the atmosphere, lifts up above the horizon the outline and the image of distant objects which, ordinarily, are not visible to the eye or through the telescope. A mirage raises before our vision objects which we had not seen before and did not think were within our ken, — ships journeying afar, or continents and islands beyond the range of our common sight.

May there not be a mirage of the mind, the soul, — as exact as this of the eye and the atmosphere, — disclosing not only natural but also supernatural things, which are absolutely real although not perceived by us before?

Perhaps it was such a condition that enabled Father Neale to see, beyond the desert or the liquid plain of years, and through the haze of the future, the duly habitated nuns of the Visitation house which he was to establish.

Let those who think the supposition fanciful or trifling examine with care the history of his achievement, which we are about to give. But first we must describe the Visitation Order and its beginnings in Savoy and France.

IV.

THE FOUNDATIONS IN SAVOY AND FRANCE.

IT was in the year 1604 that St. Francis de Sales, Bishop of Geneva, and St. Jane de Chantal, then a widow, first met. St. Francis in that year preached the lenten sermons at Dijon, whither the Baroness de Chantal had been invited, by her father, to repair and hear him. Before performing this mission of lenten preaching, for which he had become famous, St. Francis went into retreat at his ancestral home, the Chateau de Sales, situated in the centre of Savoy, and not far from La Roche. This house was a haven of rest, where the saint's most saintly mother presided happily over a large family of married sons and daughters, who lived in exquisite harmony. One day St. Francis became, in the chapel, ravished in ecstasy, receiving a great access of light upon the mysteries of the faith, and also a vision of the Order of the Visitation of the Blessed Virgin Mary. The saint was allowed to see distinctly the principal persons who were to assist him in founding the Order, so that he afterwards easily recognized them in the flesh.

On her own part, the baroness recognized in the Bishop of Geneva the spiritual director whom she had seen in a vision, when praying that God would send her some one to advise and lead her in religion.

She was now filled with joy and hope, and, sitting in front of the pulpit, gazed eagerly up at the preacher, who did not fail to notice her clear-skinned, dark-eyed young face. It happened to be to the baroness's brother that St. Francis appealed, one day, inquiring who she was, and an introduction was soon effected. This brother was André Fremyot, the young Archbishop of Bourges, and through him the two founders of the Visitation Order were enabled to meet and converse a number of times. In the attempt to learn whether the baroness was ready to renounce the world, St. Francis took occasion to remark upon certain ornaments which she wore. At the next interview these ornaments had disappeared. In every other possible way she proved most firmly her absolute desire to devote herself to religion.

Upon returning to his episcopal residence at Annecy, which is situated in Savoy (Canton of Geneva) south of the Savoy mountains, St. Francis opened a correspondence by letter which was a source of great spiritual development to St. Jane, and brought steadily forward the undertaking of the new Order.

The reasons for that undertaking were as follows: Asylums had been established for all sorts of people except delicate females, old or young, who were perhaps even seriously infirm, and who desired to devote themselves to God without the severe vows of self-crucifying observances and coporeal austerities, common to other Orders. These sisters of the human family, without winning renown in the eyes of the world, being in some cases feeble, deformed, or of

humble capacity, " might nevertheless grow beautiful
in the estimation of angels," said their friend, the
Bishop.　He exclaimed: " Oh, how I love the little
virtues which flow through the valley of our misery:
gentleness of heart, humility of spirit, and simplicity
of life and spiritual exercises ! " And these little
virtues he found indigenous to women's generosity.
Moreover, St. Francis planned to make the Order
one of usefulness to all who, outside of it, could feel
its benefits.　The name was chosen in honor of the
mystery of the Visitation, because, if the sisters
visited the poor and sick as their founder ruled, they
would try to imitate the ardor and generosity of
Mary, who, disregarding her own love of solitude,
and breaking her retreat from the world, climbed the
hills of Judea, with burning charity, to carry abundant joy to Elizabeth.　He was extremely earnest
upon this point of the active charity of this particular
Order, founded as much for the succoring of the miserable in the world, as for the harboring of delicate
nuns, although the usual law of strict enclosure would
thus be relaxed.　The innovation was emphatically
opposed by many, who thought that the religious life
would thereby lose much of its spirituality and dignity.

All attacks, and advice intended for his discouragement, were met by the saint with quiet determination ;
and yet a readiness to retire from his positions at the
first sign that such was God's will.　St. Jane was,
though so noble, often alarmed at the threatening difficulties on all sides, and received from her director
admirable words of reassurance.　" We should be,"

he wrote to her, " (if it be God's will) as willing to fail as to succeed." And also : " If it does not please God that our project flourish, it shall not please me either, and it is not necessary to lose an hour's sleep over the matter." " God makes people coöperate with him when they are least aware of it."

These were splendid answers from an enthusiasm which had perceived a vision of the Visitation and its chief personages, and kept St. Francis occupied much of the time for years in energetic planning for his undertaking. Force and gentleness were his constant companions. " I hold myself as low and very little ; I seize the humiliations which present themselves ; and if I do not meet with any, I humble myself because I am not humiliated," was the expression he once gave to his fearlessness concerning rebuff. The Visitation Order would never have been built up, if it had been built for the honor of St. Francis de Sales.

He finally, in 1616, relinquished the regulation which directed the nuns to carry holy help to the poor. Sisters of Charity were reserved for the institution of St. Vincent de Paul. The circumstances of his changing so important a clause were as follows :

One morning, during 1615, four or five French ladies, who came from Lyons, appeared at the monastery in Annecy, desiring to investigate the comparatively new Order. One of them was a religious of the Paraclete, and the others were devout widows. The Sisters of the Visitation received them with the cordiality for which they had come to be widely distinguished. Madame Colin, one of the ladies thus received, realized that she now saw the Order of which she had been accorded prophetic knowledge in a dream; one of the many visions connected with the history of the Visitation, which was so replete with them; as, indeed, seems particularly appropriate, since the mystery itself was heralded by a vision. Madame Colin had not been able to imagine where she was to look for the Order she had seen in a dream, until she found herself at Annecy. The religious was Madame de Gouffier, member of an illustrious family, who desired to leave for a more fervent Order the one to which she belonged, and which had greatly declined. She had read the "Introduction to the Devoted Life" of St. Francis, and immediately desired to study the sisterhood which he had called into being. She became a novice, remaining at Annecy. Madame d'Auxerre, another of the little company of visitors, returned to Lyons to begin the establishment of a house of the Visitation in that city. She had been fortified by several interviews with St. Francis, and she was most kindly assisted by the Cardinal de Marquemont, Archbishop of Lyons. Everything had been prepared for the reception of the sisters of the house of the Visitation at Annecy, who were to come and make the foundation; as it is the custom, in establishing a new house, to have the assistance of some most venerable members of the Order which is to be further augmented. But suddenly the jealousy of certain influential people of Lyons intervened, and the Cardinal de Marquemont was asked whether God only worked miracles through the Bishop of Geneva, and why other bishops could not

erect congregations as perfect as that of Annecy.
Without much reflection or delay, it was decided that
the Archbishop of Lyons should erect a congregation
under the title of the *Presentation*. New rules were
made, and the establishment began with much pomp,
having, in obedience to the wishes of the Archbishop,
Madame d'Auxerre as Superioress. But in a few
months this venture expired. The wise delays, the
patient reconsiderations, the heroic poverty and trust
of the true foundation were wanting. Madame d'Auxerre implored the Archbishop to at last allow the erection of the Visitation Order itself; and she and her
companions begged the forgiveness of St. Francis for
having altered his rules in their monastery. A
remarkable fact here came to view. The royal letters patent which had been expected from Paris,
authorizing the institution of the house of the *Presentation*, now arrived, and it was discovered that
wherever the word " Presentation " was to have been
inserted in the text, "*Visitation*" had been used instead. Briefly, the Archbishop asked that Mère de
Chantal and those sisters who had assisted her in the
earliest days of the Order, should come and establish
it in Lyons. This was done to the profound delight
of St. Francis, who sent, so he himself said, "the
cream of the foundation" at Annecy to this great
enterprise and first branch of the mother house. It
was at this point that the Archbishop of Lyons began
to show his disapproval of semi-enclosure, and wrote
a treatise upon the subject, in which he defended the
absolute cloistering of all nuns. He thought that
in Lyons, and other large cities, great danger might

result from allowing the sisters to pass into the outside world on errands of mercy.   St. Francis replied
by another treatise; which, however, his friend the
Cardinal, was too timid to accept as conclusive.   Then
St. Francis acceded to his superior's wishes; and he
did so, said he, "not only humbly and reverently, as
I ought, but cordially and cheerfully, in all good feeling."   Nevertheless, he insisted unswervingly, and in
spite of all controversy, upon that clause in his rule
which permitted invalids to be received, not arguing
further with the worldly who thought it unwise in
economy to do so, than to say: "Yes, it must be
done: I am a partisan of the infirm!"   Some even
of the sisters thought that they might be hampered if
many lame and blind applied for admittance to the
Order.   "Have no fear," he answered; "God shall
send a sufficient number who are beautiful and agreeable, according to the opinion of the crowd!"   And
this was particularly true.

During the time allowed them for outside beneficence, before complete enclosure was endorsed by the
saint, the sisters performed wonders of mercy, where
any other than angels would have feared to tread.

The life of a nun of the Visitation was directed, as
above stated, far more gently than that of any other
religious of that time.   Various severities were assumed by the most devout, but they were not compul-
sory, and were sometimes forbidden when discovered.
There was for her no more abstinence than in ordinary life, and scarcely more fasts.   She did not rise
before dawn; she was not less well provided for in
food or bed than the common run of people.   In con-

sequence, many persons desired to join the Order who had never before dared to contemplate entering conventual life. But in relaxing some of the chains, St. Francis created others by which human nature might be subdued, if not, as was said above, by self-crucifying observances, still by a method of moral discipline as profound as it was exquisite. The poverty which he commanded the nuns to accept was complete. Not even an individual medal, crucifix, rosary, or cell could be used by a sister for more than a year, that the idea of self might be merged in the idea of loving others even to the last step of personality. The many regulations embraced nothing which could injure the health, but also forgot nothing that could purify the spirit through renunciation. In all religious orders the presiding aim is so powerful that it even moulds the facial expression of the members. In the Visitation the presiding aim is a concord of sweetness, mutual support, and holy cordiality. It was a law that the Superioress should be always cheerful and kindly of face, though firm in her direction; full of love, but unbending in dignity. St. Francis unceasingly reiterated all this. He wished the sisters to be ever affable and gracious in consequence of deep charity. At last his inspiration reached as it were the heart of the Order, never to be lost; as we may see, after three hundred years.

To return to the still younger epoch of the Order from which this digression has been made; — the time had come, in 1610, for choosing a house at Annecy for St. Jane de Chantal and her several nuns, and fortune seemed particularly propitious. There

was an opulent family of which the three members
were strongly inclined to retire from the world.   The
father and son wished to enter the Order of the Friars
Minor ; and the mother wished to form a new Order
for women, devoted to seclusion and prayer.   Many
were anxious to join this congregation, and public
opinion enthusiastically approved of it.   St. Francis
was asked to unite his congregation to the one described.   He did not greatly fancy the measure, but,
always humble, and willing to let others have their
will if at all practicable, he at last lent himself to the
suggestion.   The requisite house was to be given to
the two combined Orders by the rich patroness, and
Pentecost had been chosen as the day for the establishment.   As the time approached, and St. Francis
heard nothing from the lady who had promised the
convent house, he wrote to her that the eve of her
sacrifice was near, and that she must decide whether
she had the courage to make it.   The lady decided
that she had not the courage.   This want of good
faith was the harder to meet, as the saint had now no
house provided in which to establish the Visitation ;
and St. Jane, thinking the pecuniary needs of the
Order would be supplied by the prospective patroness,
had deeded all her own wealth to her children.   Nevertheless, the two founders were equal to the emergency, and were really glad that the rule of poverty
was to be so completely carried out.   In the faubourg
de la Perrière, almost upon the border of the lake, St.
Francis chose, and immediately bought with part
mortgage, a little house with a court on one side, and
an orchard on the other ; the latter separated from

the house by a road, but connected by a covered gallery, thrown like a bridge over the way. It was therefore called "the little house of the *Galerie*," and has ever since been affectionately known by that name. St. Francis declared that he had never been happier in his life than upon finding "a secure cage for his doves." But in consequence of the defection of the would-be, and would-not-be nun alluded to, the foundation of the order was necessarily postponed until Trinity Sunday, which came in this year upon the Feast day of St. Claude, the 6th of June; and thus, although no one remembered it until the last moment, was fulfilled a prophecy made in vision to St. Jane long before, that she would "enter the repose of the children of God through the gate of St. Claude," — an assurance which she could in no wise understand until the event.

It had been attempted to keep secret the hour at which she and her two companions were to retire to their little convent; but, after all, a great crowd was gathered upon the streets, and devoutly watched the foundresses of the Visitation as, at evening, they passed along to the House of the *Galerie*, accompanied by the noblesse of Annecy, the magistrates, and the people of the middle classes. The three brave and devoted ladies were conducted by the three brothers of St. Francis de Sales. Benedictions were uttered around them, and all hearts were touched at this peaceful triumph of humility and charity. At their entrance into their house, Anne-Jacqueline Coste met them and threw herself at their feet; for she was to be out-sister and portress, and was one of

those seen by St. Francis in his vision of the early
members of the Order.

The house was filled with a bevy of ladies, mostly
the connections and friends of the foundresses, who
desired to be the last to embrace them as they bade
farewell to the world's customs and delights.

Night fell, and the three novices found themselves
alone with God. A great peace enfolded them.
They read the rules laid down for their immediate
use. Absolute enclosure was enjoined for this first
year of solemn test, after which they were to visit
(according to the first intention) the poor and sick,
and teach the ignorant. Mademoiselle Favre and
Mademoiselle de Bréchard promised all filial obedience to Madame de Chantal. Faithful Anne-Jacqueline Coste was embraced as a sister. The three ladies
then went to their simple little cells, and gladly put
aside their worldly attire. Mademoiselle de Bréchard
went so far as to trample her fashionably-trimmed
clothes under foot; and she often in subsequent years
spoke of the blessed content which filled her heart as
she felt herself freed forever from the dominion of
empty elegance; so that she slept more sweetly than
at any time before in her life, although upon a hard
and narrow convent bed.

All night Madame de Chantal was awake, adoring
God's mercy towards the enterprise. Yet at break
of day her joy and peace were disturbed. She was
assailed by the fear that she had tempted God by
undertaking the guidance of this religious family.
The trial was nobly borne, and after two hours of
agony she again felt profound trust and hope. She

awakened her dear daughters in religion, and they all
dressed themselves in the habit of the novitiate. It
was a simple black gown, with a white linen collar;
a black band covering the forehead half way down to
the eyebrows, and concealing all the hair. Then, a
large head-covering of black taffeta, without the least
trimming, enveloped the head and shoulders, and, if
lowered, could entirely hide the face.

At eight o'clock St. Francis came to celebrate
Mass. After dinner he returned again to visit them,
accompanied by another crowd of interested specta-
tors, and he concluded the day by ordering enclosure
for this initial year. The foundation had been happily established.

Anne-Jacqueline Coste, at sundown, set about preparing the first meal. This was a matter of some
perplexity, as there was no food in the house and no
money with which to buy it. In the morning she
had asked some advice upon the subject of St. Jane,
who had smiled and said: "My good daughter, God
will provide for us." Anne obediently tried to be
reconciled to this answer. But after ten hours she
felt that she must bestir herself, and so went into the
garden, picked a bunch of herbs, begged a trifle of
milk of a neighbor, and concocted a broth. As the
novices sat down to sup upon this fine fare there
came a knock at the door. A friend had sent wine,
bread, and meat. Anne was now a little ashamed of
her too great energy, and her want of absolute faith.

As long as six months afterwards their poverty
was equally great. Perhaps three *sous* worth of
charcoal were needed; and, according to the careful

rule, all three foundresses would take their keys and
go together in eager haste and perturbation to peep
into the money-box. St. Jane recounts that on such
an occasion exactly three *sous* were found; and she
adds that they were much relieved to discover they
had so many! Some one had given them in charity
a small barrel of wine. They drew from it for more
than a year, and the tiny barrel faithfully responded
with its contents. Then another barrel was sent
them, and the first one promptly refused to supply an
additional drop. St. Jane assured the sisters that it
would not have thus refused if its resources had still
been needed. Their poverty, be it said, was largely
voluntary. A bequest was left to the convent by a
very rich lady, who, without letting the sisters know
of it before her death, had made them her legatees.
However, her relatives began a suit to annul the will.
St. Francis would not let his religious children be
disturbed by any wrangling with mercenary greed,
and ordered the convent to cede all its rights in the
matter. None the less, the sisters offered the Mass
every Saturday in memory of their dead friend, as
her will had requested. In this way religious Orders
are built up, — by relinquishments, humility and
peace, and laboring poverty.

At the close of the year during which the community at Annecy had been faithful to the strictest
enclosure, the profession of the sisters was made with
great solemnity. The surviving children of St. Jane
were at her side at the moment when she irrevocably
dedicated herself to the life of a nun. Far from
abandoning these children, her care for them was

even more efficient than ever before. Her eldest
daughter was married to a young brother of St.
Francis, and lived in a château in the neighborhood,
from which she could easily come to visit her mother,
or to which St. Jane could go at need. Her daughter
Françoise spent her girlhood with her mother in the
convent, and was the first pensioner, or little student,
received there. Novices had already been admitted,
and the outlook for the Visitation was most hopeful.

St. Francis decided to organize still more minutely
the rule of life. He decreed that the labors for which
the sisters had been especially called together should
begin on January 1st, 1612. He had intended to
dedicate the community to the patronage of St. Martha, the model of all those who would serve the poor.
But St. Jane deeply desired that her daughters in religion might be devoted to the Blessed Virgin Mary.
She did not say so to St. Francis, but she prayed to
God that her wish might be fulfilled. Soon her
prayer was answered, and the saint told her that he
had placed the community under the care of the
Blessed Virgin, and had chosen the mystery of the
Visitation as the most appropriate illustration of their
mission. The sisters were at first called *Filles de
Sainte-Marie;* but when they began actively to carry
on their ministrations they were called Visitandines,
as has ever since been the custom. From the day of
profession, the 6th of July, to the 1st of January,
there were six months in which to add still more
amply to their numbers. The saint held council-
meetings among the sisters, to facilitate all final ar-
rangements, and the clear understanding of the rules.

The first meeting was called together in the orchard
on a lovely June afternoon, when the holy founder
arrived with his secretary, M. Michel, who was always in attendance during his visits to the convent;
and the nuns seated themselves comfortably on terraces and banks in a semicircle around their beloved
director. Thus St. Francis began: "My very dear
sisters, now that our numbers are going to increase,
we must put our affairs in order. In the first place,
we must get up at five in the morning. As for me
and my Sister Anne-Jacqueline, it is easy for us to
do so, because we are rustics from the village!"
[This was no doubt an allusion to the fact that the
nuns were all members of the highest families, and
hitherto accustomed to the usual relaxations of
wealth.] "Another thing; we must use great respect towards each other. I happen to know that the
Jesuits, if they meet the same religious a hundred
times a day, will raise their hats to him every time.
So let us incline the head each time we meet." It
was in this easy and cheerful style that all those matters were arranged which did not require solemnity.
The Catholic mind, of all others, has the opportunity
to learn where solemnity becomes ridiculous, and
where hearty cheer is fitting and refreshing. The
sisters once asked the saint what he most desired of
them. He answered: "Humility. We should seek
nothing, but refuse nothing coming from God."

"And should we warm ourselves when we are
cold?" some one inquired.

"If the fire is *already made*," he replied, smiling.
"But acts of exterior humility are not humility. They

are, however, very useful. They are the rind of virtue. Humility is not only having a low opinion of
one's self, but accepting willingly the scorn of others.
Be *joyously* humble before God and man." One day
St. Jane asked him to speak a little further about
affability, which, as has been mentioned, he considered a virtue of the first importance. The sisters
again seated themselves upon the sward at his feet, in
the orchard, where all was enchanting summer. Suddenly a thunderbolt sprang over the heavens, fright-
ening the nuns, who made great signs of the cross
upon their breasts as each flash of lightning appeared.
St. Francis laughed, and told them to take courage,
since a thunderstorm only killed saints and great sinners, and they were neither the one nor the other.
When the noise had subsided, the instruction proceeded ; that instruction which so gently introduced
divine austerities into the devoted existence of women,
whose lives had been and were still to be stories of
most excellent beauty. With such a joyous tone the
saint gave his advice ; and with such delicate freedom he formed the rules that are honored with immortal fidelity at the present time. When St. Francis
withdrew, he always left " his doves " peacefully
happy, and enthusiastic for their future labor ; — labor which should be unflinching in the midst of horror or death, although their hearts beat high at a
thunderclap, and their director soothed them and encouraged them from the abundance of his humorous
gentleness.

In her description of the early convent, St. Jane
writes that, among many lovely virtues, the sisters

made a matter of conscience of every act. One day two of them were walking in the orchard, and found some pears on the ground. They wished to decide whether it was time to pick all the pears; and each bit a little piece without swallowing it. But it was against the rule that they should eat between meals; and upon realizing that they had not kept strictly to observance, they confessed their fault to St. Francis, and asked pardon of St. Jane, who approved of the utmost fidelity in even the least matters; thus establishing a perfectly clean and healthy innocence at all moments.

The house at Annecy having been strengthened with sisters and postulants, and being enriched by good works for the suffering, St. Francis wrote to St. Jane:—

"Good morning, my very dear Superioress; God has this night given me the idea that our House of the Visitation is noble enough to deserve its coat-of-arms, its emblazonment, its motto. In fact, I have thought, my dear mother, if you are willing, that we should take for our coat-of-arms a heart pierced with two arrows, surrounded by a crown of thorns; this poor enclosed heart supporting a cross which surmounts it; and upon the heart shall be engraved the names of Jesus and Mary. My daughter, I will tell you as soon as we meet a thousand little thoughts which have come to me upon this subject; for surely our young community is a work belonging to the heart of Jesus and Mary. In dying, the Saviour created us by the opening of his Sacred Heart."

This letter was written many years before the coming of Blessed Margaret Mary, who was the inspired apostle of the Sacred Heart, in the Order of the Visitation.

Very soon the convent was subjected to slanders and persecutions from persons of low character, although it was loved and praised by the just of the neighborhood. So flagrant did the calumnies become that St. Francis finally set about writing a refutation, which he put into the form of a defense of pious congregations in general. "Time," said he to St. Jane, "spent for God is never lost. Trouble and persecutions are the fruitful seeds of righteousness." Slanders often choose points of attack that are so grotesque as to indicate the calibre of soul from which they spring. A young postulant was once told, when a storm of abuse arose from the camp of the unrighteous: "It is well known that every morning each sister is asked what she would like to have prepared for her dinner." This nonsense succeeded in somewhat disturbing the gentleness which the rule enjoined should be exhibited at all times, and the sister cried forcibly that such a report was not true ; adding that the order of life thus attacked had been arranged according to the laws of the great St. Augustine, under the guiding judgment of a great bishop (St. Francis de Sales).

The nuns admitted to the convent of Annecy a number of children as pensioners, whom their poor or rich parents hoped to dedicate to the religious life. It was a great charge; but, as St. Francis said, "is it better in our garden to have thorns because we have roses, or to have no roses because no thorns?"

He loved little children well.   One day Mère Blonay
noticed, when the saint was calling upon her, as she
sat behind the grating in the parlor, that he was
placed in a draught.   She allowed her anxiety to be
discovered by him.   St. Francis got up to shut the
door, but came back without doing so; explaining
that there was such a crowd of children looking at
him from an inner room with the best courage in the
world, that he could not "find the heart to shut the
door on their noses."   Very soon, however, Mère
Blonay managed to have the door mysteriously closed
from the other side, by sending thither little Anne,
the daughter of Madame Colin; she who had come
from Lyons after receiving her vision of the community at Annecy.   Little Anne was especially lovable,
and was often in attendance upon the foundresses of
the Order, when they went to the parlor (though ever
remaining behind their grating) to receive visitors.

Eventually, and after much demur, St. Francis
extended his hospitality towards children destined for
conventual life to children who needed to be taught
in an atmosphere of religion.   Apostacy had become,
through the assumptions of Luther, a vast evil, and
religious instruction was looked to by innumerable
parents as their children's only safeguard.   Jesuits
and others opened colleges; Ursulines and others
devoted themselves to teaching young girls.   Every
parent interested in the Visitandines implored St.
Francis to allow the sisters to become a teaching
Order.   Generosity and courage demanded the sacrifice of the sisters, and it was made.   The wisdom of
the concession was soon apparent, as the spirit of the

Visitation entered into the numerous scholars, bringing many to conventual life, and raising the others to
a sense of religious responsibility, a sense of the expe-
diency of love for the sake of God.

Two years after the foundation in the little house
of the *Galerie*, it became necessary to remove to a
larger habitation in the centre of Annecy, since the
sisters needed to reach the sick without the delays of
distance. This second house was in all respects a
monastery, although not yet all that was required.
The monastery was placed under the protection of a
powerful noble, as was frequently done in those times
of revolutionary danger. St. Francis chose for the
protectress of his Order the Infanta of Savoy, widow
of the Duke of Mantua. The brother of the Infanta,
the Duke de Nemours, ceded to the community a
large tract of land in a convenient quarter; and it
was here that the final monastery was built, whose
corner-stone was laid in 1614, with stately rites,
stately attendance of nobles, and stately music. For
the altar the Infanta gave a large crystal Crucifix, set
with precious stones. In a reliquary of crystal set
with precious stones is the heart of St. Francis de
Sales, treasured by the Sisters of the Visitation in
Venice, whither the community of Lyons fled during
the Revolution, and where they were allowed by the
little republic to remain unmolested.

Built the first of all the houses of the Order, directed for ten years by St. Francis, and during
twenty-nine years by St. Jane; and having had the
good fortune, after the death of these saints, to
take charge of their sacred bodies, the monastery of

Annecy has exercised a great influence. A name has been given to it which well describes its position among the houses of the Visitation, loving and helpful; — it is called the Holy Source. All difficulties of misapprehension of the rules and spirit were adjusted by recourse to it, and its early members lent their support to the founding of many monasteries, of which one hundred and sixty exist in the world to-day. The history of these foundations in France and elsewhere is such an interesting study that it is difficult not to select at least a few more of its pages for insertion in this chapter. The circular letters, which it has always been the rule to send yearly from monastery to monastery, written by the sisters themselves, and incorporating every item of real value, are the chief material of the history as printed in France.

St. Francis once remarked that he did not know why people called him the founder of the Visitation Order, since he had not made it what he wished, but what he did not wish. He alluded to the radical changes in regard to semi-enclosure and the visiting of the needy; and to his objection to letting the sisters teach extensively, which they after all were permitted by him to do. The usefulness of the sisterhood could not be suppressed by enclosure, since loving good-will was the inspiration it had received. Advice and courage were sought for at the grating (which screened its nuns from the world) by crowds of people. Kings and queens and their children met there to find spiritual help. Marie de Medicis and Anne of Austria came constantly to see Mère de Beaumont in the Faubourg Saint-Antoine, recommending to her prayers the affairs of the kingdom. Duke Charles de Lorraine, when he held his court at Besançon, found that no one told him the truth so well as Mère Marie-Marguerite Michel, whom he went to see every week. The Duchesse de Longueville, Queen Christine of Sweden, and Louis XIV. himself, who came with his mother and all his court, were some of those who, in spite of power and pride, discovered that the strength of courage and the wealth of faith belonging to the nuns of the Visitation (and usually joined to the greatest refinement and intelligence), made a source of holiness for the thirsty world which they themselves were eager to recognize and benefit by, as the least of us may benefit forever.

V.

LIFE SKETCH OF ST. FRANCIS DE SALES.

THE father of Francis de Sales — Bishop and Prince of Geneva, born at Château de Sales, Savoy, in 1567 — was a worldly-wise, warlike, warm-hearted noble, who regarded the tenets of the Protestant religion as palpably false, because, as he said, having sprung from the brains of certain unprincipled men, it was moreover younger than himself by as much as twelve years! Although the baron's ambition for the career of his son knew no bounds, yet he opposed each of the steps by which this divinely called youth rose to the lofty plane of his vocation. His mother, on the contrary, dedicated him from the first, in her own mind, to God. Not long before his birth she venerated the Holy Winding Sheet at Chambéry, and wept over the imprints of our Lord's wounds. In after years, St. Francis having grown to be famous for his eloquent preaching and perfect charity, the Holy Winding Sheet was exposed in his honor, and he saw it for the first time. He prostrated himself before it, and burst into tears, as his mother had done, on beholding the traces of our Lord's blood.

He was baptized when only a day old, and even then he gave to all who saw him an impression of angelic predestination. His godfather, the prior of

the Benedictine Monastery of Salengy, declared that
during the ceremony he himself felt an inexpressible
holy peace; and a strong conviction filled him that
the child was never to lose his baptismal innocence.

During the first two years of his life his blessed
nature was evident from his countenance, always
sweet, his love of holy objects (which he touched and
kissed eagerly and respectfully), and from his instant
generosity towards all the poor children whom he
met, and to whom he gave whatever he had in his
hand. His nurse was obliged to carry with her, on
their daily walks, various fruits and cakes for these
children, because he cried if they were not made
happy by some gift; and he caressed them joyously
when he saw that they were satisfied. When the
time came for him to perform miracles, if he caressed
or gently touched the cheeks and heads of mad people, he cured them. If permitted to go to the church,
he would run towards it, and was never weary of
staying before the altars; and on returning home
would imitate the services as well as he could in his
play. By such a childhood we may guess something
of the childhood of our Lord. From his infant face,
which at a day old could bring spiritual comfort to
those who looked upon its lovely peace, we can picture the tender expression on the face of the Child
Christ, that made the surrounding light seem shadow
by comparison.

He was so loving as never to overlook the claims of
those who are often imposed upon and ignored; and
showed by his charity and courtesy that consideration
for the people whom we *can* forget is the basis of

saintship. If, to his knowledge, his attendants drove a sharp bargain with a salesman, little Francis paid the difference out of his own purse. He detected unerringly, and immediately righted, all such injustice and moral vulgarity. In his mature years he said of servants: "Love as ourselves these neighbors who are so near us! Treat them as we would wish to be treated in their position."

At the age of ten he had begun to rise early in order to study, and was so avaricious of time that he economized every moment of the day. Through his insistance he received the tonsure at twelve; and he made his first sacrifice in giving up his splendid golden curls, of which he was rather vain. He bravely cut them off, realizing that this trivial beauty had prevented him from giving his heart entirely to God. It had now come to the point of choosing the Parisian college to which he should go. The College of Navarre was patronized by the flower of the nobility; but he earnestly begged to be sent to the Jesuit College of Clermont, saying that he was inclined to evil, and feared that he should succumb to temptations and follies if thrown in their way. From childhood he was wise, choosing that road and that means which saved the most time and strength for the service of God. His motto upon leaving his father's house for life work was *Non Excidet:* "He will not degenerate."

After St. Francis de Sales became a bishop, he begged his priests not only to be saints, but to be *savants* in their particular field. "That is, study on lines which will render you useful to others, or which

will sanctify you, which is also well." He evidently
believed that what a priest must do, that he should
do admirably. And as deportment is of consequence,
the priest's deportment should be perfected. Therefore, in order to train his bearing, the holy youth
took lessons in fencing, dancing, and riding; with
the result that in after years the ease and majesty of
his presence, whether at court or at the bedside of
a dying soldier, filled the onlookers with reverence.
To appropriate and serious studies of all sorts he
added another study, — that of holiness. He chose a
wise director, and under his guidance set out upon a
thorough system of religious observance. He fasted
three days in the week, wearing at those times a hair-
shirt, because he held that a body which is too gently
treated enervates the soul. When asked why he confessed and communicated so often as once a week, he
answered: "For the same reason that I would speak
to my professor or to my tutor, since my Saviour is
my teacher in the science of a saintly life."

At seventeen he was tested by the temptation of
doubting whether he was approved by God and was
in a state of grace; again fearing that, if dangerous
occasions presented themselves, he would fall into
mortal sin. And in this torment of uncertainity he
dreaded less the agonies of hell than the fact that in
hell he should blaspheme God! He lost his health,
but did not on that account relax his religious exercises; and he studied the question of predestination
in the writings of St. Augustine and St. Thomas
Aquinas, until he became convinced of the truth of
their reassuring principles and conclusions upon the

great subject. Finally he wrote "while prostrate at their feet," as he said, a beautiful prayer, expressive of his secure hope, yet his entire submission to the hidden will of God; and, moreover, expressing in prayerful adoration his determination to win from the divine mercy pardon if he should after all be consigned to hell, so strenuously would he plead for forgiveness to the Father; so that whatsoever his agony of trial, he believed he should at last be permitted to adore Him in Heaven.

He was full of courage in the affairs of daily life. Having transferred his studies to Padua, whither his father sent him to learn jurisprudence, his devout behavior there was in such great contrast to the habits of the other young men, that he was attacked in boisterous fun by his classmates, who waylaid him one evening from ambush in a retired street, through which they knew he was to pass. They supposed him to be physically incapacitated, by rigorous fasting and mental application, from defending himself.

However, he forthwith put them to flight at the point of his sword, which he would not have hesitated to use with thorough effect, if necessary; and altogether conducted himself with a determination and skill which took the place of rugged strength. He proved himself to be equally vigorous and terrible in resisting the various attacks upon his virtue which were contrived by his companions, in envy of his purity; thus answering his own doubts as to the depth of his moral endurance. Out of this experience he spoke, no doubt, when years afterwards he exclaimed: "He is happy who suffers severe temptation. When the enemy cries so loudly without, it is a sign that he is not within!" Yet he added: "Do not *force* yourself to vanquish temptations, for these efforts strengthen them. Scorn them, without considering them."

These are indeed princely moral manners, full of dignity and just indifference! In contemplating the holy men of the religious Orders whom he saw, he was fired with the desire to become a better Christian; and he struck another note in his saintly vocation by delighting to inspire his friends with the same ambition. He pointed out the example of the monks, to those who had never thought of applying it to themselves. "We trouble our consciences so seldom about salvation!" he said. "But here are men who think of nothing else! They treat with contempt pleasures and objects which pass away, and persistently remember those which last forever. Should not this sight open our eyes?" He became familiar with the works of all the great religious writers; and at this time received from Father Scupoli his "Spiritual Combat," of which, — eighteen years later — he declared: "It is a letter descended from heaven! It is my dear book, and I have always carried it in my pocket, re-reading it constantly with unfailing edification."

At twenty-five he visited Rome. It was a long hoped for and devoted pilgrimage. He armed himself with humility and gentleness; and these shields immediately protected him from death, as will be seen from the following circumstance. Some persons of the highest rank arrived at the hotel where he had put up for the night, and he was ruthlessly made to vacate his quarters for them, and go elsewhere. He submitted without dispute or ill feeling. In a few hours the Tiber had risen and had inundated the hotel, of which every one of the inmates was drowned. He fulfilled a longing of many years in visiting the Holy House at Loretto (translated from Nazareth); and he kissed the walls and the floor of this stone dwelling in which the Blessed Virgin had lived. He renewed there his vows of consecration to the church, and of chastity. His young face was overspread with an extraordinary rosy hue, and shone like a star. His tutor and companion of many years, M. Déage, never forgot this wonderful revelation of his sanctity, and always regarded him thereafter with reverence.

When he returned to Savoy from Rome, his father gave him the seignory of Villaroget, and arranged a rich marriage for him. The Prince of Savoy, also, pressed upon him a senatorship at Chambéry. But he declared that God was his portion forever, and rejected all these proud projects. He conferred his seignory upon his younger brother, and entered the Church as provost of the Chapter of Geneva.

His saintly mother had long looked forward to this step, and had some time before quietly prepared for him the cassock which he now put on at his installation. While dressing himself in the cassock, he showed so much reverence and solemnity that a witness remarked: " One would think you were donning the garb of a Capuchin ! " To which he replied that he was taking the habit of St. Peter. " It is only by dispensation that we of the Chapter are allowed to go in secular attire; and *within* we should be always under the rule and the chains of the prince of apostles." He was received into the Order of the Friars Minor a month later, on June 8th, 1593. It was then found that he was already familiar with the use of the breviary, which he held in veneration next to the Holy Scriptures.

The young saint began to evince that power of charming his listeners in religious conversation which made him one of the greatest teachers of his day. At his father's table the guests forgot to eat and drink, except of heavenly food, while he talked to them. He assumed the behavior of an apostle in all things ; visiting the sick, reconciling enemies, and suffering from the sorrows of others ; but more than all from the calamities of the Catholic Church. War, famine, and heresy invaded life on all sides. Not content with offering prayers, he conceived the idea of founding at Annecy the Confraternity of Penitents, whose members, embracing the laity, should mourn for their own sins and for those of all the world, and should constantly perform works of charity. He believed that brotherhoods of a religious nature sustain heroic measures by mutual example and mutual needs, as religion is inspired by charity, without which devotion becomes egotism. Whereas, in the philosophical world, men withdraw themselves from their fellows and occupy themselves with a wealth of words, but never with a wealth of benevolent deeds. In September, of 1593, with his usual expeditiousness, we find that his ever-growing authority had been used to erect the above Confraternity, of which his own father was the first member. He placed it under the patronage

of the Holy Cross, the Immaculate Conception, and
the apostles St. Peter and St. Paul. On the 18th of
December following, he was ordained priest, and his
labors became more and more arduous; — in inspired
preaching, in notable conversions, in the writing of
religious treatises, in the establishment of missions
in various parts of the neighboring country where
Protestantism was most rife, and in organizing con-
ferences for the priests whom he sent on these missions. At twenty-seven his zeal was fully developed,
and his life utterly dedicated to his office of brotherly
love. Realizing that special devotions of an unusual
nature keep alive the ardor of faith, and conduce to
spiritual health, he decided to conduct his Penitents
of the Cross upon a pilgrimage to Aix, where there
was deposited a relic of the True Cross, brought from
the Holy Land during the Crusades. He rejoiced to
find that the success of this pilgrimage surpassed his
hopes in impressiveness and devotion. A branch of
the Confraternity had been established at Chambéry,
and the two brotherhoods met, *en route* for Aix,
chanting the litanies of Jesus crucified, and speaking
only of divine things, their rosaries and prayer-books
in their hands.

Taking advantage of various attacks upon the
merits of the True Cross, the young priest defended
it with his superior ability, saying: "God attached
virtue to things which had belonged to his saints, as
to the mantle of Elias and the rod of Moses. How
much more, therefore, to the Cross whereon his son
had been enthroned? If the mere touch of Christ's
garment healed the sick, how much more powerful

must be the cross which has been bathed in his blood?
The Protestants say that the Holy Scriptures do not
refer to the veneration of the cross; but what of that?
There are many points of doctrine, accepted even by
Protestants, of which the Scriptures say nothing. The
early Christians made crosses and venerated them;
churches and highways bore the cross set up before
the sight of all to be honored; it was carried in procession; its image is an incentive to saintly thoughts
and useful reflections; and the sign of the cross,
when made in the name of Christ, can perform wonders. All misfortunes, looked at in comparison with
the Cross of Jesus, disappear like stars in the presence
of the sun. In short, the only enemies of the cross
are the enemies of Christ."

His preaching became so famous that he was sought
for in the highest quarters, especially during the Lenten season. He was finally asked to preach during
Lent, at court, and did so with remarkable results as
to conversions, winning at the same time the profound
admiration of Henry IV. But of flowers of rhetoric
he said: "They are of the kind which do not bear
fruit." His power was of a different order. When
he preached, he was accustomed to make a long pause
before beginning, while he looked carefully around
upon his audience. Some one happened to ask him
why he did this, and he answered: "I salute the
guardian angel of each of my auditors, and pray him
to prepare the heart over which he keeps watch. I
have received very great favors by this practice."

Among those who became devotedly attached to the
saint was M. Deshayes, Henry IV.'s secretary. The

king tried to make Deshayes tell him point-blank
whether he loved his sovereign or St. Francis de
Sales the best. M. Deshayes was very much per-
plexed, but was determined to stand true to his preference for the saintly priest, who was also very fond of
him, and he conveyed this idea to the king. Then,
with exquisite kindness, Henry IV. replied: "I am
not angry, Deshayes, — I only ask to make a third in
this friendship!" The Duchesse de Longueville offered the saint a rich present of money in recompense
for his preaching; but he insisted that he wished to
give gratuitously what he received gratuitously, and
the gift was returned. The king afterwards offered
him a pension, and this he accepted; — but he nevertheless requested that as, God be praised, he had at
present no need of the pension, it might remain in
the custody of the royal treasurer until called for.
The king was enchanted with this ingenious method
of meeting the difficulty; a method which amounted,
so gracefully, to a refusal.

He was chosen to go upon a mission to Chablais,
in which vicinity Protestantism was dangerously ag-
gressive and violent. The Bernese and Gencese were
barbarous in their hatred of Catholics, and the few
faithful who were left there were obliged to carry on
their religious observances in secret. The position
was one of the greatest danger, and the saint's escapes from assassination were narrow. But he even
preached in the open air, as if inviting death; and
traveled alone to the surrounding villages, especially
to Thonon, armed only with his Bible, breviary, and
rosary. The particular winter of this mission was

unusually severe, yet he allowed neither wind nor cold to hinder him. If snowdrifts prevented his going on his way by the highroad, he fastened ice-nails to his shoes and clambered over the rocky hills, sometimes creeping on hands and knees, until the blood flowed from his torn flesh. He once saved himself from the wolves by climbing a tree, where he remained imprisoned for the whole night, exposed to freezing winds. All these sufferings only increased his zeal and his prayers for heretics, whose hatred of him did not discourage his love. He knew that fearlessness, patience, and devotion in the priest would inspirit the persecuted Catholic laymen, and to some extent win the sympathy of his enemies. At one time, when left entirely alone on his mission, and deprived of even the necessaries of life, he "tasted an ineffable consolation in feeling himself to be thrown wholly upon the care of God."

He added, that he then had great hopes of imitating St. Paul in supporting himself by the labor of his hands. But he confessed that he was very stupid at it, and could only mend his clothes a little. His saintly mother managed to convey to him clothes and linen, and money sufficient to keep him alive, by procuring for him food and warmth. With great secrecy and precaution (and with that courage which risks all, at the will of God, for a sublime cause of mercy), she even sent her second son to see Francis several times; which proved to be an immense consolation both to him and to her.

"Suffer," he said, "for it is almost the only good we can do in this world, that is unmixed with wrong.

Our Lord is never so near us as when we suffer with patient love of Him. Patience changes our sufferings into benefits. Render thanks to God, who has deigned to give you a little portion of the Cross of His Son." He used often to say, in his eagerness to suffer for Christ, and in his consciousness of the *refining power* of suffering, that he was "never better than when little well."

Not being able, in spite of their brave promises, to induce the Protestant preachers to come and hear his sermons and enter the lists with him, he set about writing his first work, the "Book of Controversies." It was composed in spare moments and in great haste, but he therein presented the Catholic religion with irresistible force, so that the apostolic commissioners, during the process of his canonization, decided that the Athanasians, Ambrosians, and Augustinians had not sustained the faith more admirably. The Holy Father, Clement VIII., desired him to have an interview with Théodore de Bèze, or Beza, then the head of the Calvinistic sect at Geneva. The meeting was on many accounts difficult to effect. When they at last faced each other, the first question the young priest put to Bèze was this: " Can a man find salvation in the Roman Catholic Church? " Bèze long hesitated to answer, retiring to a room apart, where he excitedly paced up and down. If he replied " No," it would be as much as to say that when Luther and Calvin began their " Reformation " there was no true church; which would, further, be to say that the declaration of Jesus Christ that he would be with his church " all days, even to the consummation of the world," was a false statement. And if he said "Yes," it would be a confession that the Church of Rome was the true church of Christ, since all Protestants announced that outside the true church *no one could be saved!* Bèze concluded to reply in the following manner: "Yes; certainly a man can be saved in the Roman Church, because it is the mother church." The same answer, given by various Protestants to Henry IV., and to Louis Rodolph of Brunswick, caused many abjurations of heresy.

The saint, whose habit it was never to lose a moment in useless quiescence, instantly put another question: "If one can find salvation in the Catholic Church, why had the Calvinists shed so much blood in France to establish *their* form of religion?"

"Because," answered Bèze, "there are abuses in the Roman Church, although one can be saved in it. For example, it teaches that 'good works' are necessary to salvation. Now, some people are incapacitated by nature from performing good works, and so they are damned against their will. We are more merciful, and only require of human nature that it shall have faith."

"Holy Scripture," remarked the saint, "affirms that we cannot be saved by bad fruits, but only by the good." Of a certainty he believed the assumption to be false, that some degree of good works are not possible to every one.

His perfect equanimity was famous; yet he explained that it was the result of the utmost vigilance, and sometimes covered extreme perturbation of mind. In argument his grace and gentleness brought out

well the brilliancy of his answers. A person who
is conscious of being in the right can afford to be
self-possessed, but he does not always realize his
opportunity for ease and calmness.

Bèze, under his load of mistake, lost his temper in
a fury of anger; whereupon his visitor concluded:
" Your anger convinces me that you see the justice
of my conclusions. But I did not come here to annoy
you; so we will not discuss theological subjects any
longer." Bèze then cooled off, and begged the saint
to return frequently.

The Protestants of Geneva were incensed at his
temerity in coming among them and attempting to
convert their chief, and they sought to kill him. But
he did not fear them. That very day, being asked
in secret to take the Blessed Sacrament to a dying
Catholic, who was lodging in the house of some heretics, he proceeded to do so. As he went out of
Geneva he "wept abundantly," with a love akin to
our Lord's when leaving Jerusalem.

He desired to convert Ferdinand Bouvier. (It was
finally estimated that the number of conversions he
had made was 70,000.) Bouvier, with that childish
Protestant ignorance which advances toy arguments
to confound the grown-up wisdom of the church, flat-
tered himself that the saint was to be enlightened by
Ferdinand Bouvier; and he therefore asked him to
read a treatise on the Mass, written by Duplessis-
Mornay, distinguished as an author and soldier, and
also called " the Pope of the Huguenots." St. Francis showed that this so-called pope had falsified five
hundred passages of the writings of the fathers; and

he accordingly dubbed him "the most impudent liar of whom he had ever known." "The church," he said, "has no weapons against violence, but against calumny she has those of innocence, truth, and authority." Bouvier realized that a champion was in the wrong who won a temporary advantage only through dishonorable measures, and, having beheld with his own eyes the passages in the writings of the Fathers to which St. Francis referred, he left Duplessis-Mornay to his fate, and became himself a devoted Catholic. It was on account of such insults as the above to the Blessed Sacrament, that the saint established at Annecy the confraternity of the Blessed Sacrament, for a service of adoration, on every Thursday, not already occupied, during the year.

At Thonon now arrived the Duke of Savoy, the cardinal legate from the Holy See, and the Bishop of Geneva, to attend the devotions of the Forty Hours. Finding how much the saint had accomplished in bringing peace and religion into the midst of unchristian lawlessness, they met him with unlimited praise. The heroic young priest looked down, blushed in modest confusion, and kneeling, kissed the robe of the cardinal with all humility.

In 1602, he himself became Bishop of Geneva, being then thirty-five years of age. He was deeply moved by the responsibility placed upon him. He touched the insignia of his office with veneration, and the sight of them could plunge him into the utmost humility, or raise him to a state of rapture. He arranged his house on a basis of simplicity, and according to the utmost strictness of religious rule.

He would permit the presence of no women-servants,
however worthy; and even announced that his mother
should not dwell with him, supposing for a moment
that she would care to leave her château of Annecy;
—"because all the women who came to visit her
would not be my mother!" said he.

As a special duty of his own, he chose to hear the
confessions of those penitents who were on sundry
accounts shocking to the other priests; precisely as all
the saints have followed faithfully Christ's brotherly
mercy towards those most abandoned; because hope,
above all, is the element to be imparted to them who
have it least.   He called penitence "a second innocence."   He inaugurated Sunday-school classes,
which became, from his fascinating skill in expound-
ing the Scriptures and teaching the catechism, so
popular that no chapel would hold the crowds throng-
ing to hear him.   Two Sundays of every year he
walked in a procession of children and poor people,
singing the litanies with them, and softly reciting the
rosary.   Whenever he appeared upon the streets the
children ran from all sides, until a crowd surrounded
him as he advanced.   He was told that he lowered
the doctors of the church by putting their thoughts
into brief and simple forms for the ignorant folks
and the children, and that he lowered himself also in
descending to the motley crowds upon the streets, and
caressing the children of the masses with sympathetic
devotion.   It must have seemed strange to the saint
that the self-righteous had forgotten so easily the
words which he was obliged to repeat to them: "Unless you be converted, and become as little children,

you shall not enter into the kingdom of heaven."
He declared simply that the poor and forlorn rustic
was to him as the prodigal son, whose father did not
hesitate to embrace him, though he came home in a
disgusting state of dishevelment.

His forgiveness was of marvelous simplicity and
strength, and could not be surprised at a disadvantage. "If God," he said, "commanded me *not* to
love my enemies, I should hardly be able to obey
Him!" And certainly all those who were foes of
purity and self-sacrifice were inclined to be his enemies. On one occasion he said to an attorney, who
made an attempt to kill him because the Bishop's just
judgment in a case had overruled his own ends : "If
you tore out one of my eyes, I should look affectionately at you with the other." A gentleman of bad
habits, allied to the aristocracy, and — in spite of his
abandoned life — having considerable influence, became possessed with a desire to satisfy his heretical
opinions by persecuting the saint through the most
insulting methods. This person began his persecution
with an attack upon the residence at night, assisted
by a crowd of roughs, who threw stones, fired pistols,
and made a deafening noise with shouts and groans,
while St. Francis within, in his private room, knelt in
prayer. He refused to permit any counter attack
from his servants. Chancing the next day to meet
upon the street the apostate who had instituted this
attack, the Bishop went up to him and embraced him
as if he were his best friend. The diabolic man was
so touched by a religion which could cause a mortal
to treat cordially and gently an active persecutor, that

he returned to the church. The Bishop's mode of behavior was of that sort which it seems to us folly and even madness to adopt in *our* dealings with the outrages, petty or great, committed by our neighbors, more or less often ; and yet it was wise behavior, of the sort prescribed by Christ, as the only cure for the world's depravity. " Those," said the saint, " who cannot live in peace in the world, can at least live in patience. I am a good-for-nothing, and subject to anger ; but since I have been shepherd, I have never said a passionate word to my sheep."

A beggar who was tired of his small success in obtaining help found it an excellent plan to dress himself up as a priest, for every one then gladly responded to his appeals with alms. However, he happened to be discovered by some people who knew his real identity, and who set about punishing him within an inch of his life. The Bishop passed that way, to celebrate Mass at an adjacent chapel, and at once threw himself into the enraged crowd ; although in the confusion he was subjected to blows and insults. " What are you doing, my friends ? " he cried. " Even fellow-beings who increase their misfortunes by sin should be treated kindly ; for if we get angry with them, we add our own sin to the sum of theirs ! "

Preaching one day upon the text : " But if one strike you on the right cheek, turn to him also the other," he was addressed unceremoniously by a Calvinist, who called out : " If I should strike you, would you do as you say ? No ; like all the rest, you preach, and do not act up to your preaching." " My friend," answered the Bishop, " I know well what I ought to do, but I do not know what I might do, being full of miserable faults. However, I have confidence in the grace of God. But if, unfaithful to that grace, I did not bear the injury received from you like a Christian, still, the Evangelist in the same place from which you cite, when he reproved the preachers who *say* and do not *do* as they say, teaches you to do that which they *said*, and not that which they *did!*" When Protestants were arguing fiercely with him, he quietly remarked, according to 1 Cor. xi. 16, "But if any one seem to be contentious : — we have no such custom, nor the church of God." He called Protestants what the early Fathers had called, in their time, heretics, " Brothers ; " since, as he explained, we are all children of one Father. "I believe," he once averred, "that those who preach with love preach sufficiently against heretics, although they say not a word of argument."

When Madame de Chantal once exclaimed : " Oh, my Father, your gentleness is excessive ! " he answered : " In following the example of our Lord, we need fear no excess ! "

At Annecy he established an Academy of *belles-lettres*, philosophy, theology and jurisprudence, mathematics and the general sciences, and he gave it the device of an orange tree in flower, with the motto : " Perennial Flowers and Fruits." He called it Florimontane, to indicate that there, upon the mountains of Savoy, could be found the flowers of all useful knowledge. This undertaking he felt to be indispensable, because he saw the common run of youth leaving school without having been sufficiently

cultivated in the love of science and classic study, so
that they soon ceased to occupy themselves with re-
fining thoughts.

Another of his establishments was a Coöperative
University and Mechanic School at Thonon, on account of the custom in the large neighboring towns
of charging a higher price for commodities when
they were sold to Catholics, which became a great
temptation to the poor of Thonon.   He called the
University the Holy House, and made out the regulations after much study of other Orders, and after
asking advice of the wisest counselors, as well as
after making many prayers for God's help.   Much
as he studied and read, it is said that "he consulted
God more than books."

"Have you been long without thinking of God?"
he was once asked.   "Sometimes, almost for a quarter
of an hour!" he admitted.   He declared that most
of our faults come from not putting ourselves often
enough into the presence of the Father; which
observance he called "the garden of purity and
innocence."

So busy was he in many directions that he was
induced to mourn a little over his "dear books,"
which, as time went on, he was frequently obliged to
leave to themselves.   But even illness could not prevent him from attending to his duties and the calls
of his flock; and how much less, therefore, any self-
indulgence, however ascetic!   Everything was postponed or disregarded, except the labor of his life.
Whenever a great demand was made upon his time
and inspiration, he pressed promptly and in spite of

personal danger or barriers of storm and flood, to the post to which he was summoned.

Those who think that illness or discouragement on account of obstacles may justly debar them from efforts for their fellows, may well consider St. Francis de Sales, who suffered a continuous fever for years, in the most useful position of his diligent and long existence.

When his old friend and former tutor, M. Déage, complained that the Bishop would wear himself out with overwork, he smilingly answered: " Ah, but how much honored you would be if your pupil became a martyr in dying to fulfill his service to his God! But you have ruled me too carefully, and have made such a coward of me that I shall never procure you this glorious reputation. Martyrs are so rare, nowadays! "

He gave himself the freedom of being witty, when his sense of humor could be made serviceable. The good spirits of a good conscience have often led the saints and martyr-missionaries to see the amusing side of this mundane sojourn. A preacher who was distinguished for learning having come to Annecy during Lent, lo and behold, very few people went to hear him. However, the saintly Bishop and some other persons were present. The learned divine spent most of his time in scolding about the small audience, which amused the saint very much. Afterwards, he exclaimed: " What does he want? He punished us for a fault which we did not commit, since *we* were present. Did he wish us to divide ourselves up into little pieces? He has scolded the innocent and let the offenders go, since he might have run into the street and talked to the multitude who stayed outside the church!" He was much diverted with the fasts of a man who did not care to eat. "Do not fast!" said he. "Why, my father," the devout layman cried; "are not fasts highly recommended in the Scriptures?" "Yes," replied the Bishop. "But for those who have a better appetite!" Among the heretics who, as his fame grew, were often arrested by his sermons, and who desired to come and argue with him, was an extremely valuable old lady, so deeply impressed by a sense of her own social importance that she was hardly willing to credit any one else with having quite so much. Of all things she could not comprehend the desire of other people to be heard. After much elocution (on successive visits), at the expense of the Roman Catholic Church, she touched the subject of its abominable tyranny in insisting upon the celibacy of priests. Fearing that nobler weapons than wit might not succeed well with the self-important busybody before him, St. Francis ingeniously remarked : "But how should I, if I were married, carry on the duties of my profession, while at the same time fulfilling those of a husband and father? Should I be able, for instance, to receive from you, madam, visits so long and frequent for discussing all these interesting questions, if I had a wife and children to add to my other *pressing obligations?*" This was a ray of light to the old lady. She consented to listen to his remarks, and ended by abjuring her heresy.

At the profession of two sisters, an old ecclesiastic

wept during the ceremony of the young women's reception into conventual life. The Bishop was asked the cause of the old man's depression, and he answered that it was "because the aged priest has lost his aureole! He was once a married man, and these young women are his daughters. Then he became a priest; and so, from a *martyr* he has turned confessor!"

One day, somebody expressed contempt for the practice of praying to St. Anthony to find lost things. The Bishop replied that God had proved that these prayers were according to His pleasure, by having hundreds of times permitted things to be thus recovered. And he added: "Do let us each make a vow to St. Anthony, that he may recover for us what *we* have lost; — you, Christian simplicity, and *I*, humility."

At another time, after preaching, he was surrounded by a crowd of ladies, who asked him to solve several religious points that had puzzled them. He smiled, and asked: "Ladies, I will reply to all your questions if you will answer *one* of mine. If, in a debate, every one spoke at once and no one listened, what would be the result?" Of a young priest of high birth, who did not like to be placed in the low position of walking through the streets by the Bishop's side, instead of driving, he said, mirthfully: "See M. l'Abbé! He has still a little vanity left!"

Henry IV. showed his fine penetration in trying his best at different times to acquire St. Francis as a preacher at court. But the inspired one would not consent. He said that he "had made a novitiate of the courtly life, but that nothing should induce him to profess." At last, as the only means of learning his thoughts in Paris, and as a precaution for preserving him to the future of this world, the king ordered St. Francis to write a book on religion, which should be of the most generous application to a pious life among the affairs of ordinary routine. This was the origin of the "Introduction to a Devout Life." He blended in it all the graces of the highest social intercourse with all thoroughness in religion; and showed that we can rise from a state of mere natural goodness and fly to heaven "little by little like doves, even if we cannot mount to it like the eagle; that is, to sanctify ourselves in common vocations, when we are not called to a more perfect human destiny." His definition of devotion was this: "That love which makes us acceptable to God, is grace; that love which leads us to do good, is charity; that love which reaches the perfection of leading us to do good carefully, frequently, and promptly, *is devotion.*" "A rectitude," said he, "which is not charity, proceeds from a charity which is not truly righteous."

The saintly Bishop was very poor, and it was no easy matter for Georges Rolland, his life-long friend at service, and now his steward, to keep the Rectory going with the money available. As for his clothes, his valet locked most of them up, because he was always giving them away. However, if the weather were very bitter and the beggar very needy, he divested himself of his flannels, and would calmly shiver in this half-clad condition, until his crime of benevolence had been detected. "I use the goods of

this world," was one of his *mots*, "as the dogs of the
Nile drink its waters — *running*, for fear of being
caught by the crocodiles." He was on the alert for
the enervating influences of comfort and dazzling
emolument, and so kept his system of life altogether
meagre, though, at several points in his career, fortunes were at his command. If occasion required
that, for the dignity of the church, he should be
magnificent, he showed how easy it was to assume
princely state, if one was both noble and saintly.
Moreover, he respected prudence. "But," said he,
"I would willingly give a hundred serpents for one
dove! The serpent could destroy the dove, but the
dove would never hurt the serpent."

Some poor people came to him with a petition that
he would allow them to take the property of a priest
who had died, of whom they were only distant relatives, nor were they named in a will; under which
conditions the property of a priest always reverted to
the Bishop of the diocese. They offered a paltry
sum in compensation (twenty *ducatons*), which St.
Francis — Georges Rolland being momentarily absent — accepted; much to the subsequent horror of
his steward, who proceeded to scold him rather sharply.
"Ah, well, my friend," cried the saint, "if this good
priest had lived, should not we still have had something to live on? But, at all events, my dear Rolland, I will never do so again. As for the twenty
ducatons, I have already given them to the poor.
May God defend us from worse misfortune!"

The good spirits of a good conscience did not interfere with his outward holiness of aspect. Many times

in his life he was surrounded by rays of light, emanating from his holy body. One day, being before the Blessed Sacrament, he was filled with such an abundance of grace that he cried out: "Hold back, Lord, hold back the waves of your grace; remove yourself from me, for I cannot support the torrent of your consolations!" During the rest of the day he appeared like a seraph. His face seemed to ray out light.

Once at Annecy there was arranged a contrivance over the altar which was much in vogue, representing clouds, from which a live dove was made to descend at the moment of consecration. St. Francis was the celebrant. The dove became frightened by the music and the people, and flew about, bewildered. But at last it alighted upon the head of the saint, who stood before the altar. He did not attempt to disturb it, being absorbed in the desire to receive that which the dove prefigured. At other times, also, doves had sought to hover about him. The light which was seen now and again to emanate from him came of a blessed state which these gentle birds could perceive, and desired to bask in. It was a state resulting from determined self-purification. He believed, as has been shown, in fasting and other physical severities: and endorsed, with other saints, flagellation, that most direct and most humiliating pain of discipline, which stoops to the level of physical arrogance and indulgence. But he often gave to others very mild forms of penance; as, to a penitent soldier, that of repeating *one* Our Father and *one* Hail Mary. The soldier was astonished. However, the saint told him to rest at ease, since God's mercy was even greater than the sins committed. "Besides," he added, "I will assume the remainder of your penance for you." These few words were a revelation to the man. As soon as he had received his dismissal from the army, he returned to St. Francis and told him he was about to enter the Monastery of Chartreuse. He had met charity face to face, and longed to become a part of it, if he might. "We should always treat God as God," the saint says. While we may trust everything to God's mercy working through our charity, we may well shed our own blood as a tribute to His forgiveness of another's sin.

"Do *holily* that which you do by necessity," was another of the maxims of St. Francis de Sales. Necessity is of the earth, earthy. At the moment when we *must* do a thing, we are at the depths of humiliation, and possibly of revolt. It is then that the sublime effort of consecration to God's will makes of the earth color and light.

And so we see, at every step in the saint's life, that the heaviness of earthly rebuff was changed to the elation of heavenly endurance, because he realized that the death which is suffering must always precede the resurrection which is holiness. And when we read that, in his dying hours, he was subjected, by medical ignorance, to scorching upon the crown of the head with red-hot irons, in the endeavor to arouse him from the weakness of exhausted vitality, we discover that, instead of being filled only with horror for his agony, we are refreshed by his example of wondrous patience. His attendants asked him if his silence meant that he did not feel the pain. " Yes, I suffer," he said. " But do all that you wish to the sick man." He suffered voluntarily, as well as by necessity. He had given the following advice to a person who was subjected to constant physical anguish: "Picture to yourself Jesus Christ crowned with thorns, so emaciated that one might count his bones, and ask yourself which endures most, you or he. Imagine that the red-hot iron which singes your limb is a nail piercing his foot. You say that in your anguish you can hardly meditate upon holy things. Well, it is better to be *upon* the Cross than to *look* at the Cross. St. Paul did not congratulate himself that he was raised to the third heaven, but upon having endured much for his Master." He was true to his own advice. The example of any sort of pain nobly borne is elevating to all who witness it; and if we once dare to test the purifying efficacy of suffering, we never afterwards teach that it need be useless.

St. Francis passed from earth, November 28, 1622, at the age of fifty-five. During his lifetime he had cured nineteen deaf and dumb persons, two lepers, twenty blind, one hundred and two paralytics, thirty-seven mad people, and others. Thus he proved to the world how perfect the sacrifice was, which he had offered upon the altar of daily courage. And St. Vincent de Paul, whom he had placed in spiritual charge of the Convent of the Visitation in Paris, said of him : —

"How good God must be, since Monsieur de Genève is so good!"

VI.

St. Jane was born at Dijon, Côte d'Or, in the six-
teenth century. Her father, M. Frémyot, was president of the parliament of that city. She married
the Baron de Chantal, and for a number of years
ruled her household with a rare mingling of simplicity
and dignity, in the castle of Bourbilly, which long
afterwards was inherited by her granddaughter, the
Marquise de Sévigné, of literary fame, and only child
of the saint's only son, Celse-Bénigne. The poor of
Bourbilly said that they took pleasure in being ill,
because of their visits from the baroness. On her
side, at twenty-nine years old, she confessed : " The
longest and most wearisome day is that upon which
no one comes for my care."

Having been left a widow, she went with her four
children to Monthelon, to live with her father-in-law ;
and, laden with sorrows, and persecuted by an indulged and insolent servant of her father-in-law's ill-
regulated household, she made up her mind to think
only of others, and to suffer in silence. The culmi-
nating evidence of her heroism was her behavior
when obliged to return to Bourbilly, after some years,
to investigate the state of her children's property. She
there found great sickness among the poor. Every

morning, rising at dawn, she made her hour-long
mental prayer, and then set out to carry remedies
to the sick, and to cleanse everything about them with
her own hands. She next went to Mass; after which
she visited the most distant patients. At sundown
she again made the rounds; and on returning home
to the castle received an account of the workmen's
labors upon the estate through the day, and looked
into the financial condition of the property. She
never allowed her religious devotions to render her
less vigilant in increasing the revenues for her children. It would often happen that at evening, when
she was almost exhausted, messengers came to call
her to a deathbed; and she immediately went thither,
and passed the night in prayer, serving the dying like
a mother, and inspiring them to die holily. Seven
weeks were spent in this manner, during which there
was not a day that she did not bathe and enshroud
three or four dead. At last she succumbed, nearly
dying herself of the disease. But at the moment
when she seemed to be dying, she made a vow to the
Blessed Virgin, and was immediately restored to such
health that she arose, put her affairs in order, and
mounting her horse, rode back to Monthelon. There
she was received by her children, and the crowding
poor, and her father-in-law also, with ecstasies of welcome. At Bourbilly she had been called, " the Holy
Baroness;" and at Monthelon she was called " Our
good Lady."

Her generosity and faith were such that during a
famine she gave almost the last morsels of grain to,
the poor: the first miracle granted by Almighty God

to her ardent faith and charity was similar to that of
the multiplication of the loaves and fishes, — a single
barrel of flour remaining perpetually supplied, and,
according to her order, dispensed freely by her very
loth servants to those whose necessities compelled
them to beg. It was winter, but until the next har-
vest (six months) this miracle continued. She felt
with St. Francis de Sales that "the poor are not
merely suffering human beings; they are our Lord
himself concealed under rags." And it was this
belief which gave her courage to suffer so keenly in
the service of the poor during her whole life. She
once told a nun that the martyrs to charity are as
great martyrs as those to death; for those to charity
suffer more in living to carry out the will of God,
than if they had died a thousand times to show their
faith, their love, and fidelity. "How long," another
nun asked her, overhearing this remark, "does such
martyrdom for charity's sake last?"

"From the moment when we let the soul lean upon
God until the hour of death," said she. "But this is
only given to generous persons. Weak souls are not
so tried, for our Lord fears they will abandon him."

Here are expressed very simply but very powerfully both the honor there is in being called to suffer,
and the pathos there is in our Lord's love for those
creatures who fade spiritually as they seem about to
bloom. There is no contradiction between the desire
for this charitable mission and its pain : to suffer for
God is called, by those who know what it is, a *true*
happiness.

St. Francis said of her : "She is simple and sincere

as a child, with a solid and noble judgment, a lofty soul, and a courage for saintly enterprises unusual in her sex. In short, I have found at Dijon what Solomon could scarcely find at Jerusalem: a good woman of strong intelligence, Madame de Chantal."

St. Jane frequently received indications that she was to have a remarkable vocation. She tells us that in the little wood near the castle at Monthelon, she was praying as she walked along, when suddenly she was seized with a strong mental summons, and she stopped as if under the complete dominion of a higher power. She was then irresistibly led to the neighboring church. In the church it was shown to her that the divine love was consuming in her all that belonged to herself, and that she was to have spiritual and corporeal labors without number. (Towards the close of her life she said to a friend: "It is twenty-seven years since I have thought only of others, with no time to think of myself.") At the time of the vision her whole body trembled and shivered, probably with a forecast of the ordeals she was to meet. But her heart was filled with joy in God, because, "to die to one's self for God seemed to me the nourishment of love on earth, as praise of Him is the nourishment of love in heaven."

She strongly desired a spiritual director of greater inspiration than the one who already guided her, that she might make no mistakes and delays in fulfilling her duty as a servant of the divine will. She finally obtained the help of one of the greatest teachers in the annals of the church, St. Francis de Sales. St. Jane was long tormented with, as she supposed,

, temptations against entire faith. St. Francis always laughed these ideas to scorn, and begged her, in many a brilliant argument, to scorn them also, and pass them by. " No, no, my child," he wrote in one of his letters from Annecy, " let the wind roar, and do not imagine that the *frifilis* of the leaves is the clash of hostile weapons ! "

She afterwards cried : " Oh, how terrible the attack was ! I could find no other remedy than to take the Cross of our Lord in my hands, and say to myself : ' Child of little faith, what do you fear ? If you walk upon the waters, it is with Jesus Christ ! ' "

During her young widowhood she was sought in marriage by a number of rich suitors ; and at last one asked for her hand whom her family could not bear to have her reject. He was extremely wealthy, and proposed that (he being a widower with children) Madame de Chantal's children should form alliances with his, thus accumulating all the large estates of both families into one great aggregate. St. Jane's relatives joined in an attack upon her desires and better judgment, so that she was very nearly exhausted by the conflict. She says that the persecutions which she had suffered in her father-in-law's house were roses compared to these thorns, with which she was now torn. Escaping suddenly from a conclave of parents and cousins, she went to her chamber, threw herself upon her knees, prayed a long time with many tears, and then decided to accomplish an act which she had thought of for months past. She traced deeply, with a red-hot iron, the word *Jesus* upon her bosom. When, thirty years after, she died, the sisters discovered that these letters were an inch long, and for the most part still very distinct. "Without suffering," said Thomas à Kempis, "there is not love." She was made very ill by this severe wound ; but there was never again any doubt in her mind as to her duty in regard to re-marriage.

Both St. Jane de Chantal and St. Teresa took the vow *du plus parfait,* — to do always that which seemed the most perfect action under the circumstances. Upon reflection, it would appear that this vow could not be rejected by any one devoted to religious — and therefore Christian — development ; yet at the same time it is only such a vow that leads inevitably to immeasurable agonies of self-denial and self-expending for others. It is the very limit of all vows.

In the year 1603, — she had then become a widow, — she was affiliated to the Order of the Capuchins, as many persons in the world were affiliated to different Orders at that time in religious history, without any expectation of entering the communities to which they thus belonged. In the next year, 1604, the Carmelites had been brought from Spain by Cardinal de Bérulle, assisted by the illustrious Madame Acarie, now Sister Mary of the Incarnation ; and in 1605, Venerable Anne de Jesus, the first companion and principal confidante of St. Teresa, came to Dijon to establish the third Monastery of the Carmelite Order in France. Every one pressed into the little chapel which the Carmelites opened, wishing to hear, as they said, "the good Spanish Mothers" sing. St. Jane desired to join this Order, but St. Francis would not hear of it. He was already beginning to study her character with the hope that she would one day be found equal to the work of establishing an Order such as he had most interest in, because he considered it to be now most needed. He remembered that she resembled the Superioress of his vision. An Order such as he desired to see newly inaugurated was possibly of a higher type than those which were more severe. The latter had perhaps disciplined religious fidelity by coporeal suffering and abstinence into a condition proper for a purified gentleness. As yet he said nothing to her of his plans, and urged her to devote herself to her children and her poor. " Nothing prevents our perfecting ourselves in our vocation so much," he vouchsafed to remark, " as wishing for another." There is an astonishing difference between St. Jane's character and the intentions of the Order of the Visitation. This difference might be thought unfavorable, but it was really beneficial. The strongest type of woman was to help found one of the gentlest Orders; thus proving that the outward gentleness only covered an adamant of refined self-discipline.

" I esteem greatly," said St. Francis, " the sanctification of women, who followed our Lord in his steps even to the foot of the Cross, when he did not find there a single apostle." He declared of saintly Madame Acarie, whom he had the delight of knowing and conversing with often before she became a Carmelite, and who was eventually beatified by Pius VI. : " She inspired me with such respect for her virtues that I never had the hardihood to ask her of what she was thinking; I dared only listen to what she chose to reveal to me." With such an attitude towards the value of feminine perception and sweetness, he was able to gauge the usefulness to religion of Madame de Chantal.

When she decided to enter conventual life, and St. Francis agreed to her importunities, feeling himself that the right hour had arrived, she was considered by every one in her family and acquaintanceship almost inhuman for daring to propose to leave her four children and her father and her aged father-in-law to take some care of themselves. But the result proved her wisdom. Her service for her children, her care for them, and her inspiration given to them, were helps such as few children receive from their mothers. She not only had the capacity to be a nun, but a consummate woman of business as well. She attended carefully, for years after she entered the Visitation Order, to her children's interests.

In 1611 and 1612 she did not hesitate to leave the cloister in order to husband the estates of her children, and by her intelligent care, in a few years she doubled their fortunes. The chorus of antagonistic reproaches which went up about her was eventually changed to fulsome praises, equally loud. Said St. Francis during the storm of criticism: "If you had re-married yourself, this time to a nobleman of Gascony or Brittany, you would have abandoned all your family, and no one would have blamed you. Now you give yourself to a life which allows you to care for your children; but it being a life *for God*, every one is angered!"

At the moment of parting from her family, she suffered to the limit of human capacity. Her son threw himself upon the ground before her, and she passed, trembling and sobbing, but firm in her faith and loyalty to the divine summons, over his prostrate body. He, Celse-Bénigne, lived to acknowledge that his desperate opposition to her course was a superstitious mistake ; a superstitious regard for the conventional habits of families. He would, in any case, have been almost constantly separated from his mother by his absence at college and in the army. As it was, he saw her as often as he could absent himself from his pursuits ; and her ideally noble reputation for piety and moral power, her renown as a foundress of most important houses of the Visitation, were incentives to noble living on his own part, and gave him prestige at court and elsewhere.

She went to Annecy, and began preparations for founding the religious and benevolent Order of whose first years a brief account has been given. Her entrance into Annecy was the occasion for the collecting of a great crowd, who had heard of her remarkable kindness to the poor. The instantaneous effect of her presence upon several young girls who met her was like that of visible inspiration. Their refined, delicately-natured souls, naturally good, though in some cases deeply enmeshed in worldly vanities, apprehended her wonderful power for leading to holiness. They became the first shining lights among the postulants of the Order.

The eloquence of St. Jane was such as to arrest attention and remain in the memory. No doubt a few words from her lips could teach a young girl to look to the saint for that strength and unfaltering direction which is the acme of motherly support. In her early youth she sometimes talked badinage, and she was indeed bright and fascinating as the most enchanting of women are; but the range of her personality went far beyond this sort of value. They say that her sallies of wit were very soon diverted by herself to serious discourse. It is to be hoped that many people know in some one among their acquaintance, in man or woman, this delightful union of intellectual mirthfulness and spiritual dignity.

When scarcely five years old, St. Jane overheard a gentleman saying to her father, that he did not believe in the real presence of our Lord in the Blessed Sacrament. She then revealed that unflinching force of utterance which distinguished her so much in later life, though it was not till much later that her earnestness was invariably joined to the utmost sweetness and repose of expression. Said she, approaching the heretical gentleman with a great emotion depicted upon her little face: "Sir, we must believe that Jesus Christ is there, because he has said it; and when you do not believe it, you call him a liar!"

At the age of thirty-seven, having become a Visitandine and Superioress, her conversation with the ladies who came to see her was so noble, and deadly to the follies of worldly life, that, among many more, one young girl at once took off her ear-rings and other jewels. She broke them into pieces, lest she should be tempted to wear them again, and had a cross made of the fragments, which, years afterwards, she showed to her daughter, who was about to become a nun of the Visitation, saying: "This was the fruit of my first interview with the Mère de Chantal."

The saint's natural aptitude for verbal expression was fostered in a school of circumstances that gave her every opportunity for development in this direction. In 1619, for instance, St. Francis de Sales arrived in Paris to preside over the founding of a convent of the Visitation to which the most violent opposition was raised. He sent for St. Jane de Chantal, who gave her wonderful aid to the founding of such monasteries of the Order as were threatened with the gravest difficulties. She was just at that time in a new monastery of the city of Bourges, where her brother was Archbishop. He (fearing for her safety in Paris) refused to give her a carriage in which to travel. "Monsignor," she cried, turning upon him a firm glance; "obedience has good legs!" She would have walked the whole distance; and her brother realized it. The carriage was soon in readiness. St. Francis was surrounded, when St. Jane arrived, by the powerful help of the Cardinal de Bérulle, Père de Condren, St. Vincent de Paul, and others; and all these faultless Christians, strengthened by the magnetic and loving skill of St. Jane, met successfully the avalanche of opposition to the new monastery, which was flung upon them by the Jansenists and self-interested persons. In such a company, her genius for eloquence could not but grow more and more vigorous. The beauty of the preaching of Père de Condren was such that the Cardinal de Bérulle always knelt while he wrote down what he had heard

the saintly Father say.   On May 1st of the same year
St. Francis established the monastery as he had set
out to do.   St. Jane was placed in charge of its first
months of trial, and its spiritual direction was placed
in the hands of St. Vincent de Paul.   Not long afterwards the plague appeared, driving the friends
of the convent out of the city.   The sisters were re-
ported to be rich, but they were in reality without
the necessaries of life.   St. Jane, with the rest of
the nuns, sat upon the floor; there being no chairs.
During the fiercest cold of the winter there was almost
no fuel; and they had no covering on their beds at
night, except an occasional drift of snow, sifted
between the cracks of the insecure building.   This
was the poverty-laden monastery which its enemies so
well knew had in it the mustard-seed of irresistible
virtue, that should grow to the subduing of those
enemies, at last!   When the hour for repast arrived,
St. Jane would retire to the church and pray for
food, reciting an " Our Father " in request for daily
bread.   The moment she learned that the necessary
sustenance had been sent, she would stop the recitation
of the prayer, saying that it was not best to pray for
a superabundance.   Now comes the point for which
this allusion to the monastery of Paris was made.
When the sisters used to recount their vicissitudes,
they always assured their hearers that those of them
who had had the good fortune to sustain with St. Jane
de Chantal the poverty of this heroic experience, had
never passed happier days, because of the great cheerfulness of their Mother.   They had all been brought
up in luxury; but they had never happened to find

[Facsimile of the original circular of the Academy]

YOUNG LADIES' ACADEMY.

YOUNG LADIES' ACADEMY,

AT

THE CONVENT OF THE VISITATION, IN GEORGETOWN, D. C.

THE common branches of Education taught in this institution, are READING, WRITING, ARITHMETIC, ENGLISH GRAMMAR and COMPOSITION, GEOGRAPHY, with the use of Maps and Globes, ELEMENTS OF HISTORY, plain and ornamental NEEDLE WORK.

THE TERMS FOR TUITION of the above, and for Board, Washing, Mending, Books and Stationary, Doctors' Fees and Medicines, are $150 per annum, payable half-yearly in advance, and $5 entrance money. The parents must furnish every article of Cloathing, Bed and Bedding, (or pay a compensation for the use of it.) also, Knives, Forks, Spoons and Tumbler. The dress of the young Ladies, is, as much as possible, uniform and consists of a brown stuff Frock and black Apron;—the Sunday dress is white.

The FRENCH LANGUAGE, DRAWING, and MUSIC, form separate charges: the two first at $5, the last at $11, per quarter. Day-scholars are admitted in the School for $6 and $8 per quarter.

No deduction is made for the annual Vacation, that takes place in August, as the young Ladies are welcome to spend that time at the Academy.

Although this institution is essentially Catholic, Scholars of any other religious denomination are received, by complying with the exterior discipline of the house.

This Academy being under the superintendence of a numerous community, a selection of competent Tutoresses can always be made, whose tender and religious care of their Pupils is calculated to gain their love, and obtain the confidence of all Parents. The situation, in point of healthiness, is proved inferior to none in the United States.

All communications respecting this institution, addressed, free of postage, either to the Revd. J. P. DE CLORIVIERE, Director, or to Mrs. HARRIET BRENT, Mother Superior, or to Mrs. JERUSHA BARBER, Mistress of Pensioners, at the Convent in Georgetown, D. C., will be punctually attended to.

that luxury could command the zest of St. Jane's genius for brilliant but ever holy verbal help, and for cheer in the very heart of bitterness.

For thirty-one years she received Holy Communion every morning; and this saintly observance never ceased to be new in its inspiration to her. She had great care that there should be fine flowers in the monastery garden, which were to be placed before the Blessed Sacrament. Every Sunday, and on Feast-days, the sisters made a practice of offering her a bouquet to carry. But, after having held it a minute, she would send it by the sister sacristan to the altar. When this bouquet was faded, she had it brought and placed in her cell, before her crucifix. She always kept some of these dry flowers there. Once a sister asked her what her idea was, in doing so. To this she answered that it was not worthy to be discussed. When further urged, she said: " Color and fragrance were the life of these faded flowers, which they gave up slowly before the Holy Sacrament. I desire that my life should be given away little by little, until finished before God, in the constant honoring of Holy Church."

St. Jane must have derived her forceful speech in some degree from her father, the parliamentary president, Frémyot. He was a very devout man, and a very brave one. It is told of him that while fighting beside Henry IV. he had attracted the attention of the king by his daring. A few days after this particular battle, the king, victorious, while resting at his ease, demanded of Frémyot what he would have done in defending his sovereign if his sovereign had remained a Huguenot. "Sire," replied M. Frémyot, "I confess that if you had not cried, 'Long live the Church of Rome!' I should not have cried, 'Long live Henry IV.!'" The king could not have been more charmed than he was by this honest answer. He turned laughing to one of his cronies. "If you have any cheating to be done," said he; "find some one besides Frémyot to help you!"

Her color was uniform, brunette, and very pale; a trait of physique belonging to strong heads and hearts, to spirituality and steady earnestness. Her deportment was singularly fine, and combined with gentleness. She was as strong-willed and full of the fire of executive ability as a man, but was also in possession of a woman's lavish mercy and sensitive recognition of her dependence upon divine power. Here were two opposing forces in the noble soul of St. Jane de Chantal; and her great director, St. Francis, strove with unfailing patience and wisdom to train them into harmonious labor for God. He and his disciple were crowned, in the midst of hard effort and constant opposition from others, with success in St. Jane's development for her vocation. "Happy are those who find holy directors!" once averred Fénelon.

At the same time that St. Jane had renounced vanity, she had vowed herself to labor. Her fingers were never idle. She never allowed her diligence to be interrupted by the visits made upon her, unless quite necessary. Otherwise, she had her little work-table brought, and, after gracefully excusing it, continued to sew.

At thirty years old she had found herself in a communion with God which astonished her by its completeness. There were certain times when she felt herself raised to superior regions of feeling, of which she had not dreamed before. Miraculous visions mingled themselves with her ardent thoughts of God. Not long before her death she declared that, if she were not held back by the fear of throwing into anger and confusion those persons who had from time to time spoken to her with scorn, she would kneel at their feet and thank them with clasped hands. Yet, though so grateful for human humiliations, which lashed all traces of pride from her being, she was permitted to rest, like St. John, (as her director expressed it), upon the bosom of our Lord, in the prayerful peace which took possession of her in her contemplation of the Holy of Holies.

Eloquence was the especial impulse of St. Jane when dealing — as it was her vocation to do — with her fellow-beings. She had to perfection the art of arresting attention in personal intercourse, which is always more or less the attribute of those who are sent by Heaven to teach and lead. But her natural aptitude for social brilliancy and leadership was nevertheless chastened by constant self-mastery into humble service for the sole end of beneficence, and even nourished in the midst of its rich capacity a reverence for quiet and solitude.

> " Headstrong liberty is lashed with woe.
> There 's nothing situate under heaven's eye
> But hath his bound, in earth, in sea, in sky."

Why should we mortals desire to stand exempt

from this law of obedience to a rule which even guides the hurricane? Power guided with reference to the Highest is the only kind which does not rush to waste. St. Jane, of all personalities the best adapted to be headstrong with the greatest amount of success, very early decided that such liberty would lead her to some sort of destruction; if to no other, to that destruction of her usefulness to suffering human beings which her saintly heart considered to be the sweetest usefulness of all.

"I know a soul," she said when dying, " that charity has separated from the things that were pleasantest to it, more absolutely than tyrants could have separated his body from his soul by the wielding of a sword." If she referred to St. Francis de Sales, as she well might, yet we may apply the same phrase to her, and bless her name.

At first she was annoyed and made wretched because people cut pieces from her clothes as holy relics, and so on. Finally, as she grew in age and humility, dying to herself, she gladly held out her hands to be kissed, and gently received the honors paid her. This was because she realized a truth which was exemplified by St. Francis of Assisi. When he first went into the world after the stigmata had appeared on his body, he would try to conceal his hands from the crowds who gazed at them, blushing and confused at the attention given him. If any one cut his robe, or his cord hanging from his waist, he would murmur: "These people are foolish to honor a sinner so much." But he later met the pilgrims who came to visit him with outstretched hands, and said to a young priest who was astonished: "Do you imagine that these people are thinking of me?"

St. Vincent de Paul said of her, that of all her saintly traits her faith seemed to be the greatest, although she had all her life been tempted by contrary thoughts. In short, he had never observed in her (he was her director after the death of St. Francis) a single imperfection! Of her faith, here is an example. She lost her dear and brave young son. During many days she was utterly silent, and even at Recreation sat with eyes shut, twirling her distaff. But the joy that her son, whose salvation she had feared for, as he was hot-tempered, and frequently engaged in duels, — the joy that he had died nobly in a battle for the faith, gave her a consolation greater than her sorrow.

Of her innocence we may gain some idea from the following public confession, at the time that she forever gave up her power as Superioress, and came and knelt in the choir, before the successor to St. Francis de Sales, his cousin, Jean François de Sales, then Bishop of Geneva: —

"Monsignor, I confess very humbly my sin of having often broken silence, even that of vespers, without necessity; of my being dispensed of the Assemblies of the Community without urgent occasion; of not having served our Sisters as I should; for which I ask most humbly pardon; and from you, monsignor, pardon for the inconveniences I have given you."

Her penance was three *Paters* and three *Aves*.

Towards the end of her life she made the rounds of many convents already established. She was seventy

years old, but she often rose at two o'clock in order
to make an early start from one place to another, and
to attend Mass first. She was the awakener of all
who were with her. She frequently had no nourishment from this time until three or four o'clock in the
afternoon; and even then was often not able to find
anything but milk and black bread and cheese, in the
villages she passed through. But her cheer was unfailing; she kept every one in good spirits.

The sisters of the Visitation vied with each other
in humbling themselves; "that our lives may be
hidden with Christ in God," as St. Jane prayed.
She took her turn in all menial work; serving at
table in the refectory, sweeping stairs, cooking in the
kitchen. She called the week when she did all this,
in turn, her best week. There is a pretty story of
her guarding the cow in the early days at the house
of the *Galerie*. This cow was indeed an animal in
all respects to be envied, as it grazed near the little
fruit-trees, and was necessarily attended by first one
angelic nun and then another.

No sooner had St. Jane grown to be a part of the
Order which she helped to found by constant labors,
and increased by branches which she tended with
continued labors as fearless and devoted, than she
became subject to illnesses which made her existence a severe trial to her. We have seen that illness
did not prevail to make her relinquish ardor and
effort. In the lives of the saints this peculiarity of
trial is very frequent; and we who are not "called"
especially to give our days to God's requirements
for others, know how hard it is to press on in our

worldly responsibilities, if the body is assailed by disease. There is a proverbial belief that only *mothers* ignore physical suffering to fulfil their duties to their children. But we may learn that there are mothers who are not so by blood, who ignore their bodily pain for the sake of souls that need to know God, because these women love God so much that every soul He has created is as dear to them as a child of their own.

St. Jane went to heaven, December 13, 1641, aged sixty-nine. At her side was her cherished friend, the Duchess of Montmorency, niece of Pope Sixtus V., who had taken the veil not long before; and the beloved saint was surrounded by kneeling nuns, who prayed for her joy and peace with humble ardor and that faith which shall see perpetual light.

ANNALS OF THE GEORGETOWN CONVENT.

I. MOTHER TERESA LALOR : "THE PIOUS LADIES."

WE have shown, in our opening chapters, how the prophecy of St. Francis de Sales concerning Queen Henrietta Maria; the close association of that royal woman with the Visitation afterward; the courage and religious fidelity of her friend Madam Neale and of Madam Neale's grand-daughter, in America; together with the entrance of Leonard Neale into the priesthood, his vision, his return to the United States and appointment to Georgetown College, were all parts of a long, but clear and regular sequence, leading to the establishment of the Visitation in this country.

These were the roots from which a fine, yet hardy spiritual growth was to spring and flower here.

It remains to introduce the other persons and factors providentially brought together in order to make the culmination possible.

The foundress of this Georgetown Convent, the first Visitation house in America, was Miss Alice Lalor, known later in religion as Mother Teresa. She was born in Queen's County, Ireland; but her parents removed to Kilkenny, and there her childhood was passed, there she grew up. Her tender piety and

her bright and cheerful character won the affection
and regard of every one around her, and especially
of her pastor, Father Carroll. When at the age of
seventeen she received the sacrament of confirmation
from Bishop Lanigan, he also was attracted by her
fervor and modesty; and, having instituted with
Father Carroll a confraternity of the Blessed Sacrament at Kilkenny, he named Alice Lalor as its first
president or prefect. She soon resolved to consecrate
herself unreservedly to God, and was permitted to
make the vow of virginity, although complete renunciation of the world was not then practicable, because
there was no convent in the neighborhood. Several
of her friends took the same vow, each receiving a
ring marked with a commemorative inscription; and
she and they were looked upon as forming the nu-
cleus of a future religious community.

One of Alice Lalor's sisters married an American
merchant, Mr. Doran, who was desirous that his wife
should have the companionship of Alice in her new
transatlantic home, for a while. Alice, who was now
thirty-one, agreed to go with them, but promised
Bishop Lanigan that she would come back in two
years to aid in forming the religious community so
long contemplated. She sailed from Ireland with her
sister and her brother-in-law, in the winter of 1794.

Among the passengers on the sailing packet were
Mrs. McDermott and Mrs. Sharpe, both widows.
During the long voyage they formed an intimate
friendship with Alice, and it turned out that they,
as well as she, longed to enter the cloistered life.
On the eve of Epiphany, 1795, when their ship was

drawing near the coast, they agreed that so soon as they should land they would go to church for confession and communion, and that whatever priest they might find in the confessional they would regard as appointed to be their spiritual director.

They landed at Philadelphia, and the priest whom they found and accepted as their director was, happily, Father Neale. These three devout penitents, brought thus unexpectedly to his feet from beyond the sea, were the women destined to coöperate with him in forming the community of his vision, which he had never ceased to hope that he might realize.

It is true, Alice Lalor felt herself bound to return to Ireland, bound by the ring which Bishop Lanigan had placed upon her finger at the time of her virgin vow, and bound by her promise to him. But Father Neale saw the greater service she could render to religion in America. He asked her to remain, not to revoke her vow, but to fulfill it in this new field, under these altered circumstances; and, as her confessor, he offered to dispense her from her promise to go back to her native land. She accepted his advice. Yet a certain uneasiness lingered in her mind at the thought of her responsibility toward those who were awaiting her at home. Father Neale, perceiving this, said to her one day: "Let me see that ring, my child." She drew it off, and gave it to him. He took it, looked at the inscription; and then, to her astonishment, twisted it in two and threw the fragments away.

She felt as though her very heart were wrung; yet Father Neale's action, as he intended, destroyed the

last, reluctant tie which was drawing her back to
Ireland. The broken ring was the type of a divided
mind, which must be cast aside before she could go
forth along the pathway of her new resolve with single purpose.

Miss Lalor, Mrs. McDermot, and Mrs. Sharpe,
after this, settled in Philadelphia, hired a house there,
and lived in community. Upon entering a state in
which she could devote herself to following observances which might most thoroughly purify her heart
for the service of God, Alice Lalor made frequent
use of the discipline, the hair shirt, the cord of St.
Francis of Assisi, and fastings, watchings, and prayer.
Custom rendered these austerities, as St. Aloysius de
Gonzaga has said, "sweet and easy;" but she became emaciated, pale, and weak, having trusted too
much to her splendid constitution, and Father Neale
directed her to moderate the fervent practices. Her
rugged health and fresh bloom soon returned. Mrs.
Sharpe had her daughter with her, a child of eight
years ; and a young American postulant was admitted. Suddenly the yellow fever broke out afresh.
The postulant died, and Father Neale narrowly escaped death. Alice Lalor and her companions were
faithful to their adopted vocation of courage and
helpfulness, and remained persistently in the midst
of danger (while every one who could leave the city
fled), ministering to the pest-stricken.

When, in 1798–99, Father Neale was ordered to
Georgetown, as president of the Jesuit College there,
he sent for the three devoted, religious friends, and
domiciled them for a time with three Poor Clares,

who, being driven from France to this country by the Revolution in 1793, had set up a little convent not far from the college. The Poor Clares attempted to keep a school, as a means of support; but their poverty was so extreme, and their life so rigorous, that the scholars were mostly frightened away, and the nuns, it is told, were once reduced to such indigence that they were obliged to sell a parrot which they owned in order to save themselves from starvation. These women, barefooted, according to their rule, and abjectly poor, came of noble blood, and had been born to luxury.

A lay brother named Alexis, their protector, during the flight from France, continued with them so long as they remained in this country. For several months Alice Lalor and her two friends boarded and taught in this convent; but it soon became apparent that the austere rule of Saint Clare differed widely from that which they wished to adopt, and was uncongenial to their own spiritual attraction, as well as to the needs of the time and the locality. Father Neale, therefore, bought a house and lot near by, and installed them in it; very much as St. Francis de Sales had made provision for the first three mothers of the Visitation at the Galerie, in Annecy.

"Thus was begun by these three ladies an establishment which to the world appeared a folly, and which indeed met with many difficulties and so little assistance, that but for the invincible perseverance of Archbishop Neale and his unshaken confidence in God, the enterprise must have been abandoned."[1]

[1] Circular Letter, 1822.

In 1800 Father Neale was consecrated coadjutor to Archbishop Carroll; but, as he continued to be president of Georgetown College, he did not remove to Baltimore, but hired a dwelling near his nascent sisterhood, and acted as novice master for it.

From the manuscript records collected and kept by the nuns, it cannot be ascertained at what period, precisely, Bishop Neale formed the idea of placing this germ or bud of a community under the Visitation rule; but it is said that he had a preference for that Order. Knowing nothing of its rules, however, he conformed the life of the sisters to the rules of the Society of Jesus, with some abatements and modifications. They had regular hours for rising, for meditation, for Mass — in the Poor Clares' chapel — for reading, and silence, and for examen of conscience, with morning and evening prayers and the rosary, their fasts and mortifications, also. They opened a school, which was hailed with delight by the Catholics of the neighborhood, and received solid encouragement from them. The little group increased from three members to five, all of whom were known round about as "The Pious Ladies;" their only appellation for some years. Although the sisters kept as much as possible within their own premises, enclosure was only partially observed. They did their own shopping and marketing, went out to church, and accompanied their pupils in daily walks to the beautiful surrounding forests.

Suddenly their modest progress received a check in the long illness and the death of their principal teacher, Sister Ignatia (Mrs. Sharpe), who was buried in the parish cemetery of Trinity Church. And, although they had made a small beginning, with some favorable prospects, it must not be supposed that their condition or their slight success was in any manner easy, or free from trials, anxiety, and obstacles. In 1804, however, the Poor Clares returned to France, — where Catholicity had been restored, after a brief, wild orgy of revolutionary "reason" and a Reign of Terror. Mother Teresa (Alice Lalor) was able to buy the house and land which the Poor Clares had occupied; and Father Francis Neale purchased their simple altar and furniture, as well as their library of French books. This library, by the way, became later on the source of a "find," which was of great practical value to the sisters in ascertaining the constitution of the Visitation Order. For a time, the sisters attended Mass in the college chapel; then the Clarist altar was set up in the largest room of the "Academy" building, and afterwards was again transferred to the building which had been the Poor Clare convent, and was now occupied by "The Pious Ladies." In 1808 Bishop Neale's term as president of the college ended, and he then took a dwelling close by the convent, separated from it only by a narrow alley. This arrangement, while enabling him to be close at hand for the free access of all his parishioners, and to receive visitors from a distance on business of the diocese, and give them shelter, also made it possible for him to supervise closely these new daughters of a still unformed community, whom he was endeavoring to train for a monastic life. So it came about that "The Pious Ladies" not only began to enjoy a sequestered and well-defined little territory of their own, but that the coadjutor Bishop was able to give much more time than before to instructing and advising them.

The crude and simple convent and "Old Academy" now occupied a square of roughly cultivated ground on the heights of Georgetown. Through the middle of the plot ran, from north to south, a creek which emptied into the Potomac far below at the foot of the hill. Its banks were somewhat steep on the western side, but sloped more gradually on the eastern, where lay the convent garden, orchard, and meadow. On the west, the land rose in a series of green-sodded terraces bordered with raspberry bushes, lilacs, and other shrubbery; and here stood the "Old Academy," which was the house that Mother Teresa removed to when she and her associates withdrew from the Poor Clares. To the east, in the garden and near the street, were the convent and the Bishop's house. At first, and for a long while, both the nuns and their pupils were obliged to get over the creek as best they could in their constant passing to and fro between convent and academy, from chapel to school, or *vice versa;* though inclement weather and heavy rains, or ice and snow, sometimes made it impossible to cross. Afterwards a rustic bridge was built to span the stream. A spring and fishpond, overhung by forest and fruit trees, made this a charming spot in summer. The fishpond and the dam had been made by the Poor Clares, who needed such provision, their rule not allowing them to eat any meat.

The foliage was thronged with birds; and Sister
Agnes Brent recalled how, when a child, she used to
watch them with delight, from bridge or bank, as
they bathed in the stream or fluttered among the
trees or in the arbors of honeysuckle and grape on
the hillside. But, to offset all this prettiness of sum-
mer-time, there were many hardships in the school
and convent life of that day.

Sister Agnes Brent remembered that, when she
entered the novitiate in 1812, the buildings were in
a state of total disrepair. The monastery was but a
forlorn-looking two-story frame house, containing six
or eight rooms. To this the nuns had attached a
schoolhouse, — a still more wretched structure, built
on log foundations which had rotted and sunk, causing the building to lean so much that it was considered unsafe, and had to be propped up, inside and
out, with posts and poles. The stairway was supported in like manner, and was so rickety that Sister Agnes dreaded to go up and down its trembling
steps. It was quite necessary to do so, however, as
the dormitory — a single large room — was upstairs.
On the ground floor the space was partitioned into
an assembly room and a refectory; the assembly
room opening into the convent proper, where the
choir, chapel, novitiate, parlor, and kitchen were
situated.

None of the rooms in the old schoolhouse were
lathed or plastered at first. But in 1811 Sister Margaret Marshall — of whom we shall have something
more to say — succeeded, by her own energy and the
toil of her own hands, in lathing and plastering the

assembly room. This achievement of hers contributed greatly to the warmth and comfort of the room
in winter. Her work was well done, too, and lasted
as long as the humble old building was able to hold
itself together.

There remains now scarcely a vestige of these
primitive structures. The Poor Clares' convent and
their schoolhouse have vanished; so has the house of
Bishop (later, Archbishop) Neale; giving place to
the neat little chapel and the fine array of solid buildings which to-day present a striking contrast to the
memory-picture of that poor, bare, gloomy-looking
cloister in which the early sisters uttered their first
vows and spent their twenty long years of probation.

From the death of Sister Ignatia Sharpe in the
summer of 1802, until 1822, or somewhat later, the
community was in very straitened circumstances. The
loss of this their best teacher caused the school to
decline so that it barely yielded them subsistence.
Only the commonest branches could be taught, now;
— reading, writing, geography, and arithmetic, with
no music or other special studies. The terms were,
of course, low, but the patronage remained small;
hardly extending beyond the circle of Bishop Neale's
relatives and friends, who wished to uphold an infant
Catholic institution — for a while the only one in the
United States — where their daughters might become
well grounded in the principles of their religion, prepare for their First Communion, and be shielded from
the dangers to which their faith would be exposed if
they were sent to the non-Catholic schools of the
district. Sister Agnes Brent has recorded that her

uncle, in placing her there, told her plainly that he did so for the sake of her religion, and not with the expectation of her acquiring much literary knowledge.

Everything at the nunnery and school bore the impress of extreme poverty. Provisions were dealt out by measure; only a fixed quantity of food or fuel for each person or place. Wheat bread was never seen there. Corn bread was used, made from corn which the sisters themselves had raised, and had husked and shelled before sending it to the mill to be ground. They cleaned, salted, and put up their own fish and meat; grew all their own vegetables, and for that purpose kept a fine garden, the heavier work of which was done by their negro man or men, the lighter by themselves.

Butter was rarely a part of their diet; and when this luxury could be allowed at all, it was carefully distributed in small pieces, — one piece at the plate of each sister or child. Their coarse corn bread was divided in the same careful manner, — a single slice to each person; and if any one found this insufficient, she had to endure the lack of more. From the sketch of the life of Mother Juliana Matthews we learn that, being Refectorian and at one time Dispenser, she had charge of giving out the provisions, and that while carrying around the bread basket before meals she often felt tempted to pick out a specially large slice for herself. To avoid all fault or inequality in the matter, she used to shut her eyes and take whatever bit of bread her hand chanced upon. Sister Agnes did the same thing. "Yet," she was wont to add, laughing, when she told of it, "it never entered my mind that this stinted fare was occasioned by necessity. I thought it entirely voluntary and suggested by a desire of practicing holy poverty."

In winter, the Dispenser was obliged to stand in the cold while the sisters were getting their appointed supply of fuel for the ensuing day. When there was snow on the ground, she stood on a log in order to keep her feet dry, and watched the others as they took, each one, the quantity allowed for her apartment or office. Four sticks of wood each day were given for the large assembly-room stove. For the small stoves six or eight smaller pieces were set apart. If coal was burned, two scuttles made the daily portion. The bedclothes of the plain couches on which the sisters slept were too scanty to keep them warm. Through the crevices of their rough, unplastered, board-walled dormitory the snow blew in freely; so that the floor and the very beds were often covered with little snowdrifts. The beds, at the best, were narrow cots of straw; but most of the sisters slept on the floor, being obliged to give up their cots to the children. And so constant and severe was their exposure to the cold, that their hands frequently became purple and swelled, the skin cracking open with the frost.

We have noted how meagre was the fare with which they poorly nourished themselves to sustain these physical hardships. It may be added that their breakfast and supper consisted only of a cup of rye coffee or of milk and water, with the ever constant single slice of corn bread already mentioned. At dinner a spoonful of molasses by way of dessert, after

the salt fish or meat and vegetables, was sometimes
granted as a special dainty on the occasion of grand
festivals, and was highly esteemed. They also saved
the parings and cores of apples, and by boiling these
prepared a sweetish drink with which to vary their
simple list of beverages.

Each sister was provided with a tin cup and a
pewter spoon for use at table, besides a tin basin
and pitcher in the dormitory. But their wardrobe
was lamentably deficient. Not having underclothes
enough for even a weekly change, they changed only
every twelve or fifteen days; one half of the community, alternately. The Sister Agnes, who has been
several times referred to here, was the only one to
whom clean linen was permitted weekly; and this
exception was made only because her clothes were too
small to fit any one else. Instead of " linen," however, we ought to say cotton; that being the material
generally used for their garments, which were nearly
all home-made and often so patched that the original
pieces could not be identified.

For brooms, they used weeds; or, rather, they
manufactured very good brooms out of a particular
kind of weed; and they did not even make a pretence
of indulging in chairs. Only one chair was to be
seen in their assembly room, and that one was reserved for Mother Teresa. The other sisters sat on
trunks or chests, which completed the furniture of
the apartment. In the evenings, when they gathered
together for recreation and converse, the room was
illuminated by a " save-all; " that is, a vessel filled
with grease from the pot skimmings of the kitchen.

Yet not even this was used on moonlight nights; and if, at any time when the save-all was burning, the supply of grease that supported it gave out suddenly, the sisters contentedly sat in darkness or enjoyed the faint glimmer of the firelight. When this accident happened on Saturday nights, and any one of the sisters had a rent to draw up or some stitches to take in her severely tried wearing apparel, she lit a pine-knot reserved for such emergencies. No one thought of keeping a lamp for her private use; and the solitary candle used in the convent was burned only in the choir.

But during all the years that this condition of things continued, no word of complaint was ever heard. On the contrary, the sisters were very gay, and made merry over the shifts and inventions to which they were driven by their poverty; the absurd conduct of their " save-all," in relapsing into darkness just when it was most needed, being sure to bring out hearty laughter.

Like St. Jane de Chantal, Mother Teresa was sure to be most cheerful when circumstances were most appalling. As sighs and tears have no uses for God, and we are expected to find God's burden light, she literally shone joyously beneath a burden of discomfort. If starvation threatened, and even mouldy bread became too precious, Mother Teresa's gayety fairly changed the sisters' hunger to cheerfulness. If the " save-all " refused to dispel darkness, as above said, her amusing tales and anecdotes introduced a brilliancy which left nothing to be desired. At last the sisters used to say, when their Mother

was particularly genial with innocent entertainment :
" Ah, she has something to tell us which will give us
pain, and is trying to raise our courage first ! " All
this extreme privation was not intended by the rule ;
the nuns were entitled to better fare. However, they
remained the victims of such distress, and, moreover,
happy ones.

There were, at this time, thirteen pupils in the
school ; children delicately reared, to whom the privations and severities of life under these circumstances offered a Spartan ordeal. Yet they flourished
under it, and became strong and hardy ; in this
respect prefiguring the growth and strength that the
school and convent were to attain. The advances
made in the beginning, however, were very slow.
The little sisterhood was not yet assimilated to the
Visitation, or to any religious order whatever ; and
it was obliged to remain thus informally or partially
organized for years, often in doubt as to whether it
would be able to cohere at all, and constantly enduring the hardest of work, the most meagre of fare, the
severest anxieties.

When, after many years, Mother Teresa's motherhood was changed to obedience to young Superiors
who had been her novices, a new loveliness in her
character was manifested. She " honored, respected,
cherished them, and gave them her whole confidence
for her interior guidance."

She delighted in feeding the pigeons and poultry.
The pigeons knew her so well that they flew down
from a great height to alight on her head and shoulders, and on her hands. St. Francis de Sales was

especially loved by the doves. Mother Teresa is said to have united the humility, simplicity, and cheerfulness of a child with the prudence and dignity becoming to her station. She died when about eighty years old. A little while before her death she said to the Superioress: "My life appears to me as a dream!" Her hope of heaven had been the chief reality of her being.

II. EARLY MEMBERS: SISTER MARGARET MARSHALL.

In the first nine years only four postulants joined "The Pious Ladies." These were Sister Aloysia Neale (1801), Sister Stanislaus Fenwick (1804), Sister Magdalene Neale (1805), and a lay sister, Mary (1806–7), whose surname is unknown. She could not give the date of her birth, but stated that she was sixteen at the time of Braddock's War; and she lived to be one hundred and five. In 1808 another postulant came; Miss Catharine Anne Rigden, a convert and a native of Georgetown, who ten years later was chosen as Mother Teresa's successor. Admitted October 2, the feast of the Guardian Angels, she made the seventh in the group; and Bishop Neale, who was cheered by her arrival, decided that as they were now so many they should begin to observe enclosure more strictly.

But after this no one sought admission, for a long while; the prospect of any increase in numbers appeared hopeless, and it seemed that the Bishop's cherished design must fall through. His position resembled that of St. Stephen, abbot of Citeaux, previous to the arrival of St. Bernard. But the

interval of stagnation was broken, in the midwinter
(February) of 1810, by the unexpected arrival of a
stranger, a young woman from Conewago, Warren
County, Pennsylvania; Margaret Marshall by name
and nineteen years of age, who asked to be admitted
to the novitiate.   The story of her coming is remarkable.

Her parents were pious people, of German origin;
but as she was their only daughter, and the mother
was in declining health, they opposed her vocation to
religious life.   Finding that they were planning a
speedy marriage for her, against her will, she resolved to leave her home, since neither the parish
priest nor her brother, who was preparing for the
Jesuit novitiate, could be induced to take her part.
Her brother, however, in arguing against her purpose
of consecrating herself, gave her the very information
and the hint she needed.   "There is no convent in
this country," said he, "except the Carmelites at
Port Tobacco, Maryland; and their rule is extremely
austere.   They are forbidden to eat meat, wear no
shoes summer or winter, and go without fire.   At
Georgetown there is a small community of pious
ladies under the direction of Bishop Neale; but they,
too, are far beyond the Alleghanies."

Margaret resolved to make her way to Georgetown, in obedience to what she felt was a call from
God.   Rising early on a stormy winter Sunday, she
put on her warmest wrappings; tossed out from her
window into the deep snow a package which she had
secretly prepared containing a few necessaries; and
then, passing through her mother's room without a

word of farewell, left the house, took up her little burden from the snow, and set out on her long march. The family supposed that she had gone to early Mass; and, when she did not reappear, they fancied that, because of the storm, she must have stayed with a relative who lived near the church. But "God help the Mass I heard that day!" Sister Margaret used to exclaim, in after years. "Before church was over, I was several miles on my journey; and so afraid was I of being overtaken, that I did not stop until I had walked twenty miles, although the snow was knee-deep."

Conewago is near the northwestern boundary of Pennsylvania. At the time of Margaret's flight no stage-coach was known on the rough roads of that unfrequented wilderness. The deep gorges of the Alleghanies were filled with snowdrifts encrusted with ice, often treacherous beneath her steps. The dense forests were haunted by wolves, and the brave girl had to pilot her own route, making inquiry when she could, and putting up at night in the rude huts which occasionally gave shelter to travelers. Her hands and feet were frost-bitten, but she plodded on unremittingly, traversed Pennsylvania and, having reached a resting point in Maryland, was about to resume her journey on foot, although frightfully fatigued, — when she perceived a wagon standing at the door. She asked whither it was bound, and the answer was "To Georgetown."

This, to her, seemed a veritable ray from heaven shining on her path. "May I put my bundle in your wagon?" said she to the driver. And he replied:

"Not only your bundle, madam; but if you wish you may ride yourself."

She did not hesitate, but quickly mounted to the seat. The drive was long; yet, as they rode on and on, she and her companion hardly spoke a word, the whole way. It was not until dusk that they entered Georgetown, — too late for her to think of going to the convent for that night. Being of course without friends or acquaintance in the place, she asked the driver to draw up in front of Trinity Church, where she alighted. But as she turned to thank her unknown benefactor for his kindness, she was astonished to find that both he and his team had disappeared! "I looked up and down the street," she said, in telling Sister Josephine Barber of the episode, later, "but could find no trace of either."

Margaret was impressed with the conviction that the "unknown" who had so opportunely appeared, had befriended her, and then so mysteriously disappeared again, was her Guardian Angel made visible in homely form, to help her and bring her to what proved to be her life's destination. This conviction she always retained. Tired and possibly bewildered though she might be, by the strain of toilsome travel and the momentous act of leaving her home forever, it is hardly probable that she could have been unaware of the noise of wheels and horses turning away in a quiet street, or that her imagination could cause the wagon to vanish in an instant. And certainly imagination could not have brought her and her bundle over the long country road to Georgetown. If we admit the direct action of the supernatural on what we are pleased to call solid mundane facts, — as we must admit it, — there is nothing astonishing in the thought that an angel may use horses as well as wings, or other means of effecting results. To a rationalist, angels are a nothing, or an abstraction. To us they are realities, dealing with realities. We can therefore perceive, at times, how the words of St. Francis de Sales are verified, that " God would rather send an angel to guide us, than suffer us to want for a conductor when we are seeking Him."

Margaret's next movements did not disclose anything of bewilderment or disordered imagination. She entered the church and adored the Blessed Sacrament on the altar. Then, in simple pilgrim fashion, she applied at a neighboring house for food and a night's lodging, and obtained both.

At daybreak the next morning, Saturday, — for so energetically had she kept in motion, that she had completed this long journey of two hundred and fifty miles, or more, in six days, — she approached the convent. Here another singular thing happened. The portress of the convent, Sister Frances, heard a rap at the door, and opened it. To her surprise, no one was to be seen there. The new-fallen snow, under the early morning gleam, showed no trace of a footprint. But while Sister Frances still stood on the threshold, looking out and wondering, the stranger Margaret — bundle in hand — made her appearance, just coming in at the gate from the street. Sister Frances waited for her to come up the walk to the door and then bade her enter.

Margaret, footsore and spent, needed no further

invitation, but stepped in, threw herself into a chair, and laid down her bundle.

" What do you want, my good friend?" asked the sister.

" I have come to live and die with you," said Margaret.

" But we don't take strangers without a recommendation. At least you will have to go to the Bishop."

" Could not some one go for me?" asked the girl. " I don't know where the Bishop lives."

Sister Frances smiled, and pointed out the house, close by. Then, as Margaret rose to go, in order to obtain an interview with him, the portress — apparently doubting that the unlooked-for visitor would have any occasion to return — called to her to take her bundle with her.

" No," said Margaret. " I 'll leave that until I come back."

And come back she did ; for the Bishop, quickly discerning her strong vocation and settled purpose, granted her petition. She entered the novitiate that same day, Saturday, February 16 ; just a week from the time of her resolute departure from her distant home.

Sister Margaret was a person of strong mind, powerful energies, and robust frame. She it was who lathed and plastered the assembly room with her own hands. But her courage, vigor, and resolution were fully matched by her goodness and gentleness. She became a most useful and inspiring member of the community ; and in 1834 performed heroic and wonderful work in founding a Visitation house at Mobile, Alabama.

In all the early annals of the Georgetown convent, it seems to us, there is no stronger figure, no more striking picture, than that of this energetic, spiritual young woman appearing at the convent gate when her approach had been announced by a mysterious signal at the door beyond.

III.   DISCOVERY OF THE RULES AND COSTUME: WAR OF 1812.

Sister Margaret Marshall was the ninth member; and the next accessions were Bishop Neale's two grand-nieces, Eliza Matthews (1811), who took the name of Sister Juliana, and Henrietta Brent (1812), who became Sister Agnes.   Both of them, as found-resses and afterwards Superiors, rendered eminent service to the Order.   But at that time success appeared impossible, with only one new member gained each year.

A prime reason of this slowness and hesitation in growth was, that the American clergy would not recommend to their communicants and penitents a religious house which they believed would soon fall to pieces.   It had no papal or ecclesiastical approval, and was unable to realize its pretensions to the rule of the Visitation, of which it knew nothing more than the name.   The mother house at Annecy had been suppressed during the French Revolution, and was not restored until 1822.   The other houses in Europe were unwilling to send a copy of the consti-tutions to Georgetown, because this community had not been founded in the usual way, by professed members of the Order.

The whole undertaking, in short, was looked upon as irregular. Bishop Neale's Jesuit brethren themselves told him that it was a thing unheard of in the Church that any house of an established order should be founded except by professed members of that order. They said that Rome would never approve, and that, of necessity, he would have to alter his plans. The difficulty might have been solved, if the Bishop could have paid the traveling expenses of sisters from one of the foreign convents, who might then have brought the rules, the proper "habit" or costume, and all other necessary information, together with authority. But this, in his dire poverty and that of the community, he was unable to do.

Archbishop Carroll therefore urged his coadjutor to change the character and object of the community, and to merge it in another enterprise which was then about to be undertaken by Father Dubourg, of Baltimore. The latter had induced Mrs. Seton to come from New York and open a select school in Baltimore, with a view to enlarging it later and erecting it permanently in some neighboring place. This school ultimately became Mount St. Mary's Academy, at Emmitsburg. But Bishop Neale could not consent to abandon his own scheme, which came from an inspiration unknown . to any one but himself. The Archbishop then — still firmly convinced that the establishment was doomed to failure, from the lack of both spiritual and temporal resources — proposed another plan. A rich lady living in Baltimore, who

had been educated with the Ursuline nuns in Ireland,
had heard of the embarrassments at Georgetown, and
had offered the Archbishop her means and influence
for the benefit of " The Pious Ladies " there, if they
and their director would consent to transform their
house into an Ursuline convent. She volunteered to
go to Ireland and to return with Ursuline nuns,
herself paying all the expenses of the journey and
providing further funds to carry on the work. To
Archbishop Carroll this offer, very naturally, seemed
to be of a kind that could not be neglected or
refused. He came with the lady to see Bishop
Neale, and the generous proposal was laid before
him. But the founder of the American Visitation
was not controlled by motives of mere human prudence. Politely and respectfully thanking the Archbishop, and the excellent lady who had shown such
liberality, he told them that — notwithstanding his
deference to their views and his appreciation of their
interest in the welfare of the community — he could
never consent to the proposed change. The Archbishop found it hard to understand this refusal; and
one day, when he came with Bishop Neale, Mrs.
Seton, Mr. Cooper, and several gentlemen, to visit
the convent, the subject was again discussed before
all the sisters, who happened to be at work in the
assembly room, picking wool. But argument and
persuasion were unavailing. The Bishop remained
firm. Mother Agnes remembered well that the
Archbishop, seeing how invincible was Bishop Neale's
purpose to continue on the lines already laid down,
ended the discussion by saying: " Well, sir, I give

you power to do what you can, but — expect no help
from me ! "

Other advisers of the Bishop finally tried to get
him to unite his nuns with the Carmelites who had
been established by his brother at Port Tobacco.
But this proposition he also negatived. The Visitation idea was now too firmly planted in his mind to
be uprooted, or to be grafted upon any other growth.
And, in his unflinching refusal to accept tempting
offers of money and help, even at this time of sorest
need and trial, we see clearly reproduced the spirit
of St. Francis de Sales, who also — during the adver-
sities that beset his young Order in France — had
calmly declined to be misled into struggle and litiga-
tion even for the securing of wealth which had been
willed to his nuns ; wealth that had seemed essential
to their continuance and success.

Good Mother Teresa herself shared in the forebodings of failure which now became rife. But at
last a ray of genuine sunshine burst upon her devout
and simple household. Money the sisters of course
were sadly in want of ; but that was as nothing compared with the necessity they felt of obtaining the
rules of the Order to which they wished to belong,
and the exact costume prescribed for Visitation nuns.
In a matter of this kind, the guiding principle is
that people devoting themselves to the monastic life
must do so in every detail, even down to precision
of costume. The nun's "habit" is, to her, quite as
important as the uniform of a company of United
States soldiers, or of the National Guard, is to the
members of such organizations. The soldier has an

honorable desire that his uniform shall proclaim him, beyond possibility of mistake, a loyal servitor of his country and government, and member of a distinct regiment or corps. The nun has a desire, at least equally honorable, that her costume and discipline shall make her known, at a glance, as loyal to God, the church, and the special phase of disinterested service represented by her order.

It was, therefore, to Bishop Neale and to "The Pious Ladies," a boon beyond all computation by money values, that suddenly one day, among the books of the tiny library acquired from the Poor Clares, they found a duodecimo bearing on its title-page the name of St. Francis de Sales, and the word "Visitation." This volume, on examination, proved to contain the rules of the Visitation Order, which they had sought so long, had so ardently prayed for. The library had been bought after the death of Sister Ignatia Sharpe; and the other sisters were ignorant of French. This fact, together with their daily toils and incessant privations, probably caused them to take little account of the books, which were all French. But here at last the very thing they had most desired came to light in one of these same neglected volumes! Unfortunately, no exact record was kept of the time and manner of this discovery; though it appears to have been made certainly after the admission of Sister Catharine Anne Rigden, which was in 1808. The finding probably did not occur until 1809 or 1810, or even considerably later. But it has been remarked as an interesting circumstance, that the book came from the Poor Clares, who are spiritual daughters of St. Francis of Assisi, into the hands of these daughters of St. Francis de Sales, who was himself a special client of Francis of Assisi; had been born in a room dedicated to him, named after him in baptism, and admitted to membership in the Third Order of Franciscans, the cord of which he wore throughout his life and in death.

Bishop Neale brought into the assembly room and showed to the sisters the "Treasure volume," as it came to be called. Great was the rejoicing that ensued. Curiously enough, also, they learned from it that, in their eagerness to approximate to the monastic rule of the Visitation, they had been practicing greater rigors, fasts, and austerities than the constitutions required.

And now, having the rules, they lacked only the dress of the order. The Bishop had always been anxious to obtain this just as he had beheld it in his vision. At present, the sisters wore a quasi-conventual dress, which he had several times modified without satisfaction. The long black veil and habit, the barbette and silver cross, were wanting. At length he determined to let them wear the Teresian costume, and wrote to his brother Charles at Port Tobacco to send him a model of it, from the convent there. "A large doll, fully equipped, was immediately forwarded; and the Bishop, calling together Mother Teresa and such of the sisters as were most dexterous with the needle, had the dimensions taken, and the habit, the gimp, etc., cut out in his presence. While thus engaged, with the deepest interest, he was not perhaps aware that several of those on whom he

most depended found their courage flagging. No
wonder, when they could not get even the costume
of their own order! Mother Teresa, drawing Sister
Agnes aside, exclaimed : " My God ! Sister Agnes,
we shall never succeed. Ask him to let us become
Carmelites." [1] (The convent at Port Tobacco was a
Carmelite house, deriving its origin from one founded
at Antwerp by an intimate associate of Saint Teresa,
the Venerable Ann of St. Bartholomew.)   Sister
Agnes, however, though young, possessed a firmness
and courage that seldom yielded ; and her calm
confidence doubtless reassured Mother Teresa, thus
averting a momentary panic.

While the costume adopted provisionally at this
time was Carmelite in the main, it was changed in
one particular.   In the volume containing the rules
of the Visitation, the Bishop had found the regulation laid down : " Their bandeaus [or binders] shall
be black."   The white bandeau of the Teresian Carmelites was therefore replaced with black ; and in
this respect at least the Georgetown sisters were
able to conform to Visitation requirements.   Having
gained this much, the Bishop — undismayed by those
doubts and tremors which beset even some of his
loyal co-workers — resolved to admit the sisters to
simple vows.   This was done on the feast of St.
Francis de Sales, January 29, 1814, after they had
made a " retreat " of eight days.   As they still had
not obtained the custom book and ceremonial of the
order of their choice, the ceremony was conducted
somewhat in the Jesuit style.   The sisters donned

---

[1] MS. Annals by Sister M. Josephine Barber.

their habit and veil in private, before going into the chapel where, kneeling before the Blessed Sacrament and in presence of the Bishop, they repeated aloud in concert the formula of their vows.

His work was far from consummated; yet the good Bishop was made very happy by seeing this step taken; and, crossing the garden on the evening of that day and looking up at the sisters where they stood clad in their new dress, on the piazza above, he said with great joy; "Now I see you all as I saw you in my dream at Demerara."

But he did not relax his efforts, long continued, to procure in absolute exactness all the details of the desired monastic dress. Whenever packages of devotional objects came from Europe, he was wont to search them in the hope of finding what he needed, and was especially careful to scrutinize all pictures; insomuch that the other Jesuit Fathers, not understanding his eagerness or the object of his quest, used to laugh at him and to remark jocosely that he was "as fond of pictures as a child." There was truly a great deal of the childlike in his earnestness and trust, and this beautiful trait was rewarded. For a large box at length arrived, in examining the contents of which he came upon a handsome lithograph of St. Jane de Chantal. Raising his hands joyously, he exclaimed: "There it is, at last!"

It was the same countenance, the same stately figure, the same costume he had so long ago looked upon in his vision. When this portrait of the holy Foundress of the Order was shown to the sisters, they were pleased to find that they could trace in

it a strong resemblance to their own Mother Teresa
Lalor. In their eager study of the long-sought
costume of the Foundress, they observed, as they
thought, three or four little plaits or tucks on each
side of the gimp. Their anxiety to put every iota
of the rule and garb into practice drew their attention to this point; but, being too poor just then to
provide a new supply of gimps, they agreed that for
the present it must suffice to give the Superioress
alone this distinction. Accordingly they made for
Mother Teresa a new set of barbettes, carefully
plaited at the sides; and these she wore on festivals,
much to their satisfaction and delight, at seeing her
personate so well her illustrious prototype, St. Jane.
Not until 1816 and 1817, however, did they all receive from Europe authentic costumes and silver
crosses.

Meanwhile the secluded life of the community,
with its constant, patient, obscure struggles, and
peaceful joys, was threatened with interruption by
the War of 1812. During the winter following,
Chesapeake Bay was blockaded by the British fleet,
and the farms and villages of the Potomac were
repeatedly invaded and pillaged by Admiral Cockburn's forces, who even reached Georgetown, but inflicted little damage there. In the summer of 1814
a more formidable movement was begun against the
capital city, Washington, by Cockburn and General
Ross. The Battle of Bladensburg was fought, with
results disastrous to the Americans. The sisters,
greatly alarmed by news of this and of the enemy's
rapid advance, were roused to still keener anxiety by

seeing, that night, about dusk, a dense column of smoke rising from Capitol Hill. In a few minutes the entire summit seemed to be ablaze. The government buildings, President's house, arsenal, and great Potomac bridge, as well as many fine private mansions, were all burned to ashes; and the fierce flames lit up the country for miles around, throwing a bright glare into the convent at Georgetown, where the sisters — unable to retire to rest — watched the conflagration from their garret windows, in momentary expectation that Georgetown would also be fired. But they were spared this ordeal. The hostile army passed on to the northward; and at early morning the next day, the Vigil of the Assumption, the sisters, repairing to their chapel, offered up a heartfelt thanksgiving for their preservation from a great danger. Like other women, it may be added, out of respect to a cherished anecdote of the convent, the sisters when agitated were capable of being a little fanciful in their political perceptions. One of the elder nuns used to recount that at this time she was a child in the Academy, and she was surprised to hear the following announcement from a sister who spoke to the assembled scholars: " My children, raise your hearts to God, for the British have captured Washington, *and we are all slaves !* "

Another episode of this war ought to be mentioned here. That is, the brilliant naval victory of Commodore Jacob Jones, in capturing the British sloop Frolic off the coast of North Carolina, after an action of only forty-five minutes' duration. The victory was won October 17, 1812; the date of the

feast of Blessed Margaret Mary Alacoque, a saint
of the Visitation Order. Thirteen years later, when
Sister Agnes Brent had become Mother Superior,
Commodore Jones's daughter Wilhelmina entered the
same novitiate as a convert, in 1825, and eventually
became a valuable member of the order, with a most
interesting history, which we shall give later on.

IV. THE POPE'S INDULT: ADMISSION TO SOLEMN VOWS.

· We pass now from January, 1814, when the community took simple vows, to December 3, 1815, when
Archbishop Carroll died, at the age of eighty years,
and his coadjutor, Bishop Neale, succeeded him in his
high office, becoming Archbishop of Baltimore.

Six years earlier, — that is, in July, 1809, — French
troops, under the orders of Napoleon I., had broken
into the Vatican by night, and had carried off Pope
Pius VII., a prisoner, first to Savona, afterwards to
Fontainebleau, where the Emperor held the Sovereign
Pontiff captive, seeking to force him into submission
to make him the " puppet " (as a Protestant writer has
said) of the Emperor's own designs. There he had
kept the Holy Father all this time, under a guard of
soldiers, neither allowing him to speak with any one
alone, nor to have books or writing materials: all of
which the Pope endured with a dignity and simplicity
that commanded the respect even of his enemies.

But the day of retribution had now come. Napoleon had seen his *Grande Armée* melt away amid the
snows of Russia. He had fled from the flames of
Moscow, and, according to the very terms of his own

sacrilegious threat against the Pope, had seen the muskets fall from the frozen hands of his soldiers. On the bloody field of Leipsic he had been defeated (October 19, 1813), and six months later he beheld the allied armies of Russia, Prussia, Austria, Germany, march triumphantly into Paris. In that same castle of Fontainebleau, within which he had so long held the Pope a prisoner, they forced from him his own abdication.

It was on April 4th, 1814, that, having been dethroned by a decree of the senate, Napoleon signed the abdication at Fontainebleau, and he departed thence into the enforced solitude of a petty sovereignty at Elba.

On the 24th of May, Pius VII. returned with acclaim to Rome. But after nine months — in February, 1815 — Napoleon came back to France, rallied troops about him, resumed imperial power. Then once more the Pontiff was obliged to leave Rome, his territory being invaded by Murat. Soon, however, the combined forces of the English, Dutch, and Germans met Napoleon and crushed him at Waterloo, June 18, 1815. On the Fourth of July — anniversary of the day, thirty-nine years earlier, when freedom and independence had been proclaimed in the American colonies, as against another, but a German-British, tyrant — these victorious allies entered Paris as their predecessors had done after Leipsic; Napoleon again surrendering, and, this time, being given over to final, humiliating banishment to the island of St. Helena.

There, on that lonely rock a thousand miles from

any other land, he remained, captive to his most hated foes, the English, until his death, a period of six years; thus expiating, in measure of time at least, the six years' imprisonment to which he had subjected the Pope.

All these historic events have a significant bearing on the simple yet brave story of the Georgetown convent; for it was in December of this same year, 1815, when Napoleon was finally and completely erased from public affairs, that Bishop Neale became Archbishop Neale, and was thus brought into direct correspondence with the Pope. Throughout the six preceding years, while he had struggled on with his little community, vainly seeking to establish relations with the Visitation Order in Europe, no recourse could be taken to the Pope. Even had such recourse been allowable, the Pope was a prisoner and inaccessible. But now, through the absolute downfall of Napoleon, Pius VII. was securely enthroned again in Rome. At the same time, also, it became the duty of Archbishop Neale to report to him what had been done toward forming a sisterhood in the District of Columbia.

It is said that he had been misrepresented regarding this matter, to the Holy See, though we have no precise details. The annals report that he was " very sad " at the thought that he might thus have fallen under the displeasure of the Holy Father. But his suspense did not last long, for, on the 14th of July, 1816, Pius VII. sent him a Brief commending his zeal, and permitting his daughters of the Visitation to take solemn vows. This Brief, or Indult, was received November 10th. Even the best of tidings traveled slowly, in those days! Filled with unspeakable joy, the American Visitandines, in thanksgiving, prostrated themselves for some time before the Blessed Sacrament.

Letters of greeting, full of charity and helpfulness, and accompanied with gifts of books, rosary beads, etc., came before long from several of the Visitation monasteries in the Old World; that of St. Mary, in Paris, first; then from Chambéry, from Rome and from Shepton Mallet, England. The house of Chaillot, Paris (that which Queen Henrietta Maria founded in 1651), dispatched a complete model of the habit, together with silver crosses, which did not arrive, however, until 1817. But, before this, the Chaillot house had sent to the Archbishop the " Book of Customs " which he so earnestly desired. It came to him early in the summer of 1816.

So, when the Pope's Indult reached his hands, he set about having the sisters trained in choir duties, " both as to straight and chanting voice, upon which they entered with great eagerness." [1] It was their custom in early days to hold each a lighted candle in saying Matins and Lauds, and there was but one office book for two. One can imagine the lovely picture thus presented by them, quietly carrying the as quietly burning candles, and standing lovingly side by side, with their faces grouped two and two over the books. They began to perform these duties the first Sunday in Advent (December, 1816). Father Bestcher, formerly of the Papal choir, but now in Georgetown, was

[1] Letter of Archbishop Neale to the Monastery of Annecy, April, 1817.

requested to instruct the sisters in the chant and recitation of the office. This he did willingly; devoting
an hour or two daily to the work, and making up for
any lack of detail in the rubric by his own knowledge
of the Vatican practice. The sisters were very back-
ward and timid, especially one or two of them who
lacked an ear for music. " Having not the slightest
idea of music, they were particularly puzzled by the
term · ' key,' which the reverend Father occasionally
employed. When, at the Magnificat, it became necessary to raise the tone, the Chantress entirely mistook
his meaning, and, supposing that he required her to
give more voice, vainly endeavored to comply. This
was quite a trial to Sister Mary Joseph [the Chant-
ress], who had the best will in the world, and was
gifted with *voice*, but no musical ear to guide it.
Father Bestcher strove to make the best of the former,
making her repeat the verse again and again, leading
the chant himself. She endeavored to follow ; singing
' Ma-a-ag,' ' Ma-a-ag,' louder and louder, about
twenty times over, without any success. The sisters
pitied and sympathized with her. Sometimes they
were amused, seeing where the misapprehension lay.
. . . ' If,' said Sister Mary Joseph, ' he had told me
to *change my voice*, I should have understood what he
meant!'

" A misapprehension of the same word [key] happened later on. The community were at Matins, when
the assistant, perceiving a discord, came behind the
stalls and whispered to Sister S.: 'You've got the
wrong key.' Sister S. was Refectorian, and never
thought of any key but that of the refectory, which

she carried in her pocket. Instantly putting her hand down, she drew out the key and held it up, almost in the assistant's face, by way of reply. The latter could not repress a smile, and was obliged to withdraw from the choir for a few minutes until able to recover her gravity." [1]

Notwithstanding these little serio-comic difficulties, the industry of the sisters in studying the office was so great, and Father Bestcher was so kind and patient in training them, that they had the happiness of celebrating the office publicly, with entire correctness of chant and ceremony, on the first Sunday in Advent (as already mentioned), December 1, 1816. Ever since that moment, the office has been daily and devoutly chanted in the choir of this convent, — now seventy-seven years.

A point of utmost importance, after this had been achieved, was to complete that admission to solemn vows, for which the Archbishop had received authority. The date he fixed upon was the Feast of Holy Innocents, December 28th, which was also the hundred and ninety-fourth anniversary of the death of St. Francis de Sales. The three who were chosen for admission first were the oldest members, those who were considered to be the best fitted for the office of Mother Superior: Alice Lalor, in religion Sister Teresa of the Heart of Mary; Mrs. McDermott, in religion Sister Frances; and Henrietta Brent, Sister Agnes. The first was appointed Superior, the second Assistant; the third, Mistress of Novices. All these having previously gone into retreat, the other sisters

[1] MS. Annals, written by Sister M. Josephine Barber.

proceeded, under considerable drawbacks, to prepare their veils and habits, together with worldly attire for the " Reception." Of costumes suitable for this purpose there was almost a complete dearth. The white dresses for the two elder candidates, therefore, were made somewhat roughly out of white muslin, without regard to style, and for Sister Agnes, who like her patron saint was extremely small and slender, one of the children's dresses was borrowed.

It was a Saturday; "intensely cold, and the ground covered with snow." Long before dawn, "while the stars were still glimmering in the wintry sky, the community knelt in meditation before the altar," preparing for an event the greatest that should ever occur in the history of the Visitation in America. In repicturing that scene, the mind recalls those pure and sympathetic verses written by Alfred Tennyson, long afterward, in his " Eve of St. Agnes: " —

> " Deep on the convent roof the snows
> Lie sparkling to the moon.
> My breath to heaven like vapor goes:
> May my soul follow soon! "

The ceremonies took place before Mass: first the Reception, then the Profession; Archbishop Neale himself being the celebrant, assisted by Father Grassii, provincial of the Jesuits. No seculars were present, except the twelve or fourteen pupils. Everything was conducted strictly according to the Book of Admission. "Thus, by the happy disposition of Divine Providence," wrote the Archbishop to the monastery of Annecy, "on the anniversary day of the departure of St. Francis de Sales from this life, *exis-*

tence and life were imparted to the first established community of his Order in America."

After breakfast the Archbishop and Father Grassii called at the convent and saw all the sisters, "about thirty-three in number, novices included," in the assembly room, say the Annals. "The Archbishop, radiant with joy, said that now, like holy Simeon, he could sing his *Nunc Dimittis*, and was ready to depart; since his eyes had beheld this day 'a light to the Gentiles and a glory to Israel.'" Prophetic words! In less than six months from that time, he who spoke them had departed from this life in peace and joy.

In his letter to Annecy, the reverend prelate wrote that on the Feast of the Epiphany seventeen received the habit and white veil. "All of these had undergone a noviceship and trial for many years; some sixteen, some seventeen, others more or less." On the octave of the Epiphany, those who were in the novitiate received the habit and white veil; some of whom had already been there more than a year. At this time, April, 1817, he put the whole number at thirty-five; thirty "choir sisters," four "lay sisters," and one "out sister." Most of these were admitted to their solemn vows on the Spousals of our Blessed Lady, January 23d, 1817, and the others on the Feast of St. Francis de Sales, January 29th.

It was necessary to divide the sisters into groups and admit them to solemn vows at different times, in order that they might make a retreat previous to their profession, while other sisters attended to the school and household duties. The old Carmelite dress remained in use until the pattern of the true Visitandine costume came, in the following summer, after Archbishop Neale's death. He did not live to see it; but what he had actually accomplished justified his words to Annecy: "Thus is this house fairly established to run its course, which I hope will never be interrupted but by the cessation of time."

V. DEATH OF ARCHBISHOP NEALE : 1817.

It had been a peculiarly happy Christmas-tide, closing the old year, and a gladsome Epiphany, opening the new; for now the pure and spiritual desire formed by Father Neale, prompted of dream or vision more than thirty-five years earlier, — and so resolutely aided by the perseverance of a few sisters through seventeen years of sharp trial, — had become a triumphant reality. A new and greater happiness was about to be conferred upon the same faithful servant, now Archbishop; but it was one which, to the community, must mean inevitable sorrow.

We may call it at least an impressive circumstance that his death so closely followed the achievement of the plan so dear to him. Yet, in the natural course, it might have been expected; for he had reached his seventy-first year. For fifty years he had been a member of the Society of Jesus, for seven years rector of Georgetown College, and sixteen years a Bishop. In spite of his advanced age, however, and although he had suffered from cough and fluxion ever since his stay in unwholesome Demerara, he gave no sign of breaking health in the spring of 1817.

Before going on to speak of the change that soon

came upon him, and of his closing days, we must give
a short account of Sister Isidora McNantz, — a mere
child-sister, — whose departure from this life seems
to have been associated with his own.   Sister Isidora
was one of three children, daughters of a poor widow,
who died in 1813.   The widow was attended in her
last illness by Rev. Wm. Matthews, — the spiritual
father of the community, — who was uncle of the
venerated Mother Juliana Matthews, and related to
Mother Agnes Brent, as well as to Archbishop Neale.
He had promised Mrs. McNantz to care for her
daughters; and, at his own expense, he placed them,
when they were left orphans, as pupils in the convent
school.   All three became professed nuns; but Charlotte (Sister Isidora), although only about twelve
years old when she entered the school, was especially
remarkable for a wisdom far beyond her age.   "A
singular prudence marked her conduct and conversation," wrote the Archbishop.   "To hear her speak
was sufficient to inspire all with respect and admiration.   It was apparent how deeply she thought, and
that her sentiments emanated from a soul especially
favored and enlightened by the Holy Ghost."   So
great was her love of God, her zeal in religion, that
she begged earnestly to be received into the novitiate.
This petition was refused on account of her extreme
youth; but the promise was held out that she should
be admitted when sixteen years old.   She did not live
so long.   On the very Christmas night (1816) when
Mothers Teresa, Frances, and Agnes went into retreat
to prepare for their solemn vows, Charlotte McNantz
was taken with a violent cold, which developed into
quick consumption.

Three physicians attended her; but, finding the case difficult, they declared that there was something on her mind; which mental distress, they thought, annulled the benign effect of their medicines. Two of the doctors were Protestants; the other is said to have been an infidel. They appeared to suspect that the child (now approaching fourteen) was unhappy at being in the convent-school. To satisfy them, Mother Teresa told the medical men that anything Charlotte wished would be granted, and questioned her accordingly. "Mother," said the child, "I have never known earthly love. One sole desire consumes me: one sole love possesses my heart, — the love of my Jesus, and the desire to consecrate myself to God by the holy vows of religion. Mother, you have long known this: you are aware how it has preyed upon my mind." In compliance with this answer, Charlotte was allowed to be removed from the Academy to the Sisters' Infirmary, where she should be at once considered as a postulant and a member of the community. There she remained, greatly rejoiced by the granting of her petition, until the spring; when it became clear that she had but a short time to live. Far from being terrified, she hailed with delight the approaching moment of reunion with God, beyond the human state, and received the last Sacraments with exultant fervor. Still, she sighed for the habit and veil. In Passion Week these were granted her, and she was admitted to solemn vows.

Praying that she might depart on the Feast of our Lord's Resurrection, she died on that day, Easter Sunday, April 6, 1816. Her presence in the school and convent, the memory of her exquisite innocence and piety, left a deep impression akin to that made by some of the child saints and martyrs in the early history of the church.

Four or five weeks after little Isidora's death, Mother Teresa Lalor, while conversing on business with the Archbishop one day, noticed that his attention was withdrawn suddenly, and that his eyes became fixed upon some object, in the room apparently, but to her invisible. Struck by the strangeness of his manner, Mother Teresa exclaimed, "What is the matter?" Waving his hand to her slightly, he answered, "My child, go: *Isidora has come.*" Too much frightened to await a second bidding, Mother Teresa hurried away, although her knees trembled so that, after closing the door, she sank upon the steps without and was obliged to rest there until she recovered strength enough to go on. This occurred at eleven in the morning, and after the midday dinner she called Sister Agnes Brent, saying to her, "I am afraid the Archbishop is going to die! What could Sister Isidora have come for? Did she come for him?"

In her anxiety she returned with Agnes to the venerable prelate, and said to him, "My lord, I entreat you to explain to me the meaning of what you said this morning. Did Sister Isidora really appear to you?" He made no answer, and Mother Teresa, weeping, repeated her inquiry, asking whether Isidora had come for him. To this he responded, "My child, you must not be too curious," and would make no other answer, except that after a time he added,

" I will not be with you long." Thereupon the worthy and pious Foundress again fell to weeping; but " Do not cry," said the Archbishop. " Look at Agnes: she does not cry. Be courageous, like her." But Mother Teresa, whose attachment to her saintly Director was like that of St. Jane to St. Francis de Sales, remained inconsolable. In everything the Archbishop did, she fancied that she could see confirmation of her fears. Nor was she wrong.

Immediately thereafter he began writing and dispatching many letters, chiefly to the clergy of his diocese, but also to others, among whom were his brother Francis, together with the Rev. J. P. de Clorivière of Charleston, South Carolina, and busily made preparations as though for a final leave-taking. It turned out, afterward, that his missive to Father Clorivière contained an urgent request that the latter should come on at once and take charge of the community. He was also especially anxious to see his brother, Father Francis Neale, as to whom he made constant inquiry whether any news had come from him.

On June 16th[1] (just ten weeks after the death of Isidora) he said his last Mass, at which three of the sisters took Holy Communion. Mother Agnes, the last of the three, observed that his hand shook exceedingly as he gave her the sacred wafer. He was able to return to the altar and complete the Holy Sacrifice.

[1] The 140th anniversary of the revelation of the Sacred Heart to Blessed Margaret Mary Alacoque, of the Visitation B. V. M.

On June 16, 1875, — the thirtieth anniversary of the election of Pius IX., — the whole church was consecrated to the Sacred Heart of Jesus.

But so great appeared to be his weakness, that Father Grassii was quickly sent for from the college, and forbade him to hear confessions that day. During the forenoon the Archbishop grew better, and was able to give a short sitting to an artist who was painting his portrait, the same as that reproduced in this book; but he scarcely touched his dinner at noon, and an hour later he went to bed, never to rise again. As he grew worse in the night, a physician was called, who soon declared the case hopeless. The Archbishop was dying of apoplexy. Father Grassii came in the morning with several priests and lay brothers to administer Extreme Unction and the Viaticum, and remained with him during the twenty-six hours that he lingered alive. His brother Charles arrived fortunately, also, in time to receive his farewell and to witness his holy death, which occurred at one or two o'clock in the afternoon of Wednesday, June 18, 1817. But his brother Francis, whom he had so earnestly longed to see and confer with, did not reach Georgetown until the following day, when the dead Archbishop already lay in state in Trinity Church.

The funeral obsequies took place June 20th, the body of the Archbishop being carried to the little convent chapel, where, only four days previously, he had celebrated Mass for the last time, and then buried in the vault below the sanctuary.

That Archbishop Neale was a worthy imitator and follower of St. Francis de Sales is clear to those who have studied the lives of both. His spiritual daughters have always delighted, furthermore, in tracing certain close and specific resemblances between their

characters and careers, which we may here briefly
summarize : —

1. Archbishop Neale was remarkable for great
meekness, equanimity of soul, of conduct, and of
speech. He never betrayed irritation or impatience,
bitterness or resentment toward any one, whatever
provocation he might have ; " and the peaceful spirit
which accompanied him seemed," as the sisters have
recorded, " to extend itself to all who approached
him." " Whether it rained, snowed, or the sun
shone," says Sister Agnes Brent, " his gait was always the same, and his countenance showed that he
was conscious at every moment of the presence of
God."

2. Like St. Francis de Sales, he was blessed with
a mother of singular piety, who generously sacrificed
her feelings of natural affection to the spiritual interests of her children and their priestly vocation.

3. Madam Neale on her death-bed, like Madame
de Boisy, received the last sacraments from her son,
and expired in his presence.

4. His first labors as a priest were among heretics
and pagans, where his health and his life were in danger. So with the Apostle of Chablais.

5. St. Francis de Sales received a supernatural
intimation of God's will regarding the Order of the
Visitation, and Father Neale also beheld in vision or
dream the work to which the saint directed him.

6. His first three members at Georgetown remind
us of the first three at Annecy.

7. The opposition encountered by the holy founder
at Annecy was closely reproduced in that endured by

Archbishop Neale, against whom, in the work of the Georgetown foundation, were directed the same bitter pleasantries and malicious sneers as were flung at the Bishop of Geneva. Mother Genevieve King, who in those days was a young lady in the world and a resident of Georgetown, heard many of these sarcasms, but as she knew their falsity, they did not prevent her from asking for a place in his community.

8. Archbishop Neale was likewise denounced to the Pope, on those identical points which had been chosen long before by other men for attack upon St. Francis; lack of zeal for the spread of the faith, and a charge of non-fidelity to the church. The deep sadness thus caused to him, the loyalty evinced by him, and the complete vindication he received from the Holy Father, were all repetitions of St. Francis de Sales' experience.

9. Like St. Francis, too, the Archbishop died of apoplexy, having, like him, said Mass the very morning of the stroke; and as the founder of the Order had done, he asked to be buried at his dear Visitation.

The daughters of the convent he established lovingly dwell upon the thought and the trust that those two pure-souled Bishops are joined in heaven, and that all their spiritual children may be gathered round them there, as stars in the firmament; or, as St. Francis de Sales himself said, " covering their shoulders as a mantle of honor, and their head as a crown of glory for all eternity ! "

VI. FATHER CLORIVIÈRE.

The American Founder of the Visitation, as we have noted, sent off — only a few weeks before his death — a letter to Rev. Joseph P. de Clorivière of Charleston, S. C., asking him to come immediately to Georgetown in order to direct the community, from which he felt that he was so soon to be taken away. Meanwhile he used the precaution of speaking to the sisters about this clergyman and his merits; giving them, as it were, an introduction to him, which might prepare them to appreciate his guidance or direction.

It is thought that Archbishop Neale's anxiety to see his brother, Rev. Francis Neale, was due to his desire that he should assume at least temporary charge of the community; because, at best, Father Clorivière's journey from South Carolina would occupy some time. When Father Francis arrived on the scene, just after the death of his brother, the American Founder, he did indeed take charge. But he was an invalid, having suffered a stroke of paralysis. Another stroke soon followed, and he was obliged to give up his duties as director. Father Grassii meanwhile had gone to Europe, being appointed confessor to the Queen of Sardinia (grandmother of the unhappy Victor Emmanuel). The withdrawal of Father Francis by illness, therefore, left the nuns in a sad state of forsakenness, — " of real orphanage," as one of their annalists called it,— because the scarcity of priests in this country, at the time, made it difficult to find any one who could or would accept the spiritual charge of the house. His Jesuit *confrères* in the Georgetown

College, close by, were reluctant to add to their already numerous duties by delegating one of their number to serve as spiritual director of the convent.

These excellent Fathers, in the extreme difficulty of their situation at not being able to provide for the sisters, had recourse to citing, in self-defense, the remark of St. Ignatius Loyola, that "he had more trouble in directing five or six women, than in governing his whole institution."

Rigorously exact though this reference to St. Ignatius may have been, it was hardly adapted to bring comfort to our newly established sisters of the Visitation, who almost at the very moment when their house had been so firmly instituted, with sanction of the Pope and helpful good-will from the older monasteries in Europe, seemed to find themselves deserted at home and plunged into a new era of new trials. Like other pioneers in the foundation of monastic houses destined to possess great influence for good, the nuns were led through the noble initiation of bitter suffering for love of the suffering Christ. Before the tide of their fortunes turned, the bare necessaries of life were wanting. The sisters do not beg; they pray. If their friends desire to help them, a sharp lookout must be kept for their condition. And though assistance comes faithfully to faith, God's mercy insists upon exercising, for their greater strength, the virtues of endurance and perseverance. As one of these Visitandine scribes writes: "The consolations of heaven must always be mingled with afflictions, lest those who enjoy them might attach themselves rather to these sweetnesses than to Him who gives them."

Immediately the prophets of ill, who had all along predicted failure, resumed their song and asserted that it was evident the convent community could not survive the life of its founder.

But now, in this hour of emergency, the foresight and careful preparation of the dead Archbishop took effect and brought rescue. Father Clorivière, after a seeming delay of months,— but really as soon as he could accomplish the change and the journey,— appeared in Georgetown and took spiritual charge of the convent, in January, 1818, just when the nuns were nearing the point of despair as to the direction of their house ; if such a feeling as despair could ever really enter their devoted hearts. God never despairs ; and the true nun or priest or monk, being wholly dedicated to God, cannot despair either. Yet the trial of their human patience, the depression of their mere human spirits, was extreme when Father Clorivière came to their relief.

Let us now, in few words, tell who he was; what his life had been ; whence he came, and how.

One of his uncles, of the same name, had been confessor to the third Paris monastery of the Visitation, and Superior of the Jesuits in France ; had been imprisoned by Napoleon from 1804 to 1809 ; was made Provincial of the Society of Jesus, on its restoration in 1814, and died in Paris in 1824. Another uncle had been martyred during the Reign of Terror. Father Clorivière had gained possession of the blood-stained shirt worn by this martyr, which he kept with great reverence. His family were of the Bretagne aristocracy, and Joseph himself, in his twenty-fifth

year, being affianced to a young lady of Versailles,
was about to marry; indeed, as he was wont laughingly to tell the sisters, the day was fixed, the wed-
ding-cake and wine had been provided.   Suddenly,
the gathered fury of the French Revolution broke
bounds.   Louis XVI., so long virtually dethroned,
was made prisoner: Paris shook with tumult; priests
and religious were driven into hiding, to escape death
or outrage at the hands of a mad populace; and, among
the laity loyal to the king, many of those who could
escape at all took up arms against the revolutionists.
Such an one was Joseph de Clorivière.   As a military
officer he rendered valiant service, and in 1800 received from the Count d'Artois (afterward Charles
X.), on behalf of his brother Louis XVIII., the dec-
oration of the order of St. Louis.[1]

After Napoleon's return from Syria and election as
First Consul, Monsieur de Clorivière, suspected of com-
plicity in the affair of the "infernal machine" that
came so near ending Napoleon's life, was in great danger of himself being put to death.   For a time he was
hunted through Bretagne and La Vendée, and avoided
capture only by assuming various disguises.   Once,
dressing himself like a fop, and carelessly twirling a
rattan, he passed unrecognized in front of a detach-
ment of soldiers who were watching for him.   So
many and so narrow were his escapes from his enemies, that he was afterward disposed to regard his
preservation as little less than miraculous.   Precisely
how his engagement of marriage came to be finally

---

[1] John Gilmary O'Shea: *History of the Catholic Church in the United States.*

broken off is not certain. One account attributes this to a vow made by him, in a moment of great danger, that if his life were spared it should be consecrated to the church, and that his betrothed afterward gave her full assent to the resolution. Others have said that the vow of renunciation was made by her, for his safety.

However this may have been, when Napoleon finally seized the supreme power in France, succeeded in making a concordat with the Pope· and received the crown from his hands, Monsieur de Clorivière, loyal to the spiritual headship of the Pontiff, but still devoted to the Bourbon dynasty, so far as state rule was concerned, quitted France and came to the New World. Here, at Baltimore, he studied for the priesthood in the seminary of St. Sulpice, and was ordained in 1812. "At this epoch," says the historian O'Shea, "the church of Charleston, S. C., was torn by divisions and saddened by scandals." It was to this difficult post that Archbishop Carroll assigned the new priest, and there he remained some five years, manfully and piously battling to root out old local abuses and sow the seeds of peace. He succeeded in the work, though met by desperate opposition. But fresh difficulties arose from the fact that some among his congregation were men of revolutionary ideas, sympathizers at heart with the anti-religious party in Europe. Again, although now in the discharge of a peaceful ministry, his life was threatened. Non-Catholics in Charleston were bitterly opposed to all who professed and practiced entire loyalty to the Pope in religion, or who declared in favor of the Bourbon monarchy in France. This hostility seems to have been sharply accentuated by the final downfall of Napoleon, the restoration of the Bourbons, and the liberating of the Pope from his long imprisonment.   Father Clorivière was twice shot at by would-be assassins. Once he was compelled to remain hidden in the house of a faithful Catholic for three days, while those who designed to kill him prowled in search of him.

In these complications of political with religious sentiment, that disrupted even his own flock, he wrote to Archbishop Carroll for counsel.   The Archbishop thought the priest would in the end triumph over transient violence, by his piety, virtue, and conciliatory manners.   Nevertheless, when Bishop Neale became Archbishop, Father Clorivière appealed to him, seeking relief, once more, from his difficult position, and demanded permission to go back to France. Archbishop Neale replied, sympathizing with him, but urging him by all means to remain in this country, where priests were so greatly needed; and, in order to open to him a field where he might be freed from the strifes of his South Carolina parish, invited him to come to Georgetown and direct the Visitation Sisters.

This was the letter that the Archbishop wrote, a little before his death.   It came to Father Clorivière just when he had made up his mind that he must leave America.   He had in fact engaged passage on a vessel bound for Havre; his trunks were on board; but, on receipt of the Archbishop's message, he had the trunks immediately brought ashore, and at once made ready for the journey northward.

Had the Archbishop's letter been a day longer in reaching Charleston, it would have come too late: Father Clorivière would then have been embarked and wafted by sail-wings over sea. But, as events turned, he reached Georgetown soon after Christmas, on Tuesday, January 13th, the octave of the Epiphany, 1818, — seven months after the death of the Archbishop, but in the very nick of time to save the community from its forlorn plight.

He had not intended to take back with him to France the altar ornaments and vestments he had brought from there. But, on changing his destination, he changed his mind in regard to their removal. The ladies of his Charleston congregation insisted upon his carrying everything to Georgetown, and helped him to pack altar linen, vestments, cruets, crucifixes, altar bells; two gilt expositions; ornaments for the Repository in Holy Week; several fine paintings made by a lady of the congregation; and his whole library, containing many valuable ascetic treatises.

Near noon of January 13th, the sisters were gathered in the Assembly Room, where the tables — brought from the Refectory — had been spread with a repast somewhat out of the common; for it was a " profession day," and three new brides[1] were there, awaiting with the rest the sound of the Angelus bell. Suddenly, Mother Teresa was called out of the room; little did she or the others guess for what reason. Presently she returned, with a strange priest. It was Father Clorivière, their new director.

[1] Sisters De Chantal Corish, Xavier Hughes, and Apollonia Diggs.

With heartfelt gratitude, the sisters knelt and received his blessing.

VII. MOTHER CATHARINE RIGDEN. — THE BUILDING OF THE CHAPEL.

Father Clorivière was now in his fiftieth year; therefore not an old man; but much worn with the struggles, the fatigues, the perils, and anxieties of his active career on battle-fields, in exile, and in the churchly fold. Yet his unfailing and charming naïveté and directness are apparent in the quotations from his letters which appear in the manuscripts of the convent, and in accounts of his generous and devout conduct, giving an idea of vivacity too energetic to collapse. It was a welcome relief to him, as well as a delight, to find himself drawn by the will of God, at the hands of the departed prelate, into this peaceful solitude of the cloister, where he was to end his days in diligent and happy ministration to the sisterhood. To them, also, his coming was as welcome and as providential as to him; for he restored to them that which they had lost in Archbishop Neale, — a father, friend, and holy guide. The Circular Letter sent out from Georgetown in 1822 said of him: "He has given himself — or rather, as he says truly — God has given him to us, with all he has in the world, without our being able to make the least return. In everything he animates, assists, and encourages us. In a word, he is a true father, and makes our interest his own."

He took especial pains to initiate the sisters fully into the practice of their Rule and Constitutions, as also the Customs and Ceremonies, a portion of which he daily translated and explained. He exercised them in the chant of their office, in Gregorian music, in litanies, hymns for Benediction, and Lamentations for Holy Week. In the course of these instructions, he read to them what is prescribed as to the Annual Visit, the Annual Chapter, the triennial election, and the requirement that there should be a change of superiors every three years, or, at longest, once in six years. These points were new to them; as there had been no occasion for the questions involved to come up, between the time when the Pope's Indult was received and the date of Archbishop Neale's death.

Father Clorivière also raised the standard of the school (teaching French himself); thereby increasing the attendance. He established the " benevolent school," which Archbishop Neale had promised (to the extent at least of seven scholars) in his appeal to the Holy See, as an offset to the permission to the sisters to support themselves by taking paying scholars. This latter school finally taught, and largely clothed and fed, from one to two hundred poor children.

The Sisters of the Visitation of Chaillot, France, where, as stated, Father Clorivière's uncle had been director, and whom he also knew, often sent him linen and articles, worked by their own hands, in gratitude for their many obligations to the uncle.

It now appeared that Mother Teresa, who had continued to be Superior for nearly twenty years, during all the experimental or probationary period

of the community, was entitled — since the papal
approbation and a regular establishment had been
achieved — to remain in office three years longer.
But the humble foundress preferred to give up her
charge to other hands. Archbishop Maréchal yielded
te her simple entreaty ; and a new election was accordingly held, on the Feast of the Ascension, 1819,
when Sister Catharine Ann Rigden was chosen by
the sisters to be their Superior.

Born in 1782, of Protestant parents who lived in
Georgetown, Sister Catharine, at the age of thirteen,
had formed a friendship with a young Catholic girl,
whom — for mere pastime — she accompanied to her
catechism lessons. Then, wishing to learn how to
answer the questions of the priest, as the other children did, she began to study. The result was that,
with the aid of grace, she received conditional baptism, was admitted to the Sacraments of Penance
and the Holy Eucharist ; in short, openly professed
Catholicity.

The original sketch of her life, prepared by Sister
Mary Josephine Barber, and transcribed by Sister
Stanislaus Jones, tells us that Mother Catharine's
father and mother did everything in their power to
thwart her in the practice of her religion, and even
to compel her, if possible, to abandon it. They
allowed her to have no books except such as were
opposed to her faith ; forced her to see Protestant
ministers and listen to their exhortations ; and tried
also to turn her aside into the paths of society and
of worldly gayety, in the hope of dissipating her
serious thoughts. Catharine preferred to wear only

the plainest of gowns and bonnets. Her parents tore
these up, insisting that she should dress fashionably;
but to violence of this kind she replied by refusing
to wear what was offered to her in place of the torn
garments. So, too, when they denied her fast-day
fare, she went without food altogether. On one
occasion an aunt, with whom she was staying in
the country, declined to let her have a carriage for
returning to town, on a day appointed by her confessor; presumably a feast or holyday of the church.
Catharine, however, undismayed, set out for the city
on foot, quoting at the same time the sturdy remark
of St. Jane de Chantal: "Obedience has very good
legs."

Attractive in appearance as well as in manner and
disposition, she might easily have secured freedom
from the oppression exercised upon her at home, by
marrying; and, in truth, she had partly or conditionally formed an engagement with a young man who
had declared himself as a suitor; but when she consulted Bishop Neale, her spiritual director, on this
matter, he assured her with strong conviction that it
was not what God willed of her. The engagement,
or beginning of an engagement, was broken off; and
the unhappy suitor, in his anger and disappointment,
threatened to commit suicide. From this he was
restrained by his friends; but as he disappeared from
the neighborhood some time afterward, they feared
that he had yielded to the mad temptation, after all,
and had wrought upon himself "the act of despair."
Many years later, a little before the death of Mother
Catharine, a gentleman came to the convent parlor,

inquiring for her, and learned that she was seriously
ill. He entreated the sisters to tell her how earnestly
he wished to see her, only once more, before her
death, or his own; but this, of course, the rule made
impossible. It was then that Mother Catharine, hearing of the visit, disclosed to Father Clorivière that
the caller was her old suitor.

In the ardor of her faith, Catharine would gladly
have entered the convent as a postulant, immediately
after giving up the idea of this marriage; but Bishop
Neale delayed her doing so for several years. Then,
finding that time had no effect in reconciling her
parents, he decided at last to take her under shelter;
although these same parents, consistently with their
tyrannical and almost ferocious course from the beginning, threatened that, if she were admitted, they
would burn the convent down.

Catharine Rigden was admitted, nevertheless, on
the Feast of the Guardian Angels, October 2, 1808,
making the sixth member of the little flock, — and
the convent was not burned.

She at once entered upon the practice of all the
rules then observed; and, having excellent health,
willingly lent herself to the most fatiguing labors.
Extremes of heat and cold, and the many privations
of that early time, she bore without sign of suffering;
and when there was a special press of work on hand
she diminished even the moderate hours of sleep
allowed, in order to do extra duty. Being quick and
adroit at all manual tasks, and never making any
difficulty about them, she was constantly called upon
for every sort of service or assistance. Her equa-

nimity, meekness, and patience, Sister Stanislaus has recorded, were unalterable; in simplicity and obedience, she had the spirit of a child. Yet she reproached herself for what she believed to be her shortcomings, and was inclined to practice extreme austerities, both for her own mortification and on behalf of souls in purgatory. These her wise director felt obliged to interdict; and a cilice, or hair-cloth garment, which she wore almost constantly, was taken from her for the same reason, that it represented an excessive self-discipline. For several years she acted as "Mistress of Pensioners," and of her service in this capacity Sister Stanislaus says: "Her meekness and charity won to her these young hearts. She taught them many little practices of piety; and not a few of us who have come from the school gratefully acknowledge our indebtedness to her for impressions that led to our religious vocation."

From even this brief review of her history and her traits, it is easy to see how well the Bishop was justified in discerning her true destiny, and that the sisters' choice in making her their first duly-elected Superior was very fitting.

By her character and aspirations, she was well prepared to accept eagerly the devotion to the Sacred Heart of Jesus, which the new spiritual father of the house introduced and zealously advocated. He had brought with him from the South a Life of Blessed Margaret Mary, the originator of the devotion and eminent in the history of the Visitation in Europe. This he translated to the sisters, making them acquainted with it for the first time. It produced a deep impression upon them. Soon the practice of General Communion and Benediction on the first Friday of each month was adopted, Father Clorivière always reading aloud before the altar, while the Blessed Sacrament was exposed, the Act of Reparation of Honor. It was felt by every one in the community that there ought to be a picture, or perhaps an oratory, of the Sacred Heart in the convent; and their director himself had long been absorbed by the desire of erecting a church or chapel dedicated to the same holy object. This he inclined to think could hardly be accomplished for some years to come; but he pointed out a site upon the grounds where the chapel, if it ever should be built, would best be placed. Then he drew a sketch of the plan he had in mind, and the sisters became so interested in it that they could think and speak of little else. Meanwhile, the first Annual Visit had been made by Archbishop Maréchal and Father Clorivière; at the end of 1818, also, the first Annual Chapter was held: the Aids were given, the cells, crosses, books, beads, pictures, were all changed, — no sister, after this, being permitted to retain the same cell or furniture for more than one year at a time. The examination of accounts, made at this juncture, showed that the community was even poorer than it thought itself; so much so, that it became clear that unless Providence should send help now unforeseen, or unless the school should flourish greatly, the convent would stand in much embarrassment for means of subsistence. The prospect of even beginning a chapel, therefore, was exceedingly slight.

Yet the need of a larger place of worship was acute. The existing chapel inherited from the Poor Clares could scarcely contain its triple congregation of sisters, children, and servants. Sister Genevieve King used to recall that, at her profession, May 20, 1819, none of the family except her father could be admitted; and he was obliged to sit near the altar, with the priests. Archbishop Neale, foreseeing this need, had made humble beginnings during his lifetime toward accomplishing the object. The manner of his doing so is interesting and characteristic.

The only menial labor then obtainable in the District was that of slaves. The Archbishop had one negro slave, whom he hired out to a brick-maker in Washington; taking the amount of his weekly wage in bricks, which the negro carted back to the rude archiepiscopal dwelling, every Saturday night. By this arrangement, many hundred bricks were gathered in a promising pile, for future use.

A fine chime of bells had also been presented to the good Archbishop; and these now lay sleeping in the garret of his old home; silent, yet full of melody that was to ring forth gladly over the peaceful enclosure, soon, and to continue sounding through a long term of recurrent years. This much had been gained, then; a foothold of solid brick to serve as the basis; and a responsive peal of chimes, destined to be raised aloft as the crown of the edifice. But how, and from what, was the intermediate structure to be formed? Apparently from the stuff of dreams; for the whole project still looked visionary.

It is time, therefore, to mention here that Mother

Catharine, so long robust in health and of untiring energy, suffered a severe attack of pneumonia in the autumn of the year (1819) following her election. The same illness returned frequently; until at last she succumbed, passing away in the autumn of 1820. In the last year of her life she had many dreams of a singular and significant kind. Dreams are always debatable; but we shall not discuss these. That great master of romantic fiction, Charles Dickens, has set forth in a Christmas story how one Scrooge — a miser and curmudgeon — was transformed into a beneficent citizen, full of charitable Christian impulses, by a mere dream. This is often spoken of by critics as an impossibility; and yet they all admit that it is at least a perfectly true type of the remarkable alterations which take place in personal character or spirit, and of the effect of an idea, suddenly received, upon an individual's subsequent mood or conduct. All people — prosaic or imaginative, materialists and idealists, religious and irreligious — are disposed to regard some of their dreams with a good deal of respect, as well as with curiosity and wonder. It is undeniable that a new impression, fully grasped, whether it come to us when we are waking or when we are sleeping — often changes the whole direction of a life or a character. Mother Catharine Rigden's dreams may, according to the pleasure of one reader or another, be attributed either to ill health, or to chance imagination, or even (if it gratify anybody to entertain so unprovable a guess) to deception; although we ourselves wholly reject this last surmise as impossible, and inconsistent with her pure, exalted nature. The one thing which immediately concerns us is, that she told of her dreams simply and directly; that she seemed not always to understand their full purport, — some of them being symbolical and slightly obscure, — though their meaning soon became clear to others; and that she often dreamed that the late Archbishop was present, speaking with her and advising her. In one of these instances his counsel was definite. "My child," she seemed to hear him say; "tell the Reverend Father Clorivière to begin the church." She remonstrated at this, and fancied that she asked him how such a thing was to be done without funds. "That matters not," replied the Archbishop. "Tell him to begin. He will finish my work."

She recounted this curious dream to Father Clorivière, who, notwithstanding his predisposition to attempt the work, told her plainly that, considering the poverty of the community and its clouded outlook so far as temporal affairs were concerned, it would be downright folly to think of building.

Still, on returning to his house, he found that her recital of her dream had taken strong hold upon his mind. As he afterward wrote: "I calculated what money we had on hand and what might be coming in, and I came to the conclusion that we might at least lay the foundation of the church, and then await further supplies." As to "further supplies," evidently a new idea had occurred to him: the result of Mother Catharine's dream, or — if you choose to call it so — hallucination. It would be well for us if all human hallucinations were so sweet in kind, so beneficent. Father Clorivière owned a patrimonial estate in Bretagne. This he now resolved to sell, and apply the proceeds to the building of the chapel. He was also in receipt of a pension from the French government, paid to him annually for his past service in the army and because of a wound he had received in battle. This, also, he determined to devote to the same purpose. Even those resources, he knew, would hardly be sufficient; for they were not large. So far as they went, they would do some good : the rest he trusted to Divine Providence.

Thus, what he had at first condemned as folly, he now speedily stood committed to with all the material resources at his command, — as it frequently happens, in the case of works undertaken with a spiritual aim. But, instantly, a new obstacle was raised. The permission of the Archbishop was necessary, before the first effort at building could be made. Archbishop Maréchal immediately put a veto on the proposal, and was astonished that the sisters and their director should even think of such a thing, in their impoverished condition. Mother Catharine and her flock had recourse to prayer; and presently the Archbishop revoked his decision.

Thereupon Father Clorivière, overjoyed at the opportunity of dedicating and giving all his remaining worldly possessions to the Sacred Heart of Jesus, and of actually building the chapel, assembled the whole community in choir; whence — after the *Veni Creator*, and prayers — they moved in procession to the site long held in view; all carrying picks and spades. Mother Catharine took up the first spadeful

Rev. J. CURLEY, S.J.

of common earth; her assistant, the next; then all
the sisters, in turn, lifted with their spades a little
burden of the soil; making room for the foundation
of a hallowed edifice.

This ceremony occurred July 11, 1820; and in
such manner was the first church of the Sacred Heart,
in the United States, begun.

The completing of the chapel, however, was attended with many trials and discouragements, and
much anxiety; with alterations in the plans, and the
usual unlooked-for additional expenses. Archbishop
Maréchal laid the first stone, July 26, 1820, on the
Feast of Saint Ann, mother of the Blessed Virgin.
But as the community could not pay the carpenters
and other workmen punctually, they dared not press
them to hasten the building, and the interior therefore was not finished until October, 1821. On the
first of November, that year, the chapel was dedicated. But Mother Catharine was not of the number of those who visibly took part in the joy of this
occasion. For nearly a twelvemonth, then, her body
had lain entombed in the vault of the new cemetery
she had helped to plan, in the space formed by a
natural slope of the ground under the sanctuary.
After an illness of fourteen months, she had died in
holiness, December 21, 1820, at the age of thirty-
five; having dwelt twelve years within the cloister.
Her two sisters, then recently converted to the faith
she had so long and bravely held, came to her funeral,
and — standing in the unfinished chapel — looked
down through the open beam-work of the flooring,
upon the little cemetery-plot below, where the nuns

stood around the Mother Superior's flower-encircled coffin and chanted the Miserere.

The date of dedication was the Feast of All Saints; but the steeple of the little church was not completed until some months later. The church interior was frescoed in simple, unpretentious style. The altar, of wood at first, now of marble, stands between two Gothic windows and two pillars enclosing an altar-painting which, as previously stated, represents the Scripture scene of Mary and Martha, and was given to Father Clorivière by Charles X., who had ordered it to be painted for this purpose. High above it, in the chancel wall, is set a circular transparent window containing a picture of the Sacred Heart, painted and donated by a lady of Charleston, S. C. The nuns' choir is on the gospel side of the altar, opening upon the clerestory. Immediately over the choir-grate is the infirmary gallery, — for galleries encircle the whole interior, except at the south gable end where the altar stands; and in the gallery to the east is a convenient confessional, used on one side by the sisters and on the other by the Academy children; the sacristy, below and opposite, is on the epistle side of the altar.

When at last the steeple reared its apex and gilded cross towards the sky, there was a "christening" of the bells, three in number. The bells were named Ambrose, Joseph, and Agnes, respectively; and on this occasion they were carefully dressed in character. Ambrose was robed in purple; Joseph was clothed in a black soutane; and Agnes was draped in veil and habit, as a nun. Notwithstanding all his gravity in

the performance of church ceremonials, Father Clorivière could hardly repress a smile when he saw
these odd costumes; especially that of Agnes, with
her black bell-metal face and white barbette.

On each of the four sides of the steeple tower a
clock-plate showed the time; and it became the duty
of the bell Ambrose to answer with responsive clang
the hammer-stroke of every hour, as told off by the
clock within. Ambrose was the largest of the bells,
and was therefore called upon for the additional service of ringing for Mass and Benediction. Joseph
and Agnes rang for the conventual exercises; and on
great occasions all three sang tunefully together. The
first time that they so chimed in company is said to
have been for the election of Mother Agnes Brent,
December, 1821, although they had not then been
blest.

And so at last the convent chapel of the Sacred
Heart came into being, even when it seemed most
unlikely; the result of lofty aspirations but simple
beginnings; a monument of Mother Catharine's year
and a half of duty as Superior. This building was
no dream-work, but solid, real, and instinct with high
spirituality, though its actual construction sprang indeed from pious dreams.

VIII. MOTHER AGNES BRENT. — DANGER OF DISPERSION.

The successor of Mother Catharine in the Superi-
orship was Mother De Sales Neale; and the next,
after her, Mother Agnes Brent.

Mother Catharine's long illness, lasting through
two thirds of her brief term, had kept the community

almost in the state of "a body without a head." Yet when she died, it was not easy to replace her. By an episcopal dispensation, however, Mother M. de Sales Neale was unanimously elected, December 28, 1820; eight days after Mother Catharine's demise.

Mother Mary de Sales was a widow, whose two daughters — Sister M. Frances and Sister Sylvia — were professed in the same community. She is not known to have been connected with the family of Archbishop Neale, although of Maryland stock, but was related to the Fenwicks of that State.

The pecuniary distresses of the convent at this time were, it appears, so great that she could not endure the burden of anxious responsibility they brought upon her. So, when she had been almost a year in office, she begged to be discharged; and, another dispensation having been obtained for this purpose, Mother Agnes Brent was elected in her place, December 13, 1821.

This was only six weeks after the dedication of the church. Mother Agnes, the daughter of William C. Brent and Priscilla Neale (a sister of Archbishop Neale), was born at Port Tobacco, Maryland, October 7, 1796. At baptism she received the name of Henrietta; but, her mother dying when she was only eight, the stepmother into whose care she subsequently passed adopted in place of this the name of Harriet. At the age of ten she lost her father; but, although thus orphaned, she was happy in the tenderness which her stepmother lavished upon her, and in the almost paternal devotion of her guardian, James Neale, her mother's brother. Under their protection and training she remained at Port Tobacco until the age of thirteen. Then it was time for her to prepare for her first communion; and her guardian, observing that the sprightly and beautiful child was beginning to be tinged with vanity, against which the gay and fashionable circle who frequented her home were far from offering any safeguard, determined to place her in the convent school at Georgetown. She left her pleasant home without reluctance or regret, and, after crossing the cloister threshold, showed no desire to return. Her immediate and entire contentment there was doubtless due in part to the fact that she already had acquaintances and relatives in both the school and the community; among whom were Sister Magdalen Neale and Sister (afterwards Mother) Juliana Matthews. A simple, sincere and joyous piety reigned at that time in the school; to such degree that, of the fourteen pupils then upon its roll, eleven afterwards embraced the religious life. Among these were: Mother Juliana Matthews, Sister M. Scholastica Neale, Sister Gertrude Wight and Sister Margaret Wight, Sister Alphonsa Manning, Sisters Benedicta and Angela Boarman; Sister Clare Cummings, Sister Josephine Queen, and Sister M. Frances Neale. The three McNantz sisters also came to the school soon afterward. The conversation of the elder girls was chiefly on subjects of religion; their mutual confidences related to their possible fitness or vocation for admittance into the sisterhood. The undisguised poverty of the school, the Spartan meagreness of fare, the early hours of rising and the long walk to and from

Mass, in all weathers, all conduced to a healthy, vigorous, and spiritualized state of mind and body.

It is little to be wondered at that Henrietta Brent, after three years in the academy, entered the novitiate. This she did when just sixteen years of age, October 15, 1812. Little more than a year later, she became afflicted with a severe and persistent backache, the effect of which was so serious that it threatened to eclipse all the brightness of her conventual life. Unable to sleep at night for the pain, she was obliged constantly to rise from bed and seek relief in change of position; yet, being too weak to sit up long, she soon found it necessary to lie down again; and thus her nights were passed in moving from the bed to the chair, and from chair to bed. She lost her appetite entirely; and, being deprived in this way both of sufficient nourishment and of sleep, she grew exceedingly emaciated during the five weary, trying years that the malady lasted. In the end a very simple remedy, a strengthening plaster, recommended by an elderly lady who had become one of her novices, gave her the relief she had long sought in vain; and, in a few weeks she regained her health completely. A singular fact about this five years' backache is, that it was not accompanied by other discernible illness, and that it left her constitution unimpaired by any trace of infirmity. It resulted, amusingly enough, that as she was without experience in other kinds of physical suffering, she found it difficult afterwards to believe that any pain or sickness could be serious unless it was accompanied by a backache.

At the time of her election she was still very

young, for the occupant of so important and exacting
a post, being only twenty-five. Yet, notwithstanding
her youthfulness, great expectations were entertained
as to what the new Superior would achieve; and
these, as the event proved, were well grounded. In
later life, also, she accomplished devoted and important work at the head of the Visitation houses in
Kaskaskia, St. Louis, and Mobile, established from
Georgetown. Her career was a long, as well as a
useful one; for she lived to be nearly eighty-two,
dying September 16, 1876, on the Octave of the
Nativity of the Blessed Virgin.

Mother Agnes was remarkably prudent, and had a
genuine talent for governing. At the very outset of
her rule, however, she was confronted with perplexities that, for a time, seemed likely to end all need of
any Superior at Georgetown. Father Clorivière and
Mother Catharine, as we intimated in the previous
chapter, had drawn rather heavily against the resources of the future, in building the chapel. The
means on which the former had relied were slow in
coming, for his Brittany estate could not be disposed
of without troublesome delays. Meanwhile, several
sisters who had been recently professed advanced
funds of their own for the use of the house; but
these were used up in meeting current expenses, and
nothing, or next to nothing, remained to defray the
payments due on the chapel.

The community was now a large one, numbering
forty-eight. The sisters again felt the pressure of
absolute want, in their daily life; and, worse than
this, the bitterness of poverty was made sharper by

the fact that they were powerless to supply their sick and suffering (of whom there were many) with even the most ordinary reliefs of food or medicine. It is in truth amazing that, with the spectacle of so much privation and of harassing trial in full view before them, so many postulants should steadily have come forward, should have moved on through their novitiate with firm, buoyant step and become professed sisters, — willing and even anxious to share in all the toil, the hunger, and the bodily distress of that struggling house, as well as in its holy joys. That is, it would be amazing from the mere worldly point of view, and to people unfamiliar with the bright serenity of mind and soul, the clear, exalted aspiration that lifts up and guides women who have a vocation for monastic or conventual life. The curiously ignorant but common theory of non-Catholics, that no one can possibly enter a religious community who has not been disappointed in love, or otherwise frustrated in hope, meets with decided check in the contemplation of such women as these, gentle and devout of heart, who gave themselves — in the flower of their youth, or in middle age — to the simple, undivided service of God, through prayer and praise and perfect discipline, as well as through impersonal, unselfish dedication, to the teaching of the young. When, added to the usual expected discipline and self-denial, they gladly accepted the further burden of extreme penury and bodily distress, who can fail to see that with only disappointment or sourness, or even mere resignation as their motive, they would have been utterly unable to bear what they did for so much as a single year?

It is easy to read of those days of need and suffering, but not so easy to realize the heroism and faith
which were required in order to live through them;
not simply to live through them, either, and to crawl
along in uncomplaining silence; but, on the contrary,
to move actively and blithely about one's duties, always radiant, both at heart and in countenance, — to
hail suffering with genuine gratitude as a favor from
Christ, since borne for Him, — and to endure steadfastly, brightly, through the long, immitigable years.
Heroism, not of the moment or emergency, was
needed for this; and faith not of the spasmodic,
emotional kind, but of the kind that lives in unison
with the Infinite.

Upon all this we dwell because, if one is to gather
and embosom the true lesson and value of this Story
of Courage, one should not regard the Annals of the
Georgetown Visitation simply in the mild and mellow
light of that success which finally rewarded effort; but
must recur to, must emphasize and vividly apprehend,
the superb endeavor, the unfaltering fortitude of the
sisters during their weary time of trial. The material
success gained is but the outward manifestation of an
interior, spiritual victory won by them in the period
of obscurity, of doubt as to the issue, of patience and
fidelity.

Six or seven of the community, all young and promising, had died, even since the new cemetery was
made, and now slept there with hands folded. But,
for the living, also, — what provision could be offered
them? Let it not be assumed that either the director of the convent or Mother Catharine had ignored

the risk and possible dilemma of greater poverty and of belated income. They had looked this in the face, and had concluded that it might be better for them all than absolute, comfortable security, which often induces relaxation. Still, it is true, they had not foreseen that the strain would last so long, or that the pinch of want would bring the community to the very verge of disbandment. The hour had now come when the forebodings of those who had all along discouraged the enterprise, and in especial had criticised the building of the chapel, seemed about to receive confirmation from the result. Father Clorivière and the newly installed Mother Agnes consulted with the revered Foundress, Mother Teresa Lalor, and with other sister counselors, pondering deeply what measures could be adopted or means found for continuance. In vain! They were forced to the sad conclusion that no course remained open to them except to disperse the sisterhood, which had been brought together, maintained and enlarged by so many years of self-sacrifice, of industry, and persistent endeavor.

It would scarcely be possible for us to express the pain and sorrow with which this harsh but seemingly inevitable alternative filled them. To disperse! But whither? Were all the training and the matured faculties of these happily chosen souls to be scattered adrift? — fruitful seeds, no doubt, if sown along the highways of the world. Yet, if so scattered, they would be torn away from the perfect service of their vows, the fixed purpose of their lives. Such a dispersion as that could not be seriously contemplated, for a moment. Hence, the only thing to do was to seek refuge in some other religious order. And now that old idea of merging with the Ursulines, which had been advanced by the doubters or opponents, in the very inception of this Georgetown Visitation, was taken up again; and it was decided that it should be acted upon. For even the deepest disappointment must be borne patiently, cheerfully, wisely; and we should be ready, if God so shapes the course of things, to adopt the once rejected ideas and plans of our critics.

The resolution once taken, they wrote letters to the Ursulines of Canada and of Louisiana, begging them to take five or six of the sisters from Georgetown into each of their houses. Promptly and gladly came the welcoming answers. The Ursulines would receive with joy the daughters of St. Francis de Sales. In fact, the letters had no sooner reached them, than they assigned apartments for the Visitandines; many of the good Ursulines being ready to give up their cells to the expected refugees. The names of the latter were sent to the several Ursuline houses, and the Visitation sisters — with heavy hearts, it must be confessed — began thereupon their preparations to depart finally, in separate groups, from the dear home of their profession.

At that juncture an occurrence wholly unexpected, which appeared to them providential and must impress all unprejudiced observers, we think, as at least curiously opportune — " put an end to the project of dispersion." [1]

A wealthy merchant of New York, John Baptist Lasalla, decided to place his two daughters in the

[1] O'Shea's *History of the Catholic Church in the United States.*

Academy as boarders (and afterwards sent thither a third daughter and his own youngest sister). He wished, also, — when he perceived the needy state of the institution, — to pay their board and tuition for several years in advance. The sum which he put into the hands of the community by this act of hearty generosity gave them the amount they needed for tiding over their present indigence, until the fruit of Father Clorivière's still greater generosity in selling his estate should come to them.

When it became known that the Visitandines were not, after all, to be disbanded, the Ursulines of New Orleans did not rest content with having expressed their cordial willingness to adopt some of the Visitation members into their own house. To make their friendly and Christian intentions unmistakable and tangible, in another form, they now sent to the Visitation convent at Georgetown a large stock of provisions; sugar, molasses, ready-made clothing, altar linen, and a set of vestments.

In connection with this good deed of theirs, it is interesting to note that there was then among them a nun who had formerly — in Archbishop Neale's time — belonged to the infant community at Georgetown. She was no other than Sister Mary Joseph, whose unsuccessful efforts to accommodate her voice to the requirements of the chant, under the teaching of Father Bestcher, we have detailed in an earlier chapter. It appears that Father Bestcher's patience gave out, and he decided that Sister Joseph must leave the Visitation,— that she must go forth not as a voice crying in the wilderness, but as a voice lacking tune

and the support of an ear for harmony. She therefore betook herself to the Ursulines, and was accepted
by them in New Orleans. But, when this gentle banishment occurred (in 1816), she had been with the
Georgetown community for eleven years, and was on
the eve of making profession there. For this reason,
it was a very grievous trial to her to be obliged to
take up her abode elsewhere, and she told the Ursulines frankly that, although she was henceforth to live
with them, " her heart was with the Visitation, from
which it never could be weaned." The venerable
mothers of New Orleans took no umbrage at this,
and, on her profession, gave her the name she desired,
— that of *Sister Frances de Sales*. It was to her
that the prompting of this gift of timely supplies of
clothing and food was chiefly attributed. And so
the poor child who had been sent away from Georgetown against her will, Sister Mary Joseph, was the
person who brought aid in the day of need ; as Joseph
of old gave aid to his brethren.

It is quite worth while to pause here for a moment,
and to reflect that the rescue of the Georgetown Visitation, at this crisis, was due to a mere layman who
had hitherto been unheard of, and to a faithful sister
who had been sent away to another order because of
technical deficiency in singing. The rejected stone is
frequently found most useful, and the loyal, devout
layman — though seldom praised for his unselfish devotion — furnishes, in time of trial and impending disaster, the solid material prop which it is necessary to
put into the service of great spiritual undertakings.
The sisters themselves, in their manuscript Annals,

have been the first to acknowledge these obligations to the faithful layman, John Baptist Lasalla, and to Sister Mary Joseph (afterward Sister Francis de Sales).

As to the convent school or academy at this period, it had steadily declined since the death of Sister Ignatia Sharpe in 1802, until it was well-nigh deserted at the time of Father Clorivière's arrival. He saw the necessity of raising the standard of studies, and training teachers for the future. Therefore he at once requested the younger sisters, and chiefly the novices, to study on special lines to qualify themselves for conducting a more thorough English course. This they did, under the direction of a young convert, recently admitted, who had assisted previously in the teaching of a young ladies' school. But it took time — some years, indeed — to establish fully the repute of the academy as an institution of the first class.

It will be useful and instructive, here, to reproduce a prospectus of the academy, containing an outline of studies and of terms, on the basis established by Father Clorivière. The prospectus is given in fac-simile.

Mr. Lasalla, visiting Father Clorivière at his house on the grounds, asked him to point out "the academy" where his daughters were to dwell and study. The good Father was sorely mortified at having to show him the dreary, dilapidated building dignified by that name, and he determined, then and there, to erect, so soon as it should be possible, an edifice worthy of the title "academy." This determination was afterward carried out.

The school, assisted by Mr. Lasalla's advance payment and by the funds which eventually came to Father Clorivière from the sale of his French estate, prospered rapidly. The debts due on the church were paid from these resources. A new academy building was also erected and dedicated with merry Christmas festivities in 1823.

Many pupils were attracted by the improved facilities, the spacious rooms, and the convenient arrangement of parlors, dormitories, and refectory which Father Clorivière designed and completed. In short, an era of prosperity, destined to continue unbrokenly down to the present time, dawned upon this first House of the Visitation in America, immediately after its darkest hour of night and anxious dread.

IX. THE LASALLAS. — MIRACULOUS CURE OF SISTER BEATRICE.

Now that we have accompanied the sisters, in retrospect, so far upon the long, laborious way of their beginnings; through the frosty night of that earlier time; through the faint yet eager dawn of their great hope; have seen them in the thicket, one may say, of harsh experience, where thorns of trial and flowers of happiness interblend; but always, whether under clouded skies or sunshine, and even when thwarted or delayed by some vexatious turn of the path, pressing onward to a fixed goal with purpose unchanged, — we may pause a little in our narrative, and dwell for a while on certain interesting characters and certain miraculous cures, that became important elements in this new era of the history of the convent.

The three daughters of Mr. Lasalla who received
their education at Georgetown were Charlotte, Virginia, and Ann Louisa.   At the time of their entrance, Charlotte, the eldest, was eight years old.   She
showed remarkable natural talents, excelled in her
classes, especially in music, and was graduated, nine
years later, with the highest honors.   A friend of
hers, Miss Emily Ward of Washington, graduated
at the same time with equal rank; but the trend of
Miss Ward's mind was distinctly in the direction of
piety of thought and life, while Charlotte, returning
to her father's home in New York, plunged at once
into the gayest society there.   Not from indifference
or apathy, but from a mistaken impression that, having emerged into the world, she was in some way
bound to change her manner of existence, she ab-
stained from the sacraments, and for two years performed no religious duty beyond going to Mass on
Sunday.   It is a curious fact that her father, Mr.
Lasalla, although he would not allow his daughters to
be educated in any but this Catholic school, and had
therefore become its benefactor by his liberal advance
payments, had nevertheless completely neglected his
religious duties for a long time, and still continued to
neglect them.   In such an individuality as his, we
come at once upon the primal sources and conditions
of human nature, unspoiled yet unregenerate.   He
was a type of many negligent Catholics.   The faith
was in him, and he was loyal to it.   His heart, smit-
ten long ago in childhood by the High Priest of all
men, had gushed forth in a fountain-stream, like the
rock that Moses smote.   The living spring was there,

still, but choked with weeds and mud and rubbish that his carelessness had allowed to accumulate.

Charlotte, influenced by his example, — for, since he was a most indulgent parent, lavish towards her in all material things, and a friend of the convent, how could she criticise him? — fell in with and followed his indolent disregard of the sacraments and of confession. She felt keenly, however, the dangers and temptations of this mode of life, and often wished that she might again be brought within the shelter of the convent walls. Yet this was a passing thought, quite easily put aside again. A fit of illness at length interrupted her career of amusement and social festivity. Just then, a letter came from her friend Emily Ward, who had entered the novitiate at Georgetown and had immediately written to Charlotte in order to tell her of the difficulties, the struggles, she had gone through, and the peace and holy happiness she now enjoyed. This letter made a great impression upon Charlotte. After thinking it over carefully, she went to her father and asked his permission to go to the convent and enter the novitiate, herself.

The request was like a deathblow to him. He, the indulgent, loving parent who had never been able to deny her anything else, could not bring himself to consent to this. Seeing his agitation and dismay, Charlotte did not press the subject further. But, as the idea still dwelt in her mind and she could neither say nor do anything toward carrying it out, the repression she had to suffer broke her health down, gradually. At last, after long and obstinate delay, Mr. Lasalla, finding that even his daughter's physician insisted that the only hope of restoring her bodily health lay in acceding to her wish, took her to the convent. In the novitiate she met her old friend, Emily Ward, now Sister Bernardine, and herself received, when she took the veil, her father's name; becoming Sister Baptista. But her strength was already spent, and she lived only one year longer. During her last days, she drew from her father, who had not approached the sacraments for twenty-two years, a promise that he would receive Holy Communion for her, after her death. Even then, strange as it may seem, this man of good intentions, and of generous performance in the way of material aid to a good cause, hesitated to accede. He gave his promise, though; and, when Sister Baptista died, he made a retreat under the guidance of the Jesuit Fathers of Georgetown College, confessed himself, and received Communion. Thus, while his faith had lain dormant in him for so many years, his own act of loyalty in sending his daughters to this convent school, resulted, even against the rebellion of his self-will, in bringing him back to that visible and tangible communication with God which is vital to the soul.

It was on the 9th of April, 1837, that Sister Baptista Lasalla passed away, making her final vows of profession on her death-bed.

We will now return, briefly, to February 10, 1825, the date of a miraculous cure wrought upon Sister Beatrice Myers, a lay sister, through prayer.

CURE OF SISTER BEATRICE MYERS.

At the time of the blessed miracle manifested in her, Sister Beatrice, a native of Pennsylvania, was twenty-nine years old, and had been for about two years a professed nun of the Visitation. She was suddenly overcome by violent headaches and consumptive pains, as well as other symptoms. For the following two years she was confined to the infirmary, her malady during that time assuming such a variety of forms that the physician gave up the attempt to decide what her disease might be. She had to be lifted in her bed like an infant. On September 14, 1825, Mother Agnes Brent was called out from the chapel during Mass, and told that Sister Beatrice was dying. She hastened to the infirmary, and found the patient barely breathing. As soon as possible, Father Clorivière was asked to come from the sacristy and administer Extreme Unction to the dying nun. To this request, the Father replied, calmly, " Prince Hohenlohe will cure her. She will not die ; she will get well ! "

Here is an explanation of Father Clorivière's answer.

The princes of Hohenlohe were one of the oldest families in Germany, and were known as counts of the empire in the eleventh century. Their name is taken from the castle of Hohenlohe in Franconia, between the Main and the Tauber rivers. The Hohenlohes were among the first of the prominent noble families that embraced the so-called " Reformation " of Luther ; but in 1667 they returned to the Catholic church. Charles VII. raised them to the rank of princes of the Roman Empire, in 1744. Their house consists of two branches; that of Nuenstein, and that of Waldenburg. It is to the latter that the Rev. Prince Alexander Hohenlohe belonged. He was one of the canons of the chapter of Olmütz, and a Knight of Malta.

He was born August 17, 1793, near Waldenburg, in Hohenlohe; the eighteenth and last child of Charles Albert, then reigning prince of Hohenlohe and a general in the Austrian service. His mother — Judith, Baroness of Rewitsky — was a model of virtue. She assembled her household always, morning and evening, for prayers, and was very particular in providing for the religious instruction of her sons. When Alexander was two years old, his father died. His eldest brother, Prince Joseph, fell at Ulm, in 1800; and as the other sons were also in the army and exposed to the hazards of war, an attempt was made to divert Alexander's mind, which was already fixed upon the Church, toward worldly affairs; so that, if the succession should devolve upon him, he would be able to give his whole attention to the princedom. But he chose to become a servant of Christ, and, having passed through an eleven years' course of classics, philosophy, and theology, as a preparation for this duty, he was ordained a priest, September 16, 1815.

He was remarkable for evangelical meekness, humility, and charity. As a preacher, also, he was eloquent and powerful.

At Würtzburg he began, after a time, those extraordinary intercessions of prayer, which astonished

Europe and were known and shared in throughout the civilized world. For his companion in this work he chose a man of humble condition, one Martin Michel. Whenever any one recommended himself to his prayers, Rev. Prince Hohenlohe directed such person to make sincere "acts of contrition," and to receive Holy Communion on the same day on which he, the priest, should offer prayers, in the Holy Sacrifice of the Mass, for the individual so appealing for help.[1]

Father Clorivière was awake to the wonderful truth of Prince Hohenlohe's power through prayer, and had a prophetic conviction that Sister Beatrice was to be benefited by it. But Mother Agnes Brent exclaimed at his announcement, in greatest distress of mind: " She is dying *now*, — she may not live an hour ! " She admitted afterwards that she felt impatient, and even indignant, at the thought that Father Clorivière would so run the risk of Sister Beatrice's dying without the sacraments. The Father realized what the Rev. Mother and the Sisters were suffering in their suspense, and acceded at last to their appeals. The dying nun rallied quickly after receiving Extreme Unction and the Viaticum. Doctor Bohrer, the convent physician, coming some hours later, said to Sister Teresa Lalor that " an astonishing change had taken place, and he marveled over it." But, though a Protestant, he had much respect for the Holy Eucharist, having frequently observed its effect ; and he accepted the assurance of the sisters that Sister Beatrice had been visited by the heavenly Physician. For some months the nun remained much better, and was able

[1] *Vide* Works of Bishop England, vol. iii., p. 470.

to sit up for half an hour at a time. However, in December, most distressing symptoms returned, and in January she again seemed at the point of death. But Father Clorivière continued to have a strong faith that she could be cured by miracle, and he objected as before to giving her the last Sacraments. He promised to begin a novena for her on the 1st of February. Mother Brent and Sister Teresa Lalor protested that there was no time for a cure, and Mother Brent cried : " Begin a novena for her, when she has been placed in the tomb ! It is impossible that she can survive long enough for even the commencement of the novena ! " " She will not die yet," quietly averred Father Clorivière. " The Prince will cure her ! "

Mother Brent spoke of sending for a priest from the neighboring college. The father begged her to trust wholly in God ; and he said that he would take the responsibility upon himself of the chance of Sister Beatrice's dying without the last rites of the Church. Mother Agnes Brent thought him " most uncharitable " at this solemn moment. She regarded the matter, as she subsequently confessed, " only with the eyes of flesh and blood, while he showed sublime faith." As the Father predicted, the novena was begun on the 1st of February, both for Sister Beatrice and three other sick nuns. From its commencement she grew daily worse, and she desired to die, that she might be with God, and see the " Blessed Lady," as she said. Dr. Bohrer soon declared that if she were cured at all, it would be by miracle, and he would then become a Catholic ; — a promise which he considered extremely safe. At nearly three o'clock in

the morning of the last day of the novena, the final
preparations were made for administering Holy Communion to the four sisters. Prince Hohenlohe was
saying Mass in Germany at a corresponding hour.
The infirmary altar had been elaborately decorated
with flowers and lights. As the tower clock struck
three, the tinkling of the little bell was heard by the
patients which announces the approach of the Blessed
Sacrament when taken to the sick, and is carried before the procession of nuns which comes with the
priest from the Sacristy. Sister Beatrice was feeling
so ill that she did not expect the Father to reach her
bedside before death overtook her ; but she prayed to
live to receive the Sacred Host. As soon as it had
descended to her chest, she was a changed being.
Perfect health circulated in her blood and appeared
in her countenance. The holy sister in her humility
was silent ; for she was a lay-sister, whereas the other
three patients were choir sisters ; and so she thought
that if *she* was cured, they surely must be, and were
entitled to speak first. Father Clorivière knelt before
the Blessed Sacrament at the altar, awaiting some
word as to the cure which he firmly believed was to
come to Sister Beatrice ; but all was still. At length
he arose, and departed with the procession to the
church. The Superioress was the last to turn away
from the infirmary ; when Sister Beatrice was heard
to call to her : "Mother!" A thrill passed through
Mother Agnes Brent at this summons. The miracle,
as it were, laid its touch upon her also.

Sister Beatrice clasped her hands and cried : "I
think I am cured!" And she uttered many religious

ejaculations in thanksgiving. The sisters who had followed the Blessed Sacrament soon returned, and Sister Beatrice, rising and making herself ready, went with them into the gallery for the infirm, overlooking the sanctuary, where they all remained for some time prostrate in prayer. Father Clorivière enjoined upon the nuns "to rejoice in this great favor in silence and quiet." When he finally met Sister Beatrice, who fell at his feet for his blessing, he felt, he told the Superioress, as if he ought rather to kneel at her feet, and ask her blessing. The next morning, a Mass of thanksgiving was celebrated, during which the sister knelt almost all the time, having descended the long flight of steps to the choir with ease. That same day she did all manner of things to show her strength, and was in fine spirits. The third day, Dr. Bohrer came to see the miracle, and stood in amazement before her at sight of her radiant countenance. He found her skin, pulse, eyes, appetite, step, all those of perfect health.

"Well, Doctor," said Mother Agnes Brent; "I hope you will keep your promise of becoming a Catholic."

"That is a serious matter, Mother, and requires time and consideration," sagely replied the good man, who had been promising and reflecting for so long.

"And have you not given it sufficient time? Delays are dangerous!" said she.

"Mother," the Doctor exclaimed, still wise in his worldly regard for his own judgment, with which he was testing the value and necessity of the step which our Lord has already judged in the affirmative, "do you not think precipitation might be more dangerous than delay? In so important a concern, I do not wish to act rashly."

"Nor do I advise rashness, Doctor," answered Mother Agnes. "I would myself condemn precipitation. But you are now familiar with the truth, and have already contemplated joining the church for a long while, because of the manifestations of God which you have seen in the convent."

"The day may come," said he, "when you will see me a good Catholic."

The Mother shook her head. "Not if you continue this procrastination much further," she told him. She was right. His whole family became Catholics, and one of his daughters was received as a Visitandine; but he procrastinated until it was too late.

After her cure, Sister Beatrice continued robust for nearly ten years. She then sustained a heavy fall, while assisting an infirm nun down some stairs. She could not rally from the serious effects of this accident, until she was a second time cured by miracle. Sister Juliana Matthews had received from Mr. Frenaye, of Philadelphia, a medal of the Immaculate Conception, called "the Miraculous Medal." It was the first of the kind that the sisters had seen, and an account of the apparition of which it was the reminder, and of the cures connected with it, was read to them in the assembly-room. All the sisters came, one after another, to kneel and kiss it; but Sister Beatrice was ill in bed from her fall, and deprived of this happiness. So the Mother Superior

decided to place the medal on her neck with her own
hands, and to have a novena made in which all
should join, by saying daily the aspiration printed
around the figure: "Oh Mary, conceived without sin,
pray for us who have recourse to thee!" The patient grew worse instead of improving; but at the
time of Holy Communion on the last day, she said:
"I feel better!" She arose, dressed, and for about
twelve years, until her death, lived an active life.
She told the Superioress that at the moment of swallowing the Sacred Host an indescribable sensation
thrilled her whole frame, and she found herself entirely well.

X. SISTERS APOLLONIA DIGGS AND GENEVIEVE KING.

Another, and perhaps the most remarkable of the
miraculous cures which have occurred at the convent,
was that of Sister Mary Apollonia Diggs.

A delicate little girl, in Charles County, Maryland,
Anna Diggs, who had lost her own mother when very
young, and afterwards had been subject to an unkind
stepmother, quietly and bravely began a remarkable
life. She bore her cross with a child's touching inspiration, in a kind of novitiate of religious patience,
long before she knew she was to be a nun. Later,
moreover, she was to become a sign of God's love and
presence. When only twelve years old, she made the
choice of generosity in place of self-consideration,
which in a child often proves so much heroism. In
the house next to her father's, there was a little friend
of about her own age, Mary King, who also entered
the convent to which, in a few years more, Anna was

consigned by her relatives. Mary often heard the
unkind stepmother scolding Anna, and saw her friend
put to many unsuitable and difficult tasks, which
her frail constitution made really dangerous for her.
Mary begged the poor girl to tell her father how she
was maltreated; but Anna always answered that it
would cause him great unhappiness to know this, and
she did not wish him to be distressed. Then her
little champion declared that she would herself complain to Mr. Diggs; but Anna persisted in refusing
to have him disturbed. At last she gave this conclusive argument: "Mary, I must suffer something
for the love of God." Young as she was, she accomplished the sacrifice of justice towards herself which
most of us grow old in the effort to complete. This
angelic spirit of hers led her to make daily actions of
self-denial and piety, which purified her into a fitting
vehicle of God's power.

When about sixteen, the two friends entered (a
few months apart) their conventual novitiate. Anna
had a tendency to consumption. The disease had
already fatally attacked a number of her family.
Archbishop Neale therefore forbade her exposing herself to the morning air; or remaining more than a
quarter of an hour on her knees in devotional exercises, as this invariably brought on acute pains in the
chest; although quarter of an hour on the knees in
prayer soon becomes but a brief moment to any one
who attempts it. For eight years consumption slowly
undermined her system; yet she did not hesitate to
perform all sorts of such service for the community
as she thought it needed, regardless of the effect

upon herself, and employing a saintly subtlety in seeming able thus to labor.   How the pain and weariness of this angelic young woman blooms now, in our desire to be as brave as she could be!

During 1824, Sister Apollonia's state required that she should be bled twice a week, and use severe abstinence in the choice of food, because of her highly excited pulse, and the other dire symptoms common to consumption.   Father Clorivière supposed her to be near death, and she performed the devotions usual in this extremity.   She remained as described for several months.   Meantime, Sister Beatrice Myers had been miraculously cured, as related, by a novena made in unison with Prince Hohenlohe, far away in Germany; and Father Clorivière began to urge Sister Apollonia to have recourse to a similar novena. But she replied that she would rather die; as that seemed to be the will of God.   Still, she lived on, though now often at the point of death, always confined to her bed, and suffering from burning cheeks, coughs, debility, and all the other excessive conditions to be found in the disease.   The attending physician, Dr. Bohrer (whose Protestantism was a source of unfailing concern to the earnest nuns), noticed another appearance in Sister Apollonia, accompanying her aspect of consumption.   He called it a *moral symptom*, and said that it was an expression of *hope*, and great serenity of soul.   A sister one day solemnly exclaimed to the sick girl, that perhaps " her resignation as to death was not the service which God most desired of her: that perhaps He wished to be glorified by the reëstablishment of her health."   It was now four years or more since Father Clorivière had urged her to make the novena. Her living on, though at the point of dying, might be accounted for by this interpretation. Sister Apollonia received light from the forcible conviction which the sister had shown. She consulted the spiritual father (Father Wheeler), and the nuns' present confessor, Father Dubuisson. A novena was begun in conjunction with Prince Hohenlohe, on the 10th of January, 1831. At once the sufferer grew even worse, and the physician told her that her end was at hand. He admitted to the sisters, who again began to have great hopes of his conversion, that if she was cured by the novena, he would enter the Catholic Church. This time, it seemed as if he would and must carry out his intention. On the last night some of the sisters remained uninterruptedly before the Blessed Sacrament, praying for the cure. But their love of heaven made them do so rather to lead good Dr. Bohrer into heaven by means of the miracle to be wrought, than to keep Sister Apollonia (much as they loved her) away from its bliss a little longer. She, too, prayed fervently that the miracle might be effected; yet, while so praying, bore herself with unalterable calm. At half-past three in the morning, *every evidence of dissolution* was to be seen in her. Father Dubuisson was hastily called; and soon the little bell was heard to approach, followed by the procession of sisters. Among these were: —

Mrs. Ann Mattingly; Mother Magdalene Augustine D'Arregger, Superior; Mother Teresa Lalor (Foundress of the House); Mother Margaret Marshall (foundress of the house at Mobile); Mother Scholastica Neale; Sister Beatrice Myers; Sister Stanislaus Jones; Sister Veronica; Sister Elizabeth; Sister A. Agatha Combs; Sister Charity Waide; Sister Justine Kelly.

Being surrounded by them, and the ritual having been said, Sister Apollonia received Holy Communion. All eyes were turned towards her. In a few moments she joined her hands and cried, loudly, but tremulously: "Jesus! Jesus! My God, thou art all mine, and I am all thine!" Father Dubuisson asked her how she felt. "*Perfectly well*, Father," was her answer. Thanksgiving joy abounded among all who were witnesses of this marvelous physical change. One sister has written that, upon seeing the dying girl's ghastly countenance suddenly assume the radiance of health, she herself nearly fainted away. Numerous prayers were offered, and the sister, strong for the first time in her life, was plied with many questions. In the first hour she was allowed to rise and dress, doing so without any assistance. She said that she felt, at the instant of her cure, "as if I were lifted from the bed; and a sensation of vigor, impossible to describe, ran through my whole frame. I was delivered from all suffering, and became filled with new life." Similar expressions are almost always used by those who are thus cured. An immediate vigor and lightness of body comes, such as is felt in earliest youth. Before eating breakfast, which Sister Apollonia did very heartily, she exhibited her strength by lifting rather heavy weights (twenty-eight pounds) without any quickening of the pulse. She hastened, with a rapid step, and no difficulty in breathing, through the bitter cold January air, to visit another sister, who was in a room somewhat removed. Her breakfast, at five o'clock, consisted of two crackers, a large slice of gingerbread, two apples, and a glass of sweetened wine.

She responded to the bell for Meditation, and remained in the choir while Prime was chanted, and during Mass, kneeling for an hour. Then she took a second breakfast, and visited almost every part of the house. At nine o'clock the doctor called. He mastered his astonishment at the miracle revealed in her, and made a long examination which resulted in his pronouncing her to be in faultless health. But when he beheld her lift with ease the twenty-eight pound weight with which she had many times that morning experimented, he grew pale to the lips, and his chin trembled. Nevertheless, much as he was awed by the healing of Christ, there was in his good heart a greater awe of his own personality, and a Protestant he remained. Sister Apollonia now crossed the snow-covered yard, in the bleakest of cold air, to the Academy, where eighty children surrounded her and asked her questions, and made her lift over and over again the above-mentioned weight. She passed the entire day in a state of activity, receiving numerous visits, and attending the religious exercises, during which she knelt. A stalwart person might have been more fatigued than she was by such a variety of effort. Sister Apollonia was of frail build, and below the middle height.

The next day her labors were hardly less. She

lifted aloft a fifty-two pound weight, which had no ring in the top, only a crosspiece, without much effort. Her strength was not the result of nervous excitement, for she could show the same amount during the following eight days, upon each of which this strength was carefully tested with the smaller weight. She resumed her relinquished duties at the Academy, going across the yard in heavy falls of snow. Her pulse was always regular, and she had no pains, cough, or headache; on the contrary, "only the sweet sensations of returning vigor."

Mother Michaela Jenkins, the Superioress, had been incredulous when the wonderful news of the cure had been brought to her. She wrote of it: "I leaned my head against the wall, internally bewailing so precipitate a circulation of such a report. I thought it would only turn to our confusion, to publish such a thing. For, in my want of faith, I felt sure the cure would prove false, — that she would relapse into her old state, and die. The weather was then so cold that the pupils were not allowed to go to Mass on Sunday, that short distance from the church (or chapel), as there was then no interior or covered way from the Academy. It was during such weather that Sister Apollonia came over to the Academy, looking in the bloom of life, without even a shawl to protect her. The day previous I had seen her the very shadow of death, an emaciated skeleton, exhausted and speechless. Her sustenance for two weeks had been merely the wetting of her lips with teaspoonfuls of wine and water. While standing near me as I gazed at her, she perceived that her shoe was untied, and suddenly, with a strength and quickness of motion that took me by surprise, she stooped and tied it herself; no tottering whatever, as would be natural to any one. Shortly afterwards I found Sister Apollonia on the steps of the monastery, with her sleeves rolled up as high as they could go, and calling to another sister to come and help her ' scour the church before night.' She finished the job without any bad results, although the church was not heated, and the atmosphere was damp and frigid. I thought it most imprudent to let her do such things; that it was enough to throw her back into her former condition, and then, what would the world say of the *miracle?* I was but a few years in religion at the time, and my faith was weak. It *was* the most perfect miracle ! " When sixty-four years old, Sister Apollonia was sent as Superior to Parkersburg, Virginia, and twice served there her three years as Mother of the community. She was hampered at first by all the perplexities of being within the immediate limits of the Civil War ; the forts even encroaching upon the convent grounds, and all supplies being very difficult to obtain. She was finally recalled to Georgetown, September 2, 1889, to end her long life of usefulness — having spent about seventy-two years in the monastery — in peace and rest. The anniversary of her cure has always been religiously observed. Nothing of the peculiarities of old age marred the blessed condition which made her life miraculous, after the first moment when, as a witness said, she had " heard the footsteps of the Almighty."

SISTER GENEVIEVE KING.

Because of the beautiful lesson of Sister Mary Genevieve King's consecration to religion, which shows so well the wisdom of submitting one's self to the conventual life when one has a vocation for it, and because of her intimate friendship with Sister Apollonia, the following brief record is introduced here : —

Mary King was born on the Feast of St. Raphael, 1800. Her parents were models of Christian piety. Colonel Adam King, her father, as Sister Genevieve always delighted to repeat, never uttered a word of detraction, nor suffered any uncharitable conversation in his house. This principle was so well-known among his friends that his guests were always on their best behavior in his presence.

Sister Genevieve inherited the beautiful nature of her father. Perhaps there never was a heart more gentle and forgiving towards every one : imperfection in others did not lead her to any bitterness of thought or change of loving manner. The sight of cruelty of any kind caused her physical pain. Her kind impulses towards the poor, while she was still a child, were encouraged by her father, and even seconded by the cook of this ideal family, who, a negress of guileless soul, was so holy a woman that Father Fenwick, afterwards Bishop of Boston, used to say of her: " She is too good for this world ! "

But when Sister Genevieve entered the convent she was to cause her mother suffering that must have seemed to some people unnecessary. Ever since her birth, and that of a twin sister, her mother had been wanting in full intelligence, though always gentle and sweet. The poor invalid could not submit willingly to this separation from her lovely child. After the young girl had gone, she more than once escaped from the house at night, and wandered, weeping and wailing, under the windows of the dormitory. Sister Genevieve listened to her mother's half-suppressed call without outward response, but with what prayers may be imagined. To those who have not had experience in such cases, the daughter's persistence in separation from her suffering parent may appear fanatical; but to those who know the history, great and beautiful, of community life, the mother's loving revolt would be gauged at its true worth, and that glad resignation which is certain to ensue would be confidently looked for. There is a splendid and reassuring testimony to the fact that the holiest and profoundest happiness of parents and relatives is the knowledge that one who is so near to their hearts has also become so near to the Heart of Jesus. The religious suffers also, if bravely, for the wholly human anguish of her family (whom she loves the more truly because she loves God more), while they refuse to sympathize with the consecration of her life to adoration and labor for the glory of God. Tenderness so unchangeable as Sister Genevieve's must have caused a torture that purified like fire. At length Mrs. King became entirely reconciled, and proudly happy in the vocation of her child.

Sister Genevieve herself felt tempted to retreat from the convent a few days after she had entered it.

Her mother's distress, and the separation from her loving family, seemed more than she could bear, although she was among young companions, and her dearest friend, Sister Apollonia, was of the number. She was only sixteen, and a fit of homesickness almost overcame her. She sent a message to Mother Teresa Lalor, — the Foundress, — who was still Superior, and experienced in all sacrifice and tender care for her spiritual daughters, saying that she wished for a private interview. At the appointed hour the little novice went to the Mother's room, and knocked for admittance. "Come in, my child," said Mother Teresa. It was all she needed to say. At the sound of her maternal voice, trouble, agitation, and despondency left the heart of Sister Genevieve, and left it forever. It is easy to believe that a voice which could inspire a despairing soul so richly with courage was steeped in prayers, not tears.

The little novice became a most precious acquisition, both from a spiritual and a temporal point of view. She sang beautifully, and her fine tones were never missing at the office, the litanies, the benediction, the latter being in those days always sung by the sisters. She was a thorough and efficient teacher in the academy, and devoted, besides, much time to the "benevolent school," where almost all the poor children of Georgetown were to be found. At thirty-three years of age she was sent "far west," to Kaskaskia. Here she, in sympathy the tenderest, perhaps, of all the sisters, was for twenty-two years Infirmarian in the convent, and for thirteen Infirmarian in both convent and academy, in a climate which attacked persons fiercely in winter and in summer, so that frequently two or three patients were at the point of death. Very often, both day and night she was at the bedside of the sick, and *never* [so the record reads] did any one receive a harsh word, *a cold look,* or an unkind act from her. An expression of love was always on her face. The children had recourse to her in every little sorrow; the novices looked for her smile and caresses. She exemplified St. Paul's words: "Charity is patient." She had been inspired with a loving ability to be a Mother, and of a family infinitely larger than that of blood-relationship, though it could not be more tender. Sister Genevieve's prayers were constant, and sometimes remarkably answered at the close of remarkable devotions and evidences of faith. In her seventy-first year she was elected Superior of the community at Dubuque, and to the last day of her life she succeeded in being a joy to those about her.

XI. COMMODORE JONES. — SISTER STANISLAUS JONES.

Five weeks after the first cure of Sister Beatrice, the Convent of the Visitation joyfully received into its novitiate, March 18, 1825, Miss Wilhelmina Jones, a convert, who was then in her twenty-fourth year and was destined to become one of the most remarkable as well as cherished members of the community, under the name of Sister Stanislaus. She was the daughter of Commodore Jacob Jones, of the United States, whose capture of the British war-sloop Frolic we referred to at the close of our third chapter.

As the Commodore was one of our most distinguished American naval heroes, it is advisable here to retrace briefly some of the striking events in his career. In July, 1803, as a lieutenant, he was ordered to the Mediterranean under Captain Bainbridge, who commanded the old frigate Philadelphia ; the daughter, then just turned of two years, remaining with her baby brother in their mother's care at New York. Lieutenant Jones proceeded with Bainbridge to Tripoli, in the blockade of which port they took part with the Philadelphia. While they were chasing a Tripolitan vessel, one day, however, their own ship ran aground and was captured, with officers and crew, — three hundred and fifteen souls, all told, — who were at once imprisoned ashore. The Tripolitans then got the stranded frigate afloat once more and moored her in the harbor, with their flag at the masthead. The sight of their former consort in the control of the enemy exasperated the officers of the rest of our fleet, and they resolved to burn the Philadelphia rather than let her serve under the crescent. It was young Decatur — Stephen Decatur, the cool, the intrepid, though till then unknown — who carried out this daring project, thereby winning fame and swift promotion to a captaincy. Taking with him only twenty-one men in small boats, he made his way through the hostile squadron at night, February 15, 1804, boarded the Philadelphia, set her on fire ; and then, in full view, from the glare of the flames, rowed back ; safely regaining his own vessel.

This achievement, in turn, enraged the Bey of Tripoli, who took his revenge by treating the American prisoners in his hands with great severity. They had at first been allowed to occupy the house of the former American consul, where their confinement was not rigorous. But Harris, from whose Life of Commodore Bainbridge these and the details that follow are derived, narrates how, two weeks after the burning of the frigate, the Bey transferred his captives to a cold, damp dungeon in the City Castle, which had but one opening for light and air; an iron-grated opening in the roof. Here, closely guarded and " entombed," they were compelled to stay, throughout the sixteen months more of their captivity, albeit they did not yield to this rude necessity without making several energetic attempts at escape.

" First," says Harris, " they undertook to dig an underground passage, but had not advanced far when they perceived the utter impracticability of such a project, as well from the length of the way to be excavated as on account of the presence of guards stationed along the shore, at its intended terminus, whence they would have to swim to the American ships." Again, one night, " Captain Bainbridge and Lieutenant Jones determined to explore if possible an apartment adjoining their prison. With this view they opened a passage through a thick wall, entered the room, and discovered that the floor of the upper story was broken away, and near the ceiling was a window which, from its great height, was supposed to be beyond reach. This our prisoners resolved to make their passage of escape, climbing thence to the rampart fronting the harbor, and, by means of a rope, descending seventy feet to the water. Their plan

then was to swim for a small vessel standing in
view, take her by surprise, and trust to Providence
to be caught up by our own squadron, cruising in
the distance. None but good and strong swimmers
could engage in this enterprise, and the delay occasioned by their descending the rope in succession
would increase the risk of discovery. As, however,
this appeared their only chance of escape, it was decided on. Operations were begun, and in three or
four days, they had filed through the iron bars of the
window, so that they could be, in a few minutes, removed. Their sheets and blankets were made into
ropes; and at midnight, when all appeared quiet, the
iron bars were cautiously removed and the prisoners,
passing through, crawled in single file along the rampart. They had nearly reached the designated gun,
to which the rope was to be fastened, when the relief
guard was seen approaching. A halt was instantly
commanded. Our men for a few moments stood
silent and anxious; but finally, concluding that they
had not been observed, retraced their steps, retreat-
ing hastily through the window; and, replacing the
iron bars, returned to their prison." It afterward became clear to them that, in spite of their disappointment at the time, this frustration of their plan was
fortunate, as the ship to which they meant to swim
had weighed anchor that very night, and sailed away.

Notwithstanding their frightful sufferings from
their close immurement within limited space, with little air or light, and no means of maintaining clean-
liness or securing refreshment, amid the heats of the
African summer, and exposed to the withering influ-

ence of the desert-winds, the prisoners yet made no other attempt at self-deliverance until some months later. Then, learning that a British war-vessel was expected in port, bringing a new consul, they decided to try to reach her by cutting an underground passage to the beach, and from there swimming out to the frigate. This work was carried forward with great spirit, and seemed to give good promise of success; but just as the men were digging their way under the rampart, they unfortunately struck into a vault beneath; and, the superstructure caving in, further effort in that direction had to be abandoned. Their repeated failure left them, at last, without hope of escape by their own exertions. Finally, in August, 1804, Commodore Preble's squadron opened a fierce bombardment of the city, and in a second attack silenced the Tripolitan forts and batteries; at the same time exposing the prisoners to new perils, since the fire poured into the City Castle was very heavy. One shot struck within a foot of Captain Bainbridge's head, throwing down a large mass of débris and giving him a severe ankle wound. Nor was it until ten months after this, even, that a treaty of peace was made between the United States and the Barbary powers. Lieutenant Jones and the captain, after the release of the captives, came home, landing at Hampton; were received in Richmond, Fredericksburg, and Washington by military and civic processions, and were treated with all the honors accorded to popular heroes.

Hardly was this triumphal progress ended, than the war-worn man was called upon to face a trial sharper

than any he had yet endured.   What would have
been the chief happiness of his home-return was denied him by the sudden extinction of the light of his
household.   As he was on his way to New York, he
saw in a daily newspaper the announcement that his
young wife was dead.

Wilhelmina and her little brother were received
into the home of their aunt, Mrs. Swartout, and well
cared for.   Seven years later, Lieutenant Jones, in
one of the bravest sea-fights on record, while in command of the United States war-sloop Wasp, captured
the Frolic after a combat of forty-five minutes.   In
strange repetition of his former experience, he and his
sloop were taken, the same day, by the powerful British seventy-six gun frigate Poictiers; but his own
performance had secured him national repute.   When
he again returned, Congress voted him a special reward of twenty-five thousand dollars, together with
a gold medal commemorative of his victory.   At
Charleston, S. C., he took prominent part in the public festival offered to him with the other naval wor-
thies, Bainbridge, Decatur, and Hull.   His native
state, New Jersey, presented him a rich piece of plate.
New York and Philadelphia gave him swords.   The
Massachusetts General Assembly, the Council of Sa-
vannah, the Order of the Cincinnati and other bodies,
sent testimonials to him and to his fellow-heroes as
being "each so just, so valiant, and so honorable, that
each may boast he knows no better man."

This no doubt threw over the girlhood of Wilhelmina, then but eleven years old, a peculiar radiance,
though a radiance wholly mundane.   It is evident

that she possessed a firmness of character and a con-
scientiousness resembling her father's; for she was not
spoiled by this glamour of success and fame. Having
entered the French boarding-school of a Madame
Binse, in New York, she worked hard and made an
admirable record in her classes; emerging at sixteen
well educated and accomplished. In Madame Binse's
family, also, she had been much impressed with the
beauty of Catholic faith, well exemplified as it was
in their conduct. She had there met the Rev. B.
Fenwick, S. J. (afterward Bishop of Boston), and had
formed a strong desire to be received into the Church.

Commodore Jones, being still a widower, keeping
no establishment, and expecting at any time to be ordered to sea-duty again, readily assented to a request
made by Dr. Thomas Ewell and his wife, that Wilhelmina should live with them for a while. Here she
stayed for eighteen months. Her genial manners, her
beauty, and, perhaps even more, a noble generosity of
nature, — shown especially in her systematic charity
to the poor and suffering, — won her many warm
friends. Many tempting offers of marriage, also,
were made to her. Yet even when her own affections
were aroused and seemingly captivated, an impulse
unaccountable to her then, but irresistible, led her to
reject all such offers. She actually became engaged
to marry; yet the idea of marrying, and even the
presence of her affianced, proved to be intolerable.
This repulsion was so strong that it eventually forced
her away from all her suitors, and she afterward understood and accepted it with unbounded gratitude as
an inspiration of the Divine Spouse that she should
dedicate herself wholly to Him.

After mature reflection and prayer she decided to accept the Catholic faith, and was received into the Church, with entire openness and with great apparent fervor.

But there now ensued a singular and a seeming though not an actual contradictory episode in her history. Commodore Jones no sooner heard of the step she had taken than he expressed great anger at what he called her folly, and at once withdrew her from all Catholic influences; taking her to the eastern shore of Chesapeake Bay, where, among affectionate relatives, she was plied by them with every imaginable argument or influence that could be counted on to win her back to the Episcopal Church. Young, timid, fearing that she might be led into fatal error by opposing the wishes of her family, she at length yielded, acting with upright heart and earnest mind. To her father's gratification, she once more became an Episcopalian.

The Commodore, meanwhile, had married a Miss Lusby; and having been appointed, in 1822, naval commissioner, he established his home in Georgetown, where Wilhelmina and her brother came to live with him. The brother and his cousin, John Swartout, both attended Georgetown, where they soon became Catholics and were, straightway after that event, removed from the college by their parents. Young Jones had even expressed a strong wish to study for the priesthood; but was diverted from this, and entered the navy, where he became a lieutenant.

Wilhelmina, thus restored to Georgetown, and learning that her old friend Father Fenwick was at the college, was seized with a strong desire to convert him from Catholicity. From their meetings in New York, she retained an affectionate recollection of him, and, feeling now that she had been opportunely saved from the dangers of "popery," she was anxious to rescue him from the same. After some time she mustered her resolution to enter on this mission. He listened kindly, and patiently discussed several points of doctrine with her. But he did not yield, as she had hopefully expected he would. She repeated her visits, always with the same result; and then suddenly began to fear that she herself might be overcome in the discussion, and shaken from her present belief. Just when she had decided to avoid further peril of this kind, by not seeing him again, she chanced to meet him one day while calling upon Mother Agnes Brent. The subject was resumed. During this conversation, Father Fenwick, deeply grieved at some objection Wilhelmina had brought, simply looked at her and exclaimed sorrowfully: "Wilhelmina!" That look, that word, — reminding her, perhaps, of the glance of Our Lord on Peter, — smote her heart; and she burst into tears. The scales had fallen from her eyes; and once again, from that hour, she was to become a child of the Church, — this time, forever.

Her father seems not to have been notified of this reconversion, immediately; perhaps because of her dread that the wrath he had once already displayed might be renewed. Mother Agnes thus recalled the way in which it was made known to him, as the circumstances had been told to her. One morning in Lent, 1825, she was missed from the breakfast-table. As her father never enjoyed the meal unless she were

there, he made some comment on her absence.
Thereupon his wife — Wilhelmina's stepmother —
remarked: "You may be sure she has gone after that
Mr. Fenwick at the Catholic church."

It seems to have been, at that time, a point of great
persistence with non-Catholics to allude to a priest
always as "Mr." instead of as "Father." Mrs. Jones
had barely announced her surmise as to her step-
daughter's whereabouts, when Wilhelmina herself entered the room.

"Where have you been, my daughter?" the Commodore demanded.

"To church, papa," was the answer.

"To the Catholic church?" he asked.

"Yes."

"And do you not know that you are acting in
opposition to my injunctions? I could not allow even
a Catholic servant to remain under my roof." Then,
breaking into uncontrolled rage, stamping his foot, he
cried out: "If you *will* be a Catholic, quit my house.
Let me not see you again!"

Wilhelmina had never seen him so infuriated; had
never heard him speak in this way. The old hero had
rashly allowed himself to invade his own hearth-side
with the methods of the quarter-deck and seamen's
discipline. But his daughter quietly gave way to his
command, having already acquired a higher conception than his, of discipline and obedience. Taking up
the bonnet she had just laid down, she put it on and
quitted her home, never to return.

Thus cast out, she went to Father Fenwick, who
found shelter for her under the roof of Mrs. King, a

relative of Sister Genevieve King. But Wilhelmina's one wish, now, was to take up her abode and her part in the convent. Father Fenwick asked her, laughingly, whether she could wash or scrub. "Well, Father, I can learn," she replied : "I can try." He then suggested that it would be better for her to teach the convent pupils French and music, in both of which 'branches her proficiency was above the average. The question of her real vocation for cloister life having been well considered, she was at length admitted to the novitiate on the eve of the feast of the glorious St. Joseph, March 18, 1825.

And now what more inconsistent, yet more natural and to be expected, than that her father, the Commodore, hearing what she had done, should come hurrying to the convent to implore her to return to him? This is precisely what he did ; assuring her that he had never meant to send her away permanently from his house ; that he had spoken hastily, not expecting to be taken literally, and so on. The poor Commodore, in his sorrow, threw himself on his knees before her. He begged her not to abandon him, but to come back and be the comfort of his old age. (He was then fifty-five, and did in fact live to be eighty.) So afflicted was Wilhelmina at this sight, and at his piteous words, that she was on the point of acceding to his entreaty, at least for a few days or weeks. But the matter was too momentous for her to decide, and she referred it to Mother Agnes. The Superioress, foreseeing that, once at home again for a short time, the young novice would be exposed to the same remonstrances, influences, and struggles which had formerly been brought to bear against her faith, — to the peril of her vocation, and with no real happiness to her father, from so brief a concession, — advised her not to go. Wilhelmina complied with this counsel; although to do so cost her a sharp struggle with her own feelings.

A few nights after this, a phenomenon occurred and a demonstration began, which are most ludicrous as matters for record in this history, and would have been equally laughable at the time, had they not then involved a considerable threat of disorder and danger. The appearance of a ghost in the neighborhood of the convent was rumored, and even observed. Word went about that this was the ghost of Wilhelmina's dead mother, and plausible witnesses declared that she was seen to pass wailing and wandering around the walls, and was heard beseeching her errant daughter to return to her old church and her home. Soon, great crowds gathered to behold and listen to this obliging apparition, which had come forth at just the right time to create a " sensational " effect.

Men stood in the street in a compact mass; hundreds of them, as it seemed to the children of the Academy, who gazed out of the upper windows timorously, wondering at the unwonted crowd and disturbance. Carriages and buggies came, full of ladies, and drew up all around, the whole assembly waiting intently for the ghost to promenade, or for anything else that might kindly please to happen for their entertainment. The ghost, when visible, was duly clad in a shroud. But, whether the people always saw it or not, they at intervals joined in shouts of upbraiding, addressed to Miss Jones within the walls; informing her that she was much to blame for having, by her misguided course, disturbed her mother's rest in the grave.

Then they would all cry in chorus, under the windows: " Wilhelmina Jones, come out! Wilhelmina Jones, come out! *Come . . .* OUT! COME . . . OUT!"

This invitation, advice, or command — which, whether interpreted as any one or as all three of these things, was both impertinent and wholly irresponsible — they vociferated over and over, with great empha-. sis; afterward dispersing and retiring to their various accustomed forms of employment or idleness. It is to be hoped that, having finished this singular exercise, they were able to assure themselves of their own sanity and to certify to it, before going to sleep.

That a large crowd of American citizens, who regarded themselves as free and enlightened, and as cherishing a great respect for the civil and religious liberty of their fellow men and women, should have been capable of gathering in this way — at the beck of a supposed ghost — to hoot and howl before the walls of a quiet convent dwelling, inhabited by religious women, and studious little children and young girls, is one of the curiosities of American existence in our Republic at the close of the first quarter of this nineteenth century.

And yet, in the closing years of the last quarter of this same century, we find many people, who parade themselves as far more intelligent than their predecessors of 1825, publicly hooting and howling against

convents, against freedom of religion, and freedom of
education, in precisely the same style; except that,
instead of arriving as women in buggies, or as men
standing on the street, they band themselves in
"leagues" of high-sounding name, with passwords,
secret oaths, often with swords which they bombasti-
cally declare that they are ready to draw against
Catholics, if Catholics continue to take part in popular government and in the highest education of their
own children.

It is rather odd that these anti-Catholic folk of
.1825, who stretched their own sense of personal liberty to the point of license, in such uproar at the
Georgetown convent's doors, should have thought
themselves entitled to abridge and annul Miss Wilhelmina Jones's personal liberty; and to coerce her
into leaving the peaceful home and quiet, religious
life of her choice. It is also curious that, since their
objection to Catholic faith and convent establishments
was based on their opposition to "mummery" and
"superstition," they should have allowed themselves to
be misled by the mummery of a make-believe ghost,
and by the superstition that their momentary self-will
ought to rule the existence of every one around them.

Miss Jones heard all the noise, the unseemly tumult of her rough-and-ready advisers below the windows; but the only effect it had upon her was to
cause her to say to the sisters that it would be best
to let it pass unnoticed. As for the supposed com-
plaining ghost of her mother, this was soon punctured
and exploded.

After some four or five nights of this kind of dis-

turbance, some of the Catholics of Georgetown determined to test the nature of the apparition. They took
position on Lafayette Street, just opposite the convent, at dusk, provided with pistols and hickory clubs.
When the ghost came into sight, and found itself
closely pursued by these investigators, it was no longer
satisfied with "walking," — which is the approved
pace of ghosts. It *ran!* The investigators ran after
it, and caught it. The ghost turned out to be a man,
who begged abjectly that his name should never be
disclosed. He was let off by his captors ; and from
that moment the spectral manifestations ceased.

Another stratagem was soon resorted to, with the
object of inducing Wilhelmina Jones to come out of
the enclosure. The ghost having proved ineffectual,
a serving-maid of Commodore Jones's household came
to the convent grate, very late one night, just after
Matins, asking for Miss Jones; saying that her father
was very ill, perhaps dying, and wished to see his
daughter immediately. Wilhelmina came down to the
grate, saw the messenger, and had no suspicion whatever that the statement as to his illness could be false.
But "I will go upstairs and consult Mother Agnes,"
she said. Having done so, she waited in expectation
of some further word or summons. None came. She
soon afterward ascertained that her father was in his
usual health.

Her brother, Lieutenant Jones, was exasperated
against her and against the convent, because of her
remaining there steadfastly, and threatened — as
others had done before — to burn the convent. But
his incendiarism, fortunately, ended in words, — not

even in smoke. This brother lieutenant, as we mentioned on a previous page, had once become a Catholic and wished to study for the priesthood. Subsequently, his own son took up the holy vocation upon which his father had turned his back. The younger Lieutenant Jones's son became a secular priest.

Thus, while Commodore Jones tried to suppress Catholicity in his son and daughter, and succeeded for a while in the case of his son, his grandson became a priest, and his daughter, Wilhelmina, became a most useful and devout Visitandine.

Wilhelmina's love and solicitude for her father and brother always remained deep and tender, notwithstanding their harshness towards her. She prayed constantly for their conversion. In the case of her father, her prayers were rewarded only by his complete reconciliation to her acceptance of the faith and her choice of a religious career. In the case of her brother it is important to observe that he finally returned to the Church, and that his son, as we have said, entered the priesthood.

On the 15th of August, 1825, Wilhelmina Jones received the veil and her religious name of Sister Mary Stanislaus. On the same day in 1826, she pronounced her solemn vows. She died in the community, September 11, 1879, at the age of seventy-seven years and nine months; having been professed fifty-three years.

There is so much to be said of her extraordinary character and works, and of a miraculous cure accorded to her, that we must give a distinct chapter to the further description of her life, if only in outline.

"SISTER STANNY" was the affectionate nickname by which Sister Stanislaus Jones passed always among her Visitandine companions, even in her venerable and sweet old age. It seems happily to fit the endearing nature and quality of this nun, who, although the present writers never had the happiness of seeing her, is somehow just as vivid, as real to us and charming to contemplate, as to those who dwelt long with her and knew her well.

From the Georgetown MSS. may be quoted the following brief summary of her character, and tribute to it: "The novitiate of our dear Sister Stanislaus was passed in the faithful practice of every observance. With a generosity that knew no bounds she surrendered her heart to grace. In the convent, a model of exactitude and fervor; at the academy, devoting her mind, with its rich and varied store of treasures, her brilliant talents and accomplishments, to the high mission which led her onward and upward. While she cultivated the minds and developed the talents of her pupils, she attracted their hearts to God; and numbers have testified to her holy influence both during their school-days and in after life, by their virtuous example as well as by the faithful and loving correspondence they always entertained with their dear teacher."

She was for several years closely associated in certain charges with Sister Michaella Jenkins, afterward Superior. While Sister Stanislaus was Directress of the Academy, Sister Michaella was her first aid. So, too, in the music class. Hence there sprang up between them a strong mutual confidence and friendship. Sister Stanny devoted herself chiefly and with great ability to conducting classes in French, Italian, Spanish, German, Latin, and music. Great though her intellectual and scholarly attainments were, — a constant object of admiration, indeed, from others, — she did not pride herself upon them. On the contrary, she was so simple and unostentatious in the employment of her learning, that none of her pupils, whether Protestant or Catholic, could fail to be impressed by the sanctity and unselfishness of their teacher. She scarcely ever lost a moment of time, and kept her knitting always on hand to fill up the intervals between lessons.

Her obedience was an obedience of faith; prompt, unfaltering and unrestricted. "She was apparently equal," wrote Mother Michaella Jenkins, "in love and devotion to every Superior, showing or evincing no preference." Her tranquillity, mingled with diligence and zeal in all duties, had been acquired, nevertheless, in spite of her natural disposition, which was high-tempered. . But of this natural temper she rarely betrayed any sign, except by a flush of the cheek or a look or tone more serious than usual; and even for these hardly perceptible, almost imaginary failures of patience she would fall on her knees and ask pardon, — sometimes calling herself, in half playful yet sincere remorse, "Holy Father's little snapping turtle;" and then, in a moment, the episode was over. "How beautiful was her religious life! — all bright!" Mother Michaella continues, in the letter from which

we have just made extract. " She never complained of
what she had to do, and received very little praise or
sympathy; but she did n't seek it. Every one believed
her *au fait* in all she taught, and that it cost her no
fatigue; yet she was always delicate, and seldom entirely free from suffering. But she never complained.
Bright as a bird all the time, she never sought rest;
finding joy and happiness in every duty. I now think
it so wonderful. I never knew her to consult appetite
in anything, or to think or speak of what she liked.
Her faith was beautiful. She could so readily believe
every pious thing in the lives of the saints or otherwise.

" For many years Sister Stanislaus had charge of
the musical department, both vocal and instrumental;
guiding also the sacred music of the church choir, and
joining her voice to the sweet strains her hands drew
forth from the organ in praise of her Maker.

" In her exterior there was a rare union of seemingly opposite qualities. With the refinement and
polish of a lady of the world, there was the genial,
loving grace of a child. Her conversation, calm and
gentle, was yet animated with a certain ardor and vivacity that rendered her words more attractive and
penetrating. Her heart recollected in God, or rather
dwelling ever in the Heart of Jesus, — she seemed
little to regard what passed around her; yet when
consolation or assistance was needed, [her] charity
never failed to dictate the right word and the right
action." An exquisite instance of this inspired
faculty was when a postulant, suffering from a violent
toothache, came in to breakfast in the infirmary one

morning, and showed great confusion and anxiety lest
the sisters sitting at table with her should be disgusted
by her swollen and discolored face.   Sister Stanny, on
rising from table, went to her, caressed her tenderly,
and said in a gentle tone: "My dear child, your face
is not so bruised and swollen as the face of our Lord
was."

The words and the act brought tears to the eyes of
the sufferer, and left an indelible impression of sweetness in her heart.

Her voice was habitually soft and soothing; and,
even when oppressed with pain herself, as she frequently was, she thought first of her ailing sisters,
comforted them, and breathed silent aspirations for
them, which seemed always to bring them relief.
This trait of sympathy was probably inherited, at least
in part, from her father, whose generous and gentle
treatment of his wounded enemies in battle has been
eulogized by American historians.   To him she attributed her own active interest in the poor and
ignorant; her love for them.   She took delight in
teaching the children of the poor, and little negroes
received from her as much attention as though they
had been the brightest offspring of rich and favored
educated people.   Besides her regular Sunday instruction for them, she kept a night class in which the
catechism was explained; and this the aged as well as
the younger men and women eagerly attended.   Dealing with such folk, so near the level of the animal,
was hard work, often positively repulsive; but the
zeal of Sister Stanny for it never flagged.

Nor does the list of her tasks and services end here.

She was often called upon to give "retreats" to secular ladies who wished to spend a few days in the retirement of meditation and prayer at the convent; as also to Catholic pupils of the Academy. "Numbers presented themselves at the convent parlor to receive the words of life from her lips; and only God can know the marvels she wrought, the many sinners she brought back to God; how many she sweetly led to the sacraments, after years of absence." On this point, one secular lady wrote: "It would seem presumptuous to speak of her life as a religious, except that its benign, useful and beautiful influence on those outside the convent might not be so well known except to the witnesses of those effects outside. It is scarcely possible to estimate the weight of her example."

We shall specify only one instance; and this one because it is external and obvious enough to claim at least the curious attention of that interesting personage, "the general reader." A young lady in Georgetown (whose name is given simply as "Fanny") had a strong wish to become a Catholic; but her mother was averse to this, chiefly for the reason that it might hurt her prospects of marrying well; since, among the cultivated and well-to-do, Protestants then formed the vast majority, and Fanny's people were of that order. Sister Stanny — knowing well that the securing of a soul's true happiness in the faith is not a matter of violence or over-persuasion, or of exciting dissension in families — advised Fanny to redouble her confidence in God and the Mother of our Lord; and to offer up three Ave Marias or Hail Marys to the

Blessed Virgin, daily, for the means and opportunity
of accomplishing her religious aim peacefully.   Three
or four years passed; the young lady continually
offering her prayers for this intention.   At last, that
very power of social prestige which had been opposed
to her was brought round to her aid.   Señor Calderon de la Barca, the Spanish minister at Washington,
fell in love with her and wished to make her his wife.
She accepted him, and the match was considered by
her family most desirable.   But as Señor Calderon
de la Barca was a man of rank and the representative
of Spain, he was obliged to ask the consent of his
sovereign, who gave it only on condition that the proposed bride should become a Catholic.   Thereupon
social prestige and worldly prudence in the persons of
Fanny's family were ardently in favor of her entering
the faith she had so long wished to profess.

She, with their full consent, repaired to the convent, made a "retreat" there under Sister Stanny's
direction; was then baptized; took her First Communion; received confirmation; and, by a special
dispensation from the Archbishop, was married in the
convent chapel, where she had so long repeated her
Hail Mary for the very object of becoming a Catholic.

"Coincidence," the so-called wise folk of the materialistic sort will call it.   Well, Plato said, "God
works by geometry eternally;" and we Christians,
with a faith quite equal to his but more acutely discerning, may truthfully declare: "God works eternally by coincidences."

These are not without a deep and spiritual meaning, any more than geometry is.

Sister Stanny's wide-reaching sympathy caused her to be the leader or prompter of a movement to permit the presence and the services of Catholic chaplains in the Penitentiaries of the several States of the Union. She saw, once, a despairing letter from a prisoner in the Albany penitentiary to one of his friends. She wrote him, therefore, a letter wherein she tried to teach him resignation. This letter was lent to another prisoner, then to another; and so, before long, Sister Stanny found herself in correspondence with a number of convicts. Thereupon she aroused the interest of an influential friend, and through this friend suggested to the Bishop of Albany that he appoint a chaplain. It was done. The late Father Noethen was named to the charge; and a vast and beautiful work of charity was thus inaugurated.[1]

It appears to us very well worth while for those who have never informed themselves as to convent life, the function of monastic orders, the spiritual and the practical charitable influences emanating from them, to consider these few simple facts which we have just set down. To any honest mind it must, we think, be patent from these facts that convents and monasteries do not wish their inmates to be miserable and forlorn; that sisters who give their lives to Christ do not thereby seek to promote discord among families, or to oppose marriage and giving in marriage; and that, above all, the long years and concentred energy of devotion, prayer, and spiritual cultivation in secluded, enclosed communities are not wasted to the rest of the

[1] Files of *The Ave Maria:* Notre Dame, Indiana.

world, but result in raying out endless waves of blessed, helpful, immediate, and enduring good influence.

Reservoirs of spiritual force, stored up for all the needs of the troubled world, are just as essential for the daily welfare of mankind, as those in which a supply of water is kept to cleanse and allay the thirst of cities. And the reservoirs of spiritual force have the further advantage that they provide for the eternal as well as the transient welfare of the race.

When Sister Stanislaus had been twelve years beneficently active in the convent, indications that she was suffering from cancer in the breast aroused alarm and dread in the community. After much consultation with physicians, her superiors decided that she ought to go to Baltimore, in order to be placed under the care of Dr. Nathan Smith, then a celebrated surgeon there. An out sister accompanied her thither. It was, of course, a trying experience for her to leave the quietude of the convent, with its regular religious duties and accustomed tasks, even though she was to be sheltered in the Visitation house at Baltimore. That house was then feeble; limited in numbers and resources. But Commodore Jones was in Baltimore at the time; he employed a nurse to wait upon his daughter, and paid her board and expenses.

It was necessary to undertake an operation, in order to remove the cancer; and there was question whether she would survive the ordeal. About an hour before the operation — so Sister Eleonora, of the convent there, wrote afterward — Sister Stanny knelt in a corner of the infirmary, making an offering to God of all that she was about to suffer, and of her life also, if it pleased Him to take that. When the crucial moment came, the other sisters knelt before the Blessed Sacrament, in the next room, which was their chapel, and prayed for her; yet they did not hear a moan or so much as a sigh from her. During the operation, while the surgeon made his deep incision, she held in her hand a tiny picture of the Sacred Heart, and neither flinched nor betrayed fear.

The blood spurted forth from the cut; and two or three little specks of it fell upon the picture that she held, remaining on it, just below the wound in the Sacred Heart, as though they had been designedly painted there and were a part of it. Every one was struck by this little fact, — another " coincidence," in which the blind or the squint-eyed may not discover any serious significance, — and by the circumstance that the little painting had not been spoiled, but had been perfected, by this accident. Her brother, the young Lieutenant Jones, — who, as we have said, had been violently opposed to her entering the Visitation Order, and had gratuitously offered to burn the Georgetown convent, — so highly appreciated the importance of his sister's blood having thus been shed upon the picture of the Sacred Heart and having become incorporated with it, that he had the picture encased in a gold locket, and thereafter wore it as an amulet over his own heart. This same brother, as we have also mentioned, returned to the bosom of Holy Church, and his son took holy orders as a priest.

While she was in Baltimore at this time (1837),

Commodore Jones begged of Archbishop Whitfield that she might be permitted to dine at his house. The Archbishop consented, and himself came as a guest. This dinner was the occasion of a complete reconcilement on the part of the old Commodore and his son with Sister Stanny's monastic retirement.

Sister Stanny maintained an intense devotion to the Sacred Heart of Jesus; and during the last thirty years of her life she received Holy Communion every day; allowing no illness or suffering to interfere with her fasting preparatory to receiving the sacred bread, even though the sisters in her hours of illness besought her to take a drop of water after midnight, when the ante-communion fast begins.

Faber says: " Show me a grateful soul, and I will show you one that is holy." Gratitude was a pronounced trait in Sister Stanny, towards God and towards every one who showed kindness to her in health or sickness, or who were spiritual benefactors. So, gratefully, she lived and died, though enduring much distress from a nervous malady, for a number of years before she passed away. An impressive point, it seems to us, in this holy conventual existence of hers is that, as she reconciled her brave, autocratic and disciplinarian, yet insubordinate, warrior father and her stormy brother to her life of religious peace, so she also united in herself the gentle traits and the impassioned impulses she had inherited, but consented that the grace of God should transfuse them into a nobler existence, radiant with supernatural light.

XIII. AN OUTSIDER'S VIEW. — MOTHER JULIANA. — FATHER
CLORIVIÈRE DIES.

Before these events, — in 1826, indeed, — a quaint
little book, now rare, was published at New Haven,
which, at the dawn of the national period in our literature, gave sundry glimpses of home travel that are
still of interest.[1] It was written by a Protestant lady,
who described a call made by her at the Georgetown
convent; and her brief account is worth quoting here,
to show how the institution impressed a wholly unin-
structed outsider, who approached it in a spirit of
good will.

"From the college I went to the convent," she
says. " My curiosity was wrought up to the highest
pitch as I traced the uneven streets leading from the
college to the convent. I felt what Addison said,
viz. : 'Everything new or uncommon raises pleasure.'
I had often read of nuns and convents, but now I was
to be gratified in full. . . . A few minutes brought
me to the door of the convent, at the west end of the
town. Here, as directed, I opened the door without
knocking, and, entering a small passage, pulled a bell,
which brought a nun to the inside door, when I informed her of my business. She directed me to step
into a small room on my left, which she called the
'speaking-room.' After waiting here a few minutes,
two other nuns approached, on the opposite side of an
iron grate, which separated them from the world and
me ! I had, however, a full view of them. They

[1] *Sketches of History, Life and Manners in the United States.* By a
Traveller. New Haven : Printed for the Author, 1826.

drew up close 'to the bars, saluted, and conversed in terms of the utmost sweetness and condescension. Amongst other things, I asked them 'if they were happy.' They both replied, 'very happy; would not exchange their present situation for any earthly treasure,' and they looked so.

"Having heard that Catholics look upon all other sects as heretics, I asked them if it were true. 'No,' they answered, 'God forbid that we should think so. We believe there are many good people who are not of our religion.' [1] One of them had been in the convent eleven years, the other eight; and in all that time they would not have left if they could. They have the option in two years. They were dressed in coarse, black stuff gowns, with wide sleeves, resembling those of a clergyman's gown. Their heads were first bound with a black cloth, which came low down on the forehead. Over this a white cloth, and over all a hood. This hood is of the same stuff as the dress, and like 'a slouch bonnet.' Take the pasteboard out of one of those bonnets, fold a few inches of the front back, and you will have an idea of these hoods. They wear a small, square, white handkerchief, hardly sufficient to cover the bosom. This is

[1] The question and answer as here given convey a wrong impression. The Church *does* pronounce all sects "heretical." What "A Traveller" must have meant to ask, and the nuns doubtless understood her to mean, was whether the Church regards sects or heretics as already lost. In their reply they evidently referred to the fact that the Church, while condemning heresy, does not pronounce judgment on individual heretics or others, but believes that many outside of the visible fold are truly "invisible members" if they hold the fundamental doctrines of Christianity, and are living in good faith according to the dictates of an upright conscience.

hollowed out under the neck so as to extend up to the ears on either side. On their breasts they wear a silver cross. This, they informed me, was the uniform dress of the convent. I expressed a wish to get into the building ; but they said they dare not admit me without the consent of the mother superior,[1] and she could not be seen at that time, not even by the nuns themselves. She was gone into *retirement* [retreat], which means that she secludes herself day and night in some part of the convent for several weeks. This ceremony she performs once a year, which time she spends in fasting and prayer. I would have given much to have seen her, as she was the sister of a respected friend of mine.

" . . . These nuns dare not converse with strangers unless there be two present. I never beheld that simplicity and innocence, that humble demeanor which distinguishes these nuns, in any of the sex. They have a most heavenly expression in their looks. They are humanity itself, and well they may ; they have no earthly care, and spend their time in continual devotion." [2]

Before continuing upon the regular course of the annals, a few words may be given to that special

---

[1] Mother Juliana Matthews.

[2] The authoress inadvertently made two mistakes in her brief account. She speaks of the spiritual retreat (which she calls "retirement") as lasting several weeks, whereas the term of it is really but a few days. Further, it is not correct to say that the nuns "dare not" converse with strangers unless there be two present. It is the custom for two to be present in receiving strangers; but there is nothing to prevent *one* from entering into conversation if need be.

friend of " Sister Stanny," Mother Michaella Jenkins, who became Superior not here at Georgetown but at Baltimore, whither she went with the colony led by Mother Juliana Matthews to found a new house there in 1837.   Sister Michaella had been educated at Emmitsburg by Mother Seton, of renowned memory as a leader in education ; and Baltimore was the place of her birth.   After presiding over the new community in that city six years, she was requested to fill an unexpired term at Wheeling, and was there four times elected Superior.   Her life in religion, like that of Sister Stanislaus, was a long one : for when she died, January 3, 1881, she was seventy-seven years old, and had been a professed nun for fifty-two years.

The cloistered mode of being, notwithstanding many prevalent ideas regarding its desolateness and deprivations, would seem often to be favorable to longevity. For those who imagine that the fretful existence of the outer world is the only activity, would it not be well to ponder on the fact that, all the while, these quiet but long and busy lives are going on within sanctified enclosures ; that these lives also are bearing rich fruit of industry, of education, of beneficent self-denial   and   spiritual   development, — development undertaken not for mere selfish peace or personal salvation, but generously offered in prayer and dedicated to the welfare of all human beings ?

Another most interesting example of a useful and extended conventual career is that of Mother Juliana Matthews ; all the more so in that she, by nature, shrank from the difficult and complex duties to which finally most of her years were given.

A glance at her history will bring out its significance. She succeeded Mother Agnes Brent as Superior, being elected March 18, 1825. A grand-niece
of Archbishop Neale, she was placed in the convent
Academy by her uncle, Father Matthews, of Washington, at the age of ten. She entered the sisterhood;
finally taking solemn vows when she was twenty-two.
But, finding herself appointed Mistress of Novices
when she was only twenty, her dread of the responsibility was so great that she besought the Blessed Virgin's aid to release her from any further cares of this
kind; and for some ten years she enjoyed compara-
tive immunity. Perhaps this respite was providentially designed to give her time to mature and gather
strength for the unusual burdens that she was yet to
bear. If there was one thing she would have preferred to avoid it was apparently the having to endure
those exacting duties and anxieties inseparable from
holding important office in a community; and yet
this was the precise work which the Divine guide of
life had evidently selected for her to do.

Chosen as Superior in her thirtieth year (1825),
as we have noted, she was elected for a second triennial in 1828. Although during the latter part of
this term she largely delegated her authority to Sister
Magdalene Augustine (who had come over from
France), and even managed to hasten the regular
election by one year, so that Sister Magdalene was
installed in her place, in 1830; yet, as soon as the
latter went to Mobile, to establish a house there,
Mother Juliana was at once reëlected. Before she
had rounded out this last term, Archbishop Eccleston

appointed her to conduct the Visitation colony to Baltimore and to become its head. Later, she was also called upon to found new convents of the Order in Washington, District of Columbia, in Brooklyn, and in Richmond. Foundress of four Visitation houses, she was made Superior *ten times* during her life; once, as it happens, for each of those years during which her prayer for freedom from care had been granted.

Those who know the difficulties of constructive and executive work in the establishing and carrying on of associations among human beings, even those organized for high and ideal purposes, can form some notion of the enormous labor as well as the fine administrative skill demanded from Mother Juliana by these undertakings. Is it not curious, in looking back, to recognize that, however obedient and willing to serve in all other directions, the one particular service which she was called to was that for which she felt a deep reluctance? In the religious life, beside all the usual and expected sacrifices which are accepted at the outset, there are evidently other and special abnegations, which the disciplined and devout soul must be prepared to undergo cheerfully as emergencies arise. Perhaps the unassuming self-distrust of Mother Juliana was a means of aid to her in the success of her government. A summary of her work and character, written by Sister Stanislaus Jones, records that "in her dove-like soul there was a wonderful combination of simplicity and prudence, gentleness and firmness, talent and guilelessness. All who saw her were struck with astonishment and admiration, at discovering such

rare worth and superior endowments of mind united
to such childlike artlessness and simplicity."

Mother Juliana, too, lived long ; dying in holiness
at her Richmond convent, March 18, 1867, a little
over seventy-two years of age.

In those days of 1826, there came another change
upon the interior history of the Georgetown convent.
Father Clorivière, who had now been confessor and
director for nearly nine years, was stricken ill in May,
and died September 29th, carefully tended during his
long helplessness by priests and physicians.   Although
he suffered a paralysis of speech, his mind remained
clear, and he made known by signs that he wished
to be buried under the Chapel of the Sacred Heart.
While, his life slowly ebbing, he lay patiently in his
little dwelling (formerly Archbishop Neale's house)
adjoining the chapel, the saintly Bishop Bruté, his
bosom friend, visited him constantly.   Many a time
had this good Bishop come to see him, walking the
whole distance from Emmitsburg, over thirty miles
distant, with no refection by the way except the apples
that he picked from roadside orchards ; and many a
happy hour had they spent together in the modest,
plainly furnished sitting-room of the director's small
· abode.   Now, as death approached, Bishop Bruté
remained by his bedside, often repeating, " *Mon ami,
mon ami !   De la croix au ciel !* "

The Bishop, then simple Father Bruté, was revered
for his sanctity throughout life, and even his canonization was spoken of afterward, though never undertaken.   It must have been a great happiness to Father

Clorivière to die peacefully in the presence of so holy
a man, attended by his prayers and consolations; and it
has remained a hallowed memory in the convent, since,
that he should have been a visitor within its walls.

Father Clorivière had so well carried out, extended,
and solidified the work begun by Archbishop Neale,
through his untiring ministrations and the sacrifice of
his own property, as to merit almost the title of a second Founder. In an obituary notice of him, Bishop
England, of Charleston, justly pointed out as monu-
ments of his zeal, which would cause him to be held
in remembrance by later generations, the beautiful
chapel built by him, the Academy greatly enlarged and
increased in efficiency, a "benevolent school" put in
operation for poor children, and "a convent almost
created anew."

XIV. FATHER WHEELER. — SISTERS FROM EUROPE. — THE YTURBIDES.

In earlier years the late Father Clorivière had
made his theological studies under the Sulpitians;
and among those who stood near his bedside in his
last hours was a Sulpitian priest from Baltimore, the
Rev. Michael F. Wheeler.

Although he was a stranger to the community, the
sisters were impressed by his piety and his distinctly
ecclesiastical bearing; so much so, in fact, that they
greatly desired to see him appointed to the place
made vacant by the loss of their father and friend
who had just been taken from them. They sent peti-
tions to the Archbishop at Baltimore, who finally
granted their wish. But when Father Wheeler had

been in active service as their director some two years, his health became so precarious — and, by the way, it is astonishing how often these servants of holy aims accomplish great tasks with apparently the most inadequate strength — that his physician ordered a change of climate for him.

Father Wheeler accordingly decided to go to Rome and to France. He had for some time been troubled in mind as to the exact basis of constitution and authority on which the community stood. Pius VII., it is true, had approved it and given to it a formal foundation ; but his rescript, while granting certain privileges as to keeping schools, did so on express condition that the Georgetown nuns should follow the ordinary track of Sisters of the Visitation. This, however, it had been found impracticable to do. Owing to difference of climate, the customs of the people, and to necessities of the Academy and the free school for the poor, the minute directions laid down by St. Francis de Sales as to hours of meals could not be observed. The admission of day pupils also compelled some relaxation as to the rigid rules for enclosure.

As faith and holiness are the life-blood of a convent, so absolute obedience, respect for the rule, and close adherence to authority are the brain and the hand by which it works. Therefore, while each of the Archbishops of Baltimore succeeding Archbishop Neale had regarded the indult of Pius VII. as a sufficient warrant to the community, even in its slight departures from the original rule, Father Wheeler still felt it advisable to determine this matter with scrupulous clearness. The voyage for health which

he was now forced to take was to him the welcome
means of visiting the Holy Father and laying the
whole subject before him.

He arrived at Rome in May, 1829. Every detail
of the case was submitted to Pope Pius VIII., who
issued a rescript dated May 10th, approving all the
changes made in the Institute of the nuns, and likewise " the changes which may perhaps be made in the
process of time, on account of the circumstances of
place and government. He declares, moreover, that
these changes neither do, nor shall, prevent them
from being considered nuns of the Visitation or from
enjoying the same privileges and rights bestowed on
the other nuns of the same Institute, who follow St.
Francis de Sales as their Founder and Leader." On
the following day, Monday, May 11, 1829, the Pope
gave Father Wheeler an audience, showed great interest in the community, asked many questions about it,
and gave his blessing to all the members, a list of
their names being given to him and carefully taken
into his keeping.

From Rome Father Wheeler went to Annecy, the
mother house; and, as the result of a circular from
Mother Margaret Clanchy, there, to the convents of
Mans, Valence, and Friburg, each of these contributed
a valuable member toward a little delegation which it
was proposed to send to Georgetown. For the sisters
here in the United States cherished the longing, still,
to have some personal contact and communication with
their spiritual kinsfolk from that distant country
where the Order had originated; to learn lessons from
them in detail, and to be assured from that source, if

ACADEMY PLAYGROUND

possible, that they were working in the right way. The nuns appointed for this mission, from the monasteries just mentioned, were respectively : Sisters Agatha Langlois (Mans), Marie Regis Mordant (Valence), and Magdalene Augustine d'Arreger (Friburg). They assembled at the first Paris monastery, and embarked with Father Wheeler at Havre, July 22, 1829.

After a stormy passage of twenty-seven days they reached New York, and about a week later, traveling slowly, came in sight of the tower and steeple of the Georgetown convent; whereupon they saluted their goal with the *Salve Regina,* the *Sub tuum,* and the Litany of the Blessed Virgin ; and were soon after warmly greeted in their new home. " It would be impossible," wrote Sister Magdalene Augustine, to the European convents, " to convey to you an idea of the impression made on us by the first sight of their meek and humble Mother.[1] She is all humility and simplicity. . . . We did not expect to find so great a resemblance between our American sisters and ourselves. . . . Their docility, their zeal for the exact observance makes them willing to do anything in order to become true Visitandines."

These new arrivals — the two French sisters and the one Swiss, applied themselves first to the study of English, which they learned so rapidly that in a month's time they were able to understand conversation, as well as the religious instruction and spiritual readings given in public. The joy of the Georgetown nuns in the pleasant association with these European

[1] Juliana Matthews.

Visitandines which ensued, was great.   They followed
their steps closely, and hung upon their words as
though listening to the voice of oracles.   In fact,
there can be no doubt that the presence of such representatives from the older communities beyond sea was
of great benefit to this younger community in the
New World, — that benefit which results from direct
personal contact and mutual exchange of ideas between
those who, dwelling long apart in the separation of
geographic limits, have yet worked in common for a
supreme spiritual aim; who, when brought together,
are thrilled and revivified by a sudden and real perception of their unity in the freedom of a great, a true
development.

This meeting and this perception form a type of
that unity of all earnest, holy souls which, it is to be
hoped, and is believed, will come to pass, when those
who now bend all their efforts to misunderstanding
Catholic Christianity shall gently, simply open their
minds to a clear understanding of it and realize with
a surprised delight that, after all, this was just what
they, in their own form of sincerity, had been aiming
for and working for.   That would be a union of *all*
good souls.   This was the reunion of a few, who had
lived far asunder yet equally in reverent obedience to
the Eternal Will.   And so they recognized and rejoiced in one another; as the sunrise of each new day
beholds itself reflected in some calm surface of the
ancient sea, — both humbly, yet magnificently, true
to the unchanging law of God.

Sister M. Agatha Langlois (of Mans) was appointed Mistress of Novices.   So great was her pre-

cision in every iota of duty and obedience, that she was called " the living Rule." Her zealous and maternal guidance had the happiest results. Although she held office only for about eighteen months, she initiated her disciples so thoroughly that several of them, in after years, became eminent and admirable Superiors, both in Georgetown and in other houses. Illness, however, obliged her to return to her native climate, and Sister Marie Regis accompanied her thither, much to the regret of the Visitation here.

Toward the close of 1832, also, Sister Magdalene Augustine d'Arreger was summoned away from . Georgetown. Mother Juliana had, immediately on her coming, delegated to her many of her own powers ; sharing the administration with her so that the nuns might profit directly by her directions, her permissions or counsels, and in 1830 Sister Magdalene Augustine had been elected Superior. But now the newly consecrated Bishop of Mobile came to Georgetown, announcing that he intended to build a house of the Visitation in his episcopal city ; a legacy having been left to him for the purpose. There was not, at that time, a single Catholic church or school in his diocese : hence he was very anxious to have the aid of Mother Magdalene's experience and thorough training in the inception and management of the new enterprise. She could not refuse this appeal for help and the opportunity given by it for a new service and religion. Calling to her side, therefore, several of the sisters (among them Margaret Marshall, who soon afterward became Mother Superior at Mobile), she departed for the South ; and Mother Juliana Matthews was re-elected in her place.

This house at Mobile was the first " filiation " from Georgetown.

The three European sisters, it will thus be seen, did not abide very long within the cloistered demesne of Georgetown. But their presence there had been of good effect. It had established a vital link between this community and its congeners in the Old World. It left wholesome influences and sweet remembrances that have continued to the present time.

At the period here referred to — 1829 to 1832 — the convent Academy had given to its course of studies a range almost as extended as that which it now covers, with increased facilities, with more teachers, and recent advances of knowledge in certain departments. Mathematics, philosophy, chemistry, physics, etc., were taught; together with literature, all the modern languages, and instrumental music (the piano, the harp, the guitar). There were about a hundred pupils in the Academy. In the *free school*, or benevolent school (founded by Father Clorivière), — and it is worth while, here, when so much is said nowadays about " free schools " being the outgrowth of non-Catholic movements only, to remark that this free school simply followed the example set by the Catholic Church for centuries previously, — there were one hundred and fifty pupils; fifty more than in the Academy where fees were paid.

The community itself numbered fifty-seven, including the novices.

It is a circumstance of some historic interest that, before Father Wheeler set out for Europe, the widow of Yturbide, the self-proclaimed Emperor of Mexico, had come to Georgetown to live, and had placed her four daughters in the Academy.

Agustin de Yturbide, a native of Mexico and an officer in the Spanish army there, had taken a very important part in the war against the Mexican revolutionists, from 1810 to 1820. In the latter year, prompted by the fact that a constitutional revolution had occurred in Spain itself, he made an attempt to solve the Mexican problem by proposing to make the country an independent monarchy under the rule of a prince of the Spanish Bourbon dynasty. This plan, now famous, included this sovereignty as a part of " the three guaranties, " — the two others being maintenance of the Catholic faith and the union of Spaniards and Mexicans. It was received with great favor by the people, but unfortunately was opposed by Ferdinand VIII. of Spain, who insisted upon regarding it as another form of rebellion. Thereupon Yturbide, with the support of the army, proclaimed himself emperor and was recognized by the popular assembly, but was finally defeated by a republican uprising under General Santa Anna, his former friend and supporter. He resigned the crown, and was allowed to depart for Europe as a pensioned exile. Rashly returning to Mexico in 1824, on the plea of offering his services as a general to the Republic, in case of invasion from Spain, he was decreed an outlaw, and, on landing, was arrested and shot.

Madam Yturbide, after settling in Georgetown, spent much of her time at the convent. A little cell — and a " cell," be it known to those who have a

horror for the word, is not a place of confinement, or
dungeon, but simply a bedroom and living-room furnished in the plainest manner — was assigned to her.
Although she did not devote herself to the complete
religious life with the idea of taking vows, she was
permitted to wear the Visitation garb while in the
cloister. Her second daughter, Johanna, desired to
enter the novitiate ; but, dying quite young, before it
was possible for her to accomplish this, she received
the privilege of taking the vows conditionally and was
buried as a Visitation nun, in October, 1828, while
Father Wheeler was on his way to Italy.

Her elder sister, Sabina, some twelve or fourteen
months afterward, entered the novitiate ; but her stay
was not long.

Religious orders do not care to receive into their
membership any one who does not develop a true vocation for the high purposes of consecrated life, and
that " staying power " necessary for the fulfillment of
its regular and self-denying duties, which must be
persisted in year after year ; a persistence monotonous
in its way, perhaps, and to some natures unendurable,
— not easy for any one, yet full of peace and happiness to those who have the right qualifications and
the grace to continue in it.

Instead of reaching out right and left for new
recruits, at all hazards, — as many non-Catholics
imagine is the case, — religious communities set up
the most careful barriers, and provide every safeguard for the selection of those only who are fitted to
become members in this enduring phalanx of religion.

We have known young men and women of Catholic

parentage and ancestry, thoroughly devout, very anxious to enter religious communities and give their whole lives to these societies; who yet, after a year or two of probation, have been found lacking in the steady, persistent qualities essential to such a career, and, greatly to their own regret, have been obliged to withdraw from a task for which they were not suited.

In the next chapter we shall record something remarkable of such a woman, Mrs. Mattingly, to whom extraordinary mercies of another kind were accorded, although — notwithstanding her earnest desire — the capacity for becoming a nun was not granted to her.

XV. THE STORY OF MRS. MATTINGLY.

It was in 1829 that Mrs. Mattingly, of Washington, was admitted as a postulant at Georgetown. She was a widow, remarkable for her great piety. Her family, the Carberys, were well known in Washington, where they held honorable positions in the Church, the army, and the magistracy; and as her eldest brother, Captain Thomas Carbery, was Mayor of Washington, everything connected with her extraordinary history became a matter of public notice and interest.

Notwithstanding her rare spirituality and devotedness in her faith, Father Matthews, her confessor, told her plainly that she had no vocation for life in the cloister; but her yearning to attempt it was unappeasable; and, simply with the purpose of convincing her by a practical test that she was not qualified for this kind of spiritual service, he finally permitted her to begin the novitiate.

Doubtless, one active cause of the intense longing she felt to give herself wholly to religious seclusion was that, five years earlier, she had herself experienced a miraculous recovery from mortal illness, which was one of the most amazing as well as thoroughly attested cases of the kind recorded in recent times, with the exception of some of the miracles at Lourdes.

In the summer of 1817 Mrs. Mattingly — who was then living, widowed, in the house of her brother, Captain Thomas Carbery — began to suffer from pains in the left side, which gradually increased in severity and became concentrated on the lower and outer part of the left breast. In fine, a tumor had formed there, which was examined in September by three physicians, two of whom pronounced it scirrhus, the third also advising immediate extirpation. His counsel was not followed ; but a treatment with hemlock and mercury, according to the medical canons of that period, was entered upon assiduously. It was without effect. The malignant growth went on developing as a cancer of the most deadly kind. An account of her illness, quoted in the annals from a published report of the whole matter, drawn up afterward by Bishop England, gives in detail the threatening symptoms and the frightful sufferings that marked the progress of the disease. These having been duly recorded, and authenticated by affidavits of her brother, Mayor Carbery, of her two sisters Ruth and Catherine Carbery, and of Mrs. Sibylla Carbery, the widow of her uncle, General Henry Carbery, it is not necessary to repeat here the long and distressful enumeration of pangs endured by the patient. A brief summary will be enough to convey vividly an idea of the terrible condition to which she was reduced.

Her illness assumed an intense form in the spring of 1818, and continued with increasing virulence for six years. Throughout that time her sensations, as described by herself, were like those which might be caused if her side were bored with an augur or pinched with forceps. A seemingly permanent contraction of the *pectoralis major* kept the left arm clinging to her side, so that its pressure greatly intensified these pains. She had an incessant, racking cough, accompanied with violent spasms; also with discharges of blood and other matter from the mouth. Even in the first year she was thought to be at the point of death; and her brother Lewis, living at some distance, was abruptly summoned both then and in the following years, innumerable times, to receive her last farewell. She had no appetite; a great part of the time she could take no solid food; she suffered intense thirst and was barely able to articulate audibly. "The pulse was scarcely perceptible to the nicest touch," her brother, Mayor Carbery, testified under oath. Frequently her prostration was so great that her attendants doubted whether she were still alive, and resorted to artificial means in order to ascertain whether respiration continued. "Her physician declared that her case was out of the reach of medicine, and prescribed her only palliatives." [1]

Although, in the intervals between her severer paroxysms, she was able to occupy herself a little with

[1] Bishop England's report.

knitting and sewing, she assured Father Matthews —
as he also specified under oath — that she never enjoyed a moment's cessation of pain. During the
whole six years she never left her bed for any considerable time — so her two sisters testified — except
on two occasions ; once when she was moved from her
brother's house in which she had been taken ill, to
his new residence ; and once when she went out, with
assistance, to visit an old and favorite servant of the
family, who was believed to be dying. The place
where this servant lived was only ten yards from the
door ; yet the effort of going thither brought on a
violent hemorrhage. Even the slightest motion resulted in agonies so acute that her sisters, for fear of
such results, often had to refrain from making up her
bed for two weeks at a time.

So protracted was her illness, and so many were
the witnesses, that it is hardly possible to set up a
theory that she exaggerated her sufferings by imagination or hysteria. The visible details of physical
disintegration could not, of course, be explained, or
exaggerated, or diminished, by imagination. That
she was not nervously inclined to magnify her inter-
nal, invisible suffering seems to be clear from the
affidavit of her confessor, Rev. William Matthews,
who visited her once a week during the last year of
her illness, to hear her confession and give her communion. He says : " She apparently suffered more
than I had thought a mortal frame could endure ; and
this with heroic fortitude and edifying resignation.
*I never heard her utter a complaint. She never
showed any solicitude to regain her health.* Her

prayer was, as she told me, that the will of God might be done in her."

Clearly, she was a "patient" in the full sense of the word ; a sufferer, yet resigned. Even indifferentists, and those who have no very active belief, agree that to be "patient" means not merely to suffer, but to do so without complaint. The faithful hold the same view ; but, in addition, they look upon true suffering as a duty borne for God, a tribute offered to Him ; and they ratify the declaration of St. Francis de Sales that it is the only absolutely unselfish action we can perform. This unselfish offering Mrs. Mattingly exemplified almost in perfection.

Her eldest brother made affidavit that "he had seen her, several times a day, entirely deprived of action by the intensity of the pain ; and that she had frequently lain in such situation for twenty or thirty minutes at a time, so as to create doubts whether she was alive or dead." Ruth and Catherine Carbery affirmed that her general condition, as we have described it, remained about the same until some three weeks before her recovery, when it became much worse, and all her symptoms seemed to announce the swift approach of death.

Finally on the first of March, 1824, she began a novena of prayer to the sacred Name of Jesus. This was to be performed in conjunction with Prince Hohenlohe, whose custom of praying for the recovery of the sick, at stated times, in unison with the faithful in various parts of the world, has already been explained in our account of Sister Apollonia's cure.

Readers unfamiliar with subjects of this kind may

naturally, perhaps, wonder why, in such. an instance, — where belief in the efficacy of prayer was complete, — it was not sooner resorted to for aid. The answer is very simple and intelligible. In the first place, Mrs. Mattingly *had* resorted to prayer, all along, and had sought support by receiving the Blessed Sacrament in communion. But her prayer had been solely, as we discern from her confessor's report, that she might remain in accord with and obedient to God's will. For, strange as it may seem to others, a Catholic's first thought is not to escape suffering and be relieved from illness, but to be truly filial in accepting the divine will, and to convert the burden of pain into a cheerful offering. Secondly, although their view of prayer is very direct and practical, as applied to every detail of existence, Catholics do not regard lightly the idea of asking for a great and special favor to themselves, in the cure of illness. There is a fear of selfishness or undutifulness, in asking a favor of this kind; and therefore it is often more difficult to put up such a petition on one's own behalf, than for the health of others. It is quite possible that, feeling herself to be *in extremis*, she may have thought it her duty to seize the one opportunity remaining to her of mitigating the sorrow of her family.

Now, as to the nine days' prayer, which was to end by her receiving Holy Communion on the morning of the tenth day, — it may be well to explain its principle briefly; since we wish to enable all who glance at these pages to have at least a clear, unbiased perception of the elements and conditions in the case, whatever conclusions they may afterwards draw.

When Prof. Tyndall — as an investigator of natural science, learned and competent; as a person, amiable; as a dabbler in philosophy and theology, very incompetent, distinctly materialistic and infidel, from the pure Christian point of view — once proposed a " prayer gauge," by which a large number of Christians were to pray simultaneously for the healing of the sick in London hospitals, and were then to take account and see how many of those sick had been cured by a certain date, he shocked a large portion of human society. It was inevitable that all really thinking and reverent people should be shocked by such a plan ; because the suggestion that Tyndall put forward was simply on a level with the crude, pert inquiry of a restless boy, who for example should ask why people should not whistle in church, or conduct chemical laboratory experiments there, with the expectation of receiving some immediate reward from heaven.

Prayer is not a challenge to God ; and any attempt to treat it as such, or to use it as a defiant — or even as a materialistic and doubting — test of God's power, at once invalidates the experiment.

Any man of natural science, so intelligent as Tyndall, would scout the idea of attempting an experiment in physics or chemistry without having all the conditions of the experiment exact and logical, according to the law of the elements or compounds involved in it. Hence it was childish on his part to plan a test of prayer, from which the essential element of prayer was omitted. That essential element consists not in challenge, but in appeal ; not in doubt, but in trust.

Like many other hasty and materialistic questioners of spiritual Christian verity, Prof. Tyndall seemed to think that, in this "prayer gauge," he had sketched a method the principle of which was wholly novel. Yet — leaving out his entirely unscientific element of defiance and doubt — the method of combined prayer was as old as Christianity ; and it has been practiced from time immemorial down to the present ; with constant results of definite answer and achievement, often miraculous, in all days and in our own day.

Prayer is reciprocal action between the natural and the supernatural ; the human and the divine.   Without faith and submission, it .cannot exist at all. *With* those qualities, it may bring about results in a certain form desired by the devout human element, or it may receive answer in some entirely different form.   In either case it is God who decides the issue, without regard to time-limits fixed by an arrogant human being ; but also often with an immediate, striking, and compassionate regard for time-limits, not fixed, but ardently hoped for by religious and submissive souls.

This, then, was the basis of the novena undertaken by Mrs. Mattingly ; and no one could foretell what would be its earthly outcome.

On the night of March 9, 1824, the Rev. William Matthews, her pastor, visited Mrs. Mattingly, in order to hear her confession, preparatory to her receiving Holy Communion the next morning, in completion of the novena.   In his affidavit concerning this matter he said : " Whilst I remained at her bedside, she appeared to suffer most excruciating pains. Twice she had cramps in her breast. . . . Her voice was very low, — scarcely audible. They moistened her lips and tongue four or five times while I remained, with cold water in a teaspoon. I proposed to give her laudanum ; but her sister observed she had already taken two hundred and fifty drops that evening. I left her, about half after ten, apparently in the jaws of death." The Rev. Anthony Kohlman, superior of the Jesuits, also paid her a visit, the same evening, and stated afterward that she had all the appearance of a dying person ; in order to make out her whispered words, he had to put his ear close to her lips.

It was the Rev. Stephen L. Dubuisson, S. J., who had originally proposed the novena, in which Archbishop Maréchal and some two hundred persons, in all, took part. The prayers were said every morning precisely at sunrise, in order that all the individuals might make their offering at one and the same time. Mrs. Mattingly had felt much confidence in the undertaking, as a possible means of recovery ; yet all through the nine days she was "desperately ill," Father Dubuisson assures us ; and when, having seen her twice before (once on February 20 and again on March 7), he came to call on the night of the ninth, he found her worse than ever.

At half past two the next morning he celebrated Mass in the parish church, "after which " — to quote from his sworn account — "I carried the Blessed Sacrament to Mrs. Mattingly at her brother, Captain Carbery's, house. She was in the same state of extreme debility and suffering. I addressed to her a few words and read the letter of Prince Hohenlohe's directions." The letter had been received at Baltimore a number of days before the novena began; and this tenth of March was the day on which he was to make his special petition for the sick. " Then I administered to her the Holy Communion, withdrew from the bed, and knelt down before the Blessed Sacrament, — there being several consecrated Hosts in my pyx. Her relations and friends present knelt likewise. The tongue of the patient being exceedingly dry and hard, some minutes elapsed ere she could swallow the sacred species; but having done so — in the twinkling of an eye, she was perfectly cured.

" All pain left her. Rising in bed and joining her hands, she exclaimed: ' Lord Jesus! What have I ever done to deserve such a favor ! ' Sobs, tears, and suppressed shrieks burst from the attendants kneeling around. I arose and approached the bed, my whole frame thrilling with emotion. The patient grasped my hand. ' Father,' said she, ' what can I do to acknowledge such a mercy ? '

" ' Glory be to God ! ' I replied. I then asked her how she felt. She answered, ' Perfectly well.'

" ' Entirely free from pain ? '

" ' I am. Entirely free from pain; no pain at all.'

" ' None there ? ' — pointing to her side.

" ' Not the least, — only some weakness. Let me get up and kneel to return thanks to God.'

" ' But can you ? '

" ' I can if you will give me leave.'

" Her stockings and slippers were brought, and she put them on with perfect ease and without assistance.

She then knelt before the little altar whereon the Blessed Sacrament had been deposited, and had remained there about a quarter of an hour when her brother Thomas entered. She then arose and, advancing towards him, threw up her arms in a transport, exclaiming: 'See what God has done for me! For years I have not been able to do this.'

"Then, again kneeling before the Blessed Sacrament, she remained in prayer a considerable time, evincing not the slightest fatigue, but on the contrary appearing lost in adoration of the Blessed Sacrament.

"I confess that the impression on my soul on witnessing the entire scene, but particularly this last circumstance, was so profound, that I do not believe it could have been more so had I seen Mrs. M. raised from the dead. I underwent, I believe, the same sensation as if I had seen her rise out of her coffin. There was especially *in her look and features something which I shall not attempt to depict,* — an expression of firmness and of earnest, awful feelings, *the recollection of which it will be my consolation to preserve through life.*"

These particulars, and whatever else is cited here from Father Dubuisson, are found in his affidavit, signed Stephen Laurigaudelle Dubuisson, and sworn to before John N. Moulder, justice of the peace, in Washington, March 17, 1824.

That he was in no visionary or ecstatic state of mind would seem to be shown by the fact that, although deeply and devoutly impressed by the miracle which he had just witnessed, he remained quite practical — as a Catholic ought to, even in the presence of such a manifestation — and did not forget his duty towards another sick person, to whose house he was obliged to hurry away; and that he went on attending to his numerous engagements as assistant pastor, until eleven of the forenoon. Then he returned, with Father Matthews, to Mayor Carbery's dwelling. Mrs. Mattingly, who had been unable to walk more than a few steps at a time, for six years, and, as we have seen, had been a helpless, agonized invalid confined to her bed the greater part of that period, came to meet them at the door and knelt to receive her pastor's blessing. "Sound in mind and body, she looked and acted as one perfectly restored to health, who has only more flesh and strength to recover."

"We are now," adds Father Dubuisson, "on the 17th of March. Seven days, therefore, have elapsed since her cure. She is daily acquiring strength, as is witnessed I may say by the whole city, which flocks to Capt. Carbery's house to see her. Dr. Jones, her physician, has examined her and found no vestige of the red tumor which she had on her side, nor any sign whatever of ill health. Her breath, heretofore extremely offensive, has become sweet; and she declares that she has constantly a taste like that of loaf sugar in her mouth." He concludes his formal declaration with the words: "I now feel it a sacred part incumbent on me, to procure authenticity and notoriety to this deposition, to which I swear on the Holy Gospel of our Lord Jesus Christ, with full certitude of accuracy, and which, I trust, I would subscribe with my own blood."

The two sisters and three brothers of Mrs. Mattingly, with her aunt Mrs. Gen. Carbery, were likewise all witnesses of her instantaneous return to health, and made affidavit as to the facts. On the very day of the cure, the house was thronged with visitors, — some five hundred in number. Mrs. Mattingly received them all, and shook hands with them.

More than two months later (May 18, 1824), Father Matthews wrote, concerning his visit there at eleven o'clock that day : " Mrs. Mattingly opened to me the door, and, with a smiling countenance, shook my hand. Although prepared for this meeting, I could not repress my astonishment at the striking contrast produced in her person, in a few hours. My mind had for years associated death and her pale, emaciated face. From that day to the present, May 18, 1824, Mrs. Mattingly assures me she has enjoyed perfect health."

Every trace of bodily ailment seems to have disappeared almost immediately, including even those painful abrasions of the skin, caused by months upon months of enforced reclining in bed, which, up to that time, it had been necessary to dress with lenitive preparations, plasters, and bandages, since they had been like open wounds.

After this marvelous event, she continued in physical well-being and normal activity for almost half the length of that term assigned as the life of a generation, and, dying in 1857, was buried on March 10, exactly thirty-three years from the day of her miraculous restoration.

So far as we are aware, no attempt has ever been made seriously to question the facts narrated here ;

and surely any such attempt, at the time, must have seemed rather futile, considering the known condition of the patient, the publicity of the whole matter, the number and repute of the witnesses, the crowds of Washington people who saw her immediately after the transformation from mortal illness to serenity of health.

Still, there are doubtless minds which, with the story now laid simply before them, may obstinately impugn or refuse to accept it. Some persons who profess to believe thoroughly in God's power to work miracles in the time of Christ and the Apostles imperiously undertake to limit God's power in later times, and to deny that He has continued to exercise it. Others, who still doubt the Scripture miracles, hint that they would be satisfied if they could only obtain full documentary proof and the testimony of eyewitnesses concerning those. Yet, when precisely the kind of testimony and proof they demand is offered in the case of modern or contemporaneous miracles, they brush it all aside, on the theory that no miracle can be wrought in this age of the world, anyway, and that people who assert from their own experience the contrary must be mistaken or mendacious.

Mrs. Mattingly, as we have said, became a postulant at the Georgetown Visitation five years after her cure; yet it turned out, as her father confessor had already informed her, that the pious and eager desire which animated her did not really constitute a vocation for the career of a nun. She had to give up her attempt in this direction, but was always thereafter received as a welcome guest by the Visitation community. For, besides the congeniality of mind and soul which they found in her, the extraordinary favor she had received from heaven surrounded her with a peculiar holiness, and they felt that her presence brought a blessing to their convent home.

Such was Mrs. Mattingly's own reverence for the couch of suffering from which she had been raised by supernatural means that she never again lay upon it during the many years still allotted to her, but kept it for the use of priests or other holy persons who occasionally lodged at her brother's house.

And now we come to a point which is by no means fully authenticated, as the circumstances were which we have just reviewed ; but it is too interesting to be ignored. Sister Josephine Barber's manuscript chronicle shows that a tradition was kept alive among the Visitation sisters that, at the moment of her recovery, this bed, where a six years' martyrdom had been endured, was miraculously cleansed and sweetened. Some of them had often heard Mother Agnes Brent say that the sick-room was thereupon filled with a delicious fragrance, which she *thought* continued for a long period afterwards. Bishop England, however, in his pamphlet on the subject, makes no mention of these matters ; though it appears likely enough that he would have done so had they, at the time of his investigation, been of common report and thoroughly verified. It is regrettable that no one made research or gathered testimony regarding such a rumor, immediately after the cure. The only attempt that we are aware of, to ascertain its basis, was deferred until 1877, — fifty-three years later. The St. Louis Sisters of the Visitation then wrote to Miss Catherine Carbery, who had survived Mrs. Mattingly. Miss Carbery replied from Washington (March 22, 1877) that, for a long time previous to the miraculous restoration, the air of the invalid's room had been very oppressive, and especially so on the night before that event.

"My sister Ruth and myself," she wrote, "were sitting up with Mrs. Mattingly, and, notwithstanding the presence of camphor on my handkerchief and the use of disinfectants in the room, I became nauseated when attending at the sick-bed, and had to be relieved in my personal ministrations by my sister Ruth. This continued all night. After Mrs. Mattingly's cure in the early hours of the morning, we all noticed and remarked how pure and sweet the odor of the person and the surroundings in the bed, and in the air of the room, had become." Referring to a second question, as to a recurrence of the same phenomenon when Mrs. Mattingly died, Miss Carbery continued in her letter: "As to the second inquiry relative to the day after the funeral, 1857, — I remember most distinctly that a sister, then a Protestant, and Carbery, eldest son of Mr. Richard Lay, upon going to the room where Mrs. Mattingly died, and which had been locked, with all the fetid air from confinement, the windows being closed during the entire sickness, as also from bedclothes soiled to an extreme, were amazed at the sweet odor of the room, and called myself and other members of the family to come; and we all wondered at such sweetness from such a mass of impurity."

This is a clear, decided asseveration, which no rational critic can very well throw out entirely, unless he be disposed to suggest falsehood or delusion. The only known realities which could in any way weaken its force are, that the letter was not written until fifty-three years after the miracle, and twenty years after the recipient of the miracle had died; and that there is no concurrence of testimonies, as in the case of the healing itself. What remains incontestable is, that a rumor of this mysterious perfume had long been current, and was at last positively confirmed, so far as the word of one surviving person who had experienced the phenomenon could give a confirmation.

It is also quite conceivable that Bishop England (not a witness), and those members of the family and the reverend Fathers who were witnesses, may have thought the presence of a sudden sweet odor in the room a detail hardly worth dwelling upon, in comparison with the much greater and more astounding fact of an instantaneous transformation from disease to health. Besides, it would be a detail incapable of the same ocular and tangible proof which was at hand, as to the main fact, in the person of the restored invalid. Hence, knowing how much of skepticism and even prejudice there was in the population surrounding them, they might have preferred to pass over in silence this one particular, which perhaps would arouse dispute, seeing that as to the chief point, the actual cure, there could be no dispute whatever.

In records concerning holy persons, we often meet with the idea and the legend that a sweet, flower-like aroma was exhaled from their resting-places, whether

in life or in death.   There is nothing incredible or
against nature in such a conception ; for, since it is
well known that not only physical but also mental
conditions in the human body manifest themselves
through variations of odor, why should not spiritual
conditions do the same?   It seems probable that the
phrase " odor of sanctity " — which most people take
to be merely figurative — refers literally to a sensible
basis of fact and experience ; of that kind which tradition constantly brings to our notice.   Therefore it is
pleasant to find that certain persons at least believed
they had discerned the same thing in the case of Mrs.
Mattingly.

It probably has not often happened, in recent experience, that the same person has twice within a short
period benefited by a signal intervention of supernatural power to ward off disease which threatened a fatal
ending.   But it happened to Mrs. Mattingly, in the
eighth year following her first and most notable rescue
from death, that she again met with healing from a
source higher than human skill.

Although convinced that it was wiser for her to
withdraw from the novitiate, she remained in close
communication with religious sisterhoods.   Having
spent the night of November 29th (1831) with the
Sisters of Charity, she rose early the next morning —
the feast of St. Andrew the Apostle — to hear Mass
at St. Patrick's Church.   It was still dark ; and as
she was feeling her way down the steps of the portico,
her foot turned, causing a serious injury to the ankle.
She nevertheless attempted to walk home to her
brother's house on Capitol Hill, a half mile away.   It

took her two hours to accomplish even this short distance, as she had to stop frequently on account of excruciating pain from the hurt. Such an exertion at
such a moment of course greatly aggravated her injury. Both foot and ankle swelled ; dark spots appeared on the skin ; and the whole member finally
assumed a deep purple hue. Christmas drew near ;
and, being unable to walk or even stand, she saw that
it would be impossible to attend church on that great
festival. She therefore, on the advice of Father Matthews, decided to accept an invitation from the
Georgetown Sisters to spend some days in the convent, whither she might be removed carefully, and
there enjoy the holy season in the atmosphere of devotion she loved so well. She was lifted into a carriage,
and was again assisted by many hands at the convent
and carried to the room assigned for her, — a cell
near the novitiate.

In spite of constant care lavished upon her by the
sisters, however, she grew worse day by day. The
convent physician, Dr. Bohrer, examining her foot,
pronounced the case very serious. On the first day of
the New Year (1832), her suffering was intense, the
pain and swelling having then extended up to the hip.
Mortification seemed likely to set in at any moment ;
and, seeing this, the doctor declared that amputation
was necessary. He was unwilling, nevertheless, to undertake the operation until he could notify and consult with Capt. Carbery. For this reason it had to be
deferred until the next day, although Dr. Bohrer
agreed with the infirmarians that there was imminent
risk of her not being able to survive that long.

Answering the expressions of sympathy offered by the sisters in this emergency, the patient said: " I will place all my confidence in God. I will exert all the faith I have." When every one had retired for the night, Mrs. Mattingly placed a medal of the Blessed Virgin under her bandages, and entreated Our Lady to come to her aid; so that by her intercession, she might obtain from God either relief — should it contribute to his glory — or the grace to die a happy death. Always the Catholic thought: not seeking primarily surcease from pain, or reprieve from death, but the will of God and the ability to die firmly and well in the faith.

Hardly had thirty minutes passed, when the pangs which had afflicted her passed away. " A sensation of softness," the annals relate, " succeeded to the former rigidity. She drew up her foot; pressed it with her hand, — it was perfectly well."

" Next morning, long before daylight, Mrs. Mattingly rose, and, hastening to the choir, returned thanks to God and to Mary for this new favor. She was still kneeling in her accustomed place [probably that occupied by her while she had been a postulant] when the bell rang for the morning meditation, and the sisters entered the choir. Great was their surprise at seeing the invalid there before them. After the hour's meditation, Prime, Mass, and thanksgiving followed; during all which she knelt or stood, betraying not a vestige of her recent illness. Immediately after Mass, the community formed in procession, and, chanting the hymn *Ave Maris Stella*, went to the novitiate and to the cell where the miracle had taken place;

Mrs. Mattingly accompanying them with a heart overflowing with gratitude." [1]

Thus quickly do miracles sometimes come to pass; The moment they have occurred, they at once take their place, with all their supernatural quality, in the natural course of things. And the stream which we choose to call Time — we, who so easily obscure the fact that it belongs to the current of Eternity — goes flowing on, with or past the miracles. And sometimes they are remembered, and sometimes forgotten.

They are remembered, only to be scoffed at, by those numerous individuals who delight in puzzling themselves with every occult thing of "spiritism" or theosophy, or mind-reading, and the like, — as children are lost in pleasurable wonder at the mere mechanical toy which they cannot understand or explain. Yet those same individuals bluntly and blindly reject the marvels accomplished by pure Catholic Christian faith, which are as lucid as a clear sunrise; as natural as eyesight; as reasonable as the easiest problem of moral cause and effect of one mind upon another; as simple as the smiling of a healthy, happy, obedient child; and just as mysterious in its blessing as that smile.

XVI. ATTEMPT TO CHANGE THE ORDER. — SECESSION OF SISTER GERTRUDE.

Mrs. Mattingly — living and dying outside the bounds of the Visitation Order, for which she had so strong an affection; and receiving, by divine interposition, two such remarkable mercies as were accorded

---

[1] MS. Annals by Sister M. Josephine Barber. Vol. ii., p. 213.

to her in times of mortal illness — is a luminous example of that life, instinct with genuine and child-like religious aspiration, which may be led by one whose lot is cast in what we fancifully and limitedly call " the world."

To dignify with the title of " the world " that mass of beings who attempt to govern themselves solely or chiefly by some imagined law of their own minds, and to separate themselves in a rather select and fastidious way from the law of God, is somewhat the same as though we were to call the refuse slag of iron, pure iron, or the " tailings " of a quartz-mill, pure gold.

This " world," so-called, is loud ; and yet it is singularly dumb when recognition of eternal truth is the issue. It also calls itself, to some extent, " gay ;" and yet it is exceedingly dull when tested by its capacity to perceive The Light of the World.

To the gay, loud world which is at the same time dull and dumb, — and continually complains of its own self-imposed fatigue and misery, — the benignity of heaven, as granted to a simple and devoted woman like Mrs. Mattingly, is all but inaudible and invisible ; or, if perceived in any degree, it appears deserving only of doubt. Yet there is a considerable world of men and women, conjoined with these usurpers of the title, but representing the sincerer elements of mankind, that seeks union with God on the only terms possible, — submission. It seems to us that Mrs. Mattingly — who lived among, or in the presence of, both these kinds of people ; who could not seclude herself in the cloistered life, though she desired to — was destined to become and to remain an example and a living instance, to every one, of the doctrine and mystery of the Holy Eucharist, at the moment when she was restored to health after receiving the real yet glorified body of our Lord, in the consecrated wafer.

We have now to speak of another woman who, with an apparent vocation for the monastic religious life, and with every opportunity to consecrate herself in it wholly to God, failed wretchedly, and abandoned her post.

The contrast between the service and duty which Mrs. Mattingly was permitted to fulfill while remaining in secular life, and the dreary end of the recreant sister we are to refer to here, should be suggestive, and is worth considering.

The defection of this nun — Sister Anna Gertrude Whyte — was peculiarly painful to the community, because she was one of its most prominent and, in certain respects, most able members, and had been a child of the house, as one may say, brought up under the immediate care and supervision of Archbishop Neale and Mother Teresa. Her father having died when she was eleven years old, she was placed by her mother — with another daughter a year younger — in the care of the Archbishop, and became a pupil of " the Pious Ladies." Both the children were remarkably precocious and talented. Such piety then reigned in the school itself, that it resembled a novitiate ; and more than a majority of the girls aspired to the religious state ; cherishing hopes in that direction, which they realized before long. Thus, among others, these two half-orphans entered their postulantship when seventeen and sixteen years old, and were admitted to solemn vows in 1817. The fervor of the younger, Mary, was very great. It led to her being appointed Mistress of Novices at the age of nineteen; but she died a year later (1820).

Anna Gertrude, the elder one, seems to have developed her innate force and cleverness more especially on the intellectual side, and unfortunately — as also quite unnecessarily — at the expense of the spiritual. The highest reaches of intellectual splendor may be perfectly accordant with spiritual faithfulness or humility : as innumerable examples in the history of the human mind attest, from Dante in the secular life to Pope Leo XIII. in the sacerdotal. At the same time, even a little mere *pride* of learning may be destructive of true spiritual equilibrium; just as a great and overgrown pride of learning wrecked that once eminent and erudite ecclesiastic, Dr. Döllinger. It is to a Catholic English poet, Alexander Pope, that we owe the maxim now — by constant use — worn humbly and appropriately threadbare, that " A little learning is a dangerous thing." A little pride is equally perilous; though the remedy is not to drink deeper of pride, but to quaff from the spring of pure Christian simplicity and of wholesome, humble faithfulness.

Sister Anna Gertrude Whyte evidently suffered from, and was at last undone by, a few grains of poisoning pride that she had carelessly let fall into the well of knowledge from which she was at liberty to draw freely. During her novitiate and for some time afterwards, nothing absolutely objectionable appeared in her conduct; although ·it is hinted that there were traits or actions on her part which created misgivings as to her future, among those who observed her closely. In that obscure and quiet-loving convent she found at first no field for the exercise of the faculty she possessed — or, rather, which possessed her — for shining as a mistress and exponent of various learning. But when in the course of time a more extensive plan, a higher range of studies, was undertaken in the Academy, Sister W. was chosen to carry it out, by reason of her natural and cultivated qualification for this especial work. "She devoted her whole soul to literature," it is said ; and all the energies of her powerful mind were bent to the task of raising the Academy to the highest standard of the times.

Having first been appointed Directress of the school, and having served some time in that capacity, she was likewise made assistant or sub-prioress of the convent, in 1828. Father Wheeler seemed to entertain the most exalted opinion of her ; and Mother Juliana — saintly, unassuming, always diffident as to her own abilities — gladly entrusted to her all the exterior business of the sisterhood. That Sister Gertrude was inwardly unworthy of the confidence reposed in her did not come to light until some time afterwards ; and it is hardly to be wondered at that those who were themselves honest and unsuspicious relied upon her without question, when they knew she had passed most of her life within the convent walls, and saw her using all her brilliant gifts with seeming earnestness for the common cause. But when Father Wheeler sailed for Europe in the autumn of 1828, the actual aim she had at heart was soon made known. It turned out to be nothing less than the entire subversion of the Georgetown house of the Visitation!

The ex-Empress Yturbide of Mexico, whose advent in Georgetown has been touched upon, was allowed to take apartments with her four daughters in the Academy and even to have a cell in the cloister and to wear the conventual garb while in the convent proper. These privileges were granted to her in consideration of her great piety and the overwhelming misfortunes she had lately undergone. By the intimacy of the Academy and the cloister thus established, Madam Yturbide (as she was now called) and her children were brought into close relations with Sister Gertrude Whyte and became strongly attached to her. The Directress and sub-prioress, on her part, showed them every kindness and attention, and gave much of her time to their society. Madam Yturbide's chaplain, Father Lopez, an estimable priest, had accompanied her to Georgetown, and Father Wheeler, on his departure for Europe, asked this chaplain to act as spiritual director of the community during his absence.

So it came about that Sister Gertrude, admired by all, Madam Yturbide the friend and guest of the community, and the temporary director, Father Lopez, were brought into close association and a consensus of views. In the early days of struggle, it will be remembered, there had been a serious proposal to change the aim of this religious house and attach it to the Ursuline Order; a proposal backed, at that time, by a well-meant and very tempting offer of pecuniary aid. But it had been rejected, because of Archbishop Neale's firm determination to follow out the Visitation plan, seconded by the strong desire of most of the sisters. This idea of adopting the Ursuline rule seems to have taken deep root in Sister Gertrude's mind; and now, after so long an interval, she tried to bring it to fruition. Within a month from the time when Father Wheeler left Georgetown, she brought up in the councils of the community the old project of abandoning the institute of St. Francis de Sales. Her argument was, that the rule of the Ursulines was much better adapted to the immediate needs of this country, and that the necessity of maintaining a school conflicted with the original plan of St. Francis, which aimed to establish a contemplative order only. If an Academy on a large scale and with a high standard of studies, such as had now been started, was to be carried on to the best advantage, she thought it should be put under Ursuline guidance. It is not hard to detect, in this argument and its aim, an ambition to make intellectual and educational eminence the primary object; which object, if attained, would have given to Sister Gertrude great personal distinction and gratification.

Father Lopez and Madam Yturbide both strongly favored the change proposed; believing, no doubt, that it would really advance the cause of religion. All three were anxious that it should be carried through promptly, before Father Wheeler could return from Europe; the sub-prioress being particularly averse to his intention of bringing home with him the French sisters who, with the consent of the chapter, were expected to guide the spiritual conduct of the community. Possibly the sub-prioress foresaw that, if once the French sisters should arrive and be installed in such a capacity, there would never again be any chance of discarding the Visitation rule; and that consequently her special gifts as a teacher, instead of bringing her individual renown, would continue to be merged in the general life of the Georgetown house.

This project must have impressed the sisterhood as disloyal to their whole history, their promises, and aims. The thought of abandoning their Order after so many years of gallant struggle, when their establishment had been approved by the Sovereign Pontiff and had entered upon an era of success, was most unwelcome to them; and they rejected it so decisively, that the discussion was dropped.

But Sister Gertrude remained irreconcilable, discontented. When Father Wheeler and the French sisters were so joyously welcomed home, she alone took no share in the happiness of that event. It would seem that the wounded vanity of seeing her own desires and ambitions thwarted overcame the, discipline of a lifetime and its constant lessons of obedience. A year and a half later, she abruptly and secretly deserted the convent. In the afternoon of March 22, 1831, between two and three o'clock, she went to the Academy parlor, and, taking the key from one of the girls, in whose charge the portress had left it, sent her elsewhere. Being now alone — for there was not another individual in all that part of the house — she unlocked the door. Then, having thrown one of the children's cloaks over her head, as a partial means of disguise, she passed out into the street.

What a strange moment must that have been, —

the moment in which, after being sixteen years a professed nun and dwelling in the busy quietude, the regularity and pious devotion of the cloister, she turned her back upon it, broke her solemn vow, cast off her name in religion; and, forsaking her chosen duties, faced the outer world alone without chart or guide or any certainty as to her career!

She had walked only the distance of a square or two when Father Lucas, one of the Jesuit Fathers at the college, met her; and — notwithstanding the cloak that hid the upper part of her figure and the distinctively religious costume — he recognized her at once. She passed on silently; and he, greatly astonished and puzzled by her presence on the street, wishing also to be perfectly sure that he had made no mistake as to her identity, went around and met her again on another street. This time, apparently willing to end all doubt, she threw her cloak open, showing him plainly her face, her barbette, and silver cross. Horrified, on fully realizing the situation, he raised his hands and exclaimed: "Sister Gertrude! is it you?" As it appears from the account in the annals, she made no reply, but closed her cloak again and walked on, until, meeting a hack, she hailed the driver and told him to take her to the residence of her cousin, General Van ——, on Capitol Hill, Washington. Startled though Father Lucas was, the driver was apparently still more so on seeing her distinctive religious costume, as he let down the steps; for he stood back and made no attempt to help her into the carriage.

That same afternoon the Father Rector of the Jesuits, with another of the Fathers, called at General

Van ——'s, hoping perhaps to bring the errant nun home; but she declared that she had left the convent forever. She knelt to ask their blessing; but they did not raise their hands to make the sign of the cross over her.

Although Father Lucas, after meeting Sister Gertrude on the street, went to the convent and called for the Superior at the grate, — where, after a little, in order to relieve the suspense she would feel if she should find her assistant missing, he told her of his discovery, — it was still difficult for the Superior, Mother Magdalene Augustine, to fully comprehend the fact of Sister Gertrude's departure. Every room and corner of the convent was searched, in the hope of finding the lost sister somewhere. It was not until the evening, after supper, when the community were assembled in the recreation room, that Sister Agatha Langlois, coming in with a pallid face, exclaimed to them all: "Sister Gertrude Whyte is out. *She is gone!*"

The news was received with sobs and tears. To people who attach little importance to the most solemn obligations between the human and the divine, and regard all matters of religious faith and duty as being simply optional with each human creature, it may seem strange that the sisters should so deeply take to heart this willful secession of one of their number. But it meant, to them, the peril of her soul; because of her violating promises to God, the most sacred and profound, which involved her whole existence here and still more hereafter. All wept and prayed for her whom they had so loved and now had lost! — who perhaps had lost herself; and some went to the choir, where they prostrated themselves before the Blessed Sacrament, petitioning for pity and mercy towards her.

Madam Yturbide soon invited the fugitive to leave Gen. Van——'s, and come to her house in Georgetown, where she was treated as one of the family.

Sister Josephine Barber — at that time simply a pupil in the Academy, a girl of fifteen — called upon her there, with another of the Academy girls, some ten weeks after her sudden exit from the convent. With touching simplicity and reserve, covering a depth of grief, Sister Josephine wrote as follows concerning the sad episode : " She had known me from the time I was a baby, as also my sisters, and my mother [Sister Mary Austin Barber].   I was young enough to sit upon her knee, when I discovered that she had lost her vocation ; but the impression was never obliterated.   I mention this to show how sharp children are, and how careful one should be in their presence. . . .   On seeing Sister Gertrude Whyte in her worldly attire, smooth, glossy hair and combs, black silk dress, watch and chain, etc., I burst into tears, and could not speak for sobbing.   She and Madam Yturbide asked me repeatedly what made me cry.   At last I said : ' Sister, won't you go back to the convent ? '

" ' No, indeed,' she replied, with a peculiar shake of the head which all who knew her remember.

" She asked me many questions about the Ursuline convent in Boston, where my eldest sister was ; also about Mother St. George.   After staying about twenty minutes, we bade her good-by, and returned to the convent."

Little is recorded of her subsequent actions or employments, although she lived for thirty-six years longer. The Visitation Sisters of Baltimore wrote in December, 1867, this letter concerning her latter days and her death : —

"About the last of September she came on a visit to Mrs. N., stayed two weeks, then a few days with Mrs. L. (Gen. Van ——'s daughter). Before leaving Baltimore she came with Mrs. N. to the convent. Mother Paulina Millard said to her : 'Sister, you must come to us. I have a place for you here.' She replied : 'Oh, no !' Mother insisted : 'Oh, yes ! You must come ; you must die with us. You must either come here, or go to old Georgetown, to die.'

"She was very much agitated, and still said *No*, but not proudly. I told her I would be so happy to have her come and die with us. She then said I must come and die with her. She inquired about several of the old sisters, took the liveliest interest in dear Mother Juliana's death, and told us how devoted she was to her. Mother Paulina asked her whether she would like to have something of Mother Juliana's. She answered very eagerly, 'Yes, indeed !' Then Mother Paulina detached from her beads a medal of the Holy Family, which Mother Juliana had had about her when dying, and gave it to poor Sister [Gertrude]. Mother asked her whether she was not afraid to go to Richmond ; travelling was so dangerous. She said : No, indeed ! — she was not afraid of anything ; she loved to travel. Mother told her she put her daily 'in the wounds of Jesus.' She answered : 'I hope I *am* in the wounds of Jesus.' We saw she was very much agitated, struggling against something ; and others who saw her said the same.

"She went to church with N. twice ; made no genuflection, but knelt most reverently, and knelt at the elevation as if in deep prayer. . . . She never spoke of any religious topic whatever ; from morning to night was fixing her little articles of dress, though in deep mourning. . . . While at Mrs. M.'s, in Richmond, she had an attack of pneumonia ; but was convalescent, and able to walk across the room, when the family one day heard a heavy fall in the bedroom overhead, and going up, found poor Sister [Gertrude] lying on the floor, with her hand raised to her head. On seeing them, she exclaimed : 'Oh! Am I crazy?'—and in fifteen minutes [she] was no more. . . . She was aged sixty-eight or nine years."

From this brief account of Sister Gertrude's defection it will be seen how easy it is for the weak, the vain, or the intellectually proud to "escape" from a convent. The difficulty is not in escaping, but in getting back. For, vows once being broken and all higher purposes of self-sacrifice and duty being set at naught, the soul that imagines itself emancipated to wander freely in the common ways and market-places of earth discovers that it is really imprisoned there and can hardly return to the true liberty of pure religious devotion.

There is nothing "sensational," in the common meaning, about this story of the flight of a nun. But there is much that is deeply pathetic. Sister Gertrude Whyte, in the disruption of her conventual ties, failed to win that personal distinction for which she seems to have longed; and she came to a piteous end at last. Her old friends and companions were gentle, kind, and charitable toward her; giving their good-will and their prayers to her as to an errant soul in deadly danger; and it seems that she came back to see and talk with them affectionately. But she had willfully thrown away her opportunity, and it did not come again.

Nothing could better emphasize the truth that, even with all the safeguards of faith, the protection of religious orders and long training in submission and obedience, the individual soul must never for a moment rely wholly upon itself; for in one such moment —

like that when Sister Gertrude Whyte unlocked
the convent door and stepped out into the seeming
freedom of the street — it may lose forever that
highest joy of the free will which unites itself, humbly and through grace, with God.

XVII. LIVES OF SISTERS.

As we approach the end of that period covered by
the manuscript records at our disposal, it is fitting
and will be instructive to gather together here a few
biographical sketches of sisters whom we have not
spoken of at length in previous chapters; members of
the community who, in their several ways, left a
strong and abiding impress upon it and sometimes
upon the whole Order in the United States.

Their firm yet gentle personalities are enshrined in
the memory of the older sisters now living and in the
hearts of many American women, non-Catholic, as well
as Catholic, who in girlhood came under their beneficent care, counsel, or teaching. For this reason especially it is proper that we should offer some kind of
portrait of them, at least in outline; little though they,
in their modest self-abnegation, dreamed that their pure
and humble activity — hidden away from the world
— would ever be mentioned publicly. Such records,
however brief, may also help to make clear to those
who do not yet understand it, the vigor, the force of
character, the high quality of heart and soul constantly
wrought into the substance of a community of nuns.

From the nature of the material, an exact chrono-
logical arrangement can hardly be made. We shall
therefore present these sketches without any special

system, singly or in groups, as they happen to be drawn from our portfolio.

SISTER
MARY
ANGELA
HARRISON,
AND
OTHERS.

Sister Angela became a member of the community about the year 1819. She was one of those characters who convey to the mind the image of a soul of spotless innocence. She celebrated her Golden Jubilee, and lived for several years afterwards, retaining to the last her full mental faculties, and her child-like simplicity. She was made Superioress of the foundation in Philadelphia. On the breaking up of the house there, she was recalled to Georgetown. Then for twelve years, at different times, she served as Superioress of Georgetown Convent, and governed with a gentle firmness and a lovely spirit of forbearance; enduring the many trials incidental to authority with the utmost patience.

During the Civil War her energy and wisdom shone forth especially. She was at that time most generous in trying to aid poor chaplains; and she showed a true zeal for souls in the advice she gave to soldiers who applied to her for help. Her charity was remembered, as the nuns of Georgetown had reason to realize not long ago, during a recent encampment of the Grand Army of the Republic, when one of the veterans called to see " Mother Angela," not knowing she had been dead many years. The veteran gave as the cause of his desire to see her, that the angelic Superioress "had converted him." Whenever, worn out with marching and laden with dust, regiments halted in front of the convent during the war, a liberal lunch was served to the weary soldiers ; and, to those who wished for them, many objects of piety were sent out on the spot from Mother Angela. She, in company with Sister Cecilia Brooks, Sister Regina Neale, Sister Michaela of Wheeling Convent, and Sister Loretto Hunter, all sisters of Georgetown, was associated with everything good and holy in the community.

Sister Regina Neale went to the Mount de Sales foundation, and was for many years its Superioress, and deeply beloved. She died just after celebrating her Golden Jubilee, in 1891. Mother Loretto Hunter is the only one of the above named sisters who is still living, as Superioress of Frederick Convent. Her memory is still gratefully cherished at Georgetown.

Another long venerated inmate of this house, under the name of Sister Mary Olympia, was Mrs. Fulton, mother of the Rev. Robert Fulton, a well-known and distinguished member of the Society of Jesus. When her son, to whom she had devoted the early years of her widowhood, obeyed his vocation to enter the Jesuit Order, Mrs. Fulton herself retired to the solitude of Georgetown Convent, where she spent many years in useful service to the neighboring poor, and also as Directress of St. Joseph's Free School connected with the convent. She died at the age of eighty-five. Her name is held in benediction by her scholars and friends.

SISTER MARY GENEVIEVE WHITE. Sister Genevieve White, who was a sister of the late Judge White, of New York, as well as a niece of Gerald Griffin, the famous Irish poet and novelist, entered the convent at a time when her talents were very much needed.

For the greater part of her religious life she taught the graduating class or the first class. Her pupils will always remember her faithful care, and the great pains she bestowed on them and on many of the distinguished women of the country, who graduated under her instruction. Among these were Mrs. General Sherman, and afterwards her daughter, Mrs. Thackara; Mother Angela Gillespie, the late Superioress of the Holy Cross Sisters at Notre Dame; Mrs. Harriet Lane Johnson, and others. It was really wonderful to see her, at an advanced age, as faithful to class duties as when young, although a constant sufferer from ill health; and it is difficult to understand how she could possibly keep up and never fail to be at her post, under the stress of such bodily pain as she endured. Until she was stricken down with her death illness, she persisted regularly, to the astonishment of those who knew how delicate she was, in mounting up, lantern in hand, many flights of stairs to the Belvidere, carrying also plenty of maps, and prepared to teach her astronomy class about the constellations, as eager as if she were only twenty years of age. It was one of the secrets of Divine Providence, why Sister Genevieve, whose life had been a model of exact observance of the holy Rule of the convent, should have been burdened, as was the case, with a long martyrdom of two years of pain, before her death. Her physician, who was one of the best in Washington, and fully understood her suffering, was astonished that she could survive its ravages for so long, saying, " It is marvelous, marvelous ! " At last she died, in May, 1886, at the age of seventy-three, after having been forty-four years professed; and those who loved her best thanked God for her release.

But we should be omitting a still more important element in her character if we paused with speaking only of her academic service and her industry and perseverance in it. The *hidden* life of God's servants is known only to Himself, save for the few glimpses now and then vouchsafed to their fellow servants as an incentive to imitation. In Sister Genevieve these glimpses allowed her companions to discern an extreme delicacy of conscience, with indefatigable ardor in every duty, spiritual or temporal; an exactitude beyond comparison, involving necessarily the most heroic sacrifices, — in a word, an unceasing warfare on self. On the other hand, it was not difficult to see that her greatest fault lay in refusing offered relief when it was most craved by nature, lest some failure in stern duty might creep in.

The respect of Superiors for her excessively tender conscience prevented them from *requiring* her to give herself the care and rest that her health often called for. A development of character so sensitive yet so strong in this direction, not less than her devoted efficiency as a teacher, has caused the name of Sister Genevieve to be held sacred ever since in the community, with esteem, affection, and reverence. For a model in every Christian and religious virtue, in truth, we need scarcely look further.

Sister Mary Augustine Cleary. Sister Mary Augustine Cleary was a Virginian of good birth, and possessed in a remarkable degree the well-known characteristics of natives of that noble State, so richly endowed with men and women of brains, of generous instincts, and inbred courtesy. First a student, then a novice in the convent, she was professed in 1843.

Immediately thereafter a position in the Academy was assigned to her, which accorded with her excellent equipment of knowledge. Devoted to study and reading, Sister Augustine was veritably what might be termed a learned woman ; and the other sisters often joked about the accumulation of books to be found wherever her room might be. Like many persons given to deep thought and to reflection upon the stores of fact and information with which her memory busied itself, the good sister was often absent-minded. This trait being well known to her pupils, the mischievous among them frequently took advantage of it, greatly to their own satisfaction, if not to hers.

Scrupulously exact in following the Rule, she was a model to all religious ; and her always straightforward expression in favor of what was right won for her a general and pronounced respect. She was twice elected Superioress in Georgetown, once in 1852 and again in 1867 ; once in Frederick, Md., and twice in Abingdon, Va., — making four terms of three years each, in all a dozen years of arduous and responsible administration. From Abingdon she came back to her old home in Georgetown, very feeble and totally broken in health, and died here August 9, 1882, aged seventy-seven years. Her last illness was short and violent; but she had long been well prepared for this destined emergency, and so passed onward peacefully to her eternal rest.

SISTER
MARY
PAULINA
MILLARD.
The parents of this remarkable sister were Mr. Joshua Millard and Nancy Manning Millard, who both belonged to distinguished families among the old Colonial settlers of lower Maryland. They lived in Leonardtown, but finally removed with their numerous family to Washington. Sister Paulina, whose name before entering religion was Clotilda, was born on the Feast of the Epiphany, in 1812.

At that time, when Catholics were considered unworthy of position either social or political, the piety of the Millards shone forth fearlessly and beneficently. Mr. Millard was obliged to send his children to a secular school; but he gave them their religious instruction himself, until they were old enough to leave home for religious institutions. He was very particular about collecting the entire household for night prayers, catechism, and instruction, after which he would dismiss his children with his blessing and paternal caresses, as Sister Paulina delighted to relate. She also enjoyed giving accounts of her mother's firmness and bright example, and many other traits which rendered her saintly in character. Her mother never failed to assist at daily Mass, unless prevented by something very urgent. She would then return home and awaken her children, seeing personally to their prayers and breakfast; and prepare them for school, often sending off eight or nine at once of the whole charming group of fourteen. It is not surprising that three of these children devoted themselves to God's service in the Order of the Visitation, and that all were a credit to their home training.

Georgetown College and the Convent of the Visitation were then making their beginning ; and the older boys and girls were, as soon as possible, sent to these institutions. Clotilda was fourteen years old when she was consigned to the blessed abode of the convent. She soon desired to become a religious of this Order. In 1829, at the age of seventeen, she graduated with much distinction, receiving the " highest honors of the Academy " from the hands of John Quincy Adams, the President of the United States.

She returned to her family, and spent a short vacation with them ; after which she continued her studies for some months longer. The young girl then made a final visit of one day to her home, bidding farewell to those whom she loved best on earth, and entered the convent as a novice on the Feast of St. Catherine, November 25, 1829.

The sisters aver that Sister Paulina never once "looked back after putting her hand to the plow ; " though, when so young, she had entered God's service with such ardor that it might have been possible for her to tire, to remember with regret her easy home in the world, to feel that she had not fully understood the requirements of the convent. But no ; she had returned to her home for a single day to say good-by ; and yet had meant all that she said and did. What makes her unblemished adherence to principle and duty the more remarkable is that (as was learned from her pleasant way of telling anecdotes, although she was usually very reticent about herself) her novitiate was a particularly rigorous one ; for the Georgetown Convent was at that time governed by the French Sisters, elsewhere described, who had been invited to assist the Visitandines of America in establishing the rule of St. Francis de Sales in every iota of its demands. Some points of this rule were unsuited to American needs and climate; but the object was to keep as closely to the original decrees as possible ; and it is to be supposed that Sister Paulina was, as chance would have it, the test of how far an American nun might be capable of fulfilling them. But she was unspoiled, unselfish, and was upheld by a noble willingness ; so that, fortunately for the Order here, no unnecessary modifications were made through any failure on her part to subscribe in all things practicable. Her high degree of religious perfection, obtained through the training of these three beloved and thoroughly equipped French women, was of incalculable benefit to many souls whom she was destined to lead and teach.

At about twenty years of age, in Mobile, whither she had been transferred, she was proposed as Superioress. But she shrank from attempting it, as she was too young, and lacked the required years of profession for this post ; besides, her health was failing, under the pressure of care which had already fallen upon her. She acquainted her superiors at Georgetown with all the above facts of her position, and was immediately recalled to her first religious home. She was appointed Accountant and Aid to the venerable Sister Teresa Lalor, who was at the time Procuratrix in Georgetown.

After some six years she was appointed Directress of the academy at a new foundation in Baltimore ; and she entered upon her fresh duties with ardor.

The success of this academy, and the rapid increase of its pupils, sufficiently testified to her ability. For twenty years she earnestly carried on this labor, being also for a period simultaneously called to the office of Superioress, in which her real worth was most powerfully felt, however noteworthy her success as Directress had proved. She brought into practice many little points of observance, as soon as circumstances would permit, that were zealously cherished by her spiritual children. In 1857 she was called to the important charge of Superioress in the Washington Convent. The poignant regret of the Baltimore sisters, when she left them, was at last consoled in 1863, as they were then able once more to reëlect her to their house as Superioress.

Such a record gives amplest evidence of Sister Paulina Millard's administrative talents. These were surpassed only by her spirit of prayer and strict idea of religious observance. Her charity was boundless, and her sympathy extended to every one; but it was to the shamefaced poor that she showed what the sisters describe as more than maternal affection. Her disposition was genial, bright, and cheerful; and to her superiors she always showed a childlike deference and obedience. To her Sisters she was always kind, obliging, comforting in their sorrows, and sympathetic in their joys, as well as interested in the joys and sorrows of their dear relations in the world. She was beloved in and outside of the convent.

In 1890, after sixty years of service to the greatest number of her fellow beings possible, Sister Paulina began visibly to decline; and finally she left the community room for the last time; saying that she had preferred to endure the excessive pain of her severe illness among the sisters, and she knew that when she should once enter the infirmary she would never leave it for the community room again. She died in 1891. Although seventy-nine years of age, in death she had the appearance of one in the early bloom of youth, and her features expressed beatific happiness.

SISTER MARY LORETTO KING.
Sister Loretto, the late Directress of the Academy, who died on October 2, 1893, entered the convent in 1852, very soon after having graduated there as a pupil. In becoming a nun she gave up a happy home, in which she was almost idolized. A brother, Joseph King, also devoted himself to religion; becoming a Jesuit, and connecting himself with Georgetown College, where he died when still young. She had been reared in the most loving and delicate manner; but she bore the privations of the religious life heroically. As for labor, those who watched her declining years can best appreciate her sufferings and merits. She was in vain urged to take necessary rest; but she said she wished to die "in harness." Her appearance was commanding in manner, expressive both of firmness and gentleness; and respect and affection were the natural results of knowing her, however briefly. Many mothers who were educated at Georgetown Convent have placed their children under her care with the same enthusiastic esteem as if they were still schoolgirls themselves.

Twice she was elected Mother Superior; but continued to fill the office of Directress at the same time.

Her life was worn out in labors for the Academy; she was indefatigable in attention to what she deemed necessary and best for the house. How wasted and spent she was, those can deeply appreciate who knew her joyous nature of forty years ago. Many weary days of toil, which she could have shifted upon other shoulders, ennobled Sister Loretto, so that any one might see that her rare soul had been kept not only pure, but vigorous, in a constant effort for the good of others. All her natural vivacity had been so mingled with labor, that the labor had been transfigured; and the happy disposition, always lofty, had merged itself in healthy brain power. The former pupils who knew her best found her a true and loving friend and a life-long guide, counseling them safely in all perplexities, and seeking to instill into them an absolute confidence in God, — the strongest characteristic of her own strong heart.

SISTER CECILIA BROOKS, AND SISTER BERNARD GRAHAM. It would be impossible to name all the sisters who have been professed in Georgetown Convent, some of whom were subsequently sent on different foundations, with the details that would be gladly given if space permitted. Indeed, only a few of these sisters can be even mentioned. Some of them, however, were so long a part of the convent that it would be strange if their personalities did not find record in this account and chronicle of their home in religion.

Sister M. Cecilia Brooks was one of the much loved and much loving sisters whose lives were measured by many years of religious labor. She entered in 1819; and for the greater part of her life in the sisterhood was either the Superioress of the convent, or Directress of the school. She had great firmness of character, and great dignity; but she commanded not merely the respect of the scholars; they loved her, in return for her love. As Superioress she won the enthusiasm of the community by her genial character, her maternal thoughtfulness, and great generosity of soul; and she was highly respected by Archbishop Eccleston. Her happy government has never been forgotten. Sister Cecilia was sent as Superioress to Mount de Sales (Catonsville, Maryland), when that convent was founded. There she remained till her holy death, in 1860. She was called always by the endearing name of "Mother Cely." The beloved words "Mother Cely" have often been uttered by the older sisters in Georgetown, who have constantly quoted her as an oracle of good judgment.

Sister M. Bernard Graham was for many years Directress of the Academy. She was the daughter of the Hon. George Graham; and her mother was, by her first marriage, the wife of George Mason, of Gunston Hall, Va., by whom she was left a widow. Sister Bernard was born at Gunston Hall. She was the true type of a warm-hearted Virginian of the old school. Early in life she became a convert to Catholicity; and at the age of twenty-eight, in 1839, left friends and fortune, and the many pleasures at her command, to adopt a life of obedience and poverty at Georgetown. Far and wide, Sister Bernard's name will recall many happy memories. She possessed a sympathizing heart, and she had the ability to manifest her genial interest and tenderness in the most winning way. Her kindness to the sick was remarkable. The moment any illness among the pupils assumed a serious character, she gave up all other duty to her assistant, and watched beside the patient like a tender mother. She showed the deepest solicitude concerning everything relating to the comfort of the children.

It was most edifying to see how completely she ignored her early life of ease. Though she had learned to be accustomed to the ministration of servants, she never hesitated, when a nun, to perform any duty, however menial, if there were the slightest need of it. The older scholars, or graduates, can well remember how, on cold winter nights, Sister Bernard would go around, herself, with the coal-scuttle, and fill the stoves, to keep the dormitories and the " play-room " warm. Other loving attentions and humble kindnesses won the hearts of the children. In her last days she suffered from various infirmities ; but to the very end she insisted upon doing different services for herself which others would gladly have undertaken. She betrayed, one day, to a friend, that she was resolved thus to depend only on herself, out of a spirit of self-mortification ; for the words escaped her: " I love dearly to be waited upon." To any one who also loves dearly to be waited upon, and has been accustomed to that state of life, Sister Bernard's many years of unusually energetic labor and self-help will disclose great heroism. At her death, in 1888, on May 3, she received the last Sacraments in the utmost peace, after forty-eight years of religious life. This notice of a rarely noble soul will seem to numerous friends and old pupils too brief to satisfy their many loving memories. Sister Bernard's brother was the late General Mason Graham of Louisiana, well known as a soldier, and a thorough gentleman of the most refined culture.

SISTER FELIX COXE. Sister Felix entered the convent on June 8, 1839. She was a widow, who had consecrated herself to good works in the parish of Father Varella, a saintly priest of New York. She chose, in the convent, the rank of out-sister, as more suited to her disposition and habits of life.

The period of her religious life was long, but through it all she never relaxed her zeal for Church work; laboring for poor churches and for fairs, constantly. She was never idle. Old vestments, now darkly colored by time, attest the skill of her fingers, and prove that her eyesight well seconded her taste for fine embroidering. Her even disposition and placid temper added to her great usefulness. It would be hard to recall a single unkind word or uncharitable remark ever spoken by her. The closing years of her life were years of what the world would call terrible suffering; but the true religious is angelically spared all terror. An affection of the eye slowly disfigured her face. She who had, formerly, been the Sacristan, on whom it devolved to go forward and welcome or wait on the Bishops and priests who came to celebrate Mass, was now no longer the bright hostess and attendant, but was forced to retire into the shadows, because of a repulsive disease. Truly, this was the most beautiful, the most heroic part of her life, as her sister religious tell.

She could no longer sew for the poor, or work for the Church, — her dearest occupations: she could not even read her prayer-book, the reward of hours of fatiguing toil. But no impatient word ever escaped her; and she was very grateful for every little attention which she received. When death came, at the end of fifty years of hard work, her sisters trust that she was blessed with full consolation. Her " day," of half a century, included the time of many distinguished pupils. She taught them embroidery, accompanied them on their shopping and pleasure expeditions, and in many ways contributed to their enjoyment, before her illness drew a sharp barrier between such pleasant service and her then more sombre life, — and more profound self-abnegation.

Sister Mary Eulalia Pearce. One of the most remarkable sisters who have entered Georgetown Convent, was Miss Julia Pearce, a Bostonian, a scion of old Puritan stock. She became a member of the community in 1844.

She was most charming in manner, and had great musical ability, and was extraordinarily beloved and popular (if one should apply the latter term to a religious) among the pupils. More than one reader of these Annals will remember with gratitude that Sister Eulalia led her to the true faith. At a time when she herself had scarcely a single Catholic acquaintance, and the one or two whom she did know were converts, it seemed as if the Holy Spirit fired her soul with the gift of the true faith. This devotion to the faith never flickered for a moment in its bright flame. In the midst of ill health, keen sorrows, and the painful

changes from dear association, which the religious
who is transferred from the first convent home to a
new foundation must experience, she, as it were, held
the lamp of her belief aloft, and said in the words of
the apostle: "Rejoice in the Lord; serve Him with
gladness!" She used to tell an anecdote of herself,
which illustrates her spirit. When she was received
into the Church her joy was so exuberant that she
felt she must communicate her happiness to some
sympathizing person. But *how* was she to find one
in Boston, and fifty years ago, too, who would or
could sympathize with a Catholic convert? She
knew of no one who would rejoice with her except a
good old Irish washerwoman, and so she hurried off
to her, and threw her arms around her neck, and then
danced up and down, exclaiming, "*We are Catholics!*"

Sister Eulalia brought to the Church all the enthusiasm of her New England descent, added to which
was the holy fervor which the Faith had inspired in
her. She gave herself heart and soul to God, and
"He never failed her;" by which phrase the religious
means that despair is utterly powerless to assail the
buoyancy of ecstatic trust which blesses her whole
existence. After much suffering from a wasting disease, which the good God permitted Sister Eulalia to
endure for her greater purification, she ended her
charming and inspiring life at Wheeling Convent,
whither she had been transferred from Georgetown
many years before her death. For a long time, while
at her home in the world, she had been obliged to endure the painful opposition of prejudiced minds in the

family circle, but she finally won the happiness of being joined in the Church by her sister, who entered the Visitation Order in Frederick, Maryland.

XVIII. LIVES OF SISTERS, CONCLUDED.

There remain in our series of little portraits those of three sisters who represented distinctive types; while the personal or family associations connected with each of them, before they took up the gentle cross of monastic life, were of uncommon and striking interest.

In addition to the touch of picturesqueness and romance in the ancestry of Sister Joseph Keating and the dignified personality of her father, Baron Keating, it is to be noted that she — like Sister Felix Coxe — was a widow when she came to the convent, but did not limit herself to the labors of an out-sister. Having well fulfilled all her duties to her husband and son, and having faithfully, tenderly cared for her father all through his old age, she consecrated the last thirty-one years of her existence to a thorough participation in all the cloistral work and worship of the Visitation, and became for a time Mother Superior. A noteworthy example, this, of energy and persistence in good, both at home and within the cloister!

Sister Mary Austin Barber, who was also married long before her vocation became clear to her, affords another and singular instance of strength and determination; giving up as she did a close and happy union with her husband, and surrendering home life with her children at the same time that their father entered the priesthood. Her case was so altogether exceptional, that we must beg our readers to bear in mind the fact of its being quite out of the common, and to make no generalizations from it.

Virginia Scott, or Sister Mary Emmanuel, — the daughter of General Winfield Scott, — on the other hand, illustrates that class of vocations which are inspired in people who have been surrounded by an atmosphere apparently unfavorable to such inspiration, and perhaps even charged with elements repellent or hostile to it. Yet such a vocation may be just as commanding, just as invincible, as though it had arisen from long training or from a groundwork of every imaginable fostering condition. It may be said of Sister Mary Emmanuel Scott, as of the other two here to be spoken of, that a gift of prophecy would have been needed to foretell, from their beginnings, that any one of these would ever be affiliated with a conventual sisterhood. This is true even of Sister Mary Joseph Keating ; for although she came of heroically Catholic stock and was devoted to the faith, who could have supposed that marriage and motherhood, with their happiness or their cares, and the long responsibilities of nursing an aged father, would still leave her nearly a third of a century of beneficent life to dedicate to religion ?

SISTER MARY JOSEPH KEATING. Sister Mary Joseph Keating's family was a noble one, of Irish descent, whose titles and estates were confiscated to a Protestant relative, under the penal laws of England, imposed upon Catholics in Ireland.

The descendants of that Protestant relative — Earl Dunraven and Lord Adare — have returned to the true faith. Sister Joseph's great-grandfather, Sir Geoffrey Keating, who distinguished himself at the siege of Limerick, afterwards withdrew with the army of James II. to France. The Keatings were cordially received by the French ·monarch, and thenceforward made that country their home; though they frequently returned to visit Adare.

Sister Joseph's father, called plain Mr. Keating, or Chevalier Keating, after his settling in America, had inherited a title from his family, and was also made a Knight of St. Louis for important services in France. After the French Revolution he received a tempting offer from the Directory; but he was stanch in his devotion to the house of Bourbon, and declined all overtures. He emigrated to America, bringing letters to General Washington and others, which at once admitted him to the highest social circles. He married Miss Des Chappelles, of San Domingo, and resided chiefly in Philadelphia. He had lived " while Frederick the Great was fighting, Chatham was speaking, and Voltaire was˙writing; he was born forty years before Walpole died, and was sixty years of age when George IV. was crowned. He knew Washington and Franklin, and was nine years older than Napoleon." One of his sons married the beautiful Miss Hopkinson, granddaughter of Francis Hopkinson, a signer of the Declaration of Independence; and she was a daughter of the author of " Hail Columbia." For sixty years Baron Keating was an American citizen in name, habit, and feeling. Both as a Christian and a gentleman, he was respected to an extraordinary degree. Principle was so strong in him that he refused when in France to be presented at the court of Louis Philippe, whom he did not consider to be the lawful sovereign. The King had received hospitality from Baron Keating while in this country as an exile, and he wished to make return ; so he sent word to the Baron to come and visit him as a private citizen, — which was done, in due but simple form.

Among Sister Mary Joseph's many virtues was her indifference, with entire reticence, as to those honors of the world which had distinguished her family. One could live long in her society, and never suspect that she had sacrificed so many worldly advantages. Very rarely, in moments of intimate friendship, she would tell some pleasant items ; such as how she horrified her father, the first time he took her to France, by rising to receive the gorgeously dressed usher or footman, supposing him to be a noble guest! A sister has particularly noticed an incident which illustrated Sister Joseph's entire absence of ostentatious pride, and her reticence about the distinctions of the family. Sister Joseph, before leaving the world, had been a wife, a mother, and a widow ; and her granddaughter was now at the convent as a pupil. One morning, the sister found that the young girl had taken a good morning's nap, instead of going to Mass ; upon which she cried : " Oh, how can *you*, whose ancestors gave up titles and estates for the Faith, be so lazy about going to Mass ? " The child was utterly astonished to hear of her family's former titles and estates, for they had never been alluded to before in her presence.

We have said that Sister Mary Joseph was a widow. She came to the convent in 1843. All

the time which she had spent in the world subsequently to her husband's death had been given
to works of charity and the care of her aged father, whom she loved and honored as he deserved.
After a time she was transferred to Frederick Convent; but was ultimately recalled to Georgetown,
having been elected its Superioress in 1858. She
died in 1874. The care of the sick was one great
" attraction " for Sister Joseph. Long experience had
rendered her a most reliable judge of the best remedies and treatments. The poor, suffering, and lowly
found a sure friend in her. She was ready for any
duty, — and how much inconvenient effort that in-
volves! The sisters can remember that her skillful
hand seasoned what were really poor dishes so deliciously, during the first year or two of the Civil War,
when the school was nearly broken up and the greatest economy had to be practiced, that the retrench-
ments were hardly felt: her excellent knowledge of
housekeeping concealed the scarcity.

She was the mother of Dr. William Keating, a
well-known physician of Philadelphia ; and she was a
near relative of the saintly Colonel Garesché.

SISTER
MARY
AUSTIN
BARBER.
A word of preface seems to be necessary
in giving here our brief account of Sister
Mary Austin Barber ; because the circumstances under which her entrance to the
monastic life was made were so extraordinary. It is a
thing almost unheard of that a husband and a wife,
especially when they have children, should simultaneously feel called upon to give up their life together,
and separately devote themselves to the absolute ser-

vice of religion.   Nor would the Church permit such a sacrifice, unless there were a mutual consent between the two, and a distinct, unquestionable vocation on the part of each; for otherwise an indignity might seem to be offered to the sacrament of marriage.

One of the Church's greatest functions in this world is to build up, to conserve, and hold together the family, and sanctify it.   Therefore it does everything in its power to prevent division in families and to maintain peace, concord, and good-will in them.   Hence it would have been impossible to let Mr. and Mrs. Barber follow their vocations, if their agreement had not been complete and the circumstances exceptional. As it was, their choice seemed to be justified; and their young children also were happily provided for.

Mrs. Barber (Sister Mary Austin) was a young woman of twenty-eight, a wife and the mother of five children, when she entered the convent.   Her husband was an Episcopalian minister, Rev. Virgil Barber, who at the time of his conversion to Catholicity was president of an Episcopalian seminary and received a very comfortable salary for his services in that position. The first thing which drew his attention strongly to Catholic faith was a biography of St. Francis Xavier, "whose parallel" — as he told his wife, not a little to her distaste at that time — "could not be found in the whole Protestant Church."   When his only son was born, Mr. Barber refused to name him, because his wife would not accept for the child what she firmly declared to be " the popish name of Francis Xavier." Mrs. Barber therefore was obliged to depend on her own choice, and called the boy Samuel, after the prophet of the old law.

Mr. Barber, however, had been so much attracted and awed by the holiness of St. Francis Xavier that he justly concluded it would be wise to go still deeper into the perusal of Catholic sanctity in the records of other saints ; and also to investigate the doctrine which had produced such matchless nobility. He drew his wife eagerly into these avenues of study. She was very much opposed to Catholicity, and held back deliberately until every point was rendered clear, through careful translations made by her husband from the most important passages in the works of the early Fathers. These he had diligently read during a visit to New York and its libraries.

The day inevitably came when Mr. and Mrs. Barber found that they must either become Catholics or abjectly turn away from their conviction as to the truth. At once the Episcopal Bishop and ministers who were interested in the seminary over which Mr. Barber presided and in which he was professor, were obliged to request him to resign. He had foreseen this ; but it was with his generous wife's entire acquiescence that he relinquished the tempting competency, which thus far had made their lives comfortable. It was now necessary for them to set to work and earn a bare subsistence ; and they opened a small school in New York. Some of the Catholic clergy seemed to regard the new converts with distrust, and so allowed them to struggle on without definite encouragement ; but Father Fenwick, afterwards Bishop of Boston, was an exception. He penetrated the uprightness of Mr. and Mrs. Barber, and took a friendly interest in them, — in short he obeyed the teachings of brotherly love, by looking for and expecting virtue instead of mischief.

Nevertheless, the husband and wife must have made a peculiarly puzzling enigma to every one not blessed with far more than the ordinary gentleness and charity; since their disregard of the laws of prudence was most daring, and involved five little children. That their course with regard to these children was not really either fanatical or cruel is, we think, proved by their trust in God's care, as well as by the necessity they felt of giving Him worship in precisely the way He had commanded; which was the cause of their impoverishment. Mrs. Barber says that she considered the children as God's, rather than hers, she being but the temporary agent, as it were, of their heavenly Father; so that she would not have refused to obey his *command* to follow Him in the religious steps He had pointed out to us all, because her little family might thereby lose more than they would gain. She knew that this never could be the case where God was obeyed. Those two converts - acted with that lack of the usual forms of wisdom with which St. Peter acted, when he trusted his footsteps on the water, having received an encouragement greater than any worldly prudence can give. It will be seen that each member of this family suffered much. What they gained will also be seen.

Father Fenwick was, in the course of the following year, called to Georgetown to assume the rectorship of the college; and he wrote to Mr. Barber to ask him what plans he had for the future. In the letter which he sent in reply, Mr. Barber happened to say

that if it were not for his wife and children he should
enter the priesthood, as he felt a decided call towards
it. He had always been in the habit of reading to
his wife every letter that he received or wrote, and
did so in this instance. The sentence which spoke of
his leaning towards the priesthood, she afterwards
said, was a deathblow to her happiness. She tried to
forget it ; but everything reminded her of it. After
much delay she told her husband of the impression
upon her which his words to Father Fenwick had
made, and how she feared that if she did not act according to her belief, which was that he had been
called by God to enter the priesthood, she would be
the cause of their all losing their greatest sanctification. Mr. Barber soothed her agony of mind, and
assured her that his letter to Father Fenwick had
only expressed his lifelong predilection for the ministry ; but that he felt himself bound to his family by
all the laws of God and man. She endeavored to accept this explanation, yet found she did not believe it
was in accordance with God's will. Mr. Barber was
secretly of the same opinion, although he remained
silent while he had any doubt as to the right course
for him in the matter. But when this right course
became manifest to them both, he strengthened his
wife's courage by hopeful exhortations that she should
look forward to their reunion in heaven, after generous labor for others in this suffering world.

She, for her part, decided that her true course
pointed towards the Visitation Order, and that she
ought to become a member of it. Archbishop Neale
himself, the American founder, introduced her to the

sisters in the assembly-room, one day; and his high regard for her character was indicated by his remark to them: "Not one of you must give Mrs. Barber the black bean!"

On the day following Archbishop Neale's burial, it being the festival of St. Aloysius, the Jesuit Fathers of the college of Georgetown (where, as we have said, the kind Father Fenwick was Rector) invited Mrs. Barber to dine with them in their refectory; a privilege which, they told her, had never before been granted to any woman. After dinner three of the fathers accompanied her to the convent, and left her in the hands of Mother Lalor and Sister Agnes Brent, who was then Mistress of novices. Mrs. Barber's little son and baby daughter were in the care of Father Fenwick's mother, who rejoiced in adopting them. Mrs. Fenwick lived in a large mansion not far from the college grounds. The three other children, daughters, were received as pensioners into the convent, where Mrs. Barber, afterwards Sister Mary Austin, was able to maintain a constant care of them. Her husband had started on a journey to Rome, to begin his novitiate for the priesthood. The decision had been made; the family, loving and faithful to each other, had chosen diverse paths, which, after all, led to one goal.

Mrs. Barber undertook her novitiate with much fervor. She was so anxious to cast off her worldly attire that she succeeded in making herself a complete novice costume, without waiting for the ceremony of a formal investment. This she put on; and the community was decidedly surprised, on next meeting the postu-

CONVENT REFECTORY

lant, to find that she had literally *taken* the veil, with her own hands. Mother Lalor and Sister Agnes Brent were heartily amused at her simplicity and earnestness, and would not mar her new-found happiness by depriving her of its livery for a moment.

As she could not come across a mirror anywhere in the convent, and had some concern lest her habit was not always properly adjusted, she used to arrange it by standing before a small four-paned glass window, that overlooked the garden and could be opened in lattice-fashion, thus serving very well for a mirror. The sisters who passed her while she put herself in dainty order were never permitted by their conventual Rule to look at themselves in a glass; but the new sister was innocent of any knowledge to this effect. In a few days she was admitted to the religious habit and to all instructions. She became a shining light as a teacher in the Academy; then as its Directress, and as a trainer of novices for teaching; and was indeed of the most invaluable aid, because of her high order of culture, and her rare capacity for imparting it to others.

But her trials by repeated sorrow were very great. In the first place, she had not been in the novitiate for more than three months, when it was deemed advisable that she should withdraw to the world for a time, though much against her desire. She went to Philadelphia, where she established herself in a boarding-house. Strange to say, to this boarding-house came two gentlemen, one a Captain Baker, who rehearsed at the dinner-table the events of a voyage which they had recently made to Europe. Wholly unconscious of who

Sister Mary Austin really was, Captain Baker told how much sympathy he had felt for an Episcopal minister on board, who, having left home, wife, and children, to enter the Jesuit Order, was so overwhelmed with grief that they feared he would die. "I never pitied a man so much in my life," concluded the captain. Sister Mary Austin bore this shock with religious submission, but with intense anguish, only relieved by the good counsel of her spiritual adviser. She was now by no means sure that she might not have been mistaken in thinking that her husband had at heart approved of their extraordinary step in separating to enter the monastic life. To feel that we may be wrong in making a sacrifice which crucifies our personal happiness is certainly a most forlorn misery. It turned out, however, that Mr. Barber was fully as much in earnest as herself in offering the remainder of his life for the uses of pure generosity ; although the actual carrying out of that offering cost him great agony. When Mrs. Barber finally took her solemn vows in the convent Chapel, Mr. Barber, who had then returned from Europe, made in the same place and at the same time his own profession ; their five young children being present. Of these children the four daughters all became devoted nuns, and the son a saintly Jesuit, — a sufficient answer to any question as to the wisdom of their parents in abandoning the ordinary methods of looking after their development.

The poverty of the convent, and her own poverty upon entering it, proved to be another source of profound trial. She supposed that her husband had been able to make provision to a moderate extent for her own and the children's bare support in the convent; but this she found was not so. The community itself was enduring extreme want; so that, although her services were invaluable, there was a practical dilemma of ways and means to consider, entirely apart from hospitality and willingness. Yet Sister Mary Austin and her little daughters were dependents and must remain such. She was bitterly humbled by this thought; and, besides, grieved at the privations in regard to warmth and food which, even in sickness, her children were of course compelled to experience. Then, her naturally tender, impulsive heart was crushed at discovering, a year after she came to the Visitation, that her infant daughter Josephine, two years old, who eventually lived much with her, and wrote her life for the convent records, would not run to her arms upon being brought to see her. This was just before she took her solemn vows. She retired to her cell to give vent to her anguish; but Sister Agnes Brent followed her.

"What makes you cry?" asked Sister Agnes.

"My God!" exclaimed the mother; "to think my own child does not know me!"

"Well, why did you give her up?" was the answering query, made in kindness, to remind the postulant of the heavenly motive of her sacrifice, yet innocently bare of pathos or flattery.

There is a dearth of these quasi-consolations, in the monastic study of holiness. What is said and done for God must be absolutely meant and completely carried out, or we at once suffer for our self-deception, through the intrepid frankness of our superiors, who quietly point out our shortcoming in this respect.

But perhaps the most heroic moments of some brave people are those in which they bear the defeat of their courage without many words of regret, or many passionate tears. Sister Mary Austin has said: " I could have put myself under the feet of any one who was kind to my children ! " Yet this fervent nature kept steadily to its resolve to think first of the needs of Christ, then of her children, and of herself only as a friend towards others.

At sixteen years of age (the youngest of four daughters) Mrs. Barber had lost her father, and from this time she applied herself to comfort and please her mother, and to be *religious*, though she had already shown devotion in prayer, and was in the habit of kneeling and offering to God every new article of dress, particularly if it were likely to excite her vanity. She did not think her *actions* worthy of being offered to God. She told her children, late in life, that she believed the devil had always pursued herself and them with peculiar ferocity, causing disasters and other rebuffs to assail them all, with the hope of destroying their perseverance in faith. She had remarkable courage in enduring physical pain ; showing that her extreme ardor and sensitiveness were mastered by a calm and noble will.

Her brilliant intelligence and erudition were, after nineteen years of immense usefulness at Georgetown, eagerly sought for, in 1836, in assisting to found the house at Kaskaskia. She was there for about eight years, and then went to St. Louis, with Mother Agnes Brent, to establish still another house. When sixty years old, in 1848, she was sent to the Visitation convent at Mobile, which was then in great need of members. Wherever she was placed she showed her greatest usefulness by forming classes of sisters, who soon became, under her skill for training them, accomplished teachers, thus augmenting the strength and influence of the schools connected with the convents, and obviating the expense and inconvenience of employing secular instructors.

It will be remembered that her husband had first been led to the study of Catholicity through his knowledge of the wonderful life of St. Francis Xavier, and it was on the Feast of St. Francis Xavier that Sister Mary Austin was attacked by her last illness, through which her soul was to reach, away from the unflagging labors of this life, its reward of peace. Her patience in illness surpassed that of all others ; *her* patience, — she who had been born with the fire of strong passions within her breast! A touching episode closes her record of renunciations. While dying, she could only say repeatedly, " I want— " At last the sister who sat by her side, and had suggested to her many names and things, without hitting upon the right one, said gently : —

" Sister Mary Austin, you have made many sacrifices to God, — make this one sacrifice of not trying to express your wish, now. I cannot understand you ! "

The dying nun acquiesced.

When we are thwarted most, we may win love most.

The story of Sister Mary Emmanuel is a brief and simple one, yet in its brevity touching, and beautiful in its simplicity. She was the second daughter of

Major General Winfield Scott, commanding the United
States Army, the hero of Chapultepec and
Mexico, who until the outbreak of the Civil
War, with its new opportunities and new
leaders, was the most renowned figure in the
military chronicle of the nation since Revolutionary days.

This circumstance, no doubt, caused the social
world to take a special interest, at the time, in her
conversion and her entrance upon the religious life.
But there is a deeper reason for including in the publication of these annals some account of her career,
short and in one sense uneventful though it was.
That reason is found in the perfect example it gives
of renunciation of the world, where the world presented itself under the most smiling aspect and seemed
to offer everything that ambition could wish for.

Ambition, indeed, was at first the ruling motive
with Virginia Scott. In her girlhood she was very
beautiful, and, moreover, so gifted by nature intellectually that her companions at school could not com-
pete with her in her studies and accomplishments.
Having finished her education, she went to Paris with
her mother and three younger sisters, two of whom
were placed as *pensionnaires* or boarders in the Convent of the Sacred Heart. Through them, Virginia
became acquainted with the nuns of that institution
and was most favorably impressed with Catholicity.
Her conversion was the result, for soon afterwards at
Rome, in February, 1843, she made her abjuration
of error and profession of faith, in the chapel of St.
Ignatius, the ceremony taking place there by special

permission of Most Rev. John Roothan, General of the Society of Jesus.

Still, apparently, there was nothing to prevent her realizing all the ambitions that her father's fame and position and her own beauty and thoroughly cultivated talents would naturally open to her. In Paris, she had made a matrimonial engagement with a young man of high standing. The vista of her earthly future, therefore, seemed clearly outlined before her and glowing with rosy promise. With mind and soul at peace in the faith, with an affectionate heart ready to join itself to hers for life, with distinction, the power to charm and to command social success, why, many will ask, should she not have accepted these conditions contentedly, and indeed with elation? But there is an inspiration, a foresight of the soul, that, in a being even so happily situated as she was, may cause it to measure at a glance all the joys, the vicissitudes, the sacrifices and gains of a prosperous career in society or the world, and, having so measured, to count them as nothing compared with the service that may be rendered to God in another mode of life. From the time of her reception into the Church, Virginia Scott longed for complete spiritual devotion, with a hunger that could be satisfied only by an act of entire self-renunciation.

As a first step towards this, she obtained from her betrothed a release from her promise of marriage. Her inclination at this time was to join the Sisters of Charity of St. Vincent de Paul. But on her return to America and to Washington, she learned to know the Visitandines of Georgetown, whom she frequently

came to see at their convent. Their Order proved to
have a strong attraction for her, which in the beginning she resisted, because she believed both vocation
and duty had pointed out the work of a Sister of
Charity as that to which her efforts must be given.
At length, however, during fervent prayer in the
chapel of the Sacred Heart, it seemed to her that
the Divine Will directed her to become a member of
the Visitation; and before she arose from her knees she
had vowed never to leave this convent. She told the
superiors of her vow, at once; and when they had
satisfied themselves that her vocation was a true one,
they admitted her to her first probation.

This decision of hers, and its result, greatly agitated
her family, who opposed it with tears, entreaties, even
threats. Nothing that might divert her from her purpose was left undone; but all their efforts were unavailing. Deeply sensible though she was of the
kindness that had been showered upon her by her
parents, and anxious not to wound any one, still she
could not and would not yield; because to her vision
it was clear that a greater good was to be gained for
them and for all by her sanctification. She entered
the convent; yet, owing to the delicacy of her health
at this time, she was not allowed to wear the habit for
the first six months. Every day that she thus remained in secular garb must, she knew, defer the
period of her holy profession, for which she longed intensely; and it was therefore a heavy trial to her.
Her humility and obedience under these circumstances,
with her exact fidelity to every least observance, en-
deared her to all the sisters; and they determined to

admit her to her reception. During her retreat, preparatory to this, it was most edifying to those who had the happiness of being near her to see her delicate frame bent in prayer, or her hands and eyes raised to heaven, her angelic countenance beaming with piety while she poured forth her glowing aspirations.

At last the happy morning came when she was robed in the humble yet, to her, glorious attire of a Visitation novice. But it was not at any time her fortune to share in all the exercises of the community. If the young heroine had looked forward to severe participation in these as to a state of exquisite joy, she was obliged to give up this earthly hope, also; for her increasing ill health confined her to the infirmary. Here, nevertheless, her resignation was without flaw; she remained cheerful, obedient, grateful, although the Divine Will imposed upon her the mortification of being disabled, by physical weakness, from using even a single one of her splendid talents or accomplishments for the good of others or in aid of the community.

But that ambition which had prompted her to make progress in learning, to take the lead among her friends, — if it had disappeared, was it lost? and must this be taken as a sign of weakness? No; we should say, rather, that the early ambition had been transmuted into something finer, — it was now directed wholly towards thankful resignation, and towards implicit union with God in whatever manner He might appoint. A careless thinker, judging by common averages, might have supposed that her beauty and her former worldly station would have weakened her

capacity for humility; but, on the contrary, that
virtue now shone out brightly as a strong point in her
noble character.   So true it is that a dominant trait
of mere human nature in a person thoroughly dedicated to religious aspiration may become like a well-
tilled garden-bed from which the whitest and sweetest
flowers of spiritual being spring.

Sister Mary Emmanuel (the name which Virginia
Scott received in religion) never spoke of herself.
Her exceptional gifts, the high social place she had
quitted, the opportunities she had sacrificed, were
never alluded to by her.   This self-restraint did not
come from inertia, as might be seen from her eagerness for the things that are immortal.   She prayed
constantly for the salvation of souls ; and so ardent
was her longing in this respect that the news of a
conversion always made her face radiant.

Her father, General Scott, was admitted at times
to see her, according to the custom, which, in cases of
extreme illness, allows parents or near relatives to enter some part of the monastic precinct.   Indeed, Sister Mary Emmanuel was growing so frail, her health
was so precarious, that her loving companions in the
community feared her life would fade away before the
date appointed for her solemn vows.   Ten months of
her novitiate had gone by, when the tokens of her approaching end became so clear that it was decided not
to wait for the expiration of the year.   Her happiness
and fervor as the time approached were matters of
rejoicing among the nuns, who watched with thanksgiving her great merits and God's mercy towards her.
The Heavenly Father never permits himself to be out-

done in generosity. He gave Sister Emmanuel, in the holy experiences and perceptions of these months, a heavenly measure of bliss.

Sister Emmanuel Scott died on the very day of her profession, bearing herself, to the end, with a composure and gentleness such as are peculiar to a piety like hers. She clasped the crucifix, and pressed it to her lips with a firmness that typified her strong reliance upon Christ, enduring even while her own vital forces failed. All the aspirations she uttered were spoken in the sweetest tones. After sinking into unconsciousness, she would awaken only when the crucifix was held to her lips, and then she would kiss it fervently. Her last words, spoken gently, were, " Jesus, the God of my heart ! "

General Scott was absent from Washington at the time of her death, but returned before her burial. So remarkable a beauty had been restored to her after her decease, that the nuns delighted to gaze upon her mortal frame; but when the general arrived to take his last look at her, where she lay silent on the marble slab of Father Clorivière's tomb in the open vault below the chapel, this external beauty had vanished, being an earthly illusion. The general stood long beside her, meditating, with profound, suppressed emotion, then bade farewell to all that remained of her mortal loveliness. The immortal, the imperishable part, we trust, had ascended on high. Who would dare to say that with its purity, its prayers, and aspirations, the soul of the child may not have aided to draw the soul of the father into happy reunion with it in the light of a life beyond this ?

The history of Sister Mary Emmanuel Scott suggests the growth, the budding, the unfolding, and swift passing away of a flower. Could it have been developed equally well in the outer world? Hardly; because experience teaches us that, in all fields or departments, to obtain certain results we must have certain conditions. People spend large sums of money in order to grow rare plants and raise exquisite blossoms, in gardens of mere earth and nature, and for this purpose form rigorous enclosures which they guard jealously. The plants they cultivate there are material things that must inevitably perish forever.

In the peaceful enclosure of the Georgetown convent the soul of Sister Emmanuel bloomed, as others have done, like a lily; not to die, but to be transplanted into celestial gardens.

XIX. PAST AND PRESENT.

The life-sketches of sisters given in the preceding chapters throw illuminating rays over the years following that date, 1831, to which the formal chronicle had brought us. Many of these consecrated women lived in the diligent practice of their vocation until a time so recent, that their individual stories — carrying on the story of the convent — blend into the sunshine of the present, as the stars of morning mingle with the light of broadening day.

Little now remains to be added to the Annals; for the current of life within the enclosure flows on evenly, quietly, with so few episodes cognizable by the world, that the record of one year would read very much like that of another — until we come to the period of the Civil War. This indeed was a new time of trial to the community, which had become so well established, and to the Academy, on which its material support so largely depended.

When the war-storm burst abruptly over the land, Southern parents (who were then the chief patrons of the school) hurried to Georgetown while there was still opportunity to pass through the military lines ; and in a few days all their children were withdrawn. The number of boarding pupils fell to about twenty four, while the community to be supported consisted of eighty persons. The income from tuition fees was therefore quite inadequate to the maintenance of the house. There was no money in bank and very little coming in ; so that the situation was most perilous and aroused grave apprehensions. To the open violence of war the convent was not exposed at any time ; although in the early days of the conflict, and again in 1862, Washington and Georgetown were dangerously near to becoming the actual scene of battle. Yet it should be said, to the credit of the American people, that amid all the excitement and confusion of those times, and with large bodies of troops continually in the neighborhood, the sisters met with nothing but courtesy at the hands of every one connected with the military operations there. A special guard, even, was stationed to protect the convent.

It is true that at first the Government thought of taking possession of the convent and grounds for army purposes, as it also temporarily occupied Georgetown College ; but General Scott asked Secretary

Stanton to spare the place made sacred to him by the grave of his child ; and the convent accordingly escaped desecration.

The pecuniary problem, — the question of subsistence, and of saving the institution from wreck through want of means, — was what caused the chief anxiety of the sisters. And now, like their predecessors in the time of humble yet noble beginnings, they were true to the traditions of highest courage; trusting implicitly in God, although the way of his providing for their temporal needs could not be foreseen. Every possible economy was practiced ; all rooms that were not absolutely needed were closed, — the cost of heating them being thereby saved. The community went on bravely, patiently, with its unceasing devotions, its daily labor ; and the guardianship of Providence was soon made clear. Gifts of provisions were sent in by friends ; a kind merchant, Mr. Jacob Kengla, consented to wait for payment for supplies ; many things were done for them by others who were moved to good will. Once or twice, friends proposed that they should lease the Academy to the Government; by which they could have realized a large sum ; but the sisters resolutely chose not to do anything so discordant with the original aim of their foundation ; and their fidelity and courage were justified in the end. Rumors of possible fighting at Washington, when the war broke out, led to a general belief in some quarters that the community would have to disperse and look for shelter elsewhere. Thereupon Madam Hardy, Superioress of the Ladies of the Sacred Heart, immediately planned that they should come to her at Manhattan, and prepared for them all the rooms she had at her disposal. That these reports of dispersion were unfounded does not detract from the ready and admirable assistance offered by Madam Hardy, whose noble character made her beloved far and wide. The Visitation sisters of Georgetown wish her generosity and their keen appreciation of it to be recorded here in their Annals.

Gradually the Academy began to recover prosperity, when the war came to an end. Pupils again flocked thither as of old; a large proportion, perhaps even a majority of them, being Protestants. But the main patronage was now no longer derived from the South, where so many of the sisters' beloved friends and former pupils had suffered complete financial ruin. The West especially, which had manifested its giant strength in the national trouble and had now entered upon a career of vast development in peace, sent many children to the Academy. Before long, everything resumed its usual channel.

In 1872–73 the demands of the growing school made it necessary to replace the old Academy building with a new one, which was accordingly put up on a large scale. This edifice (described in our opening pages) not only has added greatly to the facilities of the institution, but remains a tangible proof of its prosperity. Yet a severe business panic, coming on at about the time of its erection, made the year a bad one for borrowing money; and the community was obliged to pay a high rate of interest on the funds required for the new structure. The heavy amount of annual interest came to be a very severe burden to the sisters; and they were finally compelled to attempt the negotiating of a new loan on easier terms.

It is a fact most gratifying, and worthy to be chronicled in terms of cordial praise, that the gentleman who made them this mortgage loan, on conditions very much more favorable than those under which they had been laboring, was a Protestant, Mr. John Cassels, of Washington. To his kindness and accommodation in this matter the sisters acknowledge a deep and grateful obligation. We may add, here, that such an instance of friendliness and good will from an individual Protestant towards a Catholic community, and the charming, intimate, profoundly trustful relations between the sisters and their Protestant pupils confided to them by Protestant parents, denote that true Christian charity which is not of money, which is not bound up in mere almsgiving or generosity in financial transactions, but is charity of the soul.

The Georgetown sisters of the Visitation earnestly desire to express in this place their appreciation of Mr. Cassels' great courtesy and confidence. No more thoroughly agreeable relations between debtor and creditors could have existed than those which resulted from his kindly and opportune assistance; nor could so large a debt have been more pleasantly liquidated.

If the Georgetown Convent of the Visitation had accomplished nothing else, we might almost say that its hundred years of faithful toil have borne sufficient fruit in the establishing, maintaining, and illustrating of such wholesome intercourse between Catholics and Protestants.

Another benefactor was Miss Mary Abell of Baltimore, who lived in the Georgetown convent while waiting to realize a plan cherished by her of establishing a Visitation convent without a school. Her liberal donations greatly assisted in carrying the community and Academy through a period of considerable distress. The late Dr. P. J. Murphy also left them a generous legacy; and one of the older sisters gave them the income which she had inherited. Thus at length the indebtedness was lowered to so small an amount as no longer to cause anxiety; and in later years the sisters have constantly gone on making improvements, for the comfort and health of pupils, as well as in beautifying the spacious grounds.

Here, practically, ends the Story of Courage, in a rich and fine fulfillment of the spiritual aims of the founders, with that accompaniment of a simple yet solid material basis, which is the natural result of unselfish industry. But we should miss an essential point in the many lessons this story teaches, if we failed to glance at the brilliant array of accomplished, distinguished, and eminently useful women whom this convent school received as girl students and sent forth again, equipped to take a vital and beneficent part in American life.

Mother Teresa Lalor, the venerable foundress, passed away September 10, 1846; not fifty years ago, at this writing. Even then she had long retired from supervision of the community or active sharing in its daily toil. Yet she had witnessed a remarkable growth in it, and had seen one competent Superioress after another carrying on the task that age and long service had obliged her to lay down. Before she died, or in the period from then on until the war-days, there came to the Academy the two daughters of Senator Ewing of Ohio (the first Secretary of the Department of the Interior). One of them, Ellen Ewing, afterwards married Gen. William Tecumseh Sherman. Here also was educated Harriet Lane Johnson, niece of President Buchanan, who gained social distinction at the Court of St. James while her uncle was United States Minister there, and afterwards gracefully conducted for him the social functions of the Executive Mansion, as one of the most charming in all the line of " ladies of the White House." Another graduate, famous for her exceptional beauty as well as for her social leadership in Washington, was Adelaide Cutts, who married Stephen A. Douglas, the brilliant rival of Abraham Lincoln for presidential honors. Mrs. Douglas, long after her first husband's death, became the wife of General Robert Williams, U. S. A.

General Joseph E. Johnston, eminent afterwards among Confederate military chieftains, found his wife in a Visitation graduate, Miss McLain, a daughter of Secretary McLain. Another pupil, Teresa Doyle, married Senator Casserly ; and Miss Deslonde of Louisiana, who studied here, became Mrs. General Beauregard.

" Among others who graduated before the war were Marion Ramsay, who became Mrs. Cutting of New York ; the daughters of Judge Gaston of North Carolina ; the daughters of Commodore Rogers ; Eliza and Isabella Walsh, the daughters of the United States Minister to Spain ; Minnie Meade, a sister of General

Meade, who became the wife of General Hartman Bache, U. S. A.; Albina Montholon, daughter of the French Minister and granddaughter of General Gratiot, U. S. A.; Kate Duncan of Alabama, who married Dr. Emmet of New York; the daughters of Commodore Cassin; the Bronaugh sisters, one of whom married Admiral Taylor; the Carroll sisters, one of whom became the Baroness Esterhazy of Austria; the daughters of Senator Stephen Mallory of Florida; the daughter of Senator Nicholson of Tennessee, afterwards Mrs. Martin, who became principal of a leading seminary in the South; Katie Irving, a grandniece of Washington Irving; the daughters of Major Turnbull; Mary Maguire, who became the wife of General Eugene Carr. Of the daughters of Mrs. Bass of Mississippi, afterwards wife of the Italian Minister, Bertinatti, one married a foreign nobleman. Madeleine Vinton became the wife of Admiral Dahlgren; Emily Warren became Mrs. Roebling, the wife of the builder of the Brooklyn bridge, who herself completed the great work when her husband had been stricken with illness. Nancy Lucas, who married Doctor Johnson of St. Louis, sent five daughters to the convent, as did also Major Turner. General Frost sent five representatives, one of whom married Philip Beresford Hope, son of the distinguished member of Parliament. Adele Sarpy, who became Mrs. Don Morrison, a pupil herself, later on sent her three daughters. Ellen Sherman Thackara and Rachel Sherman Thorndyke, daughters of General Sherman, followed in their mother's footsteps at Georgetown. Myra Knox became Mrs. Thomas J. Semmes of New Orleans. Ada

Semmes, who married Richard Clarke, the historian, with her sisters, one of whom was Mrs. Ives, were also pupils here. Among other leading Southern families represented at the school at this time were the Floyds of Virginia and the Stephenses of Georgia.

"Of those who have graduated since the war are Bertha and Ida Honoré; the former, Mrs. Potter Palmer, is now prominently before the country as the president of the Board of Lady Managers of the World's Columbian Exposition. Her sister is the wife of Colonel Fred. D. Grant, United States Minister to Austria. Blanche Butler, the daughter of Gen. Benjamin F. Butler, became the wife of Governor Ames of Mississippi, and Mary Goodell married Governor Grant of Colorado. Harriet Munroe of Chicago, who wrote the ode for the Columbian World's Fair, graduated in '79, having for her classmates Adele Morrison of St. Louis, now Mrs. Albert T. Kelley of New York; Ella Whitthorne of Tennessee, now Mrs. Alex. Harney of Baltimore; and Miss Newcomer of Baltimore, who, as Mrs. H. B. Gilpin, annually presents a medal for music to the school. Mary Saunders, the daughter of ex-Senator Saunders of Nebraska, as the wife of Russell Harrison, the ex-President's son, graced the White House by her presence during Benjamin Harrison's administration. Mary Logan Tucker, the daughter of the soldier and statesman General John A. Logan, is wielding as a journalist a pen as trenchant as was her father's sword.

"The portraits of Emma Etheridge of Tennessee, the daughter of Honorable Emerson Etheridge, and Josephine Dickson of Missouri, which adorn the walls of the convent parlor, were those of two young ladies noted for their beauty. The former is now Mrs. John V. Moran of Detroit, and the latter Mrs. Julius Walsh of St. Louis ; Estelle Dickson is now in Paris studying art.

" Among other pupils were Pearl Tyler, daughter of President Tyler ; Gertrude and Jessie Alcorn, the daughters of Senator Alcorn of Mississippi ; Romaine Goddard, daughter of Mrs. Dahlgren, who became the Countess von Overbeck ; Irene Rucker, who became the wife of General Philip H. Sheridan ; Constance Edgar, daughter of Madame Bonaparte and granddaughter of Daniel Webster ; Mary Wilcox, granddaughter by adoption of General Andrew Jackson. Ethel Ingalls, daughter of ex-Senator Ingalls, has reflected credit on the Academy by her literary work ; her younger sister, Constance, followed her at the school, together with Anna Randall Lancaster, and her sister Susie, daughters of the late Samuel J. Randall ; the five daughters of the late A. S. Abell of Baltimore, and Jennie Walters, daughter of W. T. Walters of the same city.

" Miss Early and Miss Ould were two gifted Southern ladies who are remembered at the school." [1] Miss E. M. Dorsey, also, a bright and winning story-writer, whose " Midshipman Bob " is well and favorably known to young readers, is one of the later graduates.

Even this partial list of some among those who have received their training at Georgetown Convent in

[1] "An Old Southern School:" *The Cosmopolitan*, October, 1892, vol. xiii, No. 6, p. 654 ; an article by Nathaniel T. Taylor. A few words have been changed in this extract, merely to adapt it to the present date.

knowledge, morals, manners, and the conduct of life, is at first sight rather surprising by reason of the high rank and average of the women educated here.   Yet on second and deeper thought it will appear to be only a reasonable result of so much patient labor, lofty endeavor, unselfish effort, and devout studiousness, offered day by day for a century, with no other thought than that of contributing to the glory of God and the blessing of the human race, in whole and in particular.

XX. A WORD AT PARTING.

The Annals which we have now brought to a close must, we think, place one fact very clearly before the minds of all thoughtful and observant readers ; and that is, the marked degree of individuality characterizing the members of such a body as the Georgetown Convent of the Visitation, — which, in some sense, may be taken as typical of all religious orders living in community.

We lay stress upon this because there is so general a notion (sometimes even among the faithful) that, in entering a sisterhood, a woman loses all individuality, and, missing those occasions for the development of varied and interesting character which the secular life affords, becomes a colorless being, a kind of cipher. But she is a cipher only to the extent and in the manner that ciphers are the token of an immense multiplication of forces and of power.   She increases her natural abilities by doing away with the selfish unit, or, rather, raising it in a geometrical ratio to something approaching the infinite.   And this she accomplishes by applying to the qualities that God has given her a spiritual motive and the effect of supernatural grace. It is not a surrender of individuality, but a dedication and development of it.

This we trust has been demonstrated by such definite examples as the steadfast endurance and guiding hope of Mother Teresa Lalor; the virgin self-reliance and bravery of Sister Margaret Marshall; the firm executive quality of Mother Agnes Brent and other Superiors; the gentle, tactful rule of Mother Juliana Matthews; the vivacious and exquisitely trustful, spiritualized personality of " Sister Stanny; " the enthusiasm for astronomical study of Sister Genevieve White, in the midst of bodily suffering; the grand, sturdy serviceableness of Sister Joseph Keating; the delicate, skillful housekeeping and responsive charity of Mother Angela Harrison; or the perfect meekness of Sister Mary Emmanuel Scott. These are but a few, among the larger few whom we have sketched in this book; and all, taken together, are only instances of the traits and capacities of numberless other sisters. They show that not only may there be pronounced individuality among the members of a religious order, but also a wide variety of development, under the uniform garb and the equal submission to a common rule and discipline.

This point it is absolutely needful to perceive and comprehend clearly, in order to understand what convent life is, — how real, how vital, how efficient. Some persons no doubt may inquire: " If these characters were so strong, so full of purpose, so capable of fine development in various directions, why could they not have been utilized in the outside world, in the common channels of secular activity ?"

We will endeavor to answer the inquiry.

As has been said on another page, it is a scientific principle that to obtain certain results we must have certain conditions. Therefore we do not believe that these personalities and lives could have been brought to the same fullness or height of spiritual growth, outside the cloister.

A closer and perhaps more tangible reason for this belief will appear, if we state to ourselves frankly and in a few words the real relation of convent or religious community life to that of the rest of the world.

We who are "in the world" do not hesitate to resign our sons and daughters, our sisters or brothers, to marriage, which in a manner cuts them off from us, and may sometimes separate them from us entirely. Marriage, or business and intellectual pursuits, — which we applaud them for adopting, — often carry them away to distant parts of the country or of the earth, so that perhaps we rarely or never see them again. Yet all this we concede to be not only in the nature of things inevitable, but we also commend it. We never for a moment assume to set up any objection to it on principle ; though we sometimes vaguely assert an imaginary principle, which would justify us in opposing our kindred who wish to seclude themselves in religious brotherhoods and sisterhoods. Now, why is this ? Why are we so inconsistent ? Simply because we are willing to sacrifice our children to the world, with all its pains and disappointments, but frequently have an innate dislike to letting them sacrifice themselves, or any part of our selfish comfort, to God and religion.

When we are pushed to a defense of this rather niggardly attitude towards God, we are apt to fall back upon, and hastily intrench ourselves behind, the idea of the family. "Of course," we say, "we are perfectly willing to sacrifice our children — as we have sacrificed ourselves — to business or adventure, to social turmoil and weariness, because that is the way the main part of the world's work is carried on. Besides, even if they are swallowed up in it and we never see them again, they proceed to form their own household and raise their own family. And everything depends on the family!" The conclusion we then leap to is, that lives given to the service of religion in convents might be spent much better in the routine of the private family.

But observe the fallacy here. The private family, essential though it is, and beautiful as it is when imbued with holiness and sacramentally blessed, is only a type of the whole human family, and hence is less important than that. We ought really, all of us, to regard the great human family with the same tenderness we have been in the habit of bestowing upon the single private family. Christ taught us that we should not restrict our love and interest to the narrow limits of the threshold of the home. But we disregard this teaching.

The commercial spirit of our personal affections is almost as strongly mercenary as the spirit of trade. We expend our affections freely, but only in that narrow circle over which we have some control;

where we may claim, as of right, a solid return in kind.

In the purely religious life alone, any one soul is as precious to each other soul, as mother or father or child. Action, here, is just as loving as in the private family; often very much more loving; and it does not offer itself in the form of what we may call specie or currency based on the obligations of blood relationship. For men and women vowed to religion, it is as though the stranger at the gate bore the same name and lineage as their own.

Just now we spoke of a certain commercial element in our personal affections, *almost* as strong as that of trade. Let us, however, take account of that word "almost," and be exact. We expect a positive and direct return, it is true. But why, after all, do we love the members of our own particular family with a sentiment so much more generous than we are ready to accord to others? Is it not because we know that, for us, their hearts reserve a trust and tenderness which remain, at any rate, more unselfish and more earnest than their love towards those not so nearly related to them as we are?

But the consecrated followers of Jesus Christ recognize no such line of demarcation. They love all souls, even though knowing that frequently they may not receive love and trust from them in return. Their reward of love is from Christ and the Holy Trinity alone. Their family circle is the beloved world which Christ blessed and beckoned upward.

Finis libri: initium operis.

APPENDIX.

I.

1795–Jan. 5.   Arrival of Miss Alice Lalor, afterwards Mother
Teresa Lalor, with Mrs. McDermot and Mrs.
Sharpe, in Philadelphia.

1798–99.   They go to Georgetown, where Father Neale
had been appointed President of Georgetown
College, to form under his guidance a Community, known at first as " The Pious Ladies."

1800.   Father Neale consecrated Bishop, as Archbishop
Carroll's coadjutor.

1801.   Sister Aloysia Neale joins the Community of the
three " Pious Ladies."

1802–July 31.   Death of Sister Ignatia Sharpe.

1804.   Sister Stanislaus Fenwick enters.

1805.   Sister Magdalene Neale enters.

1806.   "Sister Mary " enters.

1808.   Mother Catharine Rigden enters.

1810.   Mother Margaret Marshall arrives from Conewago.

1811.   Mother Juliana Matthews enters the novitiate.

1812–Oct. 15.   Mother Agnes Brent enters the novitiate.

1814–Jan. 29.   The Community takes simple vows.

1816–July 14.   Pius VII. issues his Indult for the Georgetown
Community.

1816–Nov. 10.   Archbishop Neale receives it, and informs the
Sisters.

1816–Dec. ¬   Mother Apollonia Diggs enters.

1816–Dec. 8.   Solemn vows taken by the first three members.

1817–Jan. 6.   Ninéteen sisters receive the white veil.

1817–Jan. 23.   Of these, seven are admitted to solemn vows.

1817–Jan. 29.   The rest are admitted, excepting those whose novitiate had not expired.

1817–April 6.

(Easter Sun-
day.)   } Death of Sister Isidora McNantz.

1817–June 18.   Death of Archbishop Neale.

1817–June 21.   Mrs. Barber enters.

1818–Jan. 3.   Sister Genevieve King enters.

1818–Jan. 13.   Profession of Sister M. Apollonia Diggs.

1818–Jan. 13.   Arrival of Father Clorivière.

1819–Ascen-
sion Day.   Election of Mother Catharine Rigden.

1820–Feb. 2.   Mr. and Mrs. Barber make their vows.

1820–July 11.   Mother Catharine and the Sisters, going in procession, begin digging for the foundations of the church.

1820–Feast of
St. Anne.   First stone laid by Archbishop Maréchal.

1820–Dec. 21.   Death of Mother Catharine.

1820–Dec. 28.   Mother M. de Sales elected.

1822 (proba-
bly).   The Lasallas placed as pupils in the Academy.

1824–Mar. 10.   Miraculous cure of Mrs. Mattingly.

1825–Feb. 10.   Miraculous cure of Sister Beatrice Myers.

1825–Mar. 18.   Sister Stanislaus Jones enters.
Mother Juliana Matthews elected Superior.

1826–Sep. 29.   Death of Father Clorivière, aged 58.
Madam Yturbide in Georgetown.

1828.   Father Wheeler, the successor of Father Clorivière as Spiritual Director, goes to Europe.

1829–Aug. 2.   Arrival of the three French Sisters.

1830–Ascen-
sion Day.   Mother Magdalene Augustine elected Superior.

1831–Jan. 1.   Miraculous cure of Mrs. Mattingly's foot.

1831–Jan. 20.   Miraculous cure of Sister Apollonia Diggs.

1831–Mar. 22.   Departure of Sister Gertrude Whyte.

1831–Sept. –.   Sisters M. Regis and Agatha return to France.

1831.	Rev. William Matthews appointed Spiritual Director.
1832–May 11.	Death of Rev. M. F. Wheeler.
1836.	Charlotte Lasalla returns to Georgetown.
1837.	Charlotte Lasalla dies, aged 23 years.
1838–Jan. 23.	Sister Stanislaus Jones miraculously cured of cancer.
1838–Feb. 10.	Sister Eugenia Millard miraculously cured.
1846–Sept. 10.	Death of the venerable Foundress, Mother Teresa Lalor, aged about 80 years.

II.

LIST OF MOTHER SUPERIORS.

1.	MOTHER TERESA LALOR	28th December	1815.
2.	Mother Catharine Rigden	27th May	1819.
3.	Mother De Sales Neale	28th December	1820.
4.	Mother Agnes Brent	13th December	1821.
5.	Mother Agnes Brent	19th May	1825.
6.	Mother Juliana Matthews	7th October	1825.
7.	Mother Juliana Matthews	21st November	1828.
8.	Mother Magdalene Augustine D'Arreger	11th September	1830.
9.	Mother Juliana Matthews	20th May	1833.
10.	Mother Juliana Matthews	19th May	1836.
11.	Mother Agatha Combs	15th February	1838.
12.	Mother Agatha Combs	27th May	1841.
13.	Mother Anastasia Combs	30th May	1844.
14.	Mother Agatha Combs	24th September	1846.
15.	Mother Cecilia Brooks	29th July	1847.
16.	Mother Cecilia Brooks	8th July	1850.
17.	Mother Augustine Cleary	27th July	1852.
18.	Mother Perpetua Mitchell	24th May	1855.
19.	Mother Joseph Keating	20th May	1858.
20.	Mother Angela Harrison	16th May	1861.
21.	Mother Angela Harrison	12th May	1864.
22.	Mother Augustine Cleary	6th June	1867.
23.	Mother Angela Harrison	2d June	1870.
24.	Mother Angela Harrison	2d June	1873.

25. Mother Agnes Neeson	1st June	1876.
26. Mother Liguori D'Avraireville	29th May	1879.
27. Mother Liguori D'Avraireville	25th May	1882.
28. Mother Loretto King	21st May	1885.
29. Mother Loretto King	17th May	1888.
30. Mother Leocadia Beckham	14th May	1891.
31. Mother Fidelis McMenamin	10th May	1894.

III.

IMPORTANT EVENTS IN AMERICAN HISTORY, ON THE DATES OF THE FEAST OF THE VISITATION, ETC.

THE father of Cecilius Calvert had obtained a patent from James I. for the colonization of Maryland, and his son and successor afterward petitioned for a transfer of the charter to himself. King Charles I. wished to act gratefully and gracefully towards his father's old and trusted friend ; and, notwithstanding the violent opposition of the "Virginia Company," issued his grant on July 2 (the Feast of the Visitation), 1633.

It was on the morrow of the Presentation that the Maryland Emigrants set sail, and on the Annunciation that they landed and celebrated Mass in this new region of the New World, naming the town here built, St. Mary's. The province they called Maryland, Terra Maria ; and the bay whose shores, nearly a century previous, had been sanctified by the blood of eight Jesuit martyrs, had from them received the name of " St. Mary's Bay." It was afterwards changed to "Chesapeake," but, by a singular coincidence, the names of *Virgin* and *Mary*, belonging to the States of its eastern and western bank, and given in honor of two queens, will ever remain memorials of its consecration to Mary, the Mother of God and Queen of Heaven.

On July 2, 1584, Queen Elizabeth's ships descried the coast of Virginia. On July 2, 1767, the duty on tea was fixed by Parliament, — which act brought on the American Revolution, and the independence of our country. On July 2, 1775, George Washington reached headquarters at Cambridge, and assumed command of the army.

On July 2, 1776, American Independence was *voted in Congress;* on the following day the "Declaration" was drawn up ; and on the 4th, publicly read and proclaimed.

On July 2, 1778, the French fleet, under Count D'Estaing, appeared off the coast of Rhode Island ; whereupon the penal laws against Catholics were repealed by the legislature. On the eve of the Feast of the Visitation, 1784, our American Minister, Benjamin Franklin, received a visit in Paris from the Pope's Nuncio, on the business of appointing a Bishop for the United States. Franklin writes that, on his own recommendation, Rev. J. Carroll was appointed.

The Feast of the Immaculate Conception (Dec. 8) has also been a day of special blessing.

On Dec. 8, 1774, by an act of the Maryland Convention, toleration was granted to Catholics. On Dec. 8, 1776, Washington, pursued by the British (after his disasters on Long Island and in New York), crossed the Delaware in the night ; thus saving his army, and the cause of American liberty, from total disaster. On Dec. 8, 1791, the first Catholic American Bishop was hailed in his episcopal city, having been consecrated in England, on the Feast of the Assumption, 1790.

Our United States are dedicated to Mary Immaculate ; and Columbus himself dedicated the New World to the Queen of Heaven, — the flagship of his expedition being named " Santa Maria de la Concezione."

The Feast of Blessed Margaret Mary Alacoque is, likewise, a day of note in our American history. The two decisive battles of Saratoga and Yorktown, on which the destinies of our Union depended, were accomplished on Oct. 17 (the day of the year of her death), 1777 and 1781. On October 17, 1777, the British army, under Burgoyne, surrendered to the Americans at Saratoga ; and in Irving's " Life of Washington " appears the following account of the surrender of Yorktown : " The hopes of Lord Cornwallis were now at an end. His works were tumbling in ruins about him under an incessant cannonade. He ordered a parley to be beaten on the morning of the 17th (October) and despatched a flag with a letter to Washington, proposing a cessation of hostilities for twenty-four hours ; and that two officers might be appointed by each side to meet and settle terms for the surrender."

The discussion of the terms occupied that and the following day ; and the ceremony of the surrender took place on the 19th, thus ending the Revolutionary War. Cornwallis's decision to surrender had been made, however, on October 17th, the Feast of Blessed Margaret Mary of the Visitation Order, with whom the devotion to the Sacred Heart of Jesus began.

These coincidences *prove* absolutely nothing, in the mere human sense ; yet, even to the ordinary human mind, they are of interest as showing a curious series of facts and correspondences in dates ; namely, that some of the momentous and decisive events in the history of the forming of the American nation took place on days especially devoted to the Blessed Virgin Mary, in the feasts of the Visitation and the Immaculate Conception.

IV.

REV. JAMES CURLEY, S. J.

THIS learned yet humble Jesuit was for many years Professor of Mathematics and Astronomy at Georgetown College, and founded the famous observatory of that university. A scholar of rare attainments in science, he also served the Convent of the Visitation as chaplain.

Throughout a long life he was untiring in his aid to the sisterhood, freely contributing his invaluable scientific knowledge to the Academy, the philosophical apparatus and chemical laboratory of which attest the care given by it to this branch of study. The community was greatly indebted to him on that side, as well as for his spiritual ministrations ; and his unpretentious kindness was extended to the Academy pupils. It was a charming thing to watch his venerable and benign figure as he conversed with some old-time graduate about her early days ; and so far back did his own experience and memory reach, that one of the sisters recalls how, in chatting with a young girl student, he even told her about her own grandmother's time, and related amusing anecdotes of President Andrew Jackson connected with that period.

He lived to the age of ninety-two, in the full enjoyment of his faculties to the last, always dispensing an abundance of instruction and good-will to both sisters and pupils ; beloved and reverenced by all who knew him, — so much so that the present brief memorial and the portrait of him in this volume form but a slight token of the affection with which he is remembered.